acclaim for
#1 internationally bests
cathy kelly

"[Kelly] has a gift for revealing the humor in life's most challenging moments."

—*Kirkus Reviews*

"Cathy Kelly knows exactly what women want in their contemporary romances—to escape into a world populated by believable characters in search of more satisfying lives sprinkled with romance."

—*Publishers Weekly*

"Kelly's skill as a storyteller and the rounded nature of her characters captivates and seduces."

—*Evening Herald*

"Cathy Kelly is the living definition of excellence within a genre. Her writing is infused with a kindness which allows her to make the ordinary extraordinary."

—*Irish Independent*

"[Kelly] has gained a strong following for her real life, down-to-earth characters."

—*Belfast Telegraph*

"Kelly has earned her place on the bestseller lists with her sharp understanding of behavior. . . ."

—*Publishing News*

what she wants
is also available as an eBook

what she wants

"[Kelly] knows exactly what her readers want."

—*Sunday Tribune*

"A thumping big page-turner."

—*Books Ireland*

"Funny, warm and intelligent—perfect for curling up with on a wintry, wet Sunday afternoon."

—*It* magazine

"[Kelly's] latest, rich with the emerald allure of the lush Irish landscape and tart with Kelly's sexy, bracing humor, follows four diverse women linked to the charming Kerry town of Redlion. . . . Romance fans should rejoice in this chatty, comfortable story, as warm and satisfying as Irish oatmeal."

—*Publishers Weekly*

"[*What She Wants*] empathically communicates highly charged yet recognizable emotional issues through resilient and realistically drawn characters."

—*Booklist*

past secrets

"Summer Street is the new Wisteria Lane."

—Marian Keyes, international bestselling author of *Anybody Out There?*

always and forever

"A must for Kelly's many fans; a warm, moving read."

—*Daily Mail*

"A feel-good fable about life turned pear-shaped."

—*YOU* magazine

"Kelly's skill as a storyteller and the rounded nature of her characters captivates and seduces."

—*Evening Herald*

just between us

"A compulsive read."

—*Women's Weekly*

"Enchanting, gloriously funny."

—*Books* magazine

"Plenty of sparky humor."

—*The Times* (London)

"Warm and chatty."

—*Daily Mail*

best of friends

"A warm and cozy comfort read. . . ."

—*New York Times* bestselling author Pat Gaffney

". . . touches lightly on simple truths, sensitively on death and on the destruction of relationships, and optimistically on the limitless potential of friendship."

—*Irish Independent*

"Full of credible characters and real-life scenarios that will resonate with women of all ages. . . ."

—*Evening Herald*

by the same author

Past Secrets

Always and Forever

Just Between Us

Best of Friends

Lessons in Heartbreak

Cathy Kelly

NEW YORK LONDON TORONTO SYDNEY

Downtown Press
A Division of Simon & Schuster, Inc.
1230 Avenue of the Americas
New York, NY 10020

Originally published in Great Britain in 2008 by HarperCollins*Publishers*

First Downtown Press trade paperback edition February 2009

Manufactured in the United States of America

10 9 8 7 6 5 4 3 2 1

ISBN-13: 978-1-4165-8624-1
ISBN-10: 1-4165-8624-5

To Murray, Dylan and John,
with love

Lessons

in

Heartbreak

one

The New Mexico sun was riding high in the sky when the Zest catalog shoot finally broke up for lunch. Izzie Silver stood up and stretched to her full five feet nine inches, glorying in the drowsy heat that had already burnished the freckles on her arms despite her careful application of SPF 50 sunscreen.

Truly Celtic people—with milk-bottle skin, dots of caramel freckles and bluish veins on their wrists—only ever went one color in the sun: lobster red. And lobster red was never going to be a fashionable color, except for early stage melanomas.

It was her second day on the shoot and Izzie could feel her New Yorker-by-adoption blood slowing down to match the sinuous pace of desert life. Manhattan and Perfect-NY Model Agency, who'd sent her here to make sure nothing went wrong on a million-dollar catalog shoot involving three of their models, seemed a long way away.

If she had been in New York, she would have been sitting at her desk with the rest of the bookers: phone headset on, skinny latte untouched on her desk and a stack of messages piled up waiting for her. The office was in a sleek block off Houston, heavy on glass bricks and Perspex chandeliers and light on privacy.

At lunch, she'd be rushing down to the little beauty salon on Seventh where she got her eyebrows waxed or taking a quick detour uptown into Anthropologie on West Broadway to see if they had any more of those adorable little soap dishes shaped like seashells. Not that she needed more junk in her bathroom, mind you; it was like a beauty spa in there as it was.

In between scheduling other people's lives, she'd be mentally scrolling through her own, thinking of her Pilates class that night and whether she had the energy for it. And thinking of him. Joe.

Weird, wasn't it, how a person could be a stranger to you and then, in an instant, *become* your whole life? How did that happen, anyway?

And why him? When he was the most inconvenient, wrong person for her to love. Just when she thought she'd cracked this whole life thing, along came Joe to show her that nothing ever worked out the way you wanted it to. You have no control—random rules.

Izzie hated random, loathed it, despised it. She liked being in charge.

At least being here gave her the space to think, even if she was missing her eyebrow appointment, her Pilates and—most important—dinner with Joe. Because Joe took up so much space in her head and in her heart that she couldn't think clearly when he was around.

Here at Chaco Ranch, with the vast hazy spread of dusty land around her and the big sky that seemed to fill more than the horizon, clear thinking felt almost mandatory.

Izzie felt as much at home as if she was sitting on the back porch of her grandmother's house in Tamarin, where sea orchids dotted the grass and the scent of the ocean filled the air.

Chaco Ranch, just thirty minutes away from the buzz of Santa Fe, was a sprawling, white-painted ranch house, sitting like an exquisite piece of turquoise in the middle of sweeping red ochre.

And though it was geographically a long way from Tamarin, the small Irish coastal town where Izzie had grown up, the two places shared that same rare quality that *mañana* was far too urgent a word and that perhaps the day after tomorrow was time enough for what had to be done.

While the ranch was landlocked with huge cacti and mesquite trees guarding the house and mountains rising up behind them,

Tamarin sat perilously on rocks, the houses clinging to steep hills as if the roar of the Atlantic would send them tumbling down.

In both places, Izzie decided, the landscape made people aware of just how puny they were in the grand scheme of things.

The consequent tranquillity of the ranch had calmed everyone down at least as much as two hours of Bikram yoga would.

Bookers rarely went on shoots: their work was confined to the office, living on the phone, relying on email as they juggled their models' lives effortlessly. But Zest was an important client and Izzie's bosses had decided it was worth flying her in, just in case anything went wrong on this first shoot for a whole new Zest line.

"I love this place," Izzie had said to the blond ranch owner the morning before, when the crew had arrived with enough clothes, makeup, hair spray and photographic equipment to make a small movie, and enough adrenaline to power a large town.

Mexican-inspired arches in the walls, tiled courtyards hung with Moroccan lights, and dreamy wall hangings made locally gave the place depth. Local artists' handiwork hung cheek by jowl with pieces by international artists, and there were two walls dedicated to haunting photographs of the Anasazi ruins.

The ranch owner had waved slender brown arms that rattled with silver and turquoise bangles and explained that Chaco Canyon, where her treasured photos had been taken, was home to a flea that still carried bubonic plague.

"Could we get some?" deadpanned Izzie. "Not for me, you understand, but I've got some people I'd like the flea to bite."

"I thought you fashion people had no sense of humor." The blond woman grinned.

"Only me, sorry," Izzie said. "It's a hindrance in fashion, to be honest. Some of these people cry at night over hemline lengths, and if you are not a True Fashion Believer, then they try to kill you with their Manolo spike heels or else batter you to death with their copy of *Vogue*'s new collections edition. Personally, I think a sense of humor helps."

"And you're not a True Fashion Believer?" asked the woman, staring at the tall redhead curiously.

"Hey, look at me," laughed Izzie, smoothing her palms over her firm, curvy body. "True Fashion Believers think food is for wimps, so I certainly don't qualify. I've never done the South Beach or the Atkins, and I just cannot give up carbohydrates. These are crucial in True Fashion."

In an alternate universe, Izzie Silver could have been a model. Everyone told her so when she was a kid growing up in Tamarin. She had the *look*—huge eyes, colored a sort of dusty heliotrope blue with glossy thick lashes like starfishes around them, and a generous mouth that made her cheekbones rise into gleaming apples when she smiled. Her caramel mane of thick hair made her look like a Valkyrie standing on her own longboat, curls flying and fierce majesty in her face. And she was tall, with long, graceful legs perfect for ballet, until she grew so much that she towered over all the other little ballerinas.

There was only one issue: her size. When she was twelve, she stood five feet six in her socks and weighed one hundred and ten pounds.

Now, aged thirty-nine, she wore a U.S. size ten. In an industry where skinniness was a prize beyond rubies, Izzie Silver stood out for many reasons.

With her perfect hourglass figure, like a sized-up Venus, she was proof that big was beautiful. She loved food, turned heads everywhere she went and made the hollow-eyed fashion junkies look like fragile twigs in danger of cracking inside and out.

She liked her size and never dieted.

In fashion, this was the equivalent of saying that polyester was your favorite fabric.

Joe Hansen had been mildly surprised when she told him she

worked in the fashion industry the first day they met. They'd been seated across the table from each other at a charity lunch—an event Izzie had only gone to by the strangest, totally random circumstances, which proved her point that random ruled.

She hadn't thought he'd noticed her, until suddenly, she'd seen that flicker in his eyes: a glint to add to the mirror-mosaic glints already there.

Hello, you, she'd thought wistfully.

It had been so long since she'd found a man attractive that she almost wasn't sure what that strange quiver in her belly was. But if it was attraction, she tried to suppress it. She had no time for men anymore. They messed things up, messed people's heads up and caused nothing but trouble. Work—nice solid work where you toiled away and achieved something real that nobody could take away from you—and having good friends, that was what life was about.

But if she'd discounted him, he clearly hadn't discounted her. From her position across the table Izzie could feel Joe taking her in admiringly, astonished to see that she was so earthy and real. She'd eaten her bread roll with relish, even briefly licked a swirl of butter off her finger. Carbs and fats: criminal. The city was full of fashion people, and common wisdom held that they were skinny, high-maintenance beings, always following some complicated diet. Izzie didn't try to be different. She'd just never tried to be the same.

"God made you tall so men could look up to you," Gran used to say. Her grandmother had stepped into her mother's place when Mum died of cancer when Izzie was just thirteen. Izzie wasn't sure how her grandmother had managed to steer her around the tricky path of being a big girl in a world of women who wanted to be thin, but she'd done it.

Izzie liked how she looked. And so, it seemed, did the man across from her.

He was surrounded by skinny charity queens, spindly legs set elegantly on equally spindly-legged gilt chairs, and he was staring at her. No, *staring* wasn't the right word: gazing at her hungrily, that summed it up.

Lots of men looked at Izzie like that. She was used to it; not in a cavalier, couldn't-care-less way, but certainly she barely glanced at the men who stared at her. She honestly didn't need their stares to make her feel whole. But when Joe Hansen looked at her like that, he flipped her world upside down.

The most shocking thing was that when his eyes were on her, she could feel the old Izzie—uncompromising, strong, happy in her own skin—slip away, to be replaced by a woman who wanted this compelling stranger to think her beautiful.

"You know, honey, from what I hear, that whole fashion world sounds kinda like hard work," sighed the ranch owner to Izzie now, hauling her mind away from The Plaza and the first time she'd met Joe.

"I tried that South Beach once and it takes a lot of time making those egg white and spinach muffins 'n' all."

"Too much hard work," agreed Izzie, who worked in an office where the refrigerator was constantly full of similar snacks. Quinoa was the big kick at the moment. Izzie had tried it and it tasted like wet kitchen towels soaked overnight in cat pee—well, she imagined that was what cat pee tasted like. Give her a plate of Da Silvano pasta with an extra helping of melting Parmesan shavings any day.

"Pasta's my big thing," she said.

"Spaghetti with clams," said the other woman.

"Risotto. With wild mushrooms and cheese," Izzie moaned. She could almost taste it.

"Pancakes with maple syrup and butter."

"Stop," laughed Izzie, "I'm going to start drooling."

"Bet those little girls never let themselves eat pancakes," the woman said, gesturing to where two models sat chain-smoking. Even smoking, they looked beautiful, Izzie thought. She was constantly humbled by the beauty of the women she worked with, even if she knew that sometimes the beauty was only a surface thing. But what a surface thing.

"No," she said now. "They don't eat much, to be honest."

"Sad, that," said the woman.

Izzie nodded.

The ranch owner departed, leaving the crew to it, and Izzie wandered away from the terrace where the last shots had been taken and walked down the tiled steps to the veranda at the back where Tonya, at eighteen the youngest of the Perfect-NY models, had gone once she'd whipped off the cheerful Zest pinafore dress she'd been wearing and had changed into her normal clothes.

A brunette with knife-edge cheekbones, Tonya sat on a cabana chair, giraffe legs sprawled in Gap skinny jeans, and took a first drag on a newly lit cigarette as if her life depended on it. From any angle, she was pure photographic magic.

And yet despite the almond-shaped eyes and bee-stung lips destined to make millions of women yearn to look like her, Izzie decided that there was something tragic about Tonya.

The girl was beautiful, slender as a lily stem and 100 percent messed up. But Izzie knew that most people wouldn't be able to see it. All they'd see was the effortless beauty, blissfully unaware that the person behind it was a scared teenager from a tiny Nebraska town who'd won the looks lottery but whose inner self hadn't caught up.

As part of the Perfect-NY team, Izzie Silver's job was to see the scared kid behind the carefully applied makeup. Her stock-in-trade was a line of nineteen-year-olds with Ralph Lauren futures, trailer-trash backgrounds and lots of disastrous choices in between.

Officially, Izzie's job was to manage her models' careers and find them jobs. Unofficially, she looked after them like a big sister. She'd worked in the modeling world for ten years, and not a week went by when she didn't meet someone who made her feel that modeling ought to include free therapy.

"Why do people believe that beauty is everything?" she and Carla, her best friend and fellow booker, wondered at least once a week. It was a rhetorical question in a world where a very specific type of physical beauty was prized.

"'Cause they don't see what we do," Carla inevitably replied. "Models doing drugs to keep skinny, doing drugs to keep their skin clear and doing drugs to cope."

Like a lot of bookers, Carla had been a model herself. Half Hispanic, half African-American, she was tall, coffee-skinned and preferred life on the other side of the camera, where the rejection wasn't as brutal.

"When the tenth person of the week talks about you as though you're not there and says your legs are too fat, your ass is too big or your whole look is totally last season, then you start to believe them," Carla had told Izzie once.

She rarely talked about her own modeling days now. Instead, she and Izzie—who'd bonded after starting at the agency at the same time and finding they were the same age—talked about setting up their own company, where they'd do things differently.

Nobody was going to tell the models of the Silverwebb Agency—the name had leaped out at them: Izzie Silver, Carla Webb—they were too fat. Because the sort of models they were going to represent were plus-sized: beautiful and big. Women with curves, with bodies that screamed *goddess* and with skin that was genuinely velvety instead of being airbrushed velvety because the model was underweight and acned from a bad lifestyle.

For two women who shared the no-bullshit gene and who both struggled with the part of their jobs that dictated that models had to be slender as reeds, it had seemed such an obvious choice.

Five months ago—pre-Joe—they'd been sharing lunch on the fire escape of Perfect-NY's West Side brownstone, talking about a model from another agency who'd ended up in rehab because of her heroin addiction.

She weighed ninety pounds, was six feet tall and was still in demand for work at the time.

"It's a freaking tragedy, isn't it?" Carla sighed as she munched on her lunch. "How destructive is that? Telling these kids they're just not right even when they're stop-traffic beautiful. Where is it going to end? Who gets to decide what's beautiful anymore if the really beautiful girls aren't beautiful enough?"

Izzie shook her head. She didn't know the answer. In the ten years she'd been working in the industry, she'd seen the perfect model shape change from all-American athletic and strong, although slim, to tall, sticklike and disturbingly skinny. It scared everyone in Perfect-NY and the other reputable agencies.

"It's going to reach a point where kids will need surgery before they get on any agency's books because the look of the season is too weird for actual human beings," she said. "What does that say about the fashion industry, Carla?"

"Don't ask me."

"And we're the fashion industry," Izzie added glumly. If they weren't part of the solution, then they were part of the problem. Surely they could change things from the *inside*.

"You know," she added thoughtfully, "if I had my own agency, I really don't think I'd work with ordinary models. If they're not screwed up when they start, they'll be screwed up by the time they're finished." She took a bite of her chicken wrap. "The designers want them younger and younger. Our client list will be nothing but twelve-year-olds soon."

"Which means that we, as women of nearly forty"—Carla made the sign of the cross with her fingers to ward off this apocalyptic birthday—"are geriatric."

"Geriatric and requiring clothes in double-digit sizes in my case," Izzie reminded her.

"Hey, you're a wo-man, not a boy child," said Carla.

"Point taken and thank you, but still, I am an anomaly. And the thing is, women like you and me, *we're* the ones with the money to buy the damn clothes in the first place."

"You said it."

"Teenagers can't shell out eight hundred dollars for a fashion-forward dress that's probably 'dry-clean only' and will be out of date in six months."

"Six? Make that four," said Carla. "Between cruise lines and the midseason looks, there are four collections every year. By the time you get it out of the tissue paper, it's out of fashion."

"True," agreed Izzie. "Great for making money for design houses, though. But that's not what really annoys me. It is the bloody chasm between the target market and the models."

"Grown-up clothes on little girls?" Carla said knowingly.

"Exactly," agreed Izzie.

As a single career woman living in her own apartment in New York, she had to look after herself, doing everything from unblocking her own sink to sorting out her taxes and then being able to play hardball with the huge conglomerates for whom her models were just pawns.

Yet when the conglomerates showed off clothes aimed at career women like Izzie, they chose to do it with fragile child-women.

The message from the sleek, exquisite clothes was: *I'm your equal, mister, and don't you forget it.*

The message coming from a model with a glistening pink pout and knees fatter than her thighs was: *Take care of me, Daddy.*

"It's a screwed-up world," she said. "I love our girls, but they're so young. They need mothers, not bookers."

She paused. Lots of people said bookers were part mother/part manager. For some reason, this bothered her lately. She'd never minded what she was called before, but now she felt uncomfortable being described as an eighteen-year-old's mother. She wasn't a mother, and it came as a shock that she was old enough to be considered mother to another grown-up. Why did it bother her now? Was it the age thing? Or something else?

"Yeah." Carla abandoned her lunch and started on her coffee. "Wouldn't it be great to work with women who've had a chance to grow up before they're shoved down the catwalk?"

"God, yes," Izzie said fervently. "And who aren't made to starve themselves so the garment hangs off their shoulder blades."

"You're talking about plus-sized models. . . ." said Carla slowly, looking at her friend.

Izzie stopped midbite. It was *exactly* what she was always thinking. How much nicer it would be to work with women who were allowed to look like women and weren't whipped into a certain-shaped box. The skinny no-boobs-no-belly-and-no-bum box.

Carla wrapped both hands around her coffee cup thoughtfully. The familiar noises of their fire-escape perch—the hum of the traffic and the building's giant aircon machine on the roof that groaned and wheezed like a rocket about to take off—faded into nothingness.

"We could—"

"—start our own agency—"

"—for plus-sized models—"

They caught each other's hands and screamed like children.

"Do you think we could do it?" asked Izzie earnestly.

"There's definitely a market for plus-sized models now," Carla said. "You remember years ago, nobody ever wanted bigger girls, but now, how often are we asked do we have any plus-sized girls? All the time. The days of plus girls being used just for catalogs and knitting patterns are over. And with lots of the big-money design houses making larger lines, they want more realistic models. No, there's a market, all right. It's niche, but it's growing."

"*Niche:* yes, that sums it up," Izzie agreed. "I like niche. It's special, elite, different."

She was fed up working for Perfect-NY and having daily corporate battles with the three partners who'd long ago gone over to the dark, moneymaking side. The agency's Dark Side Corporates didn't care about people, be it employees or models. Any day now, time spent in the women's room would involve a clocking-in time card and a machine that doled out a requisite number of toilet paper sheets.

Besides, she'd given ten years to the company and she felt at a crossroads in her life. Forty loomed. Life had run on and—it hit Izzie suddenly what was wrong with her, why she'd been feeling odd lately—she felt left behind.

She had all the things she'd wanted: independence, her own apartment, wonderful friends, marvelous holidays, a jam-packed social life. And yet there was a sense of something missing, a flaw like a crack in the wall that didn't ruin the effect, but was still there, if you thought about it. She refused to believe the missing bit could be love. Love was nothing but trouble. Having a crack in her life because she didn't have someone to love was just such a goddamn cliché, and Izzie refused to be a cliché.

Work was the answer—her own business. That would be the love affair of her life and remove any lingering, late-night doubts about her life's path.

"I'm sure we could raise the money," Carla said. "We haven't got any dependents to look out for. There has to be some bonus in being single women, right?"

They both grinned. Izzie often said that New York must surely have the world's highest proportion of single career women on the planet.

"And it's not as if we don't know enough Wall Street venture capitalists to ask for help," Carla added.

This time, Izzie laughed out loud. Their industry attracted many rich men who had all the boy toys—private jets, holiday islands—and felt that a model on their arm would be the perfect accessory.

"As if they'd meet us," she laughed. "You know there's a Wall Street girlfriend age limit, and we're ten years beyond it, sister. No," she corrected herself, "not ten, more like fifteen. Those masters-of-the-universe men with their Maseratis and helicopter lessons prefer girlfriends under the age of twenty-five. They are blind when women of our vintage are around."

"Stop dissing us, Miz Silver," Carla retorted. "When we have our own agency, we can do what I'm always telling them here and have an older model department. And you could be our star signing," she added sharply. "The masters of the universe only keep away from you because they're scared of you. You're too good at that 'tough Irish chick' thing. Men are like guard dogs, Izzie. They growl when they're scared. Don't scare them and they'll roll over and beg."

"Stop already," Izzie said, lowering her head back to her wrap. "It doesn't matter whether I scare them or not: they prefer nineteen-year-old Ukrainian models every time. If a man wants a kid and not a woman, then he's not my sort of man."

She didn't bother to reply to the remark about her working as a model. It was sweet of Carla, but she was too old, for a start, and she'd spent too long with models to want to enter their world. Izzie wanted to be in control of her own destiny and not leave it in the hands of a bunch of people in a room who wanted a specific person to model a specific outfit and could crush a woman's spirit by saying, "We definitely don't want *you*."

"Could we make our own agency work?" she'd asked Carla on the fire escape. "I mean, what's the percentage of new businesses that crash and burn in the first year? Fifty percent?"

"More like seventy-five."

"Oh, that's a much more reassuring statistic."

"Well, might as well be real," Carla said.

"At least we'd be doing something we really believed in," Izzie added.

For the first month after the conversation, they'd done nothing but talk about the idea. Then they'd begun to lay the groundwork: talking to banks, talking to a small-business consultancy and drawing up a business plan. So far, nobody was prepared to loan them the money, but as Carla said, all it took was one person to believe in them.

Then, two months ago, Izzie Silver had found love.

Love in the form of Joe Hansen. Love had obliterated everything else from her mind. And while Carla still talked about having their own agency, Izzie's heart was no longer in it, purely because there was no room in her heart for anything but Joe.

Love had grabbed her unexpectedly and nobody had been more shocked than Izzie.

"If it all works out, we won't be the backbone of Perfect-NY anymore," Carla had said happily just before Izzie had set off for New Mexico. "Imagine, we'll be the bosses . . . and the bookers, assistants, accountants and probably the women who'll be mopping out the women's room at night too, but, hey, we won't care."

"No," agreed Izzie, thinking that she didn't give a damn about anything because she was so miserable at having to fly to New Mexico and be away from Joe. Once, she'd have loved this chance to leave the office for a shoot in a far-flung location. Now, thanks to Joe, she hated the very idea.

"Catalog shoots are tough," Carla added. "Pity you weren't sent to babysit an editorial shoot instead. 'Cause it's going to be hard work, honey."

She was right, Izzie thought, standing in the New Mexico heat, watching the Perfect-NY model work.

Catalog shoots *were* hard work. Hours of shooting clothes with no time to labor over things the way they could on magazine shoots. On magazine shoots, Izzie knew it could easily take a day to shoot six outfits—here, they might manage that in one morning. The models had to be ultraprofessional. The girl with the cheekbones, still-eyed and silent, was just that.

During the morning, Izzie had watched Tonya in an astonishing seven different outfits, transforming her silent watchful face into an all-American, girl-next-door smile each time. It was only when the cameras were finished, and Tonya's face lapsed back into adolescent normality, that Izzie thought again and again how incredibly young she was.

Now it was lunchtime. The photographer and his two senior assistants were drinking coffee and gulping down the food brought in from outside; the other two assistants were hauling light reflectors and shifting huge lights.

No lunch for them.

The makeup and hair people were sitting outside, letting the sun dust their pedicured toes and gossiping happily about people they knew.

"She insists she hasn't had any cosmetic procedures done. Like, hello! That's so a lie. If the skin round her eyes gets pulled up any farther at the corners, she'll be able to see sideways. And talk about Botox schmotox. She never smiled much before, but now she's like a wax dummy."

"Dummy? She wishes. Dummies were warm once—isn't that how they melt the wax?"

"You're a scream!"

The woman from Zest's enormous marketing department was loudly phoning her office.

"It's fabulous: we're on target. We've the rest of the day here because the light's so good that Ivan says we can shoot until at least six. Then tomorrow we're going up to the pueblo. . . ."

Izzie's cell phone buzzed discreetly and she fumbled in her giant tote until she found it. She loved big bags that could hold her organizer, makeup, spare flat shoes, gum, emergency Hershey bars, water bottle and flacon of her favorite perfume, Acqua di Parma. The minus was triumphantly holding up a panty liner by mistake when you were actually looking for a bit of notepaper. How did they always manage to escape their packaging and stick themselves to inappropriate things? They never stuck to panties as comprehensively as they did to things in her handbag.

"How's it goin'?" asked Carla on a line so clear that she might have been in the next room instead of thousands of miles away in their Manhattan office.

"It's all going fine," Izzie reassured her. "Nobody's screamed at anybody yet, nobody's threatened to walk off in a temper, and the shots are good."

"You practicing magic to keep it all running smooth, girl?" asked Carla.

"Got my cauldron in my bag," replied Izzie, "and I'm ready with the eye of a newt and the blood of a virgin."

Carla laughed at the other end of the phone. "Not much virgin blood around if Ivan Meisner is the photographer."

Ivan's reputation preceded him. As a photographer he might be a genius who had *W* and *Vogue* squabbling over him, but the genius fairy hadn't extended her wand as far as his personality.

Nobody watching him idly caressing his extra-long lens as he watched young models could be in any doubt that he considered himself a bit of a maestro in the sack as well as behind the Hasselblad.

"He's definitely got his eye on Tonya," Izzie said, "but don't worry. I'm going to put a stop to his gallop."

"Can somebody tape that?" Carla asked. "I'd like to see him when you've finished with him. *Entertainment Tonight* would love film of Ivan having his lights punched out."

Izzie laughed. Carla was one of the few people who knew that at fourteen Izzie Silver had had a reputation for being a tomboy with a punishing right hook. It wasn't the sort of thing she'd want widely known—violence was only in fashion when it came to faking hard-edged shoots in graffiti-painted alleyways—but it still gave her an edge.

"Don't mess with the big Irish chick" was how some people put it. Izzie was more than able to stand up to anyone. Ruefully, she could see how that might put some men off. Before Joe, it had been six months since her last date. Not that she cared anymore: you had to move on, right?

"Carla, you're just dying to see me hit someone, aren't you?" laughed Izzie now.

"I know you can because of all those kickboxing classes," Carla retorted. "Sure, you're the queen of glaring people into silence with the evil eye and telling them you don't take any crap, but I'd still prefer to see you flatten someone one day. For fun. Pleeease . . . ? I hate the way Ivan hits on young models."

"He won't this time," Izzie said firmly. "He might try, but he won't get anywhere. Since the company has actually spent hard cash to fly me here to make sure it all runs smoothly, I'm going to do my best. Any news at your end?"

"No, it's pretty quiet. Rosanna's off sick so we're a woman down. Lola spotted a gorgeous Mexican girl on the subway last night. She got a photo of her and gave the girl her card, but she thinks the kid's scared she's from immigration or something, so she may not call. Stunning, Lola says. Tall, with the most incredible skin and fabulous legs."

"Oh, I hope she phones," Izzie said. As bookers, they were always on the lookout for the next big thing in modeling. Despite the proliferation of television shows where gorgeous girls turned up hoping to be models, there were still scores of undiscovered beauties, and there was nothing worse than finding one and having her not believe the "I work for a model agency" shtick.

"Me too. Lola keeps glaring at her phone. It's going to catch fire soon."

"No more news?"

"Nah. Quiet. What's the Zest marketing guy like? I heard he's a looker."

Izzie grinned. Carla had said she was never dating ever again just the previous week.

"He couldn't come. They sent a woman instead."

"You can catch up on your beauty sleep, then." Carla laughed before hanging up.

When shooting was over for the day, the entire crew repaired to their hotel's restaurant-cum-bar for some rest and relaxation. There was a sense of a good day's work having been done, but it wasn't quite party time. That would be tomorrow night when the catalog shots were all finished, when nobody had to be up at the crack of dawn and hangovers didn't matter.

Besides, the Zest marketing woman was there watching everything alongside Izzie, and there was too much money in catalog work to screw it all up midshoot.

Izzie knew what happened on shoots when party night had come too early. Someone phoned her at the office and screamed that her models had gone partying, and that the following day had been a blur with the makeup people working extra hard to hide the ravages of sleep deprivation, while general hangover irritation meant it was a miracle any shots were taken at all.

"Menus," said the Zest woman cheerily, handing them out like a prefect at school trying to quash any naughtiness in advance. "There's a salad bar too, if anyone wants anything lighter."

A line of skinny people who did their best to never eat heavy, if possible, stared grimly back at her. No mojitos tonight, then.

Food was finally ordered, along with a modest amount of wine and, thanks to the hair guy, who hated bossy women, cocktails.

"Just one each," chirped the Zest woman, who had the company credit card to pay for all this, after all.

As Izzie had predicted, Ivan wasn't long slithering up the cushioned wooden seat to where Tonya sat nursing something alcoholic from the cocktail menu.

Izzie sat down on a stool opposite Ivan and Tonya, simultaneously patting Tonya comfortingly on the knee, and giving Ivan the sort of hard stare she'd perfected after years of dealing with men just like him.

"How's Sandrine?" she said chattily. Sandrine was his wife and a model who'd miraculously staved off her sell-by date by being labeled a super. Normal models were considered elderly once they hit twenty-five; supers could get another ten years out of the industry if they were clever.

Ivan didn't appear to get the hint. He took another long pull of his margarita, gazing at Tonya over the top of his salt-encrusted glass.

"She's in Paris doing editorial for *Marie Claire*," he said finally.

Tonya, bless her, looked impressed. Izzie wished she could explain to the younger girl that she wouldn't absorb Sandrine's brilliance by osmosis. Sleeping with a supermodel's photographer husband didn't make you a supermodel. It just made you look stupid, feel used and get a bad reputation.

Izzie had another try at the subtle approach. She *was* working for Tonya's agency, after all. No point in irritating the photographer so much that he took awful shots of the girl, thus screwing up both her career and her part of the catalog shoot. Izzie knew that wasn't what her boss had in mind when she said, "Make sure nothing goes wrong."

"Ivan's married to Sandrine," Izzie informed Tonya gently, as if Tonya didn't already know this. "She's so beautiful and so successful, but she travels a lot. It must be so hard to be apart when you're married," Izzie added thoughtfully. "You must miss Sandrine so much. I bet you're dying for the moment you can phone her. How far ahead is Paris? Ten hours, eleven?"

Izzie was not a natural liar. Catholic school had done its work a long time ago, but for her job, she'd perfected the art of subtle manipulation. A tweak here, an insinuation there was all it took.

She could see the rush to Ivan's brain: Would the smooth fire of the local tequila make it there first or would her suggestion about phoning his wife overtake it?

A moment passed and Ivan reached into his jacket for his cell phone.

Izzie allowed herself a small internal smile.

Too much cocaine and general stupidity had eroded Ivan's logistic skills but still he had a certain bovine intelligence. He was aware that Izzie knew the bookers in his wife's agency and that if he misbehaved the news would reach Sandrine. He began to dial.

His wife was the sort of model Tonya might be one day, given plenty of kindness and therapy and people to stop predatory males hitting on her.

Quite why Sandrine had married Ivan in the first place was beyond Izzie. Models knew that photographers were drawn to models like flies to jam. And that DCOL (doesn't count on location) was such a given in their industry that it should have been part of the model wedding-vow thing: *I promise to love, honor, obey and look the other way if he/she has a fling doing a shoot in Morocco.* However, it didn't work quite that way with the supers; when you could have any man on the planet, you didn't stand for being cheated on.

When Tonya got up to go to the women's room, Izzie quickly slipped into the young model's seat, to make sure that Ivan couldn't get close to her when she came back.

Eventually, the rest of the group joined them, the food arrived, and the danger of Ivan getting Tonya on her own for a quiet tête-à-tête passed.

The group shared a low-key meal and Ivan wandered off with his assistant early on. Probably to score coke, Izzie guessed—and not the liquid type that refreshed, either. After all, he didn't need to look good in the morning.

Once he was gone, she left Tonya in the gentle hands of the other models and the makeup and hair people, and went to bed.

Her room was large, decorated in the soft ochre that seemed to be part and parcel of New Mexico, and looked out over a pretty pool that was surrounded by ceramic candleholders, twinkling like so many stars. Opening the double doors onto the small terrace, she stepped outside for a moment and breathed in the balmy night air.

There were two wooden loungers on her terrace, along with a little blue and yellow tile-topped table with a lit citronella candle to ward off the giant flying things that seemed to hum in the air. A heady scent of vanilla rose from below, as well as a more distant smell of garlic cooking. It was all very romantic and begging for a special someone to share it with. Even the huge en-suite bath was big enough for two. Sad for one, though.

Izzie sighed and went back into the room. She stripped off her simple belted shirtdress and sank onto the bed, trying not to worry how many other people had sunk onto the heavy Dupion coverlet—hotels were *freaky*, so many other people using exactly the same space over and over again, leaving their auras and their sweat there—and lay down. Her head felt heavy from the heat and she was tired. Tired and emotional.

She looked at her phone again. No messages. What was it Oscar Wilde said: that it was better to be talked about than not to be talked about?

Cell phones were the same. No matter how often people moaned about them, it was nicer to be phoned than not to be phoned.

She ran one unvarnished fingernail over the rounded plastic of the screen, willing some message to appear there. But there was nothing: the blankness mocked her.

He hasn't called. What's he doing?

What was the point of being wise, clever, savvy—all the things she'd worked hard at being—when she was risking it all for a married man?

Izzie closed her eyes and let the now-familiar anxiety flood over her. She loved Joe. Loved him. But it was all so complicated. She longed for the time when it would be simpler.

Of course, it was complicated simply because of the sort of person Joe was. He might be a tough member of the Wall Street elite, a hedge-fund man who'd gone out on his own with a friend to set up a closed fund and was slowly, relentlessly pushing toward the billionaire Big Boys' Club. But he was a family man underneath it all, and that was where the complications appeared.

Raised in the Bronx, married at twenty-one, a dad at twenty-two, his professional life might have been fabulous but his home life had gone sour long ago. What he did have, however, were three sons whom he adored, and while he was living a separate life from his wife, they were trying to shield their two younger sons from the breakup.

When Izzie thought about it, about the tangled mess she'd walked into when she'd fallen for Joe, she felt nauseated. She knew that people of her age or Joe's carried baggage with them, but his baggage made their relationship so difficult.

No wonder she felt nauseated.

Funnily enough, someone being sick had set it all off. That someone was Emily De Santos, one of the Perfect-NY partners.

Emily had bought a ticket for a twenty-thousand-dollar-a-plate lunch at The Plaza in aid of a child-protection charity which focused on kids from disadvantaged areas.

"Do you think those rich people would have heart attacks if they actually saw a child from a disadvantaged area?" wondered Carla when word came down from on high that Emily—a social climber so keen she carried her own oxygen—was too ill to take her place at the lunch and wanted a warm body to stand in for her.

"Carla, don't be mean," said Izzie, who was the only one without any actual appointments that lunchtime and was therefore about to race home to swap her jeans and chocolate Juicy Couture zippered sweat top for an outfit fit for The Plaza's ballroom. "They're raising money. Isn't that what matters? Besides, they don't have to do a thing for other people. They could just sit at home and buy something else with their twenty thousand bucks."

"Sucker," said Carla.

"Cynic," said Izzie, sticking her tongue out.

She was between blow-dries, so her hair needed a quick revamp, and Marcello, one of her favorite hairstylists, said he could fit her in if she rushed down to the salon.

"I'm channeling Audrey Hepburn," he announced, as Izzie arrived, having changed at home and tried to put on her makeup in the cab downtown to the hair salon.

"You better be channeling her bloody quickly," Izzie snapped, throwing herself into the seat and staring gloomily at her hair.

"You're right," Marcello agreed, holding up a bit of Izzie's hair with his tail comb as if he dared not touch it with his actual hand. Marcello was from Brooklyn, had been miserable in high school when he wasn't allowed to be prom queen and made up for it by being a drama queen for the rest of his life. "Forget Audrey. I'm seeing . . . a woman leaning into a Dumpster searching for something to eat and she hasn't washed her hair in a month. . . ."

"Yes, yes, you are so funny you should have your own show, Marcello. I have to leave here in twenty minutes to go to The Plaza—can you not channel Izzie Silver looking a bit nice? Why do I have to look like someone else?"

"The rules of style, sugar," Marcello sighed, like someone explaining for the tenth time that the earth wasn't flat. "Nobody wants to look like themselves. Too, too boring. Why be yourself when you can be somebody more interesting?"

"That's what's wrong with fashion," said Izzie. "None of us is good enough as we are. We have to be smelling of someone else, wearing someone else and looking like somebody else."

"Are you detoxing?" Marcello murmured. "Have a double espresso, *please*," he begged. "You're much easier to style when you've caffeine in your system. Fashion is fantasy." Marcello began spraying gunk on her hair with the intensity of a gardener wiping out a colony of lethal aphids.

"There goes another bit of the ozone layer," Izzie chirped.

"Who cares about the ozone layer?" he grumbled as he sprayed. "Did you see Britney in the *Enquirer*?"

They gossiped while Izzie dutifully took her espresso medicine and Marcello worked his magic.

"You like?" he said finally, holding up a mirror so she could see the back.

He'd turned her caramel ripples into a swath of soft curls that framed her face and softened it. Audrey hadn't been right, Marcello had decided early on. She was a light brown Marilyn.

"I love it! I'm grotto fabulous," Izzie joked. "Like ghetto fabulous, but the Catholic version."

"And you think *I* should have my own show?" Marcello grinned. "You're the comedienne."

The world at The Plaza that lunchtime was so not Izzie's milieu that her New Yorker cool was rattled. She stared. Used to the fashion world where wearing American Apparel dressed up with something by McQueen was considered clever, it was odd to see so much high-end designer bling in one spot.

This was a combination of stealth wealth—clothes, jewelry and accessories so expensive and elite that there was no brand visible apart from the reek of dollars—and good old-fashioned nouveau riche, where no part of the anatomy was allowed out unless it was emblazoned with someone else's name: Tommy Hilfiger, Louis Vuitton, Fendi.

Women toted rocks worth more than a year's rent on Izzie's

apartment, and it was hard not to be dazzled by the megacarats on show. Still, Izzie's face betrayed none of this.

The tallest, biggest girl in the Convent of the Sacred Heart in Tamarin had to learn to look cool, calm and collected. Izzie never raised her chin haughtily into the air—she didn't need to. She wore self-assurance like a full-length cloak, draping it round herself to show that she was happy, centered and ready for the world on any terms.

Her hair, thanks to Marcello, was fabulous. Her grape silk wrap dress—from a new designer nobody had heard of who understood draping curvy figures—might have cost the merest fraction of the clothes worn by the other guests, but she looked stunning in it. Self-esteem, as her darling Granny Lily always said, was more valuable than any diamond.

Izzie didn't have any diamonds, on purpose. No man had ever bought one for her, and somehow diamonds had come to represent coupledom in her head. Men bought diamonds in glorious solitaire settings as engagement rings for girlfriends, or a half-circle band of diamonds for the birth of babies. Strong single women bought strong jewelry for themselves.

So Izzie wore her Venetian-inspired bangles and dangling earrings with pride because she'd written the check herself. She mightn't have paid for her twenty-thousand-dollar ticket, but she was as good as anybody here.

The ballroom was beautifully formal and all cream: cream table cloths, cream bows on the chairs, cream roses rising from the centerpieces with a froth of baby's breath softening the look. It was very pretty and reeked of money.

At her table, there were six women, including herself, and two men. One was young, handsome and accompanying a beautiful, very slim woman with a youthful face, telltale middle-aged décolletage and an emerald necklace of such staggering beauty and obvious value that it was probably only out of the bank vault for the day.

The other man at the table was in a different league altogether. Forty-something, steel gray eyes that surveyed the room like those of a hawk, tightly clipped dark hair and a slightly weather-beaten face that wouldn't have looked out of place under a cowboy hat, he had a definite presence. He didn't need the exquisite perfection of his Brioni suit to give away the fact that he was a mogul of some sort or other.

Izzie knew the signs. If there was a checklist for the typical alpha male with a commanding presence, Brioni Suit Guy ticked all the boxes.

Elegance, utter self-confidence, a fleeting hint of ruthlessness: he had it all.

There was also the fact that one of the other female guests, whom Izzie recognized from the gossip pages, was flirting with him like the last ark was leaving town and she needed a man for it. Professional hunters of rich men only picked on the really rich and powerful.

The woman with the emeralds kept talking to him about superyachts. Izzie idly wondered what a superyacht was; from the odd snippet of conversation that reached her, this floating palace which needed sixty full-time staff sounded more like a liner than a yacht.

She did think of asking, just for the fun of dropping a wrench in the social works, but decided against it.

As the meal progressed, Izzie couldn't help keeping an eye on the guy, pegging him as a megarich wheeler-dealer who'd spent years in the dirty business of making money and now, finally, was shaking the prizefighter's dust from his hands and looking for some worthy charity to help him climb a much steeper ladder: the New York class ladder.

She didn't want him to see her looking. That would be so embarrassing.

But she couldn't stop.

Hello, you.

She didn't say it, but she thought it. This man was surely out of her league on so many levels. Rich guys went for young beauties: end of story. A normal New York career woman wouldn't stand a chance.

But still . . . he was looking at her, making her stomach flip.

". . . so I phoned him. I said I wouldn't, but, you know, men never take the initiative . . ." went on the woman to Izzie's left. Linda was blond and Botoxed to look forty rather than her actual fifty years. Having started by saying she loved Izzie's dress and adored her jewelry, she was now mournfully recounting her own Manhattan dating tales as she toyed with her entrée, pushing the radicchio and feta salad around her plate in the prescribed manner.

Izzie managed to swivel her head away from the hard-edged mogul and concentrated on her neighbor's story as well as her own tuna steak.

"You're going on a date with this guy, then?" she asked Linda.

"Sort of. Is it a date if he says he'll meet you at a party you're both going to anyway?"

Izzie winced. It seemed that wealthy divorcées were just like ordinary women after all. She decided to give the sort of advice she'd give a friend. "Not a date, really. More a promise of a date unless something better comes up," she said. No point in fudging. "He's hedging his bets, Linda."

Linda sighed. "That's what I think. I want to say no, but I like him. . . ."

"If he likes you, that's fine," Izzie said firmly. "But don't put your heart on the line so he can toy with you. Linda, men can sniff out dating despair the way an airport sniffer dog can home in on ten kilos of Red Leb. If you tell yourself you don't need this guy, then you've got a better chance. And if he doesn't really mean it, then you haven't compromised yourself by wearing your heart on your sleeve. Trust me."

"Yeah, been there, done that, got the T-shirt," sighed Linda. "I used to give advice like that too, when I was your age. But I'm not anymore: your age or giving that advice. Let me tell you, honey, when you get older, you get desperate. You don't care if they know it. Shit, they know it anyway. This town's full of women like me, and the guys all know the story. I don't want to be alone. Why hide that?"

Izzie's soft heart contracted. She grabbed Linda's bony arm and squeezed it. She hadn't expected this sort of honesty in such a place. Here, where it was all for show, it was strange and yet refreshing to find Linda and her straightforwardness.

"Oh, listen to me, I sound all whiny," Linda said, finally putting her fork and knife down on her pushed-around-yet-uneaten meal.

"That's not whining—that's being truthful." Izzie smiled. "I have this conversation with my girlfriends all the time. It's a toss-up between being on our own forever and getting used to it, or boarding the first plane to Alaska, where there are single men dying to meet you."

"Why can't the Alaska guys come to the Upper East Side?" Linda wanted to know.

"Because then, I guess, they'd become New York men and suddenly they'd have supermodels throwing themselves at their feet and they wouldn't want us normal women anymore."

"Oh, save me from models." Linda sighed.

Izzie laughed this time. "I work with models," she explained. "I'm a booker with Perfect-NY."

Linda looked at her with respect. "Look at me whining about being lonely when you've got to compete with that. There isn't enough Lexapro in the world to make me work with models."

"Really, they're just kids who happen to look that way," Izzie pointed out. "Lots of models are just as messed up as the rest of us. Looking amazing doesn't fix any of the stuff on the inside."

"I could deal with a lot of shit inside if I looked like that on the outside," Linda said fervently. "Still, I guess they'll get old too one day."

"You're not old," Izzie insisted.

Linda looked at her. "In this town, Izzie, once you're sliding down toward fifty, you might as well get a walker. Screw surgery and Botox: men want real youth and tight little asses and ovaries that still pump out an egg. They might not want a kid, but they want a woman who could have one if they changed their mind. They want youth, end of story."

She sounded so harsh, so bitter that Izzie could say nothing in response. For once, her appetite deserted her.

All conversation stopped while the fashion show and auction part of the lunch began. Waiters silently cleared away the dishes, African-inspired technomusic pumped out of the speakers, and the show began.

Izzie watched as the models—many of whom were from Perfect-NY, supplied free of charge for the event—stalked up and down the runway. Normally, she watched her girls intensely, scanning their moves and faces to see who looked content, who looked bored and whose pupils betrayed too many sips of the preshow champagne. But today Izzie was still shaken as she thought about her conversation with Linda and what she'd left unsaid: that she was scared of being alone too.

It had been a long time since she'd admitted that to anyone, even to herself.

Marriage had seemed inevitable when she was growing up in Tamarin: you met someone and got married, simple as that. It would all fall into place gently, without you having to do anything.

Except that she'd left Tamarin for London and then New York, a place where the same boy-meets-girl-and-gets-married rules didn't seem to apply. Now, while all of her old school friends had at least one marriage under their belts, she hadn't even come close to being engaged.

Finding the right person seemed a bit like commanding a space shuttle coming back to earth—there was a remarkably small window of opportunity, much smaller than anyone realized, and if you missed it, you had to hope you'd find another window before it was too late.

When the single guys were gone, you had to wait for the next round—the ones who'd been married, got divorced and were ready to go again. Except that they went for younger women, maybe ten years younger. And the women the same age as the guys were the ones who lost out.

Izzie thought about her forthcoming fortieth birthday in November.

A passionate Scorpio, as her astrologically mad friend, Tish, liked to remind her. Izzie and Tish had lived together on the second floor of a three-story walk-up in the West Village when Izzie had first come to New York.

They were the same age, in the same industry—Tish was a photographer's assistant—and both were immigrants. Ten years on, Tish's lilting Welsh accent was as pronounced as ever. She was also married and the mother of a six-month-old baby boy.

Tish would be forty soon too, but Izzie was facing it from a vantage point different from her friend's.

Everyone had moved their chairs to get a better view of the fashion show, so when it was time for the auction, Brioni Suit Guy was sitting much nearer to her. Izzie hadn't noticed until her auction program fell and he got up smoothly, picked it up and held it out toward her.

"Thank you," she said, startled, reaching for it.

"Unpainted nails, how refreshing," he remarked.

Izzie never polished her nails with anything but clear gloss. In a sea of exquisite manicures, her almost-nude hands stood out.

"I'm not a curly girl," she said absently. She felt too jolted by Linda's conversation to show the same level of interest in the guy.

He'd hardly be interested in her, anyway, what with her shriveling ovaries and skin that no amount of Dermalogica facials could refresh.

"What?" he asked.

"I'm not a curly girl."

"I wasn't talking about your hair." His fingers didn't reach to touch the caramel curls that were streaked with honey tones at ferocious cost in Salon Circe every six weeks. But he looked at her as if he was thinking of it.

Linda had slipped off to the bathroom, so her seat was free and Brioni Suit Guy took it, pulling it so close to Izzie that she felt her breath catch. She was a tall woman and instinctively knew if people were taller than she. He was.

"I'm Joe Hansen," he said, holding out his hand.

"Izzie Silver," she replied automatically, catching his and feeling something inside her jolt at the touch of that firm, masculine hand.

Nearly forty, but she could still feel the surge of attraction, couldn't she?

And the way he was looking at her, watching, made her think that he wasn't looking for a twenty-five-year-old. He was looking at her.

Smiling, a nice, real smile. Making her think of him with that shirt ripped off, and her close to him, kissing him, being cradled in those big arms, his mouth closed over the brown nub of her nipple. Phew.

Even now, Izzie could recall every precise detail of the moment. "So, what's the 'curly girl' thing?" he asked.

Wiping the nipple-sucking vision from her mind, Izzie grinned at him now, not her sassy New Yorker-by-adoption grin but the born-and-bred-country-girl grin her family would have recognized. "My best friend from school used to call that sort of thing 'curly.' Don't know why. She had an odd way with words. *Curly* means the sort of person who loves pink ribbons and barrettes, makes her eyes look like Bambi's and believes in eating before a dinner date so men won't think she's a great horse of a creature with a huge appetite."

"I'd warrant a guess you never did anything like that in your life," he said, assessing her with his eyes. "Not that there's anything wrong with a huge appetite."

A quicksilver flip in her stomach made Izzie think he wasn't referring to appetites at mealtimes.

"I like my food," she said flatly.

He'd get no games from her. She knew how they were played after years of dating in Manhattan. Games were games. This was for real, wasn't it?

"Favorite meal, then? Your last meal on earth?"

He was leaning back in Linda's chair by now, totally oblivious to everyone round them. The charity auction had begun. Some hideous piece of sculpture was being sold and the other alpha males in the room were practically beating their chests like gorillas trying to buy it.

But Joe wasn't interested. His total focus was on her. In turn, she couldn't take her eyes off his face, off the steel gray eyes that were making her feel like the most important person in the room. That couldn't be a trick, could it? Could a person fake absolute fascination?

Izzie sensed rather than saw the women at their table noticing the courtship going on between her and Joe, and she knew that it was time to put a stop to it all, and go back to the real world. Somebody would notice. She half recognized his name and was sure that Mr. Hansen was a big fry while she was just a shrimp in the pond. But somehow she couldn't put a stop to this just yet. It had been so long since she'd flirted with a man or felt even a quarter of the attraction she felt right now. Just a few minutes more—that couldn't hurt, right?

"Cough medicine and painkillers, probably," she joked. She joked when she was nervous.

"Not your last meal in Cedars-Sinai," he said, eyes glinting now and a smile turning up his mouth ever so slightly. He smiled with his eyes, Izzie realized. So few people did that.

"Trout caught from the stream beside my home in Ireland, with salad—arugula from the garden my grandmother set. She says it's a great cure for grumpiness, puts a bit of pep back into you. And gooseberry tart with cream."

"Real food," Joe said, and his eyes were smiling more, sending out even more warmth that hit her square in the heart. "I was afraid you might say something about rare Iranian caviar or champagne out of a small vineyard that they only stock in five-star hotels in Paris."

"Then you don't know me very well," Izzie countered. There weren't many things that surprised Mr. Hansen very much, she felt sure. *Shrewd* wasn't the word. Izzie had a feeling she'd managed a feat few people ever had, and all because she'd been herself. Normally, being herself got her nowhere with men. How lovely to meet one who liked the unvarnished, raw Izzie Silver. The on-the-verge-of-forty Izzie.

"I'd like to," he said. "Know you well, I mean."

"Sold at seventy thousand dollars!" yelled the auctioneer triumphantly. Izzie glanced up. The red-faced oil billionaire at the table next to theirs was now the proud owner of what looked to Izzie like a squashed car gearbox painted with acid yellow dribbles. Art, schmart.

"I'm boring you," Joe said softly.

"No." Izzie flushed. She *never* flushed. Flushing was manhunting girlie behavior, ranking alongside her pet hates like hair-flicking and the tentative licking-of-lip thing that men always seemed to fall for, brain surgeons and cabdrivers alike. Men could be so dumb.

"You're not boring me at all," she said quickly. He was unsettling her, though. Not that she could say that. *Hello, I haven't been on a date in six months and have given up on men, so you're not boring me, but you're freaking the hell out of me because I like you.* No, definitely not something she could say.

He was talking again; he'd think she was a total nutcase, the way she kept tuning in and out.

"That's good," he said. "I'd hate to be boring."

As if, Izzie thought with a little sigh.

The voice of the auctioneer boomed out of the sound system: "The next item in today's auction is a portrait painted by art legend Pasha Nilanhi. Who'll start the bidding at twenty thousand dollars?"

Everyone made the correct noises of appreciation. Izzie had no idea who this Pasha person was, but everyone else must from the approving murmurs. Or else they were pretending in case they looked like art philistines.

"Do you collect art?" he asked her as she craned her neck to see the picture that was now being carried round among the tables.

"Only if it's in the pages of magazines," she said with a mischievous smile. "To let you in on a secret, I didn't pay for my ticket today," she added. "I'm not one of the art-collecting ladies who lunch."

She waited for him to retreat. She was too old and not rich, either.

"I've a secret too," he murmured, moving closer so that she instinctively bent her head to hear him. "I figured that out for myself. That's why I'm talking to you."

Izzie felt another swoop deep in her belly. "You're saying I stand out like a sore thumb?" she teased.

"In a good way." He grinned. "The big giveaway was seeing you actually eat the entrée."

Izzie couldn't help herself: she let out a great roar of laughter.

"Greed was the giveaway," she laughed. "How awful."

"Not greed," he insisted. "Hey, I ate mine too."

"You're a guy," Izzie said, as if explaining experimental physics to a four-year-old. "Guys can eat and it looks macho. In our screwed-up universe, women can't eat."

"Except for you," he urged.

"Except for me," she agreed, feeling suddenly heiferlike.

"Good. Because I was going to ask you out to lunch and there wouldn't be any point if you wouldn't eat. Or if lunch isn't acceptable, we could have dinner?"

Izzie wanted to shriek "Yes!" at the top of her voice. This man, all elegance in a Brioni suit that cost more than a month's rent on her apartment, had captured her as surely as if he'd caged her. He might dress like a civilized man, but he was a hunter all the same, a predator, the alpha male.

And playing with alpha males was madness. They knew what they wanted and went after it ruthlessly. Izzie didn't want to be hurt.

To steady herself, she reached for the stem of her wineglass and twirled it. The table no longer looked pretty. It was sad now: the menus tossed aside, place names scrunched up, dirtied napkins left carelessly alongside coffee cups and untouched petits fours.

The whole shebang was nearly over and she had to go back to work afterward, back to her normal life where millionaires didn't flirt with her.

She lived in a tiny apartment with a dripping showerhead, mold in the cupboard under the sink in the kitchen, and she still owed twelve hundred dollars on her credit card, for God's sake, after splurging on those Christian Louboutin platforms and the Stella McCartney trousers. Had he mistaken her for someone else from his blue-chip world? She imagined people she knew hearing about her flirting with Joe Hansen and winced. She'd never wanted to be a rich man's arm candy: arm candy was twenty-something and ninety pounds, most of it breast enhancement, veneers and ego.

"Everything is possible," she said cheerily, the way she spoke to woebegone models on the phone when they hadn't been booked for something they were sure they'd got. "Not probable, though."

"Why not?"

Izzie thought about her words. "Because although I don't know you from Adam, Mr. Hansen, I have a pretty good idea that you live in a different world to me and it's not my world."

"What do you mean?" he asked.

Izzie threw up her hands. "OK, I've got three questions for you and if you answer yes to any of them, then we agree that you come from a different world. Deal?"

"Deal," he agreed, his eyes amused.

"You haven't flown commercial in the past year. Am I right?" She smiled and so did he.

"Yes," he admitted.

Izzie held up one finger. People needed more than the average production-line worker's salary to fly on private aviation.

"Were there three or more zeros on the check you gave for today's charity?"

This time he laughed. "You're clever."

"Is that a yes?"

"That's a yes."

She held up two fingers. "Two yeses," she said. From the way one of the table-hopping organizers had gushed over him earlier, Izzie had surmised that Joe had dropped a check for at least a hundred thousand dollars on the charity.

"Finally, do you own another home on the East Coast—say, in the Hamptons or Westchester or fill-in-the-blanks Ralph Lauren–style destination?"

He closed his eyes and ran a hand over a jaw that already had stubble shading it. Sexy, Izzie thought. Men who were smooth in every sense worried her; this guy was very real, very male. She liked that.

"You got me," he said. "None of that explains why we can't be friends."

Izzie favored him with her narrowed-eyes look that said, without actual words: *And the check's in the mail, right?*

"I'm not very good at this," he added ruefully.

"You're probably marvelous at it," she said. "I'm the one who's out of practice."

"I find that hard to believe."

"Well, believe it, Mr. Hansen," she said. "I've just had a depressing conversation about age with the woman whose seat you're sitting in. New York older women age in proportion to dog years. Once we hit forty, we freewheel downhill to becoming senior citizens, wearing elasticized waists and going on cruises so we can put on another twelve pounds at the buffet. To sum up: I am all out of sexy chat with new men."

She was sort of sorry by the time the words had left her mouth, but still, she didn't want to be toyed with. Joe was probably only amusing himself with her until a more likely prospect came along.

"You don't look forty," he said. "And I'm really not good at this. I'm out of practice too. I was married for a long time and my wife and I have, well—separated." He said it all slowly, like he was just getting used to the phrase.

"Sorry to hear that."

"Thanks, but it's been a long time coming." He shrugged. "We were married young. We've been trying to make it work for a long time but, hey, it hasn't."

"You're on the lookout for a second wife, then?" Izzie asked cheekily. "Because your neighbor"—she meant the woman with the bank-vault jewelry—"seemed to be auditioning for the role."

"Muffy?" he said. "She's sweet but not really my type."

Sweet? Muffy? She was as sweet as a rattlesnake, Izzie thought, but let it pass. She liked the fact that he wasn't the sort of guy to make a snide remark about Muffy.

"Listen," he went on, "I don't do this normally. It's been"—he winced—"over twenty years since I did."

He put one hand on her bare arm and Izzie had to hide her sharp intake of breath.

What was happening to her?

"I take risks in business, calculated ones. I try to systematically beat the markets through math. Sometimes I bet on long shots, but not often. I'm known for being straight and saying what I think. I've never sat beside a strange woman at a charity luncheon and felt like this, or acted like this. For all I know, you might have a hotline to Page Six of the *New York Post* to say Joe Hansen has lost it, but for once, I don't care because I've got to say what I feel."

There was silence. His fingers were still wrapped around her arm, warm skin on warm skin.

"This is crazy," Izzie said, shaken.

Their eyes locked and he only looked away to curse lightly under his breath and take a tiny, vibrating cell phone from his breast pocket. He scanned it quickly, then put it back.

"I've got to go," Joe said urgently. "Can I drop you someplace?"

"I've got to go back to work too," she said. Work seemed like a million miles away. "But my office is off Houston, it may not be on your way . . ." she added lamely.

"I've got time," he said.

Suddenly, they were leaving, walking out without saying goodbye to anyone. The auction was still going on. Joe made a call on his cell phone and by the time they reached the street there was a discreet black car waiting for them. It was sleek and luxuriously anonymous, like something NASA might consider sending to Mars. Izzie climbed in.

"I've lived in apartments smaller than the inside of this car," she joked, settling back into a seat of pale cream leather.

"I know the owner. We could sort out a deal," he joked back.

She sat as far away from him as she could get in the backseat, trying to appear as if she spent a lot of time being ferried round the city in luxury.

"You know about me and I still don't know anything about you, Ms. Silver. What do you do?" he asked.

Izzie gave him her spiel. Women were normally interested in the fashion world and made sympathetic noises about working with beautiful beings. Men were either bored or their faces lit up and they wanted to know—some subtly, some not so subtly—if her agency had any of the Victoria's Secret girls on their books.

Joe did none of these things.

He asked her about the agency and about the problems faced by a business where the main commodity was human beings. As the car cruised along, insulating Izzie and Joe from the rainy streets via darkened windows, she became passionate about the flaws in the industry.

Before she knew it, she'd forgotten everything except the need to explain to this man that she hated seeing so many girls messed up by fashion's predilection for using the skinniest-limbed waifs they could find.

"Officially, fashion people say it's not our fault that the big look is 'rexy'—a combination of *sexy* and *anorexic*," she explained when he looked baffled, "but of course the whole fashion industry is a factor. C'mon, if you're a fourteen-year-old and you see an airbrushed girl in every TV commercial or magazine spread, eventually you'll think that's what you're supposed to look like, even if it's physically impossible for you. So hello to anorexia or bulimia."

"I'm glad I've got sons," he remarked.

"Sons? How old are they?" Izzie recovered at lightning speed. Of course he'd have children. He'd spoken about a long marriage: children would be part of that.

"Twenty-three, twelve and fourteen," he said, his face softening. "Tom, he's the eldest. He's in France working on his French, and possibly on the girls. Matt's next, bit of a gap, I know, and he's into music in a big way. Practices guitar all the time, won't touch his math homework. Ironic, given that's how I've made my money. Josh is more into his books. His school had an extra language class this term, Japanese, and he took it." Joe couldn't keep the pride out of his voice. "Tom says his little bro is mad. Kids, huh?"

"And they live with . . . ?" Izzie probed.

"Us. We're still in the same house while we're sorting it all out," he said. "The separation has been a long time coming, but we've only recently formalized it. We've a big house," he added. "We want to get things right for the boys and this was the best way. No 'Dad moving out,' not yet."

"Ah," Izzie said. Time for her to back off. No matter what instant attraction she'd had for this guy, she didn't want to get caught up in a messy separation and divorce, or even be his rebound person. Any man getting out of a marriage after that long would be rebounding like a basketball at a Knicks game.

"That's my building," she told the driver as the Perfect-NY offices came into view.

The car pulled up. Joe put one hand on the door handle to let her out his side, the curb side.

"Would you have lunch with me one day?" he asked.

"You're still married," Izzie pointed out. "In my book, that affects the whole dating process. It gets kinda messy—I've seen it. I don't want to experience it."

"Just lunch," he said, and his steel gray eyes seemed to melt as they stared at hers. Izzie felt it again: that lurch of excitement inside her. She could honestly say she'd never felt anything like that before in her whole life, but what was the point? Their relationship could only be a friendship, it had no future. Otherwise, she'd be doing something really dumb.

"Don't move," Joe told the driver. "I'll let Ms. Silver out."

"Whatever you want, Mr. Hansen."

Whatever you want, Mr. Hansen, thought Izzie helplessly, feeling that wave of attraction spanning out from her solar plexus again.

Just one little lunch. What was the harm in that?

two

The edges of the black-and-white photograph were ragged and slightly faded, yet life shone out of it as fiercely as if it had been taken moments before instead of some seventy years previously.

Four women and five men stood around a huge stone fireplace, all clad in the evening dress of the 1930s: the women with marcelled hair, languid limbs and dresses that pooled like silk around their ankles; the men were stern-faced in black tie, with luxuriant mustaches, and an air of command lingering around them. One man, the oldest of the group, held a fat cigar to his lips, another raised his crystal tumbler to the photographer, one foot resting lazily on the fireplace's club fender, the perfect picture of a gentleman at ease.

On either side of the group stood two antique tables decorated with flowers and silver-framed photographs. On the parquet in front of them, a tiger rug lay carelessly.

The whole scene spoke of money, class and privilege.

Jodi could almost hear a scratchy gramophone playing Ivor Novello or the Kit Kat Band in the background, the music weaving a potent spell.

"Lady Irene's birthday. Rathnaree, September 1936," was written in faded ink on the back.

Jodi wondered which of the four women was Lady Irene. One of the two blondes, or perhaps the woman with a jeweled tiara woven into her cloudy dark hair like an Indian nautch dancer?

The photo had been tucked away in a copy of *The Scarlet Pimpernel,* caught in the library's elderly glued-on cover from decades ago. Jodi Beckett had nearly missed it. She'd gone to the Tamarin library one morning when her computer crashed for the third time and she'd been so angry that she just had to get out of the small cottage that still wasn't her home, even though she and Dan had lived in Tamarin for two months now. Relentless rain meant that even walking was no escape, and then Jodi had thought of the library right at the end of their street.

She'd spent many hours in the college library when she'd been studying at home in Brisbane, but in the past few years she'd rarely ventured into one. She passed the Tamarin Public Library every day on her way to buy groceries and she'd never stepped inside. That morning, she ran down Delaney Street, head bent against rain that stung like needles, and entered a haven.

The place was empty except for an elderly man engrossed in the day's newspapers and a twentysomething librarian with a clever face, dyed jet black hair, a nose ring and violet lipstick that matched her fluffy angora hand-knit sweater. Silence reigned, settling over Jodi as calmly as if a meditation CD was playing in her head.

An hour flew past as she wandered among the shelves, picking up book after book, smiling at ones she'd read and loved, making mental notes of ones she hadn't.

And then the photograph had fallen from *The Scarlet Pimpernel*, and Jodi had felt that surge of fascination she remembered from a long-ago summer when she'd joined an archaeological dig in Turkey as a student.

Archaeology hadn't been for her: she loved history but wasn't enamored of the physical digging-in-the-dirt part of it. Yet this photo gave her the same buzz, the sense of finding something nobody had seen for decades, the sense of a mystery waiting to be unraveled.

The librarian had been delighted to be asked for information and had told her that Rathnaree was the big house of the locality.

"They were known as the Lochraven family, Lord Lochraven of

Tamarin. Sounds good, huh? They were Tamarin's gentry," she'd said. "It's still a beautiful house, although it's a bit ruined now. Nobody's lived there for years. Well, since I can remember," she added.

"Are there any books about the house or the family?" Jodi asked.

The librarian shook her head. "No, not one, which is odd. The Lochravens were in that house for two hundred years at least, maybe longer, so there must be lots of interesting stuff there."

Jodi felt the surge of mystery again. "I know the photo's probably officially the library's," she said, "but could I take it and get a copy made? I'm a writer," she added, which was technically true. She was a writer, but was unpublished since her thesis on nineteenth-century American poets, and had made her living for the past seven years in publishing, working as a copy editor. "I'd love to do some research on Rathnaree. See the house, hear about the people . . . write a book about it."

There, she'd said it. Dan was always urging her to write one, but Jodi didn't know if she had the spark required for fiction and, until now, she'd never had an idea for nonfiction.

"A book on Rathnaree! Wicked!" the librarian replied. "There's a guidebook on the town with information about it, but that's all. Don't move! I'll find it for you. You'll love the house. It's beautiful. I mean, imagine living in a mansion like that."

A copy of the photo now lay on the passenger seat of Jodi's car along with a small local guide to the area which carried another photo of Rathnaree House as it had looked in the fifties. She rounded the last corner of the avenue to the house, mentally muttering about how hopeless the car's suspension was, and how bumpy the avenue. *Avenue* was really far too grand a word for it, she decided, for even though it was lined with stately beech trees and was at least a mile long, it was nothing more than a country track with a high ridge in the middle where grass grew.

And then, when she'd cleared the last corner and driven past an overgrown coral pink azalea, she saw the house. And her foot slid automatically to the brake, hauling the little car to a stop on a scree of gravel.

"Holy moly," Jodi said out loud, and stared.

The grainy black-and-white picture in the Tamarin guidebook hadn't done justice to the house. In its nest of trees, once-perfect hedging and trailing roses stood what the guidebook had described as "a perfect example of Victorian Palladianism." In reality, this meant a gracefully designed gray building with the graceful arches and stone pillars of Palladian architecture and vast symmetrical windows looking out over a pillowy green lawn dotted with daisies and dandelions.

The huge house stretched endlessly back and widened into stables, servants' quarters, a Victorian conservatory to the right and the lichened walls of a kitchen garden that led off to the left. Giant stone plinths topped with weed-filled jardinières signaled the start of a boxwood-edged herb garden designed in a knot layout, now rampant with woody rosemary and lavender that sent their hazy smells drifting into the air.

There were no ladies in elaborate flowered hats and long dresses standing about beside stern mustachioed men, nor any sign of long sweeping cars with gleaming bonnets. But this Rathnaree, although older and clearly much less tended than the version in either of the photographs, still retained the unmistakable grandeur of the Big House.

Fleets of servants would have been needed to run it and thousands of acres of farmland would have been needed to pay for it all.

It was another world, a time when Tamarin was the little town where the powerful Lochraven family sent their servants to do their bidding. Now Tamarin was a thriving place while Rathnaree was empty, the Lochravens long gone, apart from the house's owner, a distant cousin who never set foot in the place, the librarian had explained.

"Rathnaree is the Anglicized version of the name. It's really *Rath na ri*—fort of the king, in the Irish language," she'd continued. "Can't remember half of what I learned in school, but we all had that drummed into us. I had a history teacher once who was very interested in the Lochravens, said her mother had been at hunt balls at Rathnaree House in the thirties; it was very formal, with a butler and women wearing long dresses and gloves. Imagine! I like those sorts of dresses but I wouldn't be into the gloves. Do you want me to draw you a map of how to get there?"

"No," Jodi said. "I know roughly where it is. I've been living here for two months now."

"You have? Where? Tell us." The girl had leaned companionably on the counter.

"My husband and I moved from Dublin," Jodi explained, as she had so often since she and Dan had arrived in Tamarin.

No chance of not knowing your neighbors *here*.

It was all very different from the apartment in Clontarf where they'd lived for two years and only knew their neighbors from the sounds they heard through the thin partition walls. On one side, there were the Screamers During Sex. On the other side were the *CSI* addicts, who had digital television and spent entire evenings with the television on full volume so no bit of an autopsy went unheard. Neither Dan nor Jodi would have recognized either set of neighbors in the lift unless one of them had shouted, "Oh yes, *yes!!*"

Their new home in Tamarin was a crooked-walled cottage on Delaney Street with a tiny whitewashed courtyard of a garden. Within a week of their arrival, they'd been to dinner with the neighbors on both sides, had been offered a marmalade kitten by the people across the street and were on first-name terms with the postman. In their old home, they'd never even seen the postman.

"Dan, my husband, works in St. Killian's National School," Jodi explained. "He's the new vice principal—"

"Oh, Mr. Beckett! My little sister's in sixth class. Now I know you!" The librarian was thrilled. "You're Australian, aren't you?"

Jodi grinned. "Great bush telegraph round here."

"Works better than the broadband." The girl grinned back.

"Tell me about it. I work in publishing and I'm going crazy trying to connect. The engineer told me it was to do with being at the end of the line on our street, which doesn't make sense."

"He says that to everyone, don't mind him."

A group of schoolchildren and their teacher on a mission to find out about Early Bronze Age settlement remains had arrived at that moment, and the librarian, smiling apologetically at Jodi, had turned to deal with their request. Jodi had made a few gestures to signify her thanks, and left.

She'd gone home with her precious photograph, and that evening, when Dan arrived home, she'd told him about her idea.

"You want to write a book about these people," he said, sitting down at their tiny kitchen table so he could study the photograph carefully. "Sounds good to me. Ain't I always telling you that you should write a book?"

"Yes, but I never had anything I wanted to write about," Jodi said, perching on his lap.

Dan put his arms around her and held her.

"I'm sorry about today," she said. She'd phoned him at work when her computer had crashed for the third time, shouting that she was sick of this bloody town and it was all very well for him—he had a job to go to and people to see—but what about her?

"It's OK. I know it's hard for you," Dan said, his lips buried in her hair. "I love you, you know, you daft cow."

"Love you too," she'd replied, allowing herself to feel comforted by him. Since the miscarriage, she'd felt so wound up, like a coiled-wire spring, that she'd been unable to let Dan console her.

Moving here for his new job was supposed to help, but it hadn't. Here, in this watercolor-pretty town, she felt alien and out of place. Even their old home with the noisy-during-sex neighbors was better than this. She'd done the pregnancy test there: sitting on the toilet seat in their tiny blue bathroom with Dan hovering over her eagerly.

She'd been pregnant there. In Tamarin, she wasn't. Might never be again.

And now this old photo had sparked a little of the old Jodi, had made her feel ever so slightly like she could be herself again.

She leaned against Dan and closed her eyes. She'd have to do some online searching. And sort out the laptop. No way could she begin proper research with a dodgy computer.

Two days later, she was standing in front of beautiful Rathnaree House with the scent of lavender in her head.

Jodi wandered around the deserted gardens, peering in the great windows, but she could see so little: the windows were filthy and shuttered from the inside. The gloom from within meant she couldn't make out anything.

Prevented from entering the courtyard behind the house by a giant rusting gate, she stood with her hands on it, rattling it furiously.

She wanted to get inside, wanted to see Rathnaree and learn its stories.

Her list of people to see was growing. Ever since she'd told Dan about the photo, ideas had been bubbling out of her head. First, she needed to speak to someone who knew everything about the local area and would be able to put her in touch with the right people. Yvonne, who lived next door to them with her husband and two children, instantly came up with a long list of people who'd be able to help.

"Lily Shanahan, she's the one you should talk to. Nearly ninety but doesn't look a day over seventy. There's no case of her mind going, either, let me tell you. She's as sharp as a tack but in a lovely way," Yvonne added quickly. "Her family worked for the Lochravens and so did she when she was younger, although I don't think she was ever as keen on them as her mother. Her mum was the housekeeper for years and that woman idolized Lady Irene. But Lily, she wasn't a fan of Lady Irene's to-the-manor-born carrying-on. Still, she'll have some stories of Rathnaree for you, I'm sure. There isn't much around here that she hasn't witnessed."

Jodi wrote it all down quickly.

"Do you think I should call her family first, to see if she'll talk to me?" Jodi asked, thinking that such an old lady might get a shock if a strange Australian woman approached her.

"Lord, no. There's no need for formality with Lily. I'll give you her phone number," Yvonne replied. "She lives on her own out on the Sea Road. She has help these days to do little jobs around the house, but she's very independent."

"She has family, though?" Jodi still thought she might approach Lily via someone else. A ninety-year-old was bound to be frail and anxious.

"Her family are all lovely. There's her nephew, Edward Kennedy, and his wife, Anneliese. I work with Anneliese in the Lifeboat Shop on Mondays. You say her name like it's Anna-Lisa but it's spelled an unusual way. It's Austrian, I think. They're a gorgeous couple, Anneliese is a fabulous gardener. Green fingers, she has. Lily had a daughter, Alice, but she died, I'm afraid. Cancer. But Lily's granddaughter, Izzie, she lives in New York and she works with supermodels. Not that you'd think it," Yvonne said, smiling. "Izzie's very normal, despite the supermodels and everything. Lily more or less raised her, to be honest, and Lily is very down to earth."

"Do you have her granddaughter's email address or phone number in New York?" Jodi asked. "I could approach her first?"

"Nonsense." Yvonne was brisk. "Go directly to Lily. You'll love her—everyone does."

"She worked for the Lochravens, you said?"

"When she was young, she did. But she went off to London to train as a nurse during the Second World War, and I don't think she ever worked in Rathnaree again. It was all changed, anyway," Yvonne added. "Nothing was the same after that, my mother used to say."

Jodi made a mental note to study more about World War II. There was so much she didn't know and she didn't want to interview the old lady without being sure of her facts.

She'd phone Lily Shanahan as soon as she got home, Jodi decided, giving the big rusted old gate one final shove. It remained unmoved and she could only look into one corner of the courtyard from where she stood.

She only hoped that Lily had a good memory. If she was almost ninety now, she'd have been seventeen or eighteen in 1936, the date on the photograph, and that was an awfully long time ago. Then again, Yvonne had said that age hadn't diminished any of Lily's faculties. Jodi hoped that was the case. There was something about Rathnaree that made her want to know more about it and the people who'd lived and breathed inside its walls.

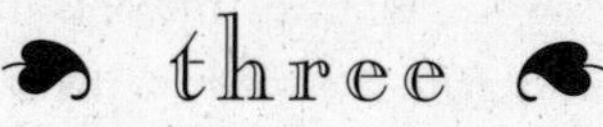

three

Anneliese Kennedy sat down in the big armchair that faced the sea and picked up one of her old flower catalogs. There was always a pile of dog-eared catalogs on the white cane table beside the chair, ready to flick through when she hadn't the energy for the newspaper.

Normally, her fingers had only to graze the pages for a feeling of contentment to flood through her. Pages of seeds illustrated with full-bodied blossoms made her think of hours spent in her garden, hands buried in the soil, nurturing and thinking about nothing more than nature.

Today the magic wasn't there. There was just a bunch of well-thumbed catalogs, and the hand that lay on them was veined with alligator skin and ragged cuticles.

"You've such pretty hands, you should look after them," her mother had sighed some thirty-seven years before when Anneliese was a young bride and prone to plunging her hands into dishwater without the time or the inclination to think about wearing rubber gloves.

Anneliese was a high-speed sort of person. Not reckless—never. Quick, practical and deft. Gloves and hand creams were for her mother's generation, not for a twenty-year-old with vast energy and a life to be lived.

"Artist's hands and green fingers," Edward said proudly as they stood in the front of the church the day their daughter, Beth, got married and Anneliese had spent hours tying barely unfurled blush pink roses into tiny posies for the pews.

Anneliese preferred growing roses in the comfort of the Tamarin Garden Center to making them into bouquets, but she'd have tied the roses together with her teeth in joy at seeing Beth walk up the aisle.

Four years ago now, it had been the best day of her life, seeing Beth finally settled. Beth was like a rose herself: one of the rare antique tea roses that Anneliese and Stephen, who owned the garden center, liked to grow in the shelter of the giant greenhouse.

Madame Alfred Carrière, very beautiful to look at with a glorious scent, but also prickly, high maintenance and needing hours of tender care. The day Beth married Marcus—gentle, strong of heart and crazy about her—Anneliese knew someone else was going to be providing that tender care, or at least sharing it with her.

If Beth was a rose, Edward was a tree, a rare oak, standing tall and strong against the sea wind. And Anneliese? When she'd met Edward, she was like a poplar: tall, slim and vibrant from the top of her fair head to the tips of her ever-moving toes.

But she didn't know what she was anymore. Time and life had changed her.

Once, when she'd started working in horticulture, she'd thought that the art of growing things was the answer to all questions. The earth taught you to be calm, to wait, that the cycles changed but it would all come round again: spring would follow a harsh winter, eventually. Nothing, not problems nor solutions, could be rushed—any more than you could rush the questing head of a snowdrop. The snowdrop would emerge sleepily into the air when it was good and ready.

That became Anneliese's motto. Things happened when they were good and ready.

And now, it seemed, she was wrong. Totally wrong.

She got up, went into the kitchen and put on the kettle. It was a reflex action. When she had nothing to do, she flicked that switch and busied herself with the ritual of tea-making. Most of the time, she barely drank more than half the tea.

Edward wasn't a tea person: he preferred coffee. There was still a jar of his favorite and wildly expensive Blue Mountain from Fortnum & Mason in the cupboard.

Anneliese hated coffee but liked the smell of it. There would be no one to make coffee now, no rich aroma lifting into the air to tell her that Edward was in the kitchen, idly listening to the radio as he brewed up.

There would be no other person to move a tea towel, reposition a cushion, unfold a newspaper. After three decades of living with another person, would she now get used to this aloneness? Perhaps aloneness was the true human state, and not the Platonic vision of two together. She hoped so.

She flicked off the kettle switch, grabbed her keys and went to the back door. Swapping her flat shoes for boots, she put on the old padded jacket that hung with a selection of others on a peg in the tiny back hallway. The back door faced the beach, and when Anneliese pulled it open, the fresh hit of sea breeze caught her breath.

The scent of sand and the tang of the sea filled her lungs and she gasped for a moment before recovering.

Her cottage was half a mile from the beach, half a mile where tenacious scrub grass and hardy sea orchids clung to the land before giving way to a crest of small stones that gleamed like precious jewels when the sea drenched them. Now the tide was out and a swath of fawn-colored sand stretched out ahead of her in a big horseshoe. This was Milsean Bay, a small cove that sat beside the much larger Tamarin Bay, the two separated by the jagged cliff that ran down to the edge of the water.

The Milsean side of the cliff was the more exposed part of the headland, where sand and sea rusted cars and pummeled paint off houses, leaving cottages like Anneliese's the same color as the driftwood that swept up onto the beach.

On the other side of the cliff sat Tamarin itself, protected from the bite of the wind and the sea by a tiara of cliffs.

The valley that ran through Tamarin down into the bay, where a chunk of glacier had carved a path millions of years ago, was occupied by both the River Bawn and the fat road in and out of town. In a sunny haven in the curve of the valley was the garden centre where Anneliese had worked until last year.

Years ago, Anneliese had thought she'd like to live safely nestled within the crook of Tamarin Bay, where the wind still rattled the windows but there were neighbors close by on the nights when the power went. In the shelter of the cliffs and the hills, what was almost a microclimate existed, and in the garden center Anneliese grew plants and flowers she wouldn't dream of planting on the Milsean side.

Her aunt-in-law, Lily, had a fig tree in her garden, for heaven's sake: hugely rotund and not so good in the fig department nowadays, like an old gentleman who couldn't be bothered with productivity now that he'd reached his three score and ten, but it was still a fig tree, still a creature of warmer climes.

Now, though, Anneliese was glad she and Edward had moved out here to the cottage twenty years before. The sense of isolation suited her. The wind couldn't scream with any more pain and anger than she did, and here at least if she wanted to sit on her weather-beaten porch and drink wine while *Tosca* shrieked in the background, nobody would call her mad or phone her relatives wondering if they "could have a quiet word."

The beach was scattered with shells and trails of slick seaweed. High on the shoreline were the hoof marks made by the morning riders who galloped along the beach from the stables three miles inland. Edward had taken photographs of them one summer: black-and-white shots of the fury of the gallop, nostrils flared and manes rippling as horses and riders thundered along, sand and surf flying.

One of the photos still hung in the cottage where she could see it every time she walked in the front door. It was a beautiful shot.

"You could take up photography," Anneliese had told him. Edward was very artistic, although there wasn't much call for artistry in the insurance business.

"I'm only an amateur, love," Edward said back, although she knew he was pleased. He hadn't been raised to compliments. Edward's mother thought praise was a word you only used in church, praising the Lord. Anneliese had always tried to make up for the lack of praise in Edward's youth.

"It's pretty good for an amateur."

"You're blind, do you know that?" Edward said, smiling. "You only see my good points."

"Selective blindness." Anneliese smiled back at him. "I see the bits I like and I like most of it."

Walking along the beach now, Anneliese knew she'd have to take the picture off the wall when she got home. It would hurt too much to see it.

The wind bit into her face, stinging her eyes. Anneliese stared down at the sand, determined to find something to shift her mind off the sharp pain in her heart. A few yards ahead of her lay a piece of driftwood, tangled up in a skein of chemical blue net from the fishing boats.

Bending slowly, she picked it up. It was a foot long, twisted like a coil of rope. Some driftwood was beautiful, sculpted by the sea, still a thing of beauty despite the battering. And then there were pieces of driftwood that were just that: wood flung on the beach after thrashing around in the surf, desolate and hollowed out, ugly and unwanted. Like this one. Like me, Anneliese knew.

She wasn't a plant at all—she was driftwood. Ugly to most people, beautiful only to the very few.

Summoning all the pent-up energy in her body, she hurled the driftwood back into the ocean and screamed at it.

"I hate you, I hate you, I hate you."

There was nobody to hear her scream. Her voice was caught on the wind and whipped away into the air, where the seagulls paid no attention.

Edward hadn't seemed to pay attention that morning when she'd got up at eight and said she was going to Sunday Mass at nine, then might call in on Lily. He'd murmured something that sounded like assent, and rolled over in the bed, bunching the snow white of the duvet around his lanky frame. Anneliese didn't mind. She was a lark and he was an owl. Opposites and all that.

Ten minutes later, she was showered, dressed and sipping a cup of green tea before she hurried out the door. She'd grown to like green tea, for all that she'd loathed it for ages after the acupuncturist had said it was good for you. Why was it that things that were good for you took a long time to get used to and things that were bad were instantly addictive?

The early service in St. Canice's in the square in Tamarin was pure and perfect. The cold spring sun sent rays of light shining through the stained-glass windows, leaving dust motes hanging in the air, an effect that was for all the world like celestial rays blessing the faithful in biblical paintings. There was no music at the early service.

The choir sang at eleven Mass, with Mr. Fitzpatrick strangling hymns on a rheumatic organ, with the congregation wincing and Father Sean smiling bravely, willing people not to laugh openly.

Dear Father Sean. He had a great sense of humor which he had to subdue because not everyone wanted a priest who cracked jokes. Anneliese felt sorry for him, having to toe some invisible line.

Eleven was the family Mass too where toddlers knelt on pews and twinkled bored eyes at the people behind them. Adorable but distracting.

At nine on a Sunday morning, the church was only a quarter full and it suited Anneliese perfectly. She loved the peace of it all. Time to think but not so much time that her mind skittered off into dark areas. No, she didn't like that. Luckily, it never happened at Mass. Something to do with the ritual of standing and kneeling, murmuring responses to prayers that were ingrained in her soul because she'd been murmuring them for so many years.

Anneliese's religion was a meditative, safe place for her to rest rather than an intense, doctrinaire version.

Then the migraine came helter-skelter into her head without warning; not the full blast that required lying down, but certainly a blistering ache that made her eyes narrow with pain.

There was no point waiting: she had to go home and lie down. She could phone Lily and apologize later. Her aunt—well, aunt-in-law strictly speaking, because she was actually Edward's aunt—wouldn't mind. Lily had many glorious qualities—she was funny, warm, had a marvelous sense of humor—but one of her absolute virtues was the fact that she never sulked or took offense at anything.

"Take care of yourself, Anneliese, and drop round when you're better," was all she'd say.

Anneliese knew so many people who cherished perceived injuries and looked for them in everything. It was comforting that Lily wasn't such a person.

Anneliese drove home slowly, feeling the car sway a bit with the wind, and hurried into the house, thinking only of the blessed relief of getting into her bed, only half registering that the car parked outside belonged to her friend, Nell. Edward would have to talk to her. Nell wouldn't mind: she and Edward were great pals and Nell knew that when a migraine hit, Anneliese could only think of lying down.

And then she stepped into the kitchen to see Edward and Nell sitting together at the table, his dark head bent toward her fair one and their hands clasped.

There was no soft music or gentle lights, no state of undress. But the intimacy of their togetherness cut into Anneliese like a knife sliding into the underbelly of a chicken fillet.

"Anneliese!" gasped Nell, seeing her.

They moved apart sharply, quickly. In another universe, Anneliese might have joked about what the speedy movement might do to Edward's sciatica or Nell's dodgy neck. But she knew, with absolute certainty, that there was nothing innocent about their closeness. The migraine pummeled louder in her head, fighting with the sense of nausea that rose instantaneously.

"We were just . . ." began Nell awkwardly, and then stopped as if she had no idea what to say next.

Nell was never short of words. In contrast to Anneliese, who preferred silence often, Nell had a word for everyone and a comment for anything.

Like the rain: "It'd be a great little country if only we could get someone to put an umbrella over it."

People loved that.

Or thoughts on money: "Spend it now: there are no pockets in a shroud."

Now Nell had nothing to say.

"Anneliese, you don't want to get the wrong idea," began Edward, his face a mask of anxiety as he moved toward Anneliese and tried to take her hands in his. His hair was wet from the shower. It was only twenty-five minutes since she'd left the house. He must have leaped out of bed as soon as she'd gone.

"Explain the wrong idea to me, so I can understand the difference between it and the right one," Anneliese said, gently detaching her hands. Her head still felt cloudy but the powerful instinctive message in her brain told her not to let her husband touch her.

"Lord, Anneliese, please don't think we'd ever do anything to hurt you," began Nell.

She looked anxiously at Edward, pleading with him to sort it out.

You could tell what people thought by their eyes more easily than by anything else, Anneliese knew.

Over the years, she and Edward had exchanged many telling

looks. And she and Nell had exchanged them too—they'd been friends for nearly twenty years, a lifetime.

Only she'd never been aware of these two important people in her life looking at *each other* in this way. Until now.

Anneliese felt as if she was watching the last reel of a movie where all the plot loopholes are tied up.

Nell and Edward were the ones sharing the telling looks now because they were the couple in this scene—not Anneliese and Edward, but Nell and Edward.

"Please, Anneliese, sit down."

Edward was still beside her, his expression anxious and his hands out in supplication.

"I wish we didn't have to do this but I suppose we have to. Now or never, right?" he said, looking defeated but determined, determined to have this awful conversation.

And that was when Anneliese knew absolutely that Edward was leaving her for Nell.

Edward hated confrontation of any kind. He'd been useless on those occasions when Beth was in floods of tears, distraught over something or other.

His facing a conversation that could easily end in shouting told her all she needed to know.

"You're going, aren't you? You're going with Nell."

Edward nodded mutely and held his hands out imploringly, as if to say, *What else can I do?*

Anneliese sat down then and placed her hands on the table. "I came home early because I've got a migraine," she said to no one in particular.

"Shall I fetch your pills?" Edward said.

She nodded.

He rushed from the room, eager to be gone.

"Tea might help," Nell added, and turned to open cupboards, finding cups and teabags easily. She'd spent so many hours here, sharing tea and life with Anneliese, that she knew where everything was as well as Edward and Anneliese did.

"Tea wouldn't help, actually," Anneliese said harshly. "Nothing is going to help."

Defeated, Nell sat down at the far end of the table opposite Anneliese.

Her hair was different, Anneliese realized. Normally, Nell's dark blond curly hair was windswept even when there wasn't wind. She rarely wore much in the way of makeup, and for a woman of her age—Anneliese's exact age, actually, fifty-six—she had remarkably clear, unlined skin with just a few freckles and the inevitable little creases that spun out from her laughing blue eyes. Today her hair was brushed carefully into shape and she wore lipstick and mascara. She looked done, ready for some event.

And that event was running off with Anneliese's husband.

"Why, Nell, why?"

"Oh, Anneliese, don't sit there and look so surprised," snapped Nell, who'd never snapped at Anneliese before in her life. "You must have known. Edward said you didn't, but I knew you did. Women *know*. You've turned a blind eye, that's all. Which says a lot about your relationship, that you didn't care enough—"

"I didn't know," interrupted Anneliese, shocked at this new version of Nell who, mere moments ago, was saying she'd never meant to hurt Anneliese. "If I'd known, do you think I'd have gone on wanting to be your friend, going for lunch with you, asking you here for dinner?" She stopped because she felt too numb to think up other examples of how she hadn't known. "How long has it been going on?" she whispered.

Anneliese knew she should summon up rage and fury, but all she felt at this moment was a terrible weakness in her legs, and the sense that she'd been totally wrong about the people in her life.

If either Edward or Nell had betrayed her individually, the

other would have been there to remind her that they still loved her. But they'd both betrayed her. Together.

"Don't let on you didn't know. You must have known," Nell hissed.

Again, Anneliese felt herself recoil at the bitterness in her friend's voice.

"Don't lie to me, Anneliese. You might lie to yourself, but you can't lie to me. If you two were crazily in love with each other, would Edward have come to me? Answer me that, then. No, he wouldn't. He came to me because you didn't need him, you cut him off. You had so much and you didn't care, didn't realize it. Well, I did and I'm not going to apologize to you for it."

Anneliese felt the weight of Nell's rage at her: at Anneliese for having the wonderful Edward all to herself and not realizing what a treasure she had, a treasure that she'd stupidly lost.

She thought of all the Saturday nights she'd invited Nell over to the cottage for dinner, making it sound as if they were three friends sharing a meal instead of a happily married couple reaching out the hand of friendship to a widow who might be sitting on her own at home otherwise. Eric, Nell's husband, had died ten years previously, and since then Anneliese had tried so hard to include Nell in their lives. Anneliese had meant it as pure friendship, but perhaps Nell had seen it as something else: as pity? Or as Anneliese showing off, as if to say, *I have a husband and you don't. Come and eat with us and feel jealous, why don't you?* What else had Nell misconstrued?

"I thought you knew me well enough, Nell, to know that if I'd realized you and Edward were—"

Saying it was hard.

"*—having an affair*, I'd have said something. I might have a lot of flaws, but I know that I'm honest. Remember how many talks we had about the value of friendship where honesty mattered? How we hated fake friends, people who said the right things at the right time and meant none of it?"

The anger that hadn't been there suddenly blazed to life in Anneliese's heart. They'd lied to her. They'd both said they valued truth, and now it transpired that truth had been missing for such a long time. Worse, Nell was trying to put the blame onto Anneliese.

"I didn't have a clue what was happening," she went on in a harsh voice. "It might make you feel better to think I did and that I was giving you tacit approval to steal my husband, but I didn't."

"I'm sorry, Anneliese." Edward stood in the doorway, the small plastic container of Anneliese's migraine medicine in his hand and a look of desolation on his face. "I knew you didn't know. I wanted to think you did because it would be easier, but I knew you didn't."

"How long has it been going on, this thing between you two?" Anneliese asked, purposely not looking at Nell anymore.

"Not that long," said Edward.

"Since the fund-raiser for the lifeboat," Nell interrupted, obviously not keen on the damage limitation of breaking it all to Anneliese gently.

Well over a year, Anneliese thought to herself.

"I presume you were waiting for a nice time to break it to me, then. My birthday? Christmas?"

"It had to come out sometime," Nell said coolly. "Might as well be now."

Both women looked at Edward, who shrugged helplessly.

Anneliese felt another surge of anger, white-hot this time.

The words were in Anneliese's mouth before she had time to think about them: "You should pack, Edward. Nell, I'd like you to wait outside, please. I don't want you in my house anymore. You could always go home and wait for Edward to come. He'll need space for his things."

Somehow Anneliese got up and went into the living room, where she broke with the habit of a lifetime and poured herself a strong brandy from the stupid globe drinks cart that Edward loved and she'd always hated. He could have that, for a start.

She heard muffled talking from the kitchen, then the sound of the kitchen door closing and the revving of Nell's car. That was some relief.

She couldn't bear Nell being in the cottage now. Her very presence was poisonous: the worst sort of poison, the sort you hadn't known was dangerous.

After the first drink, Anneliese had a second. Ludicrous to be drinking now, but she needed something to numb her. She sat on the window ledge looking out at the bay and tried not to listen to the sounds of Edward's packing.

When Beth had been a teenager, Anneliese became very good at listening. This was different from listening to a small child messing round in the kitchen: hearing the fridge opening, the milk bottle top being laboriously pulled off, the glug of milk and the intake of breath when some spilled. That was a sort of innocuous listening.

But mothers of teenagers had to listen in a different way; what CD was being played was an excellent gauge.

Oasis and Counting Crows were good signs. Anything slow and dreamy might mean Beth was in a relaxed mood. But Suzanne Vega was fatal. A signal that Beth was in turmoil.

She'd have to tell Beth about this, of course. Anneliese closed her eyes at the thought of *that* conversation.

The back door banged and she jumped at the noise. Edward had gone. She rushed to the side window to see him put one suitcase and a gym bag into his car. He could have taken very little, just his clothes, she decided. Did that mean he wanted to stay after all, or was he so desperate to be with Nell that he didn't care about his belongings? Who knew?

Evening was casting its graying spell over the beach when Anneliese left the cottage, and despite the old padded jacket, she shivered. The beach was bleak when the promise of sun had gone: like a wild kingdom that showed a softer side during the day but when evening arrived it was time for humans to clear off so the place could revert to its feral, untamed state.

The tide was coming in, slowly, inexorably. Anneliese stood at the edge of the water and watched as the waves lapped in and swept out, surging farther and farther up the darkening sand every time. It was relentless. In and out, on and on. Like life, coming at her endlessly, when she wished it would stop.

She watched as if hypnotized until the water seeped into her shoes and then she moved back, startled.

If anyone could see her now, they'd think she was crazy, and perhaps she was: a lonely woman standing half crazed at the shoreline, stuck in every sense of the word. Then she turned and walked home, leaving the dark of evening behind her.

The cottage was scarily silent and she went around turning on all the lights, anything to create a sense of warmth. In the sitting room, she picked up her knitting bag and looked forlornly at the tumbled skeins of colored wools that perched on top.

She couldn't bear the thought of the television or even the radio. But she might knit. Knitting somehow soothed her mind. It was a newish hobby. Newish in that she'd knitted things years ago: slippers, baby clothes, blankets for Beth's dolls. But she'd never been much of an expert. She'd come back to it a year ago, after she stopped working in the garden center and knew she needed something to occupy herself.

She'd toyed with the idea of learning another language or learning the computer, and then Marcus, her son-in-law, had helped by giving her an old laptop. Even though he apologized endlessly for its age and decrepitude, it still worked and Anneliese was thrilled with it.

"It's obsolete," he'd said apologetically.

"It's wonderful." Anneliese smiled.

"It's ten years old. That's practically a dinosaur in computer terms," he'd gone on.

"Like myself," Anneliese added, patting him on the arm.

She loved it, and surfing the Net—how she loved to say those words!—had taken her down a strange path one day to a craft site where she found all types of knitting that had nothing in common with the lumpen slippers and baby cardigans she used to make.

This knitting involved making felted handbags, crafting lace-like shawls, making wall hangings.

She loved it and instantly ordered a handbag kit. Then, in a might-as-well-be-hung-for-a-sheep-as-for-a-lamb moment, she'd also gone to the Crazee Knitters forum and signed herself up as a fledgling knitter. On the site, women from all over the world shared their knitting experiences.

It had taken her ages to write her first message. There was something scarily final about sending your thoughts out there where everyone could read them, but Anneliese felt safe in the anonymity of the internet.

Anneliese from Ireland could be anyone.

In her cottage with every light lit, Anneliese logged on, clicked onto her last message and felt a stab of utter astonishment at what she'd written only a few days before. It was so normal, so ordinary.

I'm halfway through knitting the pink and gray bag. It's so pretty and I can't wait to actually finish it because I want to see what it looks like when it's felted. Last night, I sat up until midnight with the TV on and kept knitting. I sort of watched two medical dramas I've never seen before at the same time and a programme about a man-made island in Dubai and I kept knitting. I wish I was faster and I'm not sure how to knit the flower—does anyone have hints for it?

Anneliese thought of that night. Edward had laughed at her manic knitting and had gone to bed, leaving her and her circular needle in front of the television. At the time she'd felt guilty leaving him to go to bed on his own. It was as bad as having separate bedrooms.

Just showed what she knew.

She'd been worried about sending him to bed alone, when he was probably grateful to escape her.

The pain of today was still too fresh to be anything but numb, but for a brief moment Anneliese felt a sharp stab of agony. Edward was gone and he'd left with Nell. And all along, she hadn't had a clue what was going on under her nose. She used to feel so intuitive, so connected with the universe. Clearly, she wasn't. That connectedness was another big misconception.

What else had she been wrong about in her life?

Suddenly, Anneliese felt that she couldn't cope with all this on her own. She needed something to dull it. She found the corkscrew and a bottle of very expensive red wine that Edward had been saving. Blast that for a game of soldiers, she thought, pouring herself a big glass.

Then, glass in hand, she sat down in front of her laptop and felt grateful for the existence of those other people around the world, who might be sitting as she was now, alone.

The wine bit as it went down. It tasted too acidy, but perhaps that was just her. She'd had a strange metallic taste in her mouth all day: Was that what grief tasted like? She drank it all the same and wondered did anyone on Crazee Knitters have any hints for what to do when your husband of thirty-seven years left you? In the five months since she'd been posting on the site, she'd only ever talked about her knitting—the pink and gray flower bag that had taken her three months because it was very complicated. Other people did talk about their lives, but Anneliese wasn't the sort of person to open herself up to others. Now, when she had this unexpected longing to share her pain, it was too big to talk about.

She scrolled down through the posts. MariLee had posted a picture of the most amazing lacy shawl with a rainbow motif and Anneliese wondered absently if she'd ever be able to make anything that complicated. The flower bag was only difficult because there were so many bits to it. There were no really hard stitches, just lots of fiddly little bits to knit, felt and sew painstakingly together.

Lily had loved the finished product.

"Isn't it a dotey little thing," she'd said when Anneliese arrived to show it off in all its glory.

"I loved knitting when I was younger although I can't knit anymore," she'd added ruefully, holding up fingers gnarled with arthritis. "It calms the soul."

"I can't knit, really," Anneliese replied. "I keep toying with the idea of getting a pattern for a sweater or something, but I'm not sure I could do anything so complicated."

"Anneliese, you can do anything you set your mind to." Lily smiled.

"Am I too old to learn?"

Lily laughed outright at that. "You're never too old to learn, darling," she said. "I'm still learning, and look at me—nearly ninety. You're only a child, Anneliese. What's it they say nowadays? Izzie said it to me once. . . ." Lily stopped to think. "Yes, I've got it: ninety is the new eighty! So fifty-six is like being a teenager, if you make yourself think that way."

Anneliese sighed. She'd have to tell Lily about Edward too.

Not that Lily would be like poor, dear Beth and need careful handling once she heard the news. Lily was quite unshockable, for all that she looked like a delicate little old lady in the flesh. While Lily had once been tall, age had withered her until she had the look of a bird about her: still with those fiercely intelligent cornflower blue eyes that missed nothing, but as fragile as a bird nonetheless. Yet there was nothing fragile about her mind or her opinions.

So it wasn't the thought of shocking Lily that made Anneliese not want to tell her—it was the pity she'd see on Lily's face. Anneliese hated being pitied most of all.

She finished her drink and began to write. Perhaps her fellow knitters had the wisdom she needed.

Sorry to bother you all with this but I've got no one to talk to and I've got to talk. You see, my husband left me today. I won't bore you with the minute details but basically I came home to find him and my best friend talking and I knew. They were having an affair. He left with her. I don't know what to do or think. I haven't told anybody yet—we have a daughter but she's very emotional. You could say she doesn't do reality very well.

The hardest thing is the sense that I didn't know him at all—or her, for that matter. It's like a death. I think I'm going through grief. I feel like people must feel when they discover someone they loved is secretly a rapist or a murderer. I'm so astonished that I didn't know, and then I wonder if everything was a lie. It must be. And I never noticed.

How could that be? How many other things did he lie about? Loving me? That I was the only woman he wanted to make love to? Wanting to be with me? Right now it all could be a lie because he managed to keep one huge lie, so how can I be sure that all the other things aren't lies too?

I can see a photo of us on the wall from here and I'm looking at it, trying to catch a glimpse of this different person who must have been there all along, except that I didn't notice him. This picture of us—me and him and our daughter, when she was about ten—is a holiday shot when we were on a picnic and it looks different now. We had that old station wagon and that really ugly tartan rug is spread beside it, and I'm smiling and so is he, and Beth's dancing—

she was so into ballet then—once, I'd have sworn tears of blood that I knew what was in his head at that moment: that he was happy with us. And now—well, I don't know.

So what he's done now has made me question every single thing in our whole shared lives. My memories are gone because they might be fake and they might not.

It's like being shown a picture of a vase in silhouette and then someone points out that it could also represent two faces in profile, and once you've seen the new picture, it's impossible to look at it and just see the vase.

And how do I tell my daughter? She's thirty-six, married—and that sounds like she should be here taking care of me right now, but the thing is, it's still the other way round. No matter what happened to me, Beth would need to be taken care of. So, does anyone have any advice for me? I'm desperate.

Anneliese was about to click Send when she changed her mind. With a single keystroke, she erased the whole message.

She could hear her mother's voice in her head, a voice made angry by Anneliese's shutting the door of her bedroom and refusing to come out: "Anneliese, you can't solve everything by shutting us all out, you know."

Shutting the door might not have worked but it made her feel better. Always had. It could again too. Instincts weren't called instincts for nothing.

She locked the doors and checked the windows were shut. That had always been Edward's job: the man's job, organizing the house before bed. Anneliese dampened down the hurt and the pain of thinking of him. They were just doors: she could lock them herself.

She went round the cottage methodically, switching off lights, then climbed the stairs to their bedroom. Her bedroom now.

The beams in the upstairs of the cottage were stripped wood, bleached pale like all the floorboards. Their bedroom was pale blue with white furniture, two denim rag rugs on the floor and white curtains that were heavily lined to keep the cold out. Anneliese took one look at the big high bedstead with its white quilted coverlet and backed out of the room. She couldn't sleep there tonight. It would be like lying in a bed of lies.

Beth's bedroom was still Beth's, even though she'd left home years before. Beth liked the comfort of her childhood things still being there: her Barbies and their various cars and wardrobes still arranged on the wooden shelves, her Enid Blyton books lined up neatly.

The spare bedroom in the cottage was barely a box room. Painted purest white, there was room only for a bed, a bleached wood chest of drawers with seashells laid on top as decoration, and a tiny one-drawer nightstand with an old brass lamp on it. In the twenty years she'd lived in the cottage, Anneliese had never slept in this room. Which made it perfect.

She unearthed a small container of sleeping tablets from the bathroom cabinet, took one and washed it down with tap water. In Beth's room, she found an old nightdress of her daughter's and pulled it on. She didn't want anything from her own room to contaminate her. She climbed into the spare-room bed, turned out the light and closed her eyes until the chemically induced sleep claimed her.

The Lifeboat Shop in Tamarin was very successful. Perhaps it was due to the loud proximity of the sea itself, but everyone—locals and visitors alike—dutifully went in to search for bargains, knowing that for every secondhand blouse they bought money went to the upkeep of the local lifeboats. Even with the sea in the bay shining serenely up at people on a summer's day, the power of the water was felt: beautiful and yet all-powerful.

Monday was one of Anneliese's days for working in the shop. She worked there Mondays and Wednesdays and had done so ever since she'd given up full-time work in the garden center. When she woke early the day after Edward left her, she knew she had to go in.

Not turning up would make everyone think she was sick, and then someone might see Edward and ask him how she was, and he might tell the truth and—

Anneliese couldn't bear that. She didn't want everyone knowing what had happened, not until she'd dealt with it in her own head. She wasn't sure when she was going to be able to do that—the sleeping tablet and the alcohol had made all thinking impossible as she'd crashed out twenty minutes after taking it, and to stave off the sense of solitude in the cottage the following morning, she'd turned on the radio loud, preferring plenty of news stories to being alone with her thoughts.

Her thoughts were dangerous, she decided: she didn't want to be on her own with them.

Anneliese preferred the mornings in the shop.

The churchgoers were sure to arrive after Mass, and the women who'd dropped children at school would pop in for a quick rummage. People who took early lunches sometimes crammed their sandwiches into a few minutes so they could rifle through the rails of clothes, or scan the shelves lined with books.

It was a nice, chatty place to work, with no real pressure, except when something of value came in and all the staff panicked slightly about getting the correct price sorted out for it, in case the original owner returned and felt their donation wasn't being prized enough.

Today there were five trash bags of stuff to be gone through, so Anneliese sat in the back of the shop where the storeroom, kitchenette and toilet were situated, and went through it all carefully. There were piles of clothes, mainly women's, soft toys still covered with dust and children's clothes alongside ornaments, some paperback books and bits of costume jewelry. About half of the stuff was in good condition and Anneliese began the painstaking job of sorting the wheat from the chaff.

It was incredible what some people thought was acceptable to donate to charity, she thought, holding up a man's shirt with a threadbare collar, several missing buttons and a suspicious yellow stain on the sleeve. Curry? Flower pollen? She threw it into the "dump" box.

Yvonne, another volunteer, was manning the front counter and kept up a steady stream of chat with the customers. Anneliese liked working with Yvonne because no response was ever required. Yvonne talked and didn't appear to care if anyone replied or not. This normally suited Anneliese because she liked working in peace with just the faint hum of the radio in the background. Today it suited her because she wasn't sure if she'd be able to have a conversation if her life depended on it.

Anneliese knew she looked wretched and said she hadn't slept to cover up the fact, even though the chemical blackjack had knocked her out for eight hours. But she looked much worse than any lack of sleep could account for. She'd been shocked at the sight of herself in the mirror that morning. Grief had aged her overnight and it was as if her very bones had thrown themselves against her skin in protest at all the pain. She felt as if the last, vaguely youthful bloom of her skin had gone, leaving nothing but sharp angles, hollows and the big indigo blue eyes her daughter, Beth, had inherited, like shining pools in an oval face. The thick white hair—once a stunning white blond, now just silky white—that she kept neatly tied back no longer looked feminine. Instead, it made her look far older than her years: older and pantomime witchy.

Anneliese could barely recognize the woman who'd been told by an admirer, many years ago, that she looked like a prima ballerina with her long, graceful neck and doe eyes. She'd been one of Tamarin's beauties about a million years ago, she thought sadly, or so Edward had told her.

Who'd have thought it now?

She should have bothered with makeup after all, she decided. Some base, a little concealer to hide the dark circles, mascara to lift her eyes and some creamy blush to bring warmth to the apples of her cheeks: Anneliese had always been very proficient with makeup.

It was the one thing she and her mother had agreed on.

If Anneliese was going to throw herself away on a job in gardening, then she should still look after her skin and never go out without lipstick, her mother had said.

Her mother had also always been firm on women not drinking hard spirits. Anneliese had kept to that dictum too and was regretting her brandies and glasses of wine the day before. Her head ached dully from the unaccustomed drinking.

"Dogs will do their business on the beach, I said," Yvonne was saying to a customer. "Signs, that's what we need; signs on the beach about doggy doo."

Anneliese was one of the people who disagreed with this point of view, preferring the dog crap to lots of ugly signs telling people off for not cleaning it up. Signs would ruin the craggy, bare beauty of the beach.

But she kept quiet and allowed herself to wonder what Yvonne would make of her news.

Edward has left me. He's living with Nell Mitchell. Yes, that Nell—my best friend. There you go. Shows you don't really ever know people, do you?

It still sounded wrong.

She tried it again, saying it more slowly in her mind, to see if she could make sense of it.

We've been through hard times, Edward and I, and perhaps it was too hard for him, and Nell is so easygoing and, after all, they know each other so well—

"Anneliese, what did you say?" Yvonne looked at her expectantly from the front of the shop. The customer was gone and it was only the two of them in the shop.

"Nothing, Yvonne. Just talking to myself."

"Oh, sure, I do the same myself, Anneliese." Yvonne sighed and went back to scanning the local paper. "Nobody pays me the slightest heed. Mum, the kids say, you talk nineteen to the dozen, and when we try to answer you keep rattling on, so we let you at it. Kids!"

"Kids, yeah." Anneliese nodded, when what she was really thinking was "husbands" and "best friends."

"But we love them, don't we?" Yvonne went on, still talking about children and not in the least aware that she and Anneliese weren't on the same wavelength at all.

It struck Anneliese at that moment that it was really quite easy to deceive people once they didn't expect to be deceived. How easy had she been to deceive? Shamefully easy, probably.

She stopped sorting out clothes to ponder this. What lies had Edward and Nell told her? Had they gone home to the cottage on days when Anneliese was in the shop, and lain on her bed having sex?

Suddenly, she had to rush into the tiny toilet to throw up. Bile, yesterday's wine and nothing else came up.

"Anneliese, you all right?" said Yvonne.

"Fine," she lied. "Heartburn. Smoked fish pie last night."

Where did that excuse come from? she wondered, unbending and looking at her red-eyed face in the tiny room's mirror. Was lying just a matter of practice?

The shop was mercifully busy all morning. Yvonne rushed about, chatting and working the till, while Anneliese gave the appearance of industriousness by tidying shelves and rails after the customers.

Her gaze often strayed out onto the streets of Tamarin, searching for the familiar figure of her husband loping along. Edward worked in an engineering company in town and sometimes dropped in on her when she was in the Lifeboat Shop.

But not, she decided, today.

Still, she stared out of the window, wondering if he and Nell would pass by.

The town was designed like half of a many-pointed star, with streets all heading down toward the harbor where they converged on Harbor Square, a wide piazza with squat Mediterranean-style palm trees, an open-air café called Dorota's, and the horseshoe-shaped harbor beyond, like two arms reaching into the sea—or like the curve of a crab's front claws, depending on which way you liked to look at it.

The Lifeboat Shop was on Fillibert Street, halfway between Harbor Square below and the tiny Church Square above, where St. Canice's stood in its mellow-stone glory.

Her shift in the shop ended at two, when Corinne Brady arrived to take over, trailing scarves, dangly bead necklaces and an overpowering scent of a musk oil purchased many moons ago in the town's health-food shop. Anneliese knew this because Corinne was always telling her that modern perfumes were bad for you and that eau d'elderly musk was where it was at.

"Natural smells are best, Anneliese," Corinne would say gaily, waving a tiny bottle sticky with age. "Modern perfumes cause cancer, you know."

Normally, Anneliese tolerated Corinne's eccentricities and her bizarre medical theories, but she couldn't cope today. She was all out of the milk of human kindness and she wasn't sure if any of the local shops stocked it.

"Hello, Yvonne, look at this! A new consignment of black cohosh. Now, Yvonne, I know you don't want to talk about the whole menopause thing . . ."

In the background, Anneliese winced. Poor Yvonne. There was no chance of a discreet talk about female problems when Corinne was involved. Corinne didn't do volume control. She roared, even when attempting to whisper.

"This is fabulous," Corinne was saying.

"Shout a bit louder," Yvonne said crossly, "I don't think the whole town heard you."

"Tish, tish," said Corinne, unconcerned. "We're all women here and we're proud of our bodies. It's the cycle of life, Yvonne. The great life force that moves inside us because Mother Nature put it there."

Normally, Anneliese would have been grinning by now. Nobody could deny that Corinne was marvelously entertaining when she went into her whole Mother Nature routine. Mother Nature was responsible for all manner of things, including Corinne's addiction to milk chocolate and Dr. Shepherd from *Grey's Anatomy*. Mother Nature would, undoubtedly, be responsible for Edward running off with Nell, if Corinne had a chance to think about it. The great life force would be in flux or something. Anneliese shuddered at the thought of having this raw pain slapped up on Corinne's mental chopping board for examination. She wondered if she could leave without being seen. Too late—

"Hello, Anneliese . . . ohmydear, you look soo tired. Poor you. I have just the thing in my bag—" began Corinne, reaching into the enormous patchwork leather handbag she hauled around with her. The bag smelled plain bad after too many little bottles of oil and potions had spilled in it. "It might look a little odd, dear, but it's a fungus and you keep adding water to it and drink the juice and—"

"Corinne, thank you," said Anneliese quickly, thinking she might have to throw up again at even the thought of drinking fungus juice. "I'm afraid I can't stop, not now. Bye."

She almost ran out of the shop, holding her jacket and bag in her hand. She couldn't deal with Corinne. Not now.

For all Corinne's bulk, she was very fast, and fear of Corinne running after her made Anneliese rush down Fillibert Street looking blindly for somewhere to escape. The bookshop. The Fly Leaf was a small, quirky establishment with a big crime section and darkish windows so it was hard for anybody from outside to see in. Perfect. Nobody would talk to her there.

It was a Bookshop Rule: smile and nod only.

She rushed into the silence of The Fly Leaf, and made blindly for the shelves at the back. The Classics section. She fingered the spines of the books, asking herself how long was it since she'd read Jane Austen?

Eventually, she felt calmer. Corinne hadn't followed her. Now that she was out of the Lifeboat Shop, she could stop pretending and be herself again. Except she wasn't sure who herself was. It was a strange, disconcerting feeling. Anneliese felt fogged up, not real somehow. Like she'd been teleported into this body and this life and none of it was even vaguely familiar.

Oh no, please, no.

She moved on from Classics and found herself in Self-help. Her breathing was getting faster again. No. Breathe deeply. In, count to four, and out. After a while, she refocused on the shelves. Self-help. She'd looked in this department many times before and knew that there was no *Meditations for People Who Are Pissed Off With the Whole Planet*.

A definite gap in the market, she thought grimly. And no *100 Ways to Kill Your Husband and Former Best Friend*, either.

But there were plenty of books on depression, which could be cured by therapy, positive visualizations or eating exactly the right combination of supplements, depending on which book you read.

Anneliese had read lots of them, wanting to be fixed. She scanned the shelves, thinking that she probably had all of these volumes at home, apart from the newer ones. None of them had worked. Depression wasn't something you could sever from yourself merely by reading a book.

It was so much darker and deeper. She stared angrily at the books, furious with their authors for daring to pretend that they *knew* what it was like.

Bloody psychiatrists and mental health gurus wrote books on depression, not real people who'd actually been in that cavernous underground: a place where you couldn't imagine ordinary, happy life; a place where functioning was almost out of the question.

Anneliese, come on out of your room and talk to me, please. Her mother's voice in her memory again. Dear Mother. She'd tried so hard, Anneliese knew, but she'd been stuck with a daughter with a cloud of darkness inside her, and their family—ordinary, kind, simple really—hadn't known what to do with someone like her.

"If only you'd tell me what's wrong," Mother would beg.

"I don't know what's wrong," Anneliese would reply. Because she didn't. Nobody had hit her or hurt her. But she felt everything so deeply, more deeply than Astrid, her older sister, who was nearest in age to her. There were days when there was simply a cloud in her head, a cloud of fear and anxiety and darkness. She didn't know why—it was just there.

It was more than forty years since she'd had that realization. She'd been fifteen when she discovered that everyone else didn't feel the same, that she was different.

And then, in The Fly Leaf bookshop in Tamarin, Anneliese Kennedy had that familiar, jarring sensation of darkness in her head, and something else—the onset of sheer panic. Behind her eyes came a thrumming sensation, like drums beating far away. A slow, constant noise that wasn't real—she knew that—but felt more real to her than anything else at that exact moment. She hadn't heard it in so long, normally only heard it in nightmares now, but she knew what it was: fear and panic.

She'd once read that certain types of situation made the lizard brain dominate. The lizard brain was the core survival part of human beings, lower down the totem pole than the limbic system and the cerebral cortex.

The lizard kicked into place when people reached a deep primal fear. There had been so many other hugely long medical words in the article that Anneliese had slightly tuned out, but she'd remembered that bit: that the lizard brain was basic survival and came out when the person was mortally threatened.

Like now. When a panic attack swept over her with raging force. No sooner had she thought the words than the breathlessness hit and she began to wheeze, feeling her chest tightening. She couldn't breathe, her heart was racing.

Anneliese moved so quickly that she bumped into a man bending over looking at the sports books.

"Sorry," she half gasped, whisking past him. She had to get out and home. She needed to be in a safe place so she could make this fear and darkness go away.

It was *years* since she'd had a panic attack, years. She'd forgotten how horrific they were, how she always felt as if she was going to die.

Her hands were shaking so much, it was hard to get her keys from her bag, almost impossible to keep the key for the car at the right angle to slip it into the lock. But she did. Safe, she was a bit safe.

She sat in the driver's seat shaking, trying to calm her breath.

Breathe in, count to four, breathe out.

When she'd felt recovered enough, she started the engine, keeping the volume turned up loud on talk radio, willing the discussion to block out her own head. She didn't want to think.

The house was silent when she got there—not the silence of a home where another person might be back soon, but the deadening silence of a place where only one person lived. Anneliese made herself a mug of herbal tea, the Tranquility tea that Edward used to gently tease her about. About to put the pack back in the cupboard, she took another teabag and stuck that in the mug too. She needed a double dose of tranquillity.

Then she took the mug and an old fleecy blanket outside to sit on the deck.

With her feet curled up under her, mug in her hand and the

blanket wrapped around her, Anneliese stared out at the crashing waves and let herself breathe slowly.

Breathe. In and out. Slowly and deeply. *Concentrate on each breath, let your lungs fill and exhale slowly through your nose.* In and out. That was all you had to do every day—breathe.

Shit, *shit,* it wasn't working. Despite the deep breathing, she could feel her heartbeat fluttering along at speed, and the darkness was still in the back of her head, coming closer now.

Fuck you, Edward, for doing this to me, Anneliese thought bitterly.

She huddled into the fleecy blanket for warmth.

She was not going back on the tablets, not again.

Edward had been so good and understanding about her depression, even if he'd never entirely got it.

"I feel a bit sad too sometimes, you know," he'd said early on in their marriage. "It's not the same as you, love, but I understand, or at least I'm trying to."

Anneliese, who'd chosen her words carefully when she talked about being depressed so that she didn't scare him or make him think he was married to a complete nutcase who needed access to a straitjacket at all times, had to stop herself from laughing out loud.

He couldn't know or understand that depression was a part of her: she could go about her daily life like anybody else but while some people had freckles or lovely olive skin as part of their genetic makeup, she had depression. A part of her: sometimes there, sometimes not. She could go months, years, without feeling that overwhelming darkness, but when she did, it was far more than feeling a bit sad. And yet she loved him, loved him for trying.

"I love you, you darling man," she said to him fiercely. He'd laughed too and hugged her, and Anneliese had ended up sitting on his lap, their arms wrapped round each other, and she'd felt really loved.

This kind, complex man didn't really understand what she

went through, but he was doing his best. That was love: trying to understand your mate, even if the understanding was outside your scope.

She remembered talking to Nell about it too. That hurt: thinking of bloody Nell knowing about Anneliese's inner pain and then still walking off with her husband. Anneliese shuddered under her fleecy blanket.

She was beginning to hate Nell.

"How can you be feeling like that, you know, down, and still go out and be normal?" Nell had asked once, when Beth was a little girl and Anneliese had brought her to a classmate's birthday party and gone home to cry for two straight hours, which was where Nell had found her when she dropped round.

"You put your game face on," Anneliese said simply, her face raw with tears. "You can't sit in a corner and stare into nothingness when you've a child. You just can't."

Not that she hadn't felt like it many times, but mother love was a potent force. Anneliese might have had many days where she'd have liked to stay in bed, drag the duvet around her like armor and sit out the bleakness. But she couldn't do that to her daughter.

When Beth grew older and it became clear that she'd inherited her mother's depression just as she'd inherited her indigo eyes, protecting Beth had become Anneliese's life. Beth, who needed huge love and attention, came highest on the totem pole.

Next came Anneliese herself, sometimes staying on top of it all, sometimes falling into the pit so that she'd reluctantly have to go to the doctor and take some of those damned antidepressants, and she hated them. It was like admitting to failure, and if she read one more article that said depression was like diabetes and if you had diabetes you wouldn't mind taking insulin to fix it, then she'd kill someone.

Edward, dear, kind Edward, had become a very definite third in his wife's list of priorities.

Women's first love and concern would always be their children, if they had them, Anneliese had realized, while men's would be their women. The two equations weren't even on the same page.

Had that driven Edward away—always being third in their marriage? How could he not have known that he wasn't third through choice but because of the rules of simple survival?

Anneliese sighed and stared out at the view that sold the house to her and Edward all those years ago. In the sharp light, Milsean Bay was like a mirror set in a valley that changed from white sand to the peaty green of the fields.

Beyond lay the Atlantic Ocean where seagulls swooped and flecks of white foam whisked up dramatically. *Be careful*, roared the water. It was a lesson that locals never forgot. Tourists took boats out to explore the sheltered bay, and kidded themselves that the waters were safe, only to have to be rescued when their boats were swept out into the fierce tempest of the Atlantic.

Basking sharks could sometimes be seen from the cliffs above the point, where a dolmen stood in grandeur. Anneliese could remember the day she and Edward had taken Beth to see the dolmen when she was small, wanting to instill a sense of pride in her.

"This is our history, Beth," Edward had explained.

And now he'd rewritten their family history. Anneliese didn't know if she could ever forgive him for that. There was no justification, none.

Of course, it didn't matter to Edward if she forgave him or not. He wasn't in her life anymore.

four

Izzie's Manhattan apartment was cold and looked bare after the warmth of the New Mexico hotel. Even her beloved New York was coolly impersonal today, she decided: the cabdriver who'd picked her up at the airport hadn't been classically eccentric, just dull, and it was raining too, the type of flash flood that could drown a person in an instant.

Wet and tired, Izzie slammed her front door shut and set her luggage down, trying to put a finger on the sense of discontent she felt. There was something about the friendliness of the pueblo, a small-town kindliness that Izzie missed from home. She was a small-town girl, after all, she thought, feeling a rush of homesickness for Tamarin. She thought about home a lot these days. Was it because she felt so alone when Joe left late at night and her thoughts turned to her family, the other people who cared for her?

Or was it because she felt a growing anxiety over what was happening: a relationship that was so hard to explain that she hadn't tried to explain it to anyone, not Carla, not her dad, not Gran.

She stripped off her dripping jacket and only then allowed herself to look at the answering machine. The message display showed a big fat zero. Zero messages.

Horrible bloody machine. She glared at it, as if it was the machine's fault that Joe hadn't rung.

Turning on the lamps to give her home some type of inner glow, Izzie stomped into the bathroom, stripped off her clothes and got into the shower to wash away the dust of the mesa. She was becoming obsessed with cleaning herself. Was obsessive-compulsive disorder a product of tangled love affairs? She'd never had so many showers in her life, always showering and scrubbing and oiling in the hope that, once she was in the shower, the phone would ring. It always used to. But not now. Joe hadn't phoned in five days.

Five days.

"I'll talk to you," he'd murmured the morning she flew to New Mexico.

"You do that," she'd murmured back, wishing she could cancel, wishing something would happen so she'd be close to him, because there was a cold, isolating feeling from not being in the same city as him. What was that about?

But he hadn't phoned.

Not even on the last night when they all let their hair down, when the noise of partying would have made any normal absent lover slightly jealous. Izzie had hoped he'd phone then, just so she'd have the chance to move away from the hubbub and casually say that Ivan was playing the limbo-dancing game, and make it all sound like fabulous fun. So fabulous that Joe would be jealous of her being there without him . . . Except he hadn't played the game. He hadn't phoned.

Izzie clambered out of the shower, still irritated.

No, a shower wasn't the right thing. A bath, that would be perfect.

She started to fill the tub, poured in at least half of her precious Jo Malone Red Roses bath oil, opened a bottle of white wine and made herself a spritzer for the bath, and finally sank into the fragrant bubbles.

She sipped her spritzer, lay back with her eyes closed and tried to relax. But the blissful obliviousness baths used to bring her, a sinking-into-the-heat thing that made her forget everything else, evaded her. As ever, since she'd met Joe, he was the only thing in her mind.

For that first lunch, they'd met in a small, quirky Italian restaurant in the Village, the sort of place Izzie hadn't imagined Joe would like. She'd guessed he'd prefer more uptown joints where the staff recognized every billionaire in the city. It was another thing to like about him, this difference.

Over antipasti, they chatted, and the more he talked, the more Izzie felt herself falling for him.

He'd got a business degree, then joined J.P. Morgan's graduate training program.

"That's when the bug hit me," he said, scooping up a sliver of ciabatta bread drenched with basil-infused olive oil. "Trading is all about instant gratification, and I loved it."

"Isn't it stressful?" she asked, thinking of losing millions and how she'd have to be anesthetized if she did a job like that.

"I never felt stress," he said. "I loved it. I'd trade, lose some, win some, whatever, I'd go home and go to sleep. People burned out all the time—the hours, the work-hard, play-hard mentality. It got to a lot of them but not me."

At twenty-nine, he'd been running his own trading fund, a hedge fund.

"That's what it means," said Izzie, delighted. "I never knew."

The higher up the chain he went, the more risk, but also bigger percentages to be earned, until finally he ended up as head of trading for a huge bank. "Basically, you're trying to systematically beat all the markets through math," he explained. "You name it, we traded it. We were a closed fund."

Izzie, mouth full of roasted peppers, looked at him quizzically.

"Means we only reinvested profits and no new investors could get in."

"Oh." She nodded. This was like a master class in Wall Street. How many years had she known all those money guys and never had a clue what they were talking about?

Finally, he and a friend named Leo Guard had started their own closed hedge fund, HG.

"Eventually, we were doing so well, we changed the fee structure from two and twenty to five and forty."

"I add up using my fingers," Izzie explained. "I have no idea what that means."

He grinned and handed her some more bread.

"That's the typical fee structure: two and twenty means you get two percent for management and twenty percent of profits from performance."

"Wow," she said. "And you were trading in millions?"

He nodded. "Imagine having six hundred under management."

Izzie hated to look thick. "Six hundred million dollars?" she said, just to check.

He nodded.

"You're rich, then," she said, hating herself for eating all those antipasti as she already felt full and the main courses would be coming soon.

Joe laughed.

"You're the real deal, Izzie Silver," he said. "I like that."

"Honest," she said, pushing her plate away. "Not everyone likes it."

"I do. Yes, you could say I am rich."

"You don't own a superyacht, though?" she asked, with a twinkle in her eye.

He laughed again. "No. Do you want one, or do you simply want to date a guy with one?"

Izzie smiled at his innocence. "You haven't a clue, do you?" she said coolly. "I am so far away from the type of woman who wants a man with a superyacht that I am on a different continent." She rearranged things on the table, pushing the salt and pepper around. "The pepper is me." She stuck it at the edge of the table. "And the salt"—she moved it to the other side completely—"is the sort of woman who wants to know a guy's bank balance before she meets him for a drink. See? Big gap, big difference. Enormous."

"Sorry."

"Just don't do it again," she joked. "I have never in my entire life gone out with a guy because of the size of his bank balance. Ever. I did briefly—one date—go out with a guy from next door in my old apartment building because he knew how to work the heating, and he'd fixed it for me one day when the super wasn't around and I went out on a date with him, but that was it. A one-off."

"You came out with me because I gave you a ride back to the office, then?" he teased.

"Exactly," she said. "Keep going with this life story of yours. Tell me some personal stuff."

He was forty-five, his wife was a couple of years younger, and they'd married young, kids, really. Izzie was sorry she'd asked for personal stuff.

"Then Tom came along quite quickly," he said proudly. "It all changes then, you know. Do you have children?"

Yes, in my handbag, Izzie wanted to say. "No, 'fraid not. So I don't know how it changes everything."

"Take my word for it, it does. It changes the couple dynamic, you get so caught up in the kids. But, hey, I didn't come here to talk about my boys," he said.

"OK, what did you come here for?" she asked. She wasn't sure why she was here. He was too complicated, there was too much going on in his life. She needed a rebound guy like she needed a hole in the head.

Besides, he wasn't even at the rebound stage: he was still in the nursing-the-broken-relationship stage. A man on the hunt for a rebound relationship didn't necessarily want to talk about his wife and kids.

Pity, she thought sadly. He was lovely, sexy, made her stomach quiver in a way she could never quite remember it doing before.

It just proved what she knew and what Linda had confirmed to her: all the good ones were taken. But he was a charming guy and she could enjoy lunch and mark it down to experience.

"You still don't know what I came here for?" he asked.

Izzie shot him a wry look.

"I might want to know more about the modeling industry so I can invest in it," he continued.

"You might just want to be introduced to long-legged models?" she countered. "I'm normally quite good at working out if a man is interested in me only as a means to get to the models. Although you"—she surveyed him—"aren't the normal type. You're too nice."

He pretended to gasp. "*Nice?* That's not a word people usually use about me. I've been called a shark, you know."

"You're nice," Izzie said, smiling back at him. It was true. For all that he was an alpha male, with all the built-in arrogance and intelligence, he had a solid, warm core to him, a devastatingly attractive bit that said he might be a rich guy but he'd been brought up to take care of people, to protect his family and his woman. Izzie felt a pang that she would never get to be said woman. There would be something wonderful about being with a man who'd take care of her.

"You might pretend to be a shark but you're a pussycat," she went on, teasing a little. "Besides, I know you don't need me to get you introduced to the supermodels. You're rich enough to buy all the introductions you need. Money is like an access-all-areas card, isn't it?"

"My, but you're cynical for one so young." He grinned.

"I'm not young, I'm nearly forty," she said. If she'd thought he was interested in her, she'd have said she was thirty-nine. "It's creeping up on me every day. I'm going to be over the hill soon."

A few days ago, it might have been a joke. But since The Plaza and Linda, Izzie no longer felt complacent at the thought of her approaching birthday.

"You'll never be over the hill," he said in a low voice that made her think, ridiculously, about being in bed with him and having him slowly peeling off her clothes.

"Are you flirting with me, Mr. Hansen?" Izzie squawked to cover her discomfit. "I thought this was a friendly lunch."

"Cards on table," he said, "I am flirting with you."

"Well, stop," she ordered. "You've just told me about your wife and fabulous kids. I don't know what sort of women you're used to meeting, but I'm not in the market for part-time love. I've got through thirty-nine years without dating a man who's still tangled up with his wife and I'm not planning on starting now."

"Do you think I'd be here if my marriage was still viable?" he asked in a low growl. "Give me some credit, Izzie. Yes, I have a wife and kids, but we're separated and we're only living together for the sake of those kids. Didn't you listen to me? I told you Elizabeth and I married young. We haven't been a couple for years. Nobody's fault, it just was inevitable. We finally agreed a few months ago that it wasn't working on any level and we needed to formalize things."

"Oh," said Izzie, waiting. Was he serious? Or was he really still in that awful postbreakup stage where he was trying to convince himself it was over and that a rebound would sort him out?

"I love her, I'll always love her," he said, "but it's like loving your sister. We've had twenty-four years together and counting; it's a lifetime, but the marriage part is long over. We try to appear together for the younger boys. Tom would be able to cope with it if we split up, but Matt and Josh, no. The New York house is so big, it's not a problem. Lots of people do it: if you have enough space, you can all exist happily together. I have my life, she has hers. Elizabeth's parents divorced and she didn't want our boys to come from a broken home. That's why we stayed with each other, I guess, but it's too hard. I can't do that anymore."

"What if one of you fell in love and wanted to be with another person?" Izzie asked, trying to understand this strange arrangement. She felt like she was standing on a cliff and was about to fall. She didn't want to fall without knowing he was going to be holding his arms out.

"That's never happened. Before." He added the last word deliberately slowly. "If it happened, then everything would have to change."

"Do people know about this?"

"Most of our circle know. We're not broadcasting it, but it works for us. Matt and Josh are still so young. They think they know it all now they're twelve and fourteen, but they're still kids. Now they can see their parents living amicably in the same house, they've got stability. That's our number one priority."

"I see," she said, thinking with a sudden flash of sadness of her life when she was between twelve and fourteen.

"Do you?"

She nodded and somehow he instantly picked up on the fact that she'd become suddenly melancholy.

"What is it?" he asked.

"I was thirteen when my mother died," she explained. "Cancer. It was sudden too, so there was no time. Six weeks after we found out, she was dead." She shivered at the memory. It had taken her years to be able to say the word *cancer*: it had held such terrifying connotations, like a bad-luck charm, as if just saying it brought danger and pain. "My father and my grandmother tried to protect me from that, but they couldn't."

"I'm sorry," he said. "It must have been tough."

She nodded. Tougher than anyone could imagine. In a way, she'd dealt with it by not dealing with it: locking herself up tight inside so nothing could hurt her, not crying, not talking much to anyone, even darling Gran, who was so devastated herself and was trying to hide it for Izzie's sake.

Dad, Uncle Edward and Anneliese had all been there for her, ready to talk, laugh, cry, whatever she needed. Only her cousin

Beth—quirky, irritable, easily upset—had been her usual self. Beth had actually helped the most in the first year. She'd made Izzie cry one day by screaming at her, and that simple act of one person in her life not tiptoeing around her brought Izzie back.

"Is your father alive?" Joe asked gently.

Izzie smiled. "Yeah, he's great, Dad. A bit dizzy sometimes; runs out of sugar and cream endlessly and has to rush over to my aunt Anneliese's house or to my gran's. Between them, they take care of him—not that they let him know or anything. He'd hate that. But they do. They tell me how he's getting on."

"Coffee, dessert? More wine?" asked the waiter.

When he was gone, having cleared their plates and taken coffee orders, Joe leaned forward again.

"Tell me more about you," he urged.

But Izzie felt she'd revealed enough about herself. She rarely talked about her mother, certainly not to someone she'd just met.

"Hey, that's enough of me," she said, trying to sound perkier. "You're more interesting, Mr. Mogul. So tell me—are you interested in buying a model agency?"

"No," he said.

"I didn't think you were but—"

"But you needed to know where you stood?"

"Convent education—it gets you every time," she sighed.

"Would Sister Mary Whatever approve of me?" he asked. She could feel his foot nudging hers under the table.

"I think you're probably the sort of guy they had in mind when they told us to bring a phone book out with us on dates," Izzie quipped.

When he looked puzzled, she filled him in: "If you had to sit on some boy's lap, you placed the phone book down first, then sat. An inch of paper barrier."

"More like five inches if you lived in Manhattan."

"Don't boast." She was smiling now.

"So you might see me again, Ms. Silver, now you know I'm kosher?"

"I might," she said.

"Listen, I have an art collection in my office building—"

"You didn't bid on that Pasha picture at the charity lunch," she interrupted.

"I might have, except I was distracted," he growled. "I have to go to an artist's studio to look at some paintings tomorrow afternoon. Would you like to come?"

Izzie took the plunge. Looking at art—where was the harm in that? "Sure. What time?"

"Say eleven o'clock?"

"You said 'afternoon,' " she said, confused.

"He lives in Tennessee, in the Smoky Mountains. We'll have to fly."

Izzie had never been on a private jet before. First, she and Joe were picked up by helicopter and flown to Teterboro airport, where a Gulfstream sat waiting on the tarmac. Inside, apart from the crew, there were just the two of them.

"It's fabulous," Izzie said in awe as she stepped into the cabin. On the inside, it looked smaller than she'd imagined but the luxury was something she couldn't have dreamed up. Entirely decorated in calm cream shades, there were only eight or nine vast cream leather seats.

The light oak cabinets were topped with marble instead of airplane plastic. It was luxury cubed. Even the blankets laid on the seats felt too soft to be ordinary wool.

"Cashmere?" she asked the stewardess standing to attention with a smile fixed to her face.

The stewardess nodded. "The seats are a blend of wool and leather, for added comfort."

"There's nothing you can't do on this plane," Joe said, sitting down and reaching out for the glass of cold beer the stewardess had ready for him without him even asking for it. "Watch DVDs, phone outer space—you name it. They've even got a defibrillator on board. Have you had to use it, Karen?" he asked the woman.

"Mr. Hansen, you know I can't tell you that," she said, grinning.

They flew into Gatlinburg but Izzie could only glance at the pretty streets of the historic town before they were driven out of town for twenty minutes to a property set on its own in the foothills of the Great Smokies.

"I can see why a painter would want to work from here," Izzie said, taking in the sweep of awesome mountains ranged all around her as they walked to the door of the ranch-style house. The greenery reminded her a little of home, but there were no mountains in Ireland like these, no giant peaks that dominated the landscape.

The artist, a man named AJ, made them drinks and ambled round his studio, talking in a laid-back Tennessee drawl. Izzie had worried that the artist might wonder who she was and she imagined an awkward conversation ensuing, but no such thing happened. It was as if once she was with Joe, she was instantly a member of whatever club they were in at the time. She found that she liked that.

Joe wanted to buy a lot of paintings.

AJ hugged him in a loose-limbed way. Izzie wondered how much it had all cost, but decided against asking. She wasn't sure if she could take it.

On the flight home, over Cajun blackened fish, a Gatlinburg favorite recipe that the galley staff had prepared in honor of their destination, Izzie idly mentioned her initial anxiety that AJ would wonder who she was.

"Who cares what other people think or wonder?" he said, genuinely astonished at such a concept.

"No reason," Izzie said cautiously. "It's just—"

She stopped. She was scared of so many things around Joe: how intensely she liked him, how powerfully attractive she found him. But there were all those complications to consider. Izzie felt she was on a slippery slope now—she didn't want to fall in.

Also, she was afraid that just by being with him she'd appear like the sort of person she disliked: the all-purpose rich man's girlfriend. Not that she was his girlfriend or anything yet. He hadn't so much as touched her, and she wasn't sure if this was on purpose or not.

I have a career and my own life, she wanted to yell. *I like him for who he is, not for how much money he's got.*

He dropped her home in the limo. Neither of them moved. Izzie felt so conflicted: on one hand, she wanted to invite him in and see what happened next. On the other, she wanted to go slowly because this felt so special, so different.

If only he'd do something, say something, then she'd know how to respond.

But he seemed to be playing some gentlemanly game, waiting for *her* to do something.

"Have you talked to your wife about meeting me?" she asked. *Why did you say that?* she groaned inwardly. How to kill a romantic atmosphere in ten seconds flat.

"We don't talk about the people in our life," he said brusquely. "It'd weird me out."

"Because you'd be jealous?" Izzie asked tentatively.

"Because we're trying to keep a reasonable family unit together for the sake of the boys and that might add extra pressure," he replied.

And then he leaned over and kissed her softly on the lips, not a Mr. Predator kiss but a gentle "Till tomorrow" sort of good-bye. Izzie closed her eyes and waited for more, waited to sink into the kiss. But there was no more.

"I'll call you tomorrow, and thanks for coming with me."

"Thanks for asking me," she said coolly. She was still trying to work out why he hadn't kissed her properly. "I've never been to Tennessee before. Does a two-hour flying visit count as being somewhere?"

He looked at her thoughtfully.

"Yes," he said.

"Cheerio," she said, getting out as the driver opened the door. *"Cheerio?" What's wrong with you, Izzie? First the weird question about his wife and then "cheerio."*

He phoned the next day.

"Would you like to go on another date?" he asked.

Date? It had been a date after all. Izzie hugged herself with delight.

"Yes," she said, and squashed the feeling that she'd just fallen down the slippery slope.

From the comfort of her bathtub, sipping her spritzer, Izzie thought about those first days when she felt like the luckiest person on the planet.

Joe was in her head all the time, edging more mundane matters out of the way, like a problem with a model sinking into depression because she'd been dropped from a beauty campaign or a big screwup which saw five models miss a plane to Milan because they'd been out late partying.

It was a fabulous secret that she hugged to herself. Izzie found herself behaving as if her life was a movie and Joe would be watching her every move.

She wore her best clothes every day, so she'd look fabulous on the off chance that he'd phone. The spike-heeled boots she moaned about were hauled out of her wardrobe to go with the swishy 1940s-inspired skirt that hugged her rear end and made construction workers' mouths drop open.

They had lunch and dinner twice a week, holding hands under the table, and kissing in the car on the way back to her office or to her apartment. They talked and talked, sitting until their coffees went cold.

But she'd never brought him to her home, had never done more than kiss him in the back of the car. Something held her back.

That something was her feeling that Joe and his life were more complicated than he'd told her. Why else were they having this low-key relationship? she asked herself. It only made sense if Joe wasn't being entirely truthful about everything and she couldn't believe that. He was so straight, so direct. She didn't want to nag him like a dog with a bone. She said nothing and just hoped.

They'd had a month of courtship—only such an old-fashioned word could describe it: walking in the park at lunchtime and sharing deli lunch from Dean & DeLuca.

And then, on a sunny Thursday, they'd visited another artist in a giant loft apartment in Tribeca and Izzie had wandered round looking at huge canvases while Joe, the artist and the artist's manager discussed business. Izzie felt a thrill that had nothing to do with admiring the artist's work: the fact that Joe had brought her here showed that she wasn't a dirty little secret in his life. Otherwise, he wouldn't have brought her along, would he?

Silvio Cruz's giant abstract paintings had prompted some critics to compare him to the great Jackson Pollock. Even Izzie, who knew zip about art, could see the power and beauty of his canvases, and she loved listening to Joe talk about them.

Joe hadn't grown up with art on the walls, he'd told her: food on the table in his Bronx home was as good as it got. So she loved hearing him talk passionately about a world he'd come into late thanks to his sheer brilliance.

Finally, she, Joe and Duarte, the manager, took the creaking industrial elevator down to street level.

"The Marshall benefit for AIDS is on tomorrow night," Duarte said to Joe. "You and Elizabeth going?"

Izzie froze.

"Yeah, probably," murmured Joe.

"I hear Danny Henderson's donating a de Kooning. I mean, jeez, that's serious dough. Danny's been here too, but he just doesn't get Silvio's vision," Duarte went on, oblivious to the sudden temperature shift in the elevator.

Elizabeth was probably going with him? What happened to the separate lives thing?

On the street, Izzie looked around for Joe's inevitable big black limo and then realized she couldn't possibly sit in it with him. She wasn't sure what was worse: the feeling that Joe had wanted to shut Duarte up and not talk about the party or Duarte's assumption that she, Izzie, wouldn't be going.

If Joe Hansen was officially unattached, then why would anyone assume he'd take his wife to a benefit? And why would he say "Yeah, probably" when asked?

There was only one answer and it made Izzie feel sick.

Without saying a word, she turned and walked briskly away from the two men and the limo which had slid noiselessly into place.

"Izzie!" yelled Joe, but she kept walking.

He caught up with her, hurt her arm as he grabbed her roughly and turned her to face him.

"Don't go," he begged.

"Why not?" she demanded. "You've been lying to me. It's not over with your wife. You lied to me."

"It's over with me and Elizabeth," he insisted.

"Fuck you and your lies!" Izzie threw back at him.

"They're not lies." He let go of her and his hands dropped limply to his sides. "It's deader than any dodo, Izzie, it's just hard to end it all. Elizabeth's different from me, she finds it difficult to let go. I've told her she can have the house here, the place in the Hamptons, whatever she wants. It was over long before you, that wasn't a lie. But she's trying to get her head around the fact that I want to leave."

"So you're leaving now? First, you were all staying together for the kids," Izzie said, trying not to cry.

"We did try but it didn't work. Elizabeth kept getting upset about it—she wants all or nothing—and now it's a matter of her accepting it and us telling the boys. I promise, Izzie. Don't go, please."

Izzie stared at him. She was a good judge of character, damnit, and he wasn't a liar, for all he pretended to be a shark in business.

"Why didn't you tell me the truth straight up?" she demanded.

"You wouldn't have gone out to lunch with me," he said, with a small smile that recalled the Joe she knew and loved.

Loved. She loved him, Lord help her, she loved him. Without meaning to, she'd got tangled up in this mess and now she couldn't just walk out. Still, she needed time to think.

"I've got to go back to work, Joe," she said. "I'll call you later."

"Let me drop you," he said.

"No, I'll get a taxi."

As if sent by an angel, a taxi with a lit sign appeared in front of her and Izzie stuck out her arm. She waved at Joe as she sat in the back and the driver sped off.

"What's up with you?" snapped Carla at work that afternoon. "You don't listen, you don't talk, you stare into space like a moony high schooler. What gives?"

Izzie hesitated. She and Carla had sat up nights talking about men, dissing men and generally deciding that no man at all was better than changing who you were in order to capture one.

"Surrendered wife, my butt! Why pretend to be Pollyanna to get him, so you can go back to being Mama Alien once he's married you? Who needs a man that much?"

They knew each other. But something had stopped Izzie from telling Carla about Joe. Perhaps it was a sixth sense, or else it was her feeling that this was all too good to be true.

She'd had a feeling that explaining Joe's complicated family setup would trigger Carla's internal Men Are Assholes alarm and there would be no stopping her. Carla wouldn't understand the nuances of it all.

Well, she would now, Izzie thought bitterly. Now it wasn't so complicated at all—just another guy trying to mess around on the side, only Izzie Silver, who'd never done the married-man thing, was the person he was messing around with.

And how could she explain all that to Carla, along with how she felt about him despite today? That thinking of Joe made her burn with heat. That his voice made her want to melt. That she was falling for him like the sort of soppy woman she'd never been in her life before. That she was furious with him for lying to her, but somehow her traitorous mind kept thinking, *What if she stayed with him anyway . . . ?*

No, she couldn't tell Carla until she knew what she was going to do next.

"Was I staring into space?" Izzie said. "I was only thinking about Laetitia. We'll need to keep an eye on her because her acne has flared up again and it really upsets her. I told her about the facialist who did wonders with Fifi's skin, but she says she's thinking of getting a prescription for something. . . ."

Models using antiacne drugs to combat skin problems were guaranteed to occupy Carla's mind. Carla felt that skinny girls who lived on cigarettes and diet drinks didn't need more medication.

"She doesn't need drugs!" Carla went off, yelling and being angry.

Izzie was able to tune out of her job and into Joe.

Carla's instinctive reaction—if she were told—would be the correct one. There was no future in this relationship. Izzie had to end it, tonight.

The sad thing was, she believed Joe. She believed his feelings for her, but it was all too complicated, too tangled, and he wasn't ready to walk away from his past yet.

If Izzie stayed, she'd be the evil woman who'd ruined his marriage. The evil-woman story played better than the marriage-falling-apart one.

"Izzie, you're tuning out again. What's up?" demanded Carla.

"Just tired," Izzie said, flustered.

It wasn't enough that Joe was messing up her heart, he was messing up her job too. She had to get out because somewhere deep inside Izzie knew that Joe had the power to hurt her like no man had ever hurt her before.

She was grateful now that their relationship had never become physical. Ironically, she'd thought that tonight might be the night that it would. Still, she was grateful for small mercies. It was as if some psychic force had kept her from making love with him because once that happened there would be no going back. Now she had to get out, fast, while she still could.

Before the fight in Tribeca, they'd discussed going to dinner somewhere fancy at half nine. Izzie couldn't wait that long. She needed to do this soon, after work, or else she'd explode. She had to get Joe out of her life and try to forget him. Although quite how she was going to do that, she had no idea.

She left a message on Joe's cell phone for him to meet her at seven in a small bar at Pier Nine. Anonymous and quiet, it would be the perfect setting for telling Joe she never wanted to see him again.

At seven that night, the bar contained a mixed crowd, with student types, men and women in work clothes and people for whom fashion wasn't a mission statement. The walls were jammed with nonironic movie posters like *Love Story* and *Flashdance*, and there wasn't a cocktail shaker in sight.

Carla would love this place, Izzie thought briefly, then realized she couldn't tell Carla about it because there would be nothing to tell after tonight.

There was no future in this for her except heartbreak. God, she earned her living telling young beautiful girls that there was no future in it for them with the moguls they met at parties. They were just fodder for the rich, disposable people in a world of disposable income.

Look who's talking now. Stupid, stoopid.

She sat there with her drink for fifteen minutes, hating herself, and finally moved on to anger because Joe was late. How dare he?

After everything he'd put her through, how dare he be late now?

Furiously, Izzie moved off the banquette, pulling her handbag after her.

"You leaving? I'm sorry I'm late." His body, solid in a charcoal gray coat dusted with tiny diamonds of rain, blocked her way. He looked penitent, tired. He wasn't playing a game with her, she knew instantly. But their whole relationship was based on mistruths and she hated that.

"Joe." She slumped back into the seat, suddenly exhausted. "I wanted to see you to say I can't do this anymore. It's not right, it's not me. I was never comfortable with the idea that you still lived with your wife, split up or not, and today made it plain that I was right about that. I don't want to be the other woman. I never auditioned for that."

He'd moved in to sit beside her.

"I know, I'm sorry," he said, sounding resigned. "Go, Izzie, you're right. I've nothing to offer you."

He *had* something to offer her, she thought, a moment of yearning in her heart. He had. But he was still married to someone else, still involved with someone else because of their children. Why couldn't this be easy?

Joe was off the banquette and on his feet in one fluid gesture. He moved with such elegance; he was comfortable in his own skin.

When she'd woken up that morning with their dinner ahead of her, Izzie had decided that she wanted to feel that skin naked against hers. She wasn't a silk underwear sort of woman. She did simple black, white or nude briefs and bras. No frills or lace. Until some invisible magnet had drawn her into Bloomingdale's and the lingerie department, where she'd gone crazy, doing more damage to her credit card bill. She could feel the results of that craziness, soft and very different under her clothes.

Going to bed with him now, the first and last time, was a strange idea. Yet maybe not. If she could have him, feel him touching her just one time, then perhaps she could leave. Like immunotherapy: one touch and she'd be forever immune to him. Her heart would send out little antibodies so she wouldn't want him again.

An anti–Joe shot.

Izzie closed her eyes.

"Do you want to go?" he asked. Softer, definitely.

"Do you want me to?"

"No." Low with wanting her.

"Really?"

"Really. I wanted to be honest with you, but when I met you, I knew you wouldn't see me again if I told you how it really was. It's over with me and Elizabeth, I promise. But I didn't think you'd believe me, not at first."

She kept her eyes closed and thought about his wife, Elizabeth, and his sons, the duplex in Vail, the listing in *Fortune*, the assistant's assistant, all the things that were making this impossible. Then she opened her eyes and looked at him, that face she felt as if she'd known in another lifetime because how could you commit someone's face to memory in such a short time? Reincarnation made sense suddenly. She and Joe had known each other in another life, for sure.

Perhaps he was meant to come into her life sooner, but he was here now. He was the one, she knew it.

"I don't want to go."

He didn't sit beside her: he bent and took her head in his hands, fingers cradling her skull with passion and gentleness, and crushed her mouth to his. She was just as ferocious, hands digging into his shoulders, dragging him down to her. This was what they hadn't done, this type of kissing. They'd been so careful, dancing around it, both knowing that if they touched, properly, there would be no going back.

Izzie moaned, knowing she was lost.

They pulled apart, two sets of bruised lips, two pairs of eyes black with desire.

"Let's go," Izzie said.

There was a car waiting outside the bar for him: a discreet Town Car that smoothly drove up as soon as Joe raised his finger. It was always a different driver, Izzie realized, as he helped her into the leather backseat. Someone like Joe would absolutely have a regular driver, but that driver would know his wife, run errands for her, take the kids to school.

He couldn't risk *that* driver seeing her again after the Plaza lunch. She was a guilty secret, to be hidden until it was all sorted out with his wife, the wife who didn't want it to be over. Izzie, who'd never been hidden in her life and who'd often longed to be small for a day just for the experience, forced herself to brush the thought away. She was a secret. So what? It wouldn't be for long, just long enough for Joe to end what was already over.

In her apartment, she didn't think twice about saying, "I bet you didn't know they made apartments in this size, huh?"

"I didn't come for the real estate," he said.

"What did you come here for?" she said.

"For this." With one effortless move, his arms were around her waist, crushing her tightly against him. Izzie felt the surge of being plugged into some heavenly main supply and with her back against the wall, she hungrily pulled his head down to hers and kissed him. His face was hard but his lips were soft, melting into hers, consuming her. Izzie flowed into the kiss, then suddenly pulled back.

She wanted to be in charge, in control for a moment, to show him that she would not be messed around with. She shoved him until he was against the facing wall, and she was on her toes, reaching and kissing.

"Me first," he murmured, wrenching his mouth away. Her hands were behind her back, pinioned at the wrist with one of his big hands, the other cradling her head as he kissed her. He half carried her against his body until she was at the other wall again.

"Rough stuff?" she gasped, struggling to free her hands.

"No," he said, stopping to stroke her cheek tenderly. "Never. I don't want to hurt you, but I want you under me. Does that make me a Neanderthal in these sexually enlightened times?"

Izzie laughed. She took his hand and led him into the tiny living room. "I'm the sort of girl who goes on top."

He hauled her close again. "Maybe the second time," he growled.

"I'm not like other women," Izzie said. Still in his embrace, she managed to unwind her scarf and unbutton her coat. He ripped his coat off.

"Never thought you were."

"So don't tell me what to do or what not to do," she added.

"Not even in bed?"

He was pulling his knotted tie loose and the sight of this normally buttoned-up businessman turning primeval made her weak at the knees.

"Maybe in bed," Izzie teased, slipping her fingers down to untie the ribbons of her blouse. A complicated thing made of navy polka-dot silk and laced up the front, it was the sort of garment that begged to be torn off. Joe's eyes darkly followed her fingers as they loosened the navy ribbons.

"I hope it's not expensive," he said heavily, grabbing her again and pulling at the ribbons urgently, ripping the fragile fabric. Her full mouth caught his again, hot breath and hot tongues melding. He tasted like more. She wanted him like she'd never wanted anyone before.

Izzie felt every nerve ending on fire with desire. Her nipples were hard buds of lust and underneath her sedate pencil skirt she could feel her skin burning in its silken lingerie, wild to be set free and naked.

"I can afford a new one," said Izzie, which wasn't true, but now wasn't the time to split dollars.

"Good."

He'd pulled the blouse apart, and his hands and mouth were roaming the soft skin of her breasts, kissing, licking and then sucking. Then his hands slid under the pencil skirt and his fingers cupped her pubic bone, making her feel the moisture pooling inside her.

Izzie groaned with pleasure. If this was her vaccination, then she wanted it to go on for a very long time.

She hadn't shut the drapes and afterward the lights of the city provided a gentle illumination for their crumpled bed. Joe lay propped up on her pillows, the sheets reaching up the muscled tan of his waist. Izzie lay on her side, head on her elbow, not quite looking at him but gazing away. It was an odd moment: at once both intimate and oddly formal.

Izzie, who'd had no difficulty sitting astride this man's hips and letting him watch her face as she screamed with ecstasy, felt the awkwardness of afterward. Suddenly, she wondered how pure physical lust and attraction could make people do what they'd just done. There were so many things they didn't know about each other. She didn't know how he liked his coffee in the morning, the name of his first pet, did he love his mother?

None of that had mattered before. Now the gap of that knowledge made what had gone before seem seamy, dirty. What was the protocol?

Thanks a million, honey: the money's on the mantelpiece? It might be different for billionaires. *The mink coat will be biked over, sweetie, good-bye—*

She shivered involuntarily. She'd never, ever wanted to be that sort of woman. And now she was, wasn't she?

"I don't suppose you have a cigarette?" he asked.

"I didn't think you smoked," she said, surprised. Whatever she'd expected, it hadn't been this.

"I don't. I quit ten years ago. But sometimes . . ."

"Like when you're in bed with women other than your wife?" Izzie said, cut at the insinuation. "How many packs do you go through a month?"

"None," he said evenly. "Don't be like that, Izzie."

"Like what?"

"That."

"I can't help it." She couldn't. Now she'd crossed over to the other side, the side of loving him. Now he could hurt her and she felt naked, raw. She wanted to hurt first.

"I'm sorry I wasn't honest with you from the beginning," he said. "I wish I'd told you everything."

"Me too," she said bitterly, but at least now she was bitter at herself.

"Are you sorry that we made love?" he asked.

"Yes," she said, and burst into tears.

"Izzie," he said, cradling her close to him, murmuring her name as he held her.

Then, when she'd managed to stop crying, he continued to hold her and slowly his hands massaged her back, tenderly rubbing out aches, until they moved down to the curve of her buttocks, and then they were making love again with more intensity even than before. As Joe arched over her, forearms rigid with muscle as he lunged into her, and Izzie was about to let go of herself and let her body soar into orgasm, she realized that she couldn't give this up. This sort of love and passion—this was the most addictive drug of all.

That had been two months ago. Since then, no one could have said that Izzie Silver and Joe Hansen were having half an affair—it was 100 percent, for sure. They talked every day, met as often as Joe could manage, and Izzie tried very hard to cope with both the insecurity of her own position and the fact that making love to another woman's husband went completely against her moral code.

"Oh, Izzie, you pathetic idiot," she said aloud. She was staying in a cooling bath in case the man in her life phoned. What was modern, grown-up and independent about that?

If he phones, he phones. She drained her spritzer and then stood up, letting the rose-scented water slide off her body. She'd just wrapped a towel around herself when the apartment phone rang.

"Hi, it's me."

Izzie felt the relief sweep from her head to her toes.

"Hello," she said softly, as if she were the one whispering as she made an illicit call. "How are you, Joe? I missed you."

Probably not the right thing to say, she knew, but she refused to play games.

"I missed you too."

He didn't play them, either.

"Why didn't you call?" OK, so that was a bit of game playing. But she couldn't help it. Why *hadn't* he called?

"I'm sorry," he said softly.

"That's not an answer," Izzie replied, feeling the familiar anxiety claw its way up her throat. She'd never been this way in a relationship before. But then, she'd never had a relationship like this before: a hidden one.

"It's complicated."

"O-K."

"Really. I can't talk now. I'm at home."

Why did that word hurt so much? *Home*. He had a home that was where she wasn't. How could that be right? When she felt as if nowhere was home except when she was with him? When had this all become so one-sided?

"Well, if you can't talk . . ." she said sharply, knowing she was cutting off her nose to spite her face. She'd *longed* for this call, blast it.

"I can't, I'm sorry," he said evenly.

"Why did you phone, then?" The words just snapped out of her.

"Right now, I'm asking myself precisely that question," Joe said, a slight edge to his voice. "We should talk when you want to talk to me."

"I do want to talk to you—but not with you whispering in case somebody hears," hissed Izzie. And that was the crux of it: the great love of her life was talking quietly on the phone to her when she wanted him yelling his love from the rooftops. How bloody hard could it be for him to tell his wife that he was formalizing what they'd talked about for years?

"I'm sorry you feel that way," he said, still calm. His calmness infuriated her. He was in control, in every way. Whereas she felt wildly out of control over the depth of her feelings for him. And she had no control over their relationship because he called the shots. It was like walking a tightrope with no harness and no safety net.

"I have to go," she said suddenly, wanting to goad him into begging her not to go. "I just got out of the bath and I'm dripping bathwater on to the floor."

He didn't take the bait.

"Fine," he said.

"No, it's not fine. Nothing's bloody fine!" she snapped back, and hung up. Then, because she so desperately wanted to phone him back and say she loved him but couldn't because of how awful she'd just been, she burst into tears. If she wasn't so fiercely in love with Joe, she'd wish she'd never met him. Because surely there wasn't much more pain than this, was there?

The next morning, her eyes looked red as a coal miner's and her face was puffy with tiredness. She'd barely slept all night and during the hours she'd lain in bed, awake, tears had kept welling up in her eyes. It was like having a geyser in her head.

"Ugh," she said, grimacing at her reflection in the bathroom mirror. Emergency measures were required. As the most up-to-date beauty-fixing products were spilling out of her bathroom cabinet, Izzie had no trouble finding balms, soothing eye creams and drops, and antipuffiness masks.

Half an hour later, she looked marginally better.

"Like someone with a migraine," she decided grimly, peering at herself. Her eyes weren't red anymore—those eyedrops made her cry, but, wow, they worked—but the rest of her still looked rough.

Rough, tough and dangerous to know, she decided, pulling on a masculine trouser suit. She'd never wear this for Joe; for him, she let her feminine side out, reveling in silks and lace, spike heels and figure-hugging styles.

But he didn't want her, so she'd go for tough instead.

"You sick?" asked Louisa, Perfect-NY's receptionist, when Izzie stalked in, menacing in her charcoal boy's suit.

"Yes. And tired."

"Eight messages for you on your desk. The Zest catalog people want you to phone, like, yesterday, and Carla's got a virus, so she won't be in."

Izzie breathed a sigh of relief. Carla had X-ray vision which could detect bullshit anywhere. With her out sick, poor love, at least Izzie had some hope of telling people she simply hadn't slept well. Keeping her relationship with Joe secret was turning her into a liar and she hated that.

Joe phoned at ten: "I need to talk to you."

"Fuck off."

"That's nice," he said mildly.

"I don't mean to be nice," she retorted.

"I'll hang up and phone again when you're less pissed off with me."

"You do that."

Izzie hung up first, which gave her a certain childish satisfaction that lasted for a second, whereupon she moaned softly at the thought of having hung up on him. She loved him, blast it. Needed him. Didn't he know that she was just saying those things? That she wanted him to need her so badly that, in spite of her anger, he'd rush downtown to Perfect-NY's office, throw himself on his knees in front of everyone, and tell her he loved her? That Elizabeth would have to deal with it? That his kids—and Lord knew, she admired how he did things for his kids, but it could still hurt—would get over their parents splitting up? Kids weren't stupid. They knew when people weren't getting on, didn't they? Surely she'd read that in a psychology magazine. It was better for children to see their parents facing up to the problems than hiding them, pretending it was all fine. But she couldn't say any of that to Joe because she wasn't supposed to be the kid expert, after all. He had to work it out for himself.

Her cell phone rang again.

"Yes?" She'd hit the button before it could attempt a second ring.

"Izzie, this is Amanda from Zest—"

Get off the fucking phone in case my lover is trying to contact me!!! was what Izzie wanted to say. Instead, she went into professional mode.

"Hi, Amanda. Recovered from New Mexico yet? And has Ivan sent over the photos from the shoot?" she asked calmly.

At lunchtime, Izzie deliberately went out and had a sandwich in the diner she'd told Joe she loved most, in case he was waiting for her and wanted to see her. She sat in one of the front booths, forced to share with three suited guys because the place was so busy, and pretended to read a magazine, all the time aching for Joe to come in and drag her out onto the street.

I love you, I don't care about anything else. I want to be with you, he'd say, and everyone would smile at this proof of true love on the streets of Noo Yawk, and it would all be perfect because he'd chosen her.

Wait, he'd beg. *Please wait for me, Izzie. It will work out, I promise.*

He didn't turn up.

Izzie went back to work but couldn't concentrate on anything until she flicked through the *Post* and found an article about a benefit in the Museum of Natural History the following night.

The great and the good would be at it, the *Post* told her breathlessly, including Elizabeth Hansen, who was on the charity committee, and her husband, Joe, who was a major benefactor. Izzie could feel the blood draining from her head. She'd never fainted in her life but she might just faint now. Joe was going to this charity thing with Elizabeth after he'd sworn that he'd told Elizabeth they'd have to stop doing that. She'd been so hurt when he'd gone to the AIDS benefit the night after they made love.

"I had to," he'd said.

"If you live separate lives, you don't have to!" she'd yelled back.

"I know, I'm sorry. I'll tell her we can't do that again. It's just . . . she's on lots of committees and there are lots of functions—"

"Joe, if you and Elizabeth are over, then that's fine," Izzie had said coldly. "If you're not, get the hell out of my life."

"We're over," he'd said. "Over. Promise. It will work out, Izzie, soon, I promise."

"I think I've got Carla's flu," Izzie announced blindly, closing the *Post*. She just had to get out of the office, where she jumped every time a phone rang.

Izzie had never attended a function at the museum, although she'd seen pictures in the papers and magazines and knew the form. The vast Romanesque steps spread majestically down to where the cars lined up, with fat red carpet laid for the rich to step on.

It was nearly eight in the evening and she stood with all the onlookers and waited, feeling crazier by the minute. It was just like being a celebrity-obsessed person waiting for their favorite movie star, standing in line in the rain and cold for just a glimpse of a person adored on screen. Why would anyone do that? It was sad, such a sign of not having a life.

And then she thought of how sad she was: standing waiting for a glimpse of her lover and his wife, to see if she could detect the truth. She was pathetic.

Hating herself at that moment, Izzie turned, leaving the small crowd of onlookers, not thinking where she was going in her misery, and found herself close to a dark limo that was disgorging four passengers going to the gala.

Two men and two women, all with the waft of privilege and dollars around them. On one side of the limo were Joe and a blond woman who could only be his wife. She looked better than she had in the Google pictures: thin, tall, with the racehorse legs these East Coast society women inherited from their mothers, and high, high shoes with the telltale red soles that marked them as Christian Louboutins. Izzie had only one pair. They were things of beauty but too expensive for someone on her salary. She felt envy at a woman who wore them carelessly in the rain. And her clothes—Izzie gazed enviously at her clothes. Elizabeth wore a beautiful evening coat—tailored plum silk, definitely Lanvin, beyond fashionable. Of course she wouldn't be a bling-bling tastefree person. As if anybody in Joe's life could be that.

Izzie thought of the knockoff of that same coat that hung in her own wardrobe, one she'd worn once with him. He'd said it was sexy but he preferred what was underneath, and he'd untied the big bow belt and they'd made love on the rug in her living room.

Hers had been cheap. Like her. She'd got a fake Lanvin, lots of pairs of pretend Louboutins and a fake boyfriend. Which was just right for someone who was cheap.

Exactly then Joe turned his face away from the rain and she knew without a doubt that he'd spotted her in the crowd. For a flicker of a second, their eyes met before he turned away. His face didn't really alter, but she knew he'd seen her. Standing in the crowd like a dirty-faced urchin with her nose pressed up against the sweetshop window looking at forbidden treasures.

His face was expressionless, and Izzie felt as if she was the cheapest whore on the planet.

So cheap, she'd been free. She should print cards and leave them in phone booths. *For a good time, no fee, call Izzie Silver . . .* Even joking couldn't make it better.

His wife said something to him, and clutched his raincoated arm with her hand, a sparkly hand that glittered with a fat diamond the size of a robin's egg. Tiffany, Izzie thought. Engagement ring or just cocktail ring? She wasn't sure which finger it was on.

Joe instantly turned to Elizabeth, his head bent the way it bent when he talked to Izzie.

How could she have been so stupid?

He'd said he loved Elizabeth, that after twenty-four years, he still did, but that their relationship was over and that he wanted out. He'd said he needed and wanted Izzie.

Izzie had imagined that no man could love two people at the same time, simply because she wouldn't have been able to. She'd assumed it was the same for him.

She was obviously wrong.

Joe could love his wife and simultaneously lie to and fuck Izzie. Simple as that. Izzie turned away, furiously blinking back tears. This time she wouldn't cry. She was done crying over Joe. Falling for him had made her abandon all her principles. She'd known it was complicated, messy, but she'd gone out with him anyway.

She was as bad as those predatory women who hunted men, using anything to get a ring on their fingers. Izzie had thought she was above all that. It had turned out she was just as bad. At least they knew what they were doing, and she hadn't. She was dumb as well as a stupid whore.

five

Lily Shanahan sat on a wooden bench in the tiny courtyard beside St. Canice's in Tamarin and let the April sunlight wash over her. It was nearly half ten and the courtyard was empty, apart from a couple of pigeons poking around the gray slab paving stones looking for crumbs. Everyone else was inside the church, listening to the gentle tones of Father Sean. Lily could hear the drone of the small Thursday-morning congregation murmuring along to the service.

She'd been on her way into the church when she'd felt a little light-headed and had a strange compulsion to sit outside in the sun instead, and worship another way.

You didn't have to talk to God in a church. If God had made the sun and the sky, it was only right to enjoy them. So she'd walked slowly to the wooden bench and decided she was taking a different sort of pew today.

God would understand. The church would be warm and the stuffiness might make her light-headedness worse. St. Canice's was architecturally very beautiful but flawed when it came to heat and cold. In the winter, it was freezerlike, elderly radiators notwithstanding. In the warmer months it became a hothouse, and many a bride had found that it was fatal to dress the church with wedding flowers the night before the wedding because even the buds that liked heat wilted in the fierce warmth of the church and slumped in their arrangements on the day itself.

Once she'd settled herself on the bench, Lily took off her beige cotton hat and closed her eyes, turning her face to the sun. Before she'd left the house, she'd meant to use some of that expensive cream that Izzie had given her the last time she was home—marvelous stuff, Izzie had said.

"Skin Replenish. Keeps wrinkles at bay. You should mind your skin, Gran."

Eyelids still shut tight, Lily smiled at the memory. Izzie didn't come home often enough these days. She was busy with her life in New York, and while Lily missed her, she was able to accept it. Lily's job as a grandmother standing in for Alice, Izzie's dead mother, had been to give her darling granddaughter roots and wings.

She used to say it to Izzie when Izzie got a fit of guilt over missing some big event in the Tamarin world: "Roots and wings, darling: that's what love is," she'd murmur, and feel grateful that she had the strength to mean it and that the words comforted Izzie.

Besides, there was no point saying that type of thing if you whined when the wings part meant the person built their own life away from you. Lily had no time for people who liked spouting such truths but didn't like living them. It was the hypocrisy she disliked—like telling Izzie to get on with her life and then being discontented because she did.

No, Lily wasn't a woman for hypocrisy. Probably not a woman for expensive moisturizer, either, she thought with a little chuckle.

Izzie's precious cream felt beautiful on Lily's skin when she actually used it, but she'd generally left the house before she remembered and she could never be bothered to go back to apply it. At her age, time, gravity and life had done damage that no expensive cream could fix—unless there was alchemy at work in the pretty glass jar.

What was nice was that her granddaughter still thought her skin worth saving. Izzie, who worked with beautiful women with skin as velvety as newborn babies', hadn't written her off as an old woman.

Some people did—as if wrinkled skin was an invisibility cloak. Like the maids' uniforms of so long ago, Lily thought wryly. She'd learned that early on. Once a person slipped on a servant's garb, they faded into the background.

The maids' uniforms at Rathnaree had been plain navy gabardine dresses with buttons up the back and a white collar that had to be laundered and starched to within an inch of its life. Lily's mother, Mary, didn't have to wear the same uniform because of her valued position as housekeeper, and Lady Irene had provided her with two navy serge skirts—"From *Harrods*," Mary would say, in awe at the very thought of owning a garment from a shop where the gentry themselves shopped.

Mary wore the skirts with pristine white blouses and a gray woolen cardigan.

The memory of her mother in that outfit, keys dangling from her belt, glasses on a ribbon round her neck, used to make Lily wince at the subservience of it all.

The Rathnaree housemaids liked their uniforms and the fact that it saved their own clothes.

Even Vivi, Lily's best friend, liked hers.

"Keeps my things nice, Lily," she said cheerfully, squashing her curls under the starched maid's cap. "Will you ever tell me why you have such a bee in your bonnet about the uniform?"

"I don't," Lily would say, which wasn't the truth at all.

Vivi was such an uncomplicated soul and Lily knew it would be impossible to explain that she hated the way putting on a uniform turned her into a piece of the furniture, which was what Lady Irene wanted: lots of blank-faced servants rushing around doing her bidding. Lily might have been born into the servant class, but she didn't have to like it.

Lady Irene wouldn't have forgotten to put expensive wrinkle cream on, Lily thought, smiling to herself outside St. Canice's.

If ever there was a woman keen to keep the ravages of time

at bay, it had been Lady Irene. In those long-ago days when Lily worked in Rathnaree, creams like Izzie's gorgeous Skin Replenish were definitely the preserve of the upper classes. An ordinary woman from the town would never wear any cosmetics, never mind expensive face cream. Lily's mother washed her face in water and soap, and that was it. She tidied up Lady Irene's walnut dressing table with its many potions and silver-topped bottles but never expected to use such things herself.

Lily could remember herself at twenty, defiantly buying Max Factor cosmetics and arranging them on the windowsill beside her bed. She'd have loved Lady Irene to see them and understand that the girl from the cottage was as entitled to beauty as she was.

"See, they're not just for the likes of you, Lady Irene," she'd have said, holding up the Chinese Red lipstick she loved and painted on in the same way Joan Crawford wore hers, with that elongated, sultry bow. The Crawford Smear, they called it, and it was the devil to clean it off your mouth, leaving a dark red stain that made you look as if you'd been pigging out on raspberries.

Had she ever been that young and fierce? That angry? She'd hated the Lochravens and all they stood for then: wealth, privilege and a blithe, careless approach to life. Lady Irene was the worst. From the moment she got out of bed, leaving her teacup teetering on the edge of a dresser, casting off silken bedclothes onto the floor, the lady of the house went about her business with the unassailable knowledge that someone would be following behind, tidying up. Lily hadn't cared so much when *she* was the lady's maid following in her employer's wake. She was young, energetic and with supple limbs: she could button her lip if need be. But how she'd hated it when her mother, Lady Irene's housekeeper, was the one stooping and tidying up.

"You'd think she'd pick up her things the odd time," Lily would say, scowling, when her mother came down to the big Rathnaree kitchen late at night, worn out after her day but not ready to go home yet.

"Hush," Mum would say, anxious lest anyone hear, although there were plenty of other people in the house who agreed with Lily and said nothing, but just took their wages. "Her ladyship wasn't reared to tidy up after herself."

"More's the pity," Lily would snap. She was fed up hearing how Lady Irene, a lady in her own right and not by marriage, had been raised in a palatial home in Kildare with three times the number of servants she had in Rathnaree. In the run-up to hunting house parties, her ladyship could be heard moaning about life at CastleEdward, where her mother, Lady Constance, had so much time to herself because the vast household almost ran itself.

"Why doesn't the stupid cow go back there, then?" Lily would snap at Vivi.

From the vantage point of age, Lily was able to smile at the memory of her angry younger self. At the time, she thought she knew it all, but she didn't. She hadn't understood that money and privilege didn't buy escape from the pain of life. There were some things a person had to live through and nothing could ease the agony, be they lady's maid or ladyship. They were all sisters under the skin.

The murmuring was louder in the church.

The congregation was reciting the Creed, Lily realized. In another ten minutes, the Mass–goers would be out and they'd fuss over Lily, worrying about whether they should call the doctor or not.

Lily's friend Mary-Anne would twitter with anxiety at Lily's mention of feeling light-headed, and would probably get faint with the shock of it all, and need to sit down herself. Everyone had to have a hobby and Mary-Anne's was hypochondria. At eighty-six, she was a slave to her pills and a torment to her GP.

Lily was the opposite. She didn't want a fuss. She'd move before everyone emerged, perhaps walk slowly out down the lower left side of the courtyard and on to Patrick Street. A cup of strong tea in Dorota's might revive her.

She could sit and look out at the harbor and watch the fishing boats come in. Thursday was the day Red Vinnie—so called because of the bright red slicker he wore—brought in his lobster pots. Vinnie always had time for a chat and he'd talk of the seals he'd seen basking out beyond Lorcan's Point, or the gulls with the strange yellow stripe on their wings the like of which he'd never seen before in his thirty-five years as a fisherman.

He was still young enough to find change shocking, Lily reflected. She'd lived long enough to see that there weren't as many changes in life as people thought: the world moved on a cycle and everything came round again. Only someone of her age could see that. Wait long enough and the past had its turn again and became the present.

The past—Rathnaree, Lady Irene, dear Vivi—had been taking up space in her mind lately because of that sweet Australian girl who'd been so softly spoken on the phone, scared of ringing such an ancient old dear as herself.

Jodi Beckett, the girl's name was, and she had a photograph, she said, of Rathnaree in 1936, of Lady Irene's birthday party.

"It's all beautiful and glamorous, like people from a film," Jodi had added excitedly. "They're standing in front of a fireplace with a tiger rug at their feet. I don't like that because it's a real tiger. It's so cruel, but the rest is so amazing. The clothes are incredible, glamorous. . . ."

It had been all that, Lily agreed, smiling wryly: very glamorous, although not so much so when you were the person sweeping up the ashes from those once-blazing fires at six on a cool morning, knees hard on the marble hearth, trying to be quiet lest you wake the household, who wouldn't care less about waking you if they needed something.

But that wasn't the thing to say to the girl. Jodi, pretty name, so confiding too, had told Lily that she'd married an Irishman, who was the new deputy headmaster in the local secondary school. And that her great-great-grandparents had come from County Cork and her family in Brisbane considered themselves Irish and loved all things Celtic.

"Investigating the past in Ireland is what I'm meant to be doing," Jodi had said on the phone. "I knew so much about Ireland before I came here. I love it."

Lily thought of how the past got romanticized into the rich vibrancy of Technicolor and Hollywood, where the servants weren't seen—except to doff their caps and be meekly happy with their peasant lot—and the rich got to be glamorous and have fun.

There were so many stories she could tell young Jodi about those times, but they might not be the stories Jodi was expecting.

Yes, there were silk gowns that bared pale, pampered backs, and the glitter of family diamonds and emeralds hauled out of jewelry cases for parties and balls. But that was only one side of the story. The less glamorous side was of whole families practically born into service by virtue of being born on the grand estates, families who were expected to have subservience in their blood. Except that not all of them wanted to wear a uniform, bob endless curtsies and do the bidding of people who were exactly the same as them except that the gentry had money behind them.

Lily knew that feeling all too well, because that was how she'd felt about the likes of Lady Irene.

She sighed, thinking of her younger self and all the anger and resentment she'd carried inside then. People now didn't really understand class the way older people did. Money could buy you anything now. But then money was nothing against the wall of the fierce class divide. When you were born one of the peasant class, you died that way too. Raging against such cast-iron barriers made little difference. Such complex memories weren't what Jodi was anticipating.

"I've made a start on the history of Rathnaree, but there's not much about it. No books—isn't that incredible? I'm sure you've so many stories and things. I'd love to hear them but . . ." Jodi paused. "Only if you'd like to talk to me. I wouldn't want to tire you out."

"Ah, pet," Lily said kindly, "talking doesn't tire me out. Let me look and we can talk about it all then."

Jodi would love the box Lily had kept hidden in her spare room: full of letters, photographs and her precious diary, along with programs from the theater, menus, a fake gold compact that had once been filled with Tea Rose face powder, dried flowers from her tiny wedding bouquet, her old ration book, bits and pieces that made up a life lived fifty years before. When she'd been speaking to Jodi, Lily's mind had instantly run to the box.

She'd taken it from its hiding place and put it beside her armchair in the sitting room, planning to open it up and look at its contents again. But somehow she hadn't. The box was still there, its dusty flaps closed.

Lily decided she'd meet the young Australian girl, but she wasn't sure if she wanted the precious contents of her box out there in the world. There were secrets in there—nothing that would threaten the state, she knew. But secrets nonetheless. Things she'd never told anyone.

There was just one person she'd trust with those secrets and that was Izzie.

Perhaps the best thing would be to write a note to Izzie and tape it onto the box so that one day, when Lily was gone, Izzie would find it. But then, maybe Izzie wasn't ready for her grandmother's secrets just yet.

Besides, Lily was sure Izzie had secrets of her own to occupy her. Izzie had been subtly different the last few times she'd phoned from New York: a little preoccupied, a little awkward, the way she used to be when she was younger and had something to hide.

"Is everything all right, love?" Lily had asked the last time they'd talked, on Sunday night.

"Fine," Izzie had said in a brisk tone that reminded Lily, with an ache, of Izzie's mother, Alice. Izzie sounded exactly like her mother when she spoke: the same soft tones, the same way of emphasizing certain words so her voice flowed like water, rapidly like quicksilver. When Izzie's voice had grown up, a few years after her mother's death, it was sometimes unbearably poignant for Lily to hear her speak: it was like Alice come back to life.

They'd looked so different: Izzie was tall and strong with eyes like Lily's own and the milky Celtic coloring that was set off by that marvelous caramel hair of hers. Alice had been small and fine boned, with dark hair and the olive skin of Lily's own grandmother, the fearsome Granny Sive.

Granny Sive was descended from the fairy folk, people used to say when Lily was a child, which was one way of saying they were scared stiff of her.

Lily had never been scared, though. Granny Sive had simply been uncompromising and different, a modern woman in olden times. No wonder they were all scared of her.

Granny Sive, now there was an old lady who'd have had a lot of great stories in her life.

What a pity nobody had come along to hear her tales.

Lily sighed. She hoped she'd done the right thing with the diary and the box. It was hard to know what the right thing was. But Lily had been feeling so unsettled since the phone call from Jodi Beckett. There was—how could she describe it?—a sense of time speeding up, an urgency in her heart, since then. Like she needed to phone Izzie and talk to her, but it would sound strange if she rang up midweek and said she'd been feeling odd. Poor Izzie would think she was going gaga.

She'd phoned Anneliese the previous evening to say how she felt but Anneliese and Edward's answering machine came on and she hung up without leaving a message. She hated answering machines, they were one of the modern inventions she'd never liked, and how could a person leave such a message on a machine anyhow?

Anneliese, I feel scared and anxious. Please tell me I'm not going gaga, will you?

It would sound too strange, definitely senile. She dreaded losing her mind: it had happened to so many people she knew. Even lovely, lively Vivi had succumbed and was now in the nursing home outside town. Laurel Gardens, it was called. A gentle-sounding name for a place Lily never wanted to be.

The diary. Her mind kept drifting back to it. If only she'd phoned Izzie after all. Izzie would know the right thing to do. Darling Izzie, who'd said she was going to New York to live, no matter what.

"I don't care if I'm living on threepence and sleeping in a teeny apartment where you couldn't swing a hamster, never mind a cat," she'd said all those years ago. "I'll be doing it *in New York*. You went and lived abroad, Gran, you must know what I'm talking about?"

Lily had nodded. "You're right, Izzie darling, forgive me. I'd forgotten."

"Gran, you never forget a thing," Izzie had laughed.

Sitting now in the sunlight, Lily wished that weren't so true. It might be nice not to remember.

She thought so much about the past nowadays. Did that mean she was very close to the end of her life? Did the voices of the past come to warn her? She saw them all in her dreams now: Mam, Dad, Tommy, Granny, Uncle Pat, Jamie, Robby and her beloved Alice. Alice was the worst. No parent should ever have to bury a child. The place where Alice had been was a part of her heart that Lily couldn't bear to touch, even now that Alice was twenty-seven years gone.

There had been so much death in her life, Lily reflected. All those young, healthy people dying because a bomb had landed nearby, or men shipped home with injuries everybody could see and scars on the inside where nobody dared to look but that killed them just the same.

As a girl who'd grown up in the countryside, Lily was familiar with death. There had been no question of keeping children away from the coffin at a funeral—everyone, young and old, bent to kiss the icy forehead of the corpse nestled in its wooden box. Lily had sat quietly at wakes and listened to old songs sung and watched the dead being mourned. But she'd never seen an actual person die until those first days on the wards.

She'd been amazed to find that life didn't ebb out of people with a fanfare—it slipped away quietly, leaving nothing but a body growing colder as the doctor moved swiftly on to the next patient. It was only much later, when the bloodied gauze and instruments were being cleared up and the amputated limbs were being carted off to the incinerators that anybody had time to tidy up the dead patients.

Lily used to find herself thinking about them later, when she'd be sandwiched between the girls—Maisie and Diana—drinking hot tea in the tearooms, or sharing pink gins—then she'd allow herself to remember. Of course, remembering was always a mistake.

Each young man could be her younger brother, Tommy, who was somewhere in the Mediterranean, she thought, although he couldn't tell her in his letters, and her mind would leap to the what-ifs—what if it was him lying cold on a table . . .

Which was why they'd all order another round of pink gins.

"*Nil bastardi carborundum!*" Diana would cry, which was dog Latin for "Don't let the bastards get you down."

Despite all the death, they'd been so young that they didn't think about dying themselves. Death was for other people. They were going to be lucky, and just in case, they'd live each day to the full.

And now death was waiting for her, except that she wasn't afraid to go. That was the one great gift of old age: readiness to move on. There was nobody left for her to take care of. Nobody would sob that it was too early when she died. God had let her live to care for her baby; she would have to thank Him for that, if she saw Him. Although she might be heading for the other place, the one with fire and the devil. Lily grinned to herself. She wasn't afraid of the devil—he'd been laughing in her ear for years.

If everything she'd heard in churches all her life was true, she'd meet all the people she'd loved in the past. Like her darling Alice. Letting Alice go had been the hardest thing she'd ever had to do.

Lily closed her eyes against the sun and let herself dream until it all turned dark inside her head.

six

Four miles away, Anneliese was in her kitchen clumsily making strong tea in the hope that it might wake her up. She'd slept badly again, staring at the alarm clock for much of the night, and had only dropped off to sleep when dawn began creeping over the horizon.

Now she was dressed and determined to go for a walk along the beach to get her out of the house, but her head felt heavy and muzzy. Normally, she might have sat down on the porch and read a book or a magazine until she felt more energetic, but she couldn't enjoy those pleasures now. Every magazine she picked up had some article in it that pierced her.

Yesterday a seemingly innocent magazine that came free with the daily newspaper had carried an interview with an actress starring in a film about infidelity.

Sickened, Anneliese had thrown the whole magazine into the trash.

The library books by her bed were no help, either: she'd never realized she'd been so drawn to novels about relationships. If asked, she'd have said she read everything, but all the books she'd taken from the library recently, with the exception of a thriller and a biography of Marie Antoinette, had dealt with families, couples and the relationships therein.

She had her second cup of tea outside on the porch. It was a beautiful sunny morning with a feeling of real warmth in the air, and when she set off for her walk Anneliese didn't bother with her light rain jacket. Her gray fleece was enough; she'd soon warm up. If she walked along the beach away from Tamarin, right down to the outcrop of rocks that marked the end of little Milsean Bay and back, she'd have walked two miles. That would be enough to warm her up.

As she left, she noticed several people on the town side of the beach, more than the normal morning dog walkers. Anneliese strained to see what was going on. There were definitely six or seven people gathered together on the high ground between the two bays and it was as if they were looking out to sea for something.

A boat. Oh no, she thought. A fisherman's boat had gone missing. It was the awful fear that haunted any seaside town.

Once a boat went missing, the whole community came to a stop as people prayed, the air and sea rescuers searched, and families sat numb. Anneliese could remember a vigil being held in the church once when a boat with three generations of fishermen capsized; what felt like all of Tamarin had crowded into the wintry cold of St. Canice's, as if the intensity of prayer could carry the boat and its crew back home. It hadn't. Only one of the crew had returned when his body had been washed up on the rocks five miles south.

She had no business to be feeling low when all she'd lost was a husband—who still lived—while some poor soul in Tamarin was readying herself for the real loss of a man.

Although Anneliese felt too raw to deal with the pain of a fishing crew lost, she felt a responsibility to walk down to the people on the beach. She was a local, and if help or vigil was needed, she had to be there too.

But as she walked quickly through the sand, down to the damp swath of the beach, she realized that the people weren't looking desolately out to sea: they were looking at something in the water.

"What is it, Claire?" she asked a woman who lived several miles inland and who was often on the beach walking three black and white collies who danced around the surf in delight.

"Hello, Anneliese," the woman said. The dogs were at her feet, whimpering because they wanted to keep walking and not stand. "It's a whale, look. She's come in too far and now she can't seem to get out."

"Poor whale," said someone else, moving so that Anneliese could stand on the highest part and see for herself.

There in the waters of Tamarin Bay was a dark shape circling in slow, aimless arcs. It was huge, had to be, because they were easily half a mile away from the shape and it was easily visible. Just as Anneliese was wondering how anybody could tell for certain what the creature was, it moved gracefully up in the water, a gleaming mound of darkest, silky blue, and she could see that it was clearly some sort of whale.

A tall fountain of water sprayed up from the whale's blowhole before the huge mammal sank back beneath the waters of the bay.

"They rise when they're in distress," said a voice, explaining. "She won't know what to do."

Anneliese hadn't noticed the man before in the group of local people. He could be taken for a fisherman in his dark pants and bulky sweater, but she knew most of the fishermen and she'd never seen him before. He was tall and grizzled-looking enough to be one of them, with a graying beard that matched thick, slightly too long hair.

"What should we do?"

"I'm sorry to say, there's not an awful lot we can do," he said.

"But there must be!" said Anneliese, furious at the resignation in his voice. Didn't he care? That poor whale was like her, lost and alone, and now nobody wanted to help. It just wasn't good enough. "Has anyone phoned the maritime wildlife people to tell them about her?"

"That would be me," the strange man said. "I'm the local maritime expert. I'm living in Dolphin Cottage."

Dolphin Cottage was less of a house and more of a barn,

nestled among the sand dunes on Ballyvolane Strand, the next horseshoe-shaped bay up from Milsean. A squat wooden building, painted blue by man and washed beige by God, Dolphin House was one of the local houses that were permanently rented out.

"I'm Mac," he added. "Mac Petersen."

Anneliese glared at him, not taking the hand he held out. She'd done polite all her life: she wasn't doing it anymore.

"And you can't do anything to help?" she snapped.

"When whales become stranded in shallow harbors, they often die," he said, calmly ignoring her rudeness.

"So this is it?" Anneliese demanded, waving her arms to encompass the whole group. "Us standing around watching her die? That's great. Well done, Mr. Marine Specialist."

As she turned to see the whale's dark shape move silently through the water again, Anneliese felt more empathy with the great creature than with any of the human beings around her. They knew *nothing*. Pain, loss, fear—they knew nothing about it. But the whale, circling in fear, she understood.

The man began to speak again but she didn't want to hear.

Tears bit at the corners of her eyes as Anneliese stormed back up the beach.

She knew she'd lost it, but she was past caring. Bottling up her feelings had got her nowhere in life. She didn't care enough about the world to hide who and what she was. Let the bloody world deal with it.

As she got in the door of the cottage, she caught the final ring of the telephone before it clicked into answering-machine mode. The message was still Edward's voice, telling everyone that he and Anneliese were busy and couldn't come to the phone, but to leave a message. Strangely, it was Edward's own voice that came on the phone then, leaving her a message.

"Anneliese, love—sorry, don't know how to tell you this, but just had a cell phone call from Brendan and . . . I'm really sorry, darling . . . Lily's in hospital, they think she had a stroke. She was sitting outside the church in town and they found her there this morning after Mass. Anyway, she's in the hospital, they took her in by ambulance. Brendan's on his way there now. I can't go just yet, I have . . ."

He paused. ". . . something else to do, but I'll drop in this afternoon, if that would be all right, if . . ." He paused again. "If you wouldn't mind me being there, I mean. Nell won't be there, obviously, but I'd like to be there for Brendan and for you. OK, goodbye, Anneliese. Sorry to be bringing you such horrible news."

The phone call ended. Anneliese stared at it for a moment before rushing over and hitting one of the speed-dial buttons to ring Brendan's number. Brendan Silver was Lily's son-in-law, and Anneliese's cousin—well, cousin-in-law, if such a thing existed. He was actually Edward's cousin. A good, kind man, but not the sort of person you'd need in a crisis, and poor darling Lily was in a crisis. Anneliese felt her heart ache for her darling aunt. Lily mightn't have been a blood relation to Anneliese, but she was one of the dearest people in her life. Strange how Lily—who had virtually raised her granddaughter, Izzie, when Izzie's mother had died—seemed to understand how difficult life had been for Anneliese and Beth. Anneliese couldn't imagine Lily ever suffering from panic attacks or depression. She was so calm, so serene, and yet she did understand. She'd been through the darkest thing a person could deal with: the death of her daughter, Alice. Lily understood darkness.

When Beth and Izzie were teenagers, Lily often stepped in and invited Beth to come and stay when Izzie was spending a few days with her. Anneliese hated the sleepover concept, but with Lily it was different: when Beth was in her house with her cousin, Anneliese could relax. The two girls were like chalk and cheese, mind you, and Izzie was three years older too, but they loved each other and got on well despite the squabbling. It was also a welcome distraction for Beth. Lily never said why she was doing it, nothing so bald as saying: "You're clearly depressed, I'll take your child off your hands."

It had never been like that. But she had understood that Anneliese sometimes needed the space to recover, so she could get her life back on track again. Lily had been such a part of Anneliese's life ever since she had first come to Tamarin, thirty-seven years ago, and now Lily needed her.

Brendan's mobile phone was turned off, but she left a message anyway. "It's Anneliese here, I've just heard about Lily, I'm on my way to the hospital. I'll run by her house first and pick up some things for her."

Anneliese grabbed a few things for herself first. Coins for the phone in the hospital, the plug for her mobile phone charger, a few of her Tranquility teabags, a big sweater and socks in case she had to stay overnight, her knitting and the spare keys Lily had given her years before for emergencies. Then she locked up, put her overnight bag in the car and drove off. In the distance she could still see the people standing on the high dunes, looking down into Tamarin Bay, and she thought of the whale circling aimlessly in the water, not knowing where she was or how to get out. Even with all the people watching her and all the ocean life teeming in the Atlantic out beyond Tamarin Bay, Anneliese knew, the whale felt lost and alone in the world.

It had only been a week since Anneliese had last visited Lily's house. So much had happened in that week. Edward had left her and now Lily herself lay in hospital. Anneliese felt the guilt again, guilt that she hadn't gone out and talked to Lily about her and Edward's splitting up. She just hadn't been able to face it, to face the pain and pity in Lily's beautiful old face.

"Oh, love, I'm so sorry for you. Is there anything I can do?"

Anneliese had known all the things Lily would say, and she was afraid that they wouldn't be any comfort to her, so she'd told Lily nothing. Now her stupidity and fear meant that she mightn't ever be able to say any of it. Lily was nearly ninety. At her age, a person who'd had a stroke might never recover. And all the pain Anneliese had inside her might remain bottled up there forever.

As she drove, she let the tears flow, unchecked, down her cheeks. It wasn't like the tears she felt with the panic attacks or the depression; those tears she tried to stifle, as if she could physically push them back into her body and stop the pain from escaping. But these tears for Lily were cleansing, they were a tribute.

Anneliese and Edward had always loved the road out to Rathnaree, which headed west of Tamarin along the top of the hill from where you could see the swath of both Tamarin and Milsean Bays. Then the road dipped into woods and fields and parkland, bordered by huge hedges that stretched long tendrils out onto the road, making the road itself very narrow and forcing cars into the hedges in order to pass each other.

Lily's house was the family home she had grown up in, a former forge that had once been a part of the huge Rathnaree estate. The Old Forge was no longer owned by the Lochraven family. They'd sold a lot of the land off years ago and now the house and the four acres of land it sat on belonged to Lily. That mattered a lot to her, she'd told Anneliese once.

"I don't think I'd be happy here if it was still part of the Lochraven estate," she'd said. "I know it's crazy. I'm old enough for it not to bother me, but there's peace in the fact that it's mine now, nobody else's. There's nothing like owning your own little bit of God's green earth.

"My mother, Lord rest her, would turn in her grave to hear me saying that. But I like the fact that it's my own land and my own house. It gives me immense joy, actually, to own it."

"Why did the Lochraven family never give the house to your family?" Anneliese asked. It didn't quite make sense to her, that these incredibly wealthy people would never gift the homes to the loyal workers who had served them for years.

Lily had laughed loudly at that.

"Oh, Anneliese, the number of times I wondered about that. I finally came to the conclusion that those sort of people don't gift anything, that's how they stay rich. They hold on to it and we're just the peasants who do their bidding, working our fingers to the bone and getting nothing but a pittance in return. Well, I used to think that. Long ago. But I know a bit better now."

There was something final about those last words, as if she didn't want to be drawn on the subject of how she'd learned those lessons, but Anneliese had to know more. Thirty-seven years ago, Anneliese would ask anyone anything. She plowed on.

"Both your parents worked for them, didn't they?" she said.

"My mother was the housekeeper from 1930 to 1951," said Lily. "Until she died, actually."

"She must have seen some amazing things, working in that big house," Anneliese added.

"Oh, she saw lots of things, all right," Lily said. "She saw everything. That was how I learned my first French. Lady Irene used to say things like, '*Ne pas devant les domestiques*.' Not in front of the servants. I worked as a maid there for a while and I got used to hearing that. Lady Irene never seemed to realize that eventually some of us might learn French and know what she was saying. Lord, but my mother used to go mad if I'd complain about them," Lily added. "First, she'd be scared someone would overhear. Then she'd say: 'Where's your gratitude?'

"I had no problem with gratitude. It was just that gratitude was a one-way street. My mother and my father worked hard up at Rathnaree and they just accepted that they'd never receive any gratitude for it. They got exactly what they were due, nothing more. The Lochravens liked to say their servants were part of the family, but they weren't treated like that. They were just words, and words mean nothing. Oh, don't mind me, Anneliese," she said. "I used to think if you were rich and from the gentry, you had it all. I know better now. Life hurts them the same way as it hurts us all."

Anneliese thought of that now, as she turned off the road, up a narrow, hedge-lined lane to Lily's cottage. It was such an enigmatic thing to say, but there had been a sense that Lily had a lot more to say if she were asked.

Anneliese wished she'd asked now. A person didn't get to Lily's age without learning a lot of life's wisdom, and right now Anneliese could have done with some wisdom. Anneliese had never known how Lily, after losing her only child, didn't crawl up into a ball of bitterness and die.

It had been a long time since Lily's home had been a forge but the name stuck: the Old Forge. Her father had been a blacksmith, the last in a long line of blacksmiths, who had come to work for the Lochravens. In his time it had been a working forge, complete with picturesque horseshoe-shaped door and the tang of hot metal in the air. Eventually, though, the forge itself had shifted to Rathnaree with its huge stables. Over the years, the original forge had been absorbed into the family home, until it was hard to tell where the forge ended and the house began.

There was an herb-filled front garden, because Lily loved herbs, and a fine big vegetable garden at the back that she no longer had the energy to dig or sow. When Lily's husband, Robby, had been alive, the couple had kept cows and hens and Lily had become proficient at selling free-range eggs, making her own butter, doing anything to get by in the lean years when Robby hadn't been able to find much work as a carpenter.

He was long dead, at least twenty years, Anneliese thought, remembering Lily on that bleak day in St. Canice's, when winter rain had lashed against the church's stained-glass windows and Lily's face looked as if it had been carved from the same wood as her husband's coffin as she stood and stared at it.

All I've done is lost a husband, and he's not lost forever, he's just run off with someone else.

She tried this idea out in her mind, seeing how it felt. Edward wasn't gone forever: he had just chosen to leave her. Was that worse or better than if he'd died? Because if he'd died, and he still loved her, she'd have that comfort to help her along as she dealt with the pain of being on her own. Yes, she thought, grinning, feeling some crazy sense of relief, in the midst of all this madness, death certainly trumped separation.

On the outside, the forge looked much the same as it had in those pictures Anneliese had seen of Edward and Alice standing outside it as children, laughing as they stood beside the big rain barrel where Lily kept the water that the family used for everything from washing their hair to bathing. Inside, it was different, full of character and warmth in the way only someone like Lily could fill a house, with lots of books and pictures of the family, and flowers, mixed with herbs, from her garden, scenting the air. There was a beautiful bathroom too.

"I always swore that if I had to live in this house I'd have an inside toilet," Lily used to tell Anneliese. "When we were kids, we were used to it, nobody had indoor toilets. Except up at Rathnaree; they had the most amazing bathroom installed for Lady Irene, all marble and mirrors replacing the old wooden paneling and a huge cracked tub. None of us had ever seen anything like it. I think everyone on the estate went in to have a look. It was just sheer luxury. I swore, one day I'd have a bathroom like that!"

And she had, thought Anneliese with a smile. Well, it wasn't quite like the fabled Rathnaree marble version, but it was pretty luxurious: pure white tiles and a swirling chocolate brown Deco pattern running along the edges. She was glad that Lily had had her lovely bathroom—it was nice at the end of your life to have had the things you dreamed of having. You could look at them before you died and say, "I wanted that when I was twenty, and now I have it!"

"Stop," Anneliese said out loud as she stood in Lily's home. She was talking as if Lily was already dead, and she wasn't. But Lily was very old, and maybe this was the way for her to go. Quickly was always better for the person who died, but it was horrible for those left behind. It would break Izzie's heart if her darling gran died before she had a chance to say good-bye.

Anneliese wondered if she should have offered to phone Izzie to tell her the news. She had an idea from her last conversation with Lily that Izzie was away on a shoot: Mexico, New Mexico . . . she wasn't sure about the place or time. Time had escaped her these past few days. She barely knew which day of the week it was.

If Brendan hadn't phoned Izzie to tell her what had happened, she would when she got to the hospital. But now she had to rush, not stand here looking at old photographs and thinking back on Lily's life. That was no good for anybody. She hurried upstairs into Lily's bedroom and packed some nighties, underclothes, bed jackets and soft slippers. *Hurry*, a voice inside was telling her.

Lily looked so frail in the hospital bed when Anneliese walked into the intensive care unit. Even though she'd thought about the possibility of Lily not waking up, the realization hit her forcibly when she saw that frail body lying doll-like under the covers, winking and beeping machines all around her. The ICU hummed with activity, with nurses hurrying back and forth, quietly and efficiently, while patients lay still in the ward's four beds. There was no sign of Brendan at his mother-in-law's bedside and Anneliese was glad for that. She didn't want to have to comfort Brendan. Instead, she could sit quietly on the chair beside the bed and look at Lily. The older woman's eyes were closed and yet she looked more than asleep; the animation that normally shone from her face was absent today. She'd always seemed somewhat ageless in normal life, yet now she looked like a very old lady, with fragile bones and skin delicate as tissue paper. An IV was stuck into the back of one of her fragile hands and Anneliese winced at both the pain of the needle and the ache of the bruise that had already settled around the sharp metal.

"Oh, Lily," she said, taking Lily's other papery hand in her own and stroking it. "I'm so sorry, darling. I'm so sorry you're here and that I haven't been talking to you. Things have been so dreadful with me and Edward, and I didn't know how to tell you. I'm sorry, that's not fair. And now you're here and I don't know what you'd want me to do. We never talked about this. I don't know if you want heroic measures to bring you back, or if you're happy to go, my love. I wish I knew. You deserve the dignity of choice."

It was odd because Lily could talk about anything. Not for her the ostrich-in-the-sand mentality or thinking that if you didn't face an issue it would disappear. Lily faced everything head-on. But death, and what to do in the run-up to death, was one of the last taboos.

Anneliese held the old woman's fragile hand and prayed for guidance. She wasn't equipped for this, not now. Because of Edward, she felt as fragile as Lily herself.

"Oh, Lily, what do you want me to do?"

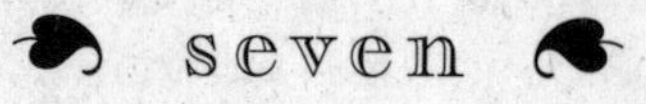

seven

Cosmetics contracts were the holy grail of the industry. There might be huge kudos at landing a photo shoot for *Vogue* but the honor was supposed to make up for the lack of cash involved in such a high-profile shoot. Editorial was great for a model's portfolio, but mascara ads meant a whole lot more cash.

Once a model had signed on the dotted line with one of the cosmetics giants, she never had to worry about badly paid photo shoots again. Cosmetics contracts guaranteed a lot of money up front and some security in an industry not known for it. A contract made a model more valuable in that a million billboards made her famous, made her a name. Once a model became a name and not just another slender beauty, she had a chance at the big time: more advertisements, television, endorsements. When that happened, everyone—including the model's agency—got to laugh all the way to the bank.

The day after she'd stared at Joe and his wife outside the museum and had felt her life crashing painfully around her, Izzie had to put her pain aside for a big meeting with a cosmetics company client about a megamillion-dollar campaign aimed at teenagers. The Jacobman Corporation wanted a new model to front their new cosmetic line and Perfect-NY was, through a fabulous piece of luck, in the running to find the girl.

It was a huge slice of business for Perfect-NY and exactly the sort of job that Izzie didn't want to be doing the day after her heart had been broken.

As she marched into Jacobman's giant office block on Madison, she looked the part—on the outside. She was fashion perfect in black Marc Jacobs with her hair sleeked back, wearing a solid four ounces of Bobbi Brown nude makeup in order to look as if she was wearing no makeup at all.

On the inside, however, she was tired, dead eyed and felt as if she had barely enough energy to lift her coffee cup to her lips.

The meeting was in the Jacobman Corporation's third boardroom—the first and second ones were big enough to host a Yankees game—and there were only four people present: Izzie, representing Perfect-NY, two people from the SupaGirl! brand and a Jacobman bigwig, Stefan Lundberg.

Cosmetics companies spread their net wide when looking for the right girl for their products. But Perfect-NY had been invited to showcase any of their girls who filled the brief because the current Mrs. Rick Jacobman Jr. had once been a model at Perfect-NY and had, astonishingly, never forgotten the agency which had launched her career, a rather short one which had then launched her into the arms of Rick, heir to the Jacobman millions. Around the model agencies, Svetlana Jacobman was seen as a model who'd won the ultimate cosmetics contract. Even with a cast-iron prenup hanging over her should it all go horribly wrong, Svetlana had joined the ranks of the truly rich.

"Yeah, she's fresh faced, but she's sorta kooky, isn't she?" snapped one of the SupaGirl! executives, tossing aside the third model card they'd looked at. "We're not about kooky. We want a normal American teenager."

On the other side of the boardroom table, Izzie stuck her nails into the palms of her hands to make herself keep schtum. Normal teenager—yeah, right. She'd seen the brief, and no matter how they pretended they were looking for normal, what they really wanted was a fifteen-year-old goddess who'd never seen a zit in her life in order to advertise oil-free foundation.

"Lorelei is actually very versatile," Izzie said, once she'd managed to get her temper under control.

"We're not about kooky," agreed the other SupaGirl! person, who looked about twelve years old and was clearly a yes-woman for the other executive.

"No, definitely not. Let's skip her. Who else have you got?" snapped the first executive.

After another half hour of this, Izzie had only four models left to show them and couldn't face doing it, and being rejected again, without a hit of caffeine. Perfect-NY wasn't getting an early chance to place one of their models with SupaGirl! after all. This whole thing was a PR exercise to please Svetlana Jacobman and the bitchy executive had never had any intention of doing business this way.

"I need a coffee," Izzie said, forcing a smile onto her face and rising abruptly from the conference table.

"Yeah, me too," said Stefan, following her.

Outside the conference room was a small kitchen that was, nevertheless, bigger than the one in Izzie's apartment.

"No good so far, but hey, you never know, we might hit gold yet," Stefan said as he leaned against the doorjamb and watched Izzie making her mind up between machine espresso or filter. She'd known him for a few years; he was good-looking in an outdoorsy way, but he was too obvious: blond hair carefully gelled, shirt opened to show his impressive chest. Izzie had a vision of him in front of the mirror in the mornings, working out exactly which button to open down to on his shirt. She hated that: she preferred her men rougher, as though they could afford nice suits but really couldn't be bothered trying to look so smooth. Unfortunately, that type of guy clearly couldn't be bothered about her either, if Joe Hansen was anything to go by.

Irritation with Joe spilled out onto the general population.

"I'm not holding out much hope for us hitting gold," she snapped. "Your Laurel and Hardy team don't seem to like any model I show them."

"Ouch. Laurel and Hardy. That's harsh. Bad day?" said Stefan.

"You could say that." Izzie went for filter coffee. She might start to shake if she had any more espresso inside her.

"Man trouble or office trouble?" Stefan asked.

Izzie shot him a glare. Stefan was straight, therefore not allowed to broach the "Having man trouble?" conversation.

With guys like him—straight, women-mad with access to a corporate gold card—man conversations always ended up with him offering himself, clothed or otherwise, as a shoulder to cry on.

"I don't have man trouble, because I don't have anything to do with men."

"Pity."

"Pity, schmity."

"You sure you don't want to talk?"

"Stefan," she snapped. "I'm not talking about this with you. We are not friends."

"Ouch." He feinted grabbing his bruised heart at that.

Izzie laughed. "What I like about you is that I can say anything and you can take it."

"I'd love you to say anything to me, but you always turn me down. Like that time I asked you to have early drinks with me before the Ford party . . ."

"I had to work. Besides, when I turned up, you'd found yourself a date."

She'd been tempted by the invitation at the time, during another date drought, before she'd given up on men altogether. But Stefan had cut a swath through more than one model agency. She'd often wondered if he had his own wall with model cards on it and a merit rating system.

The night in question, she'd showed up at the party to find him being consoled by a Texas model who had legs up to her armpits, a curtain of platinum hair down to her coccyx and a body made for lingerie ads.

"She was on the subs bench," he said. "You were first team."

"You've an answer for everything, Stefan," she sighed. "You do realize that if it was anybody else but me you'd be facing a sexual harassment suit right now? You're lucky I'm so easygoing."

"You, easygoing? Hey, Irish, never get hardgoing, will you?"

"Let's concentrate on what we're doing."

"Not over coffee," he groaned. "We're supposed to be doing the brainstorming in the conference room."

"It's hard to think creatively with that pair wrecking my buzz. Can't you hire executives whose facial muscles allow them to smile?"

"Point taken. They are kinda miserable. Hard to believe, but there's a lot of competition to get onto the SupaGirl! team. Great package, great health care, gym in the basement . . ."—Stefan pretended to flex a muscle—". . . guys like myself, looking decorative and available for dates because hot girls from the model agencies keep turning them down—"

"That's it!" Izzie banged her cup down, spilling coffee onto the counter. "A *competition.* What about a find-a-model-for-SupaGirl! competition?"

Even as she was saying it, her mind was flipping the idea over. Was it a stupid idea or a clever one? There was such a fine line between the two.

"Brilliant!" said Stefan, clearly not thrown off track by his meanderings being interrupted. Izzie wanted to give him a hug. He might be a macho male in some respects, but he was an out-and-out professional.

"Absolutely brilliant. Publicity and launch in one fell swoop."

No, hugging would be a mistake, she reckoned. Stefan might misconstrue it. She patted his arm instead in a filial gesture. "Glad you like the idea."

"Like it? I love it."

"Perfect-NY will represent the girl who wins and we'll help you set up castings all around the country," Izzie went on. No point in her coming up with a fabulous idea and letting the SupaGirl! executives take over.

She almost danced out of the building an hour later and was on her cell phone to the office before she'd got a cab.

Everyone was on a call, so she left messages on people's voice mails and then sat back on the scuffed black seat and realized that she had nobody else to phone. Carla was her closest friend and she'd just left an ecstatic message on her voice mail.

But there was no one else to talk to. No special someone to phone and murmur that she'd had a brilliant idea, nobody to tell her they were proud of her. Gran loved to hear about her work, but she felt a shaft of misery at the idea of phoning home in order to connect with people who loved her. The deep gloom that had lifted briefly in the conference room descended again.

Before Joe, she'd never needed to phone anyone to tell them her news. But she'd got used to it with him, and now, without him, she felt the lack of it deeply. Damn the rest of the coupled-up world. She was fed up with them.

When she got to the office, the team happily discussed Izzie's idea before people raced off on their lunch breaks.

"Hey, you going out for lunch?" Carla asked her.

"No."

"Good. I want to talk to you."

Carla led a dead-eyed Izzie out onto the fire escape for a bit of privacy.

"Yeah, what's up? said Izzie, wrapping her arms around herself. She felt cold—no matter what she did, she hadn't been warm since last night. It was like the combination of rain and sheer emotional pain had sent a chill into her bones. Even the buzz from the SupaGirl! idea couldn't warm her up.

"There's a bit of prime gossip going around," Carla said, " 'bout a certain married Wall Street gentleman who's having a hot thing with a model agency booker. Seems somebody's driver said to another driver who said it to a hairdresser who told a client—possibly lots of clients. Hey, you know this town, everybody loves to talk—and this particular everybody happens to be a friend of mine and said it to me."

"New York whispers are deadly, huh?" Izzie quipped nervously. There was no way Carla could know about her and Joe.

"Tell me it's not you," Carla said.

Izzie bit her lip. It was only a momentary pause, but it was enough for Carla.

"Oh fuck, it *is* you, isn't it?"

Izzie didn't want to look Carla in the eye. She couldn't face the reproach she knew she'd see there. How could she explain this?

I didn't know the full story that first day—dumb, I agree, but I didn't know. I didn't think. He was so charming and sexy and we connected, and by the time he said he was with his wife but not with her, well, I was hooked. . . .

"Izzie, you cannot be serious! What has happened to you? I should have known," Carla raged. "I knew something was wrong and I hoped you'd tell me what it was, but I never thought it was a man. A married man! Are you nuts? How many women do we know who've gone that route, and it always ends up bad. Always. The only person who wins is the guy."

"Look, he's married, but they're not together—" began Izzie, thinking that it was a bit rich that her secret was out now that she'd finally decided it was over between her and Joe.

"Puhleese!"

"It's not like it sounds," snapped Izzie. "You know me, Carla: I'm not the sort of woman who's looking for a *Fortune* 500 guy to tear him away from his wife so I can cut up my subway pass and never work again. I just thought he was a guy, he liked me, we saw each other, and—"

"—and he told you it was over with her?"

"Living separate lives. Together for the kids."

Carla actually hit her forehead with the palm of her hand, the international "You are a moron" gesture. "And you believed him?"

"Yes! He's not a liar, honestly."

"Why didn't you tell me about him, then? I heard nothing 'bout Mr. Wall Street. Why? Because you *knew* something wasn't right, didn't you? And you knew I'd talk you out of it."

Izzie shot her friend an anguished gaze. "I thought it was the real thing, Carla. You can't fake love, and he loved me. I loved him."

"So why not tell me?"

"It was all so complicated. He loves his kids and he wants to make it all right for them, Carla. He's not a bastard, honestly. He's the real deal and I knew he needed time," she said lamely.

"Time? Yeah, time to play an away game until he rolled back to his wife."

Izzie burst into tears, a move which startled both of them.

"Jeez," said Carla.

"It's over anyway," Izzie said, weeping. "I believed him about needing time and then I found out he was going to a party with his wife, and it didn't seem like such separate lives anymore, so I finished with him."

"That's something," Carla remarked.

"No, it's not," sobbed Izzie. "Because I've never felt worse in my whole life. I still believe him, but it's too much, too complicated. I can't be involved in that and I had to get out before . . ."

She couldn't finish the sentence. *Before I fell so painfully in love with him that I'd stay no matter what,* was what she wanted to say. Except she'd already done that, it seemed. She didn't care what was going on in Joe's life, she just wanted to be part of it. Her moral compass was broken and she didn't care.

"Izzie!" a voice rang out from inside. "Urgent call for you from Ireland. Some emergency. . . ."

Izzie gratefully took the cup of coffee that Carla offered her and wrapped her hands around it. Their cube farm in the Perfect-NY offices wasn't cold, but she was icy inside at the news. Darling Gran, one constant in an always messed-up world, was in hospital back home in Tamarin and she might die.

The news had shocked all thought of Joe out of her mind.

Instead, she thought of Lily, frail now more than slender, with those faded blue eyes staring out wisely at the world. Kindness shone out of her: kindness and wisdom.

Izzie couldn't bear to think that her grandmother's wisdom would be gone forever when she needed it so much.

There were so many things she still needed to know, so many things she wanted to tell Gran—now she might never be able to.

And the one thing she desperately wanted to share, how she felt about Joe, she'd never be able to tell. To a woman of her grandmother's generation, there could be nothing worse than infidelity, and Izzie simply couldn't bear to see Gran's eyes cloud over with the knowledge that Izzie was having an affair with a man who was still married. If Carla, who was as liberal as it was possible to be without being a radical lesbian feminist, had been shocked by the news, imagine how devastated Gran would be. Granted, Carla's anger was only because she felt Izzie had been conned, but still.

"Oh, Gran," Izzie prayed, willing magic into the air as if that might breathe health into her grandmother thousands of miles away, "please, please don't go."

"It was a massive stroke," Dad had said on the phone. "They found her in the courtyard outside the church. Luckily she'd fallen against the back of the seat or else she'd have cracked her head on the slabs and then, well . . ." His voice had trailed off.

Her father couldn't say ". . . she would certainly have died." Not dealing with the hard stuff was Brendan's forte. Izzie knew it was not by accident that she'd fallen for an alpha male with vigor, courage and the ability to face life.

The noticeable differences between the man she loved and her father was the stuff undoubtedly covered on the first day of the Psychology Made Simple class.

"When did it happen?"

"This morning after Mass."

"What do the doctors say?" Izzie steeled herself.

"Not much. . . . She's in intensive care and they've got all these tests to do, but nobody will really say anything to me. . . ."

Izzie could imagine her father, taller than she was but without a shred of her fierce energy, looking round the ICU for a doctor, but not able to find anyone to ask because they were all rushing and he didn't like to bother anyone.

Sweet and gentle was a lovely way to live, but it didn't work in the high-speed, intensely pressured atmosphere of an emergency room.

"Is anyone with you? Like Anneliese or Edward?"

Uncle Edward was a more forceful individual than her father and would certainly get things done. Darling Anneliese was even better: she was calm in any crisis and she'd certainly needed to be, Izzie knew.

Her cousin, Beth, would have gone under if her mother hadn't been made of such stern stuff.

"No-o." Her father made the word into two syllables.

Izzie waited.

"Anneliese is on her way. I phoned Edward, you see, and told him and said to tell Anneliese, and he went all quiet and said since it was an emergency he would, which sounds strange, but I didn't have time to ask him—"

"But Anneliese is on her way?" Izzie was impatient with these details. She needed to know that her aunt would be there, looking after things, looking after Lily.

"Well, yes. I suppose. You know how Anneliese loves your gran."

"*I* should be there," Izzie said.

"I wouldn't dream of asking you to come home. You're so busy with work," her father said quickly, which made Izzie feel bleak at this perceived notion that her job, only a bloody job, was more important than her beloved grandmother. Had she made them all think that? That Perfect-NY was higher on her list of priorities than her family?

"I'm coming," she said fiercely. Damn the bloody job. If she had to swim across the bloody Atlantic to reach her grandmother's hospital bedside, she'd do it. "Gran needs me."

What she didn't say was: *And I need her because my heart is broken*.

"Go home," advised Carla. "You look wrecked. Lie on the couch and chill, and call me if you need me, right?"

Izzie nodded. "I will, thanks—for everything." Thanks for not mentioning Joe again, she meant.

She got a cab home instead of battling it out on the subway, and all the way home she wondered if God was so vengeful that her grandmother's stroke was his way of getting at her for being involved with Joe.

No, don't be crazy, she told herself. That's like saying *only you* are important, so that God punishes other people to get at you. But still the thought hammered away in her head with the intensity of a horror movie watched late at night. She'd always jokingly described herself as a submarine Catholic—one who only comes up when there's trouble. Now she realized it was true, and then some. Trouble made her Catholicism seep out of her pores and make her question everything.

At home, she checked the airlines and found that she'd never make that evening's flight to Dublin, but that there were seats on the next evening's.

She booked, feeling a strange sense of relief that she couldn't leave New York just yet. She felt too unraveled to go, so much of her life still hung out there, threads flying in the wind.

She began to pack for the trip and found that she couldn't concentrate. What would the weather be like was normally an important packing question, but the major one—how long would she be gone—was unanswerable. It depended on her grandmother's survival.

Oh, Gran.

The silence of the apartment was closing in on her. Izzie was rarely at home on a weekday afternoon; she was always out there, being New York City Girl, rushing and racing. For what? she thought bitterly. To be alone, dealing with this horrible news, preparing to make a journey home alone too.

Where was her lover now that she needed him? With his wife, that's where.

Izzie sat down on her small couch and cried. All the romance and the excitement counted for absolutely nothing at that moment. She could tell herself it didn't matter that she didn't have a husband, 2.5 children and a crippling mortgage, but at moments like this it did matter.

She knew she wasn't the only woman to fall for a married man, but it felt like it—she was in a club with only one member, a spectacularly stupid member.

Still, when her cell phone rang she leaped to it, hoping that it might be him, eyes too blurry to focus on the number.

"Hello?"

"Hey, girl, how are you doing?" Carla's smoky Marlboro Lights voice was warm with concern.

Izzie slumped against the wall beside the phone. "OK," she mumbled.

"I'm sorry I told you to go home. I got to thinking that you'd be climbing the walls by now."

Izzie laughed. "How'd you know that?"

"Instinct."

"Whatever it is, it's spot-on," Izzie replied. "I can see the lure of the barstool now. All those people I used to think were losers for sitting in bars in the afternoon—they have a point."

"You could join me on a barstool tonight? First, we eat, then we hit a club or two. Might take your mind off things."

"Count me in," Izzie said. If she stayed at home, she would cry herself to sleep, she knew.

They arranged to meet in SoHo at eight, and when her phone rang moments later, Izzie answered it without looking, thinking it was Carla ringing back.

"Hi," she said warmly.

"Hello."

It was him. Colder than he'd ever sounded before, but still him.

The driving rain hitting her face outside the museum benefit came starkly back into her mind. She thought of his arm on his wife, the stunning WASP blonde with racehorse legs, and the blank look on his face as he stared at Izzie.

Then she remembered her father's voice on the phone, along with the vision of Gran lying in a coma, and all the vicious things she'd planned to say to Joe vanished. She needed him like she'd never needed him before.

"I'm sorry," she said, starting to sob. "I'm sorry, Joe. It's awful, my grandmother back home in Ireland is sick: she's had a stroke and they don't know if she's going to be all right, and it's awful . . ."

"Oh, my love," he murmured, frost gone. "I'll be right over." He was there in ten minutes.

At the door he said nothing, just held out his arms and let her come to him, where he drew her into the tightest bear hug she'd ever experienced.

"Baby," he kept saying over and over again, his hands tenderly stroking her as if she were a child.

Finally safe, she cried until her face was raw and she felt too tired even to stand.

He brought her over to the couch and they sat, Izzie curled

up on his lap. The comfort from feeling small and loved was immense.

"Thank you." She sighed, her head bent against the wall of his chest.

Curled up against him, she talked about Gran: about how she'd practically lived in Lily's house after her mother died, and how Gran had been the only person who didn't shy away from talking about her mum.

"Dad didn't know what to do. He thought that if we talked about Mum, I'd get upset, so it was better if we didn't. That was fine for the first year when I couldn't talk about Mum, but afterward, when I wanted to, he'd change the subject so fast. Maybe he couldn't talk for his own sake, either."

"What was she like?" he asked.

"A lot like my dad: vague and artistic. She painted. She'd walk around with paint smudges all over her clothes and on her face and not even notice. She'd go to the supermarket in her slippers and laugh if you mentioned it to her. Bohemian, I guess. She had quite dark skin, not like me, and she loved the sun. She had a mole on her back that went very dark, and she didn't think anything of it. By the time they realized it was cancerous, she had only weeks to live."

Joe said nothing, just kept on gently stroking her hair.

"Dad went to pieces, like today," she sighed. "Nothing new there. Gran stepped in and took over. She raised me."

"Tell me about *her*," he said, moving so that they were both lying on the couch now, his long legs hanging over the end, Izzie feeling fragile against him, the way she always did because he was such a big man.

So she talked: about Gran blazing a trail in Tamarin by leaving to train as a nurse in London during the war, of the stories she'd told of being a twenty-one-year-old in another country, and how she'd coped.

"That's probably why I wanted to travel when I left school," Izzie said. "I'd grown up hearing Gran talk about another world outside Tamarin, and it felt like what I had to do."

"She went back to Ireland, though, didn't she?"

Izzie nodded. "She went back after the war, married my granddad and has been there ever since."

"I know you're going home, but not for good, right? I don't want you to leave New York," he murmured. "Your grandmother needs you now, but not to stay. I need you even more, Izzie."

He moved his hand from stroking her hair to gently tracing the curve of her waist and hip, settling around the firm swelling of her buttocks.

Fear and death made people think of love, Gran had told her once. That thought flickered through Izzie's consciousness as she felt her body answering Joe's hunger.

People regularly went home from funerals and made love, she knew, to banish the cold, hard reality of death. Gran wouldn't die, she just couldn't. As if the fierce passion of their lovemaking could keep her grandmother's heart beating through some spiritual intervention, Izzie Silver kissed her lover back with more hunger than ever before.

Life and love couldn't end, they couldn't.

They ended up in the bed after all, since the couch was too small for both of them. Joe had lifted Izzie up and carried her to the bed, throwing off the pretty pillows that decorated it so they had more room, pinioning her to the bed with his weight as he adored her body, kissing, sucking, licking. The second time was gentler, more loving and less fierce.

When he was inside her, he cradled her face in his hands and gazed into her eyes with such love that Izzie wanted to cry, but he didn't say anything, only called her name as he came.

After their exertions, Joe lay beside her, breathing deeply. Izzie was sure he was asleep, and she lay curled against him.

As she lay there, she allowed herself to dream. What if he said that this was the time for him to leave his home and come to her?

You need me now, Izzie. I'm going to be there for you. I'm coming to Tamarin too.

And Izzie, who knew she'd never, ever have asked him for that because she wasn't the sort of woman to walk round with a chisel in her purse, trying to prise him off his wife, would say: *Thank you, I'd hoped you'd say that, but I'd never ask.*

If she'd asked, she'd be no better than the sort of woman she hated: the professional girlfriend who picked a married man with a big bank balance and used skills like safecracking to get her hands on the money. That wasn't Izzie.

But if he came to her now, how wonderful it would be. She'd be able to cope a little better if he were with her, holding her hand, sitting beside her in the hospital with Gran.

"This is the man I love, Gran," she'd whisper, and even, *God forbid,* if Gran never woke up, Izzie would have brought Joe to meet her. She so wanted Gran's approval of the man she loved. Even though it was all so unconventional and difficult, it would work out, because love found a way, didn't it?

The love of her life stretched beside her and then moved so that he was propped up on one arm, staring down at her.

She gazed up at him happily, eyes tracing the familiar lines of his face and loving what she saw.

"Izzie, I need to know why you came to the museum last night," he said.

"*What?*" she asked, her happy daydream crashing to the ground. "Can't you guess?"

"Well, no."

This time she sat up and pulled the sheet protectively over her breasts.

"Oh, come on, Joe," she said. "It's not rocket science. You're one of the smartest people I know. Surely you can figure it out."

"You wanted to look at my wife?"

He couldn't say her name: couldn't say "Elizabeth." As if saying it here in Izzie's apartment would taint her. Elizabeth was the one to be protected, not the other way round.

Izzie shivered at what this meant.

"I could look at her in any magazine, Joe," she said calmly. "I wanted to see you *together*—don't you get it? You and her, together. Wouldn't you want to see me and him together if I was the one who was married?" she asked incredulously.

"If you were married, we wouldn't be together," Joe said bluntly.

"What?"

"I wouldn't want to share you." He shrugged. "That wouldn't be an option. I'd never see someone who was involved with anyone else."

Rage boiled up inside her.

"You bastard!" she hissed. "I get to share you, but you'd refuse to share me. You are so hypocritical."

"Me, hypocritical? I don't think so." Joe's eyes were like cold steel and they bored into her.

Izzie was shocked by the ferocity of his glare.

"What I didn't think we were getting into was you turning up like a stalker to watch me and my wife with our friends."

His words actually hurt her physically. She hadn't known words could do that.

"I can't believe you're saying this to me," she said. She no longer felt angry, just very scared and very shocked. This was not how it was supposed to be. Where was the Joe who'd looked down on her as they'd made love, as if he'd like to gaze at her face with love forever.

The words just slipped out. "I thought you loved me."

The silence gaped like one of the valleys near the New Mexico pueblo where she'd been just days before. Outside, police cars roared past, droning sirens into the afternoon.

"I thought you and Elizabeth were just together for the kids? That's what you told me. Is that the truth or not?"

"Izzie," he began, "I do love you, but it's not that simple."

And then she knew for sure. Carla had been right. He hadn't loved her. He'd loved making love to her, sure, but as for the Real Thing—that was all one-sided. Her side.

"Don't say anything." She scrambled out of the bed, dragging the sheet with her, wrapping it around her body as if she were an Egyptian mummy. She didn't want him looking at her naked body ever again. She felt so ashamed: ashamed, humiliated, stupid. He'd used her. She loved him, thought he loved her too. But she was wrong.

"Let's not fight," he said gently. "I didn't come here for that."

The shred of dignity left to Izzie stopped her saying: *What did you come here for, then?* Because the answer was simple: to fuck you, my handy little girlfriend. That's all she was. A convenience store—available for late-night drinks, dinner and free sex. For the first time ever, she had respect for the hard-boiled Identi-Kit New York girlfriends of married men. At least they understood the rules of the game and they considered it a profession. Get your man and get something from him. She'd considered herself different: his true love. She was his equal and she wasn't the sort of woman who wanted *things* from a man. She wasn't in it for gifts—she was in it for love. Except he was in it for something different. No shit, Sherlock.

"No," she said, reaching inside herself and finding one last thread of calmness. "Let's not fight. I have to pack."

Pack? She didn't care if she traveled on the flight without a single item of luggage but the clothes she stood up in. Still, it was a good excuse.

"Of course," he said, sliding gracefully out of the bed. He was such a handsome male animal, she thought, watching him. Everything she found physically attractive—no fat, just hard muscle and a hard business brain, and now, she'd just found out, a hard heart.

"What time is your flight?" he murmured.

"Five forty tomorrow evening," she said.

"Nothing earlier."

"No."

"If you want, I could get you on the private plane," he said.

Like a computer finally downloading a big email, the litany of vicious things she'd planned to say earlier came online in Izzie's brain. The thread of calm vanished.

"But not the company plane, right? That might really let people know that you were screwing me. No, you'd have to take a favor from someone or else pay to fly me home, because God forbid that any of your employees should find out about me, the boss's whore."

"Izzie," he said, sounding hurt, "I never made you feel that way. I never meant to."

"I know, but that's still how I feel," she said.

"Guess we're fighting after all."

"No, you're leaving," she said. "In fact, I am too. I've got things to buy." She grabbed a sweatshirt and sweatpants from her closet and went into the tiny bathroom. Twenty seconds later, she emerged, wearing the tracksuit, her hair messy from where she'd hauled it over her head. Who cared about her hair? Bed hair and life-is-over hair looked pretty much the same. "I'm going. You can let yourself out."

"Don't go," he said urgently.

"Tough, I'm going," she said. "I don't want to wait here and listen to more of your lies."

"They're not lies, Izzie. I love you. It's just difficult now. Complicated—"

"I'll undo some of the complications, then," she snapped. "Consider me out of your life, Joe. Does that make it easier?"

She snagged her purse from the hall, grabbed her keys and was gone.

She ran down the stairs to the street in case he came after her, and then ran two blocks to a coffee shop they'd never been to together, just in case he came after her.

But he wouldn't, she realized, as she stood at the counter and tried to summon up the brainpower to actually order something.

"Er . . . skinny latte, please," she said to the barista. Joe wouldn't follow her. He didn't want an emotional girlfriend who had expectations, he wanted an easy lay who wouldn't cause trouble. Or did he? She'd trusted him, had been sure he was telling the truth. But if he was, and if he loved her, wouldn't he walk away now to be with her?

She sat at a table and stirred sugar into her latte. What a hideous day this had turned out to be. First, darling Gran, now this.

Oh, Gran, she said to herself, *I've let you down so much. Let both of us down, actually. Bet you thought you'd taught me better, huh?*

A mother with a baby in a stroller and several bags of groceries underneath sat tiredly down at the table beside her. Izzie watched the mother and child sadly. *She'd* never have that, not now. Motherhood was a destination getting farther and farther away from her. Once she'd thought it was a right, inevitable. Women got married and had children. Then it became a challenge: harder than originally thought, but still possible. And now—now it looked impossible, unless she went it alone.

Suddenly, she could understand women who reached forty and went looking for donor sperm to father their babies. If there was no man on the scene to be your baby's daddy, and the time bomb that was worn-out ovaries was ticking away, what else did you do? Wait like Sleeping Beauty for a nonexistent prince? Or save yourself.

The baby wriggled in her stroller and Izzie caught sight of her properly. Downy African-American curls framed an exquisite face with chubby cheeks and huge dark eyes like inky pools. In her peachy pink sleepsuit, she looked like a little doll.

"She's lovely," Izzie said to the tired mom, who instantly brightened.

"Yeah, isn't she? My little princess."

"Does she sleep?"

What Izzie knew about small children could be written on the head of a pin with room left over for the State of the Union address, but she knew that sleep patterns were as important to mothers as New York Fashion Week was to her.

"She's getting better," the mother said, warming to her theme. "She went six whole hours last night, didn't you, honey?" she cooed to her baby. "You got kids?" she asked Izzie.

Izzie felt the prickle of tears in her eyes.

She shook her head. "No," she said.

"Not everyone wants 'em," the woman agreed.

Izzie nodded. She didn't trust herself to speak. She pushed her barely touched latte away from her. "Bye," she said with a gulp, and ran out.

It was too late for her to have a baby, she thought, wild with grief. It wasn't that her eggs were too old or that her body was too decrepit; it was that her heart was a dried-out husk and she couldn't nourish another human being when there was nothing left in her.

"Don't go yet, Gran," she whispered up to the Manhattan sky. "Please don't go yet. I need to see you one last time, please."

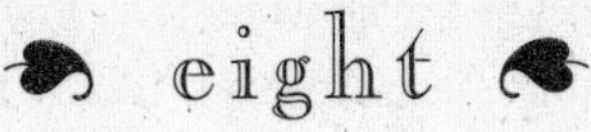

eight

Izzie's in-control façade had stayed in place throughout the entire flight, the roller-coaster turbulence of their descent into Dublin airport and the long march through the glass hallways of the airport to the baggage claim.

She traveled so much for business that she could adopt her woman-business-traveler look easily. With her pink silk eye mask for sleeping on the flight, her moisturizer to cope with the dryness of the cabin and her flat shoes (socks in her carry-on bags), she had traveling down pat.

It was only when the airport double doors swept open and she was suddenly out of the international no-man's-land of the airport and into the actual country of her birth that it all hit her.

This wasn't a routine work trip or even a planned trip home; this was an emergency visit because her beloved grandmother might be dying.

Directly outside the doors, standing right in front of lots of moving human traffic crossing the road, Izzie Silver stopped pushing her cart and started sobbing for herself.

A hundred miles away, Anneliese sat at her aunt-in-law's bedside and talked softly about how she felt, and how she simply wasn't able to cry.

"It's like I've this black hole inside me," she whispered, even though there was no need to talk so quietly.

"Crying would be better," Anneliese went on. "Therapeutic or something. But I can't. It's like being full of nothingness. No matter what I do or how I try to buoy myself up, it's hopeless. Gray, dismal desert with only blackness everywhere. Oh, Lily," she sighed to the still, silent figure in the bed. "I wish you were here so I could tell you—well, you *are* here, but not in the same way."

Lily's pale, lined face didn't flicker.

Anneliese didn't know if she was present or not. Were people in comas *there*? Even so, talking to an almost-not-there Lily surpassed talking to everyone else.

"The oddest things occur to me about it all. Like the fact that Nell was so bitter," Anneliese whispered. "She said I must have known about her and Edward. That was almost the worst thing. She kept insisting that I knew and allowed it to go on. I *didn't*. I swear on the Bible, Lily, I didn't. How could I let Edward have an affair and not say a word to him about it? I wouldn't, and not with Nell.

"She was my friend. Was," Anneliese added bitterly. "Nobody's going to believe me if she's my best friend and she says I knew all along. I won't be believed, and if I deny it, she'll say I'm just a vengeful ex. She might even tell Edward that she and I had talked about it. She could tell him anything, and how would he believe me over her?"

It wasn't a relief to say these horrible things. They hurt as much in the telling as they did in the thinking. The ache was still there, the ache of aloneness.

What was worse was *how* she'd become alone.

The evening before, she'd sat on the veranda and stared out at the sea, trying not to think about the beautiful trapped whale still circling sadly in the harbor, and she'd thought about her Worst Case Scenarios.

It was a trick of hers when she felt depression looming: to think of the very worst things that could happen and visualize herself coping with them. A person could cope with anything, she knew, making herself think of people who'd gone through every pain possible from torture to seeing people they loved murdered.

Edward's death was one of her Worst Case Scenarios.

She remembered seeing an interview with a woman who'd been widowed in the World Trade Center attacks and it had almost hurt to watch it. The woman's pain was so raw, so open, and she spoke of how her life had changed and how now she expected the worst.

Her words had resonated with Anneliese for two reasons: because she was speaking of widowhood, and Anneliese knew too many widows of her own age not to fear it, and because Anneliese had felt that sense of fear all her life: that pain was just round the corner, waiting its time. She'd felt like that forever. Waiting for the blade to fall.

She'd been so cautious, pushing Edward with his healthy heart and his healthy diet to have blood tests every year at the doctor's. She'd cooked giant lumps of broccoli, bought him fish oil tablets, stocked the fridge with blueberries. She'd done everything to keep him with her, warding off disease.

He'd been taken anyway. He might as well have died. It was like he *had* died, in a way.

"How did you manage, Lily?" Anneliese asked. "How did you manage when Alice and Robby died? Forgive me, but I keep thinking that death is almost easier. You can grieve. How can I grieve?"

And then she checked herself: Lily had done her grieving privately because she'd had to keep calm for Izzie.

"Forgive me, Lily," she said now. "That was terrible of me. Nothing could be worse than losing Alice. I'm sorry. There's no comparing my loss to yours. I'm sitting here whining and I haven't had as much taken from me as you. But I can't help feeling devastated. I only wish you were here. You could make sense of it all for me before I go totally crazy."

"Good morning. How are we all doing here?" said a cheerful young voice.

Anneliese looked up, startled by the interruption. A nurse hovered, and from the ultrafriendly set of her face, Anneliese guessed she'd heard the end of the monologue. Anneliese was too sad to feel embarrassed. She guessed that nurses were used to hearing people murmuring hidden thoughts at hospital bedsides.

"I just want to check on your mother-in-law's vitals," the nurse said, still smiling.

Anneliese nodded and moved out of the way, not bothering to correct her. "Aunt-in-law" sounded ridiculous. "Will you be long?" she asked.

"We might be a while. You should take a walk outside," the nurse said, resiliently cheerful. "It's a lovely day."

"Yes," said Anneliese. Lovely day for throwing yourself over a cliff. What would the poor girl do if she said that? Probably find the on-call psychiatrist and tell him there was a madwoman in-house, and could they find her a bed, a straitjacket and a needleful of benzodiazepine.

She collected her bag and went into the corridor, not knowing quite what to do with herself. Somehow she ended up in the small hospital coffee shop, at a table with a cup of frothy white coffee and a scone that looked hard enough to bounce off the walls. She wasn't in the slightest bit hungry, but she buttered the scone anyway and bit into it.

Keep putting the fuel in, she remembered someone saying to her once. But why? Old worn-out cars got scrapped. Why couldn't old worn-out people get scrapped too? Why bother putting fuel in when the engine was gone?

She shoved the scone away and, to occupy herself, switched on her mobile phone. Brendan had sent her a text message. He was hopeless with phones, spent so long sending the simplest message that the time involved far outweighed the benefits of texting versus actually phoning.

Once, she, Beth and Izzie had laughed gently with him over his hopelessness in this area. Now Anneliese wondered if she'd ever laugh at anything again. What did laughing actually feel like? Would she ever do it again?

Marvelous news. Izzie has arrived. She will be at the hospital by four.

No text shorthand for Brendan.

Anneliese thought of Izzie, who was strong on the outside and soft as a marshmallow on the inside, and how she'd cry at the sight of her darling Gran in the hospital bed. Then she thought of Beth, who'd sobbed when she'd heard the news on the phone, but who couldn't come until the weekend.

"Of course, don't rush," Anneliese had reassured her. Reassuring her daughter was what Anneliese did best. "Gran will be OK."

Another lie. Who knew if Lily would really be all right or not? But there was method to her madness: the longer Beth stayed away, the more time Anneliese would have before she had to tell her daughter the horrible news about her parents' separation.

It was ridiculous that she still hadn't told Beth about her and Edward, ridiculous. Beth would be furious with her, but Anneliese just hadn't had the heart to do it. As if telling her daughter would make it all true.

Anneliese knew she could not be strong enough for both Izzie and Beth.

That was what she'd wanted to tell Lily before the nurse interrupted them.

"Beth doesn't need me," she half whispered to herself in the hospital coffee shop. "She has Marcus to look after her and he adores her. Nobody needs me anymore. I don't have to be here. For the first time ever, I don't have to be here."

It was both liberating and terrifying at the same time.

She didn't need to be there. Be anywhere. She could jump off the cliff or walk into the sea and keep walking, and it wouldn't really matter.

"How did you manage, Lily?" she wondered out loud.

She partly knew the answer: Lily had thrown herself into raising Izzie. She'd had to bury her own grief and deal with her granddaughter's instead. But Anneliese had nobody to take care of. She had only herself and right now she didn't care what happened to Anneliese Kennedy.

The first person Izzie saw when she went into the four-bed ICU was Anneliese. Sitting by a bed with knitting on her lap and a faraway look on her face, she seemed so wonderfully familiar that Izzie had to bite her lip to stop herself crying again and ruining all the repair work she'd done with makeup on the way there.

Then she saw her grandmother, tiny and frail as a child in the bed, with no hint of the vital woman she'd known all her life. Shock leached the color from Izzie's face and her emotional armor came tumbling down.

"Anneliese," Izzie gasped, grabbing her aunt's hands in horror and stopping beside the bed. "Oh God, poor Gran, my poor Gran."

Anneliese could do nothing but pat Izzie's shoulders as the younger woman held on to the little body in the bed, sobbing, "Gran."

It was almost too private to watch, Anneliese thought, and she began to turn away, hoping nobody else would approach so that Izzie could mourn in peace.

"Anneliese! She's talking!"

"What?" Anneliese rushed to the other side of the bed. "She hasn't woken up, Izzie, not since . . . We should call the doctor."

"Yes, Gran." Izzie wasn't listening to Anneliese. She was bent close to her grandmother's face, trying to decipher the faint words.

Lily's mouth was moving and her eyes were open, shining out of her face with a vitality undimmed by nearly ninety years of life.

"We're here, Lily," Anneliese said gently. "You're in hospital. You had a stroke, love, but you're going to be all right."

Lily stared up at the ceiling as if she was looking at somebody neither of them could see.

"Jamie," she whispered in a voice as faint as paper rustling on the wind. "Jamie, are you there?"

Izzie and Anneliese stared at each other across the bed. *Jamie?* Neither of them knew of a Jamie.

"Jamie?"

"Gran, it's me, Izzie." Izzie stroked her grandmother's cheek softly, but Lily's eyes closed slowly shut and the brief moment of vitality faded from her face.

"I don't understand," Izzie said. "Dad said she was still unconscious . . ."

"She was. She still is," Anneliese said. "That wasn't really waking up, was it? Your voice reached her, for sure, but she wasn't talking to us. She was seeing someone else—"

"Jamie." Izzie sat heavily down on the chair beside the bed. "Who the hell is Jamie?"

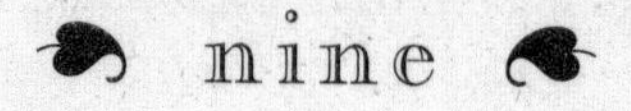

nine

October 1940

Lily Kennedy rested her stockinged feet against the base of the cream Aga in the huge kitchen in Rathnaree and sipped her tea from a flowered china teacup. It was early morning and the room was silent except for the ticking of the clock on the wall and the occasional crowing of the cockerel outside in the yard.

The ten-minute walk from the Forge to the big house had been cold, with Lily and Mam hurrying along in their heavy outdoor boots, the cool of dawn biting into their faces and a weak sun lengthening shadows in the dark woods along the avenue. Lily wasn't afraid of the dark: a girl raised in the countryside had no fear of shadows, although there were plenty of stories about bogeymen and spirits that gave her pause on the nights she bicycled from her friends' homes in Tamarin. But looming dark shapes beside the road were often as not a cow or an innocuous blackthorn bush.

Tommy had written in his letters about the city lights of London and how there was almost a glow above the houses in the sky from the streetlights. They were all gone now, he said, nobody wanted a glow as a signal for Mr. Hitler. Lily couldn't imagine a city the size of London: Dungarvan was the biggest town she'd ever seen in real life, although she'd seen London, Paris and New York through the magic of films in the Ormonde Cinema.

And now she'd be seeing it herself in a few days. She hugged the thought to herself, excited and a little bit anxious. Tommy, who'd helped her find out about the nurses' training in the Royal

Free Hospital, wouldn't be there to meet her. His regiment, the Royal Irish Fusiliers, was being sent overseas, although he couldn't say where to.

Dad had read Tommy's last letter and then crumpled it up and thrown it in the direction of the fire.

"Tommy's gone, why are you setting off too, Lily?" he'd demanded gruffly. "We've had enough wars of our own to keep us going. We don't need to be sending our children off to fight anyone else's battles."

Lily hadn't replied. She knew her father's pain was over losing his beloved son to be a soldier rather than any diatribe against a war in which the Irish Free State was taking a neutral stance.

Mam understood it better. She knew that Lily was passionate for another life, one away from Rathnaree.

"A person would never believe the cold of this house if they didn't experience it," said her mother now, hurrying into the room, dressed in her housekeeper's uniform. "The beds are all damp despite it all, and there'll be hell to pay if her ladyship comes home before it's all settled."

Lily jumped to her feet and poured tea into another cup and saucer. Her mother didn't bother with china cups usually, but Lily loved the delicate feel of the bone china.

"Here's your tea, Mam. Sit down."

"I've no time to sit," her mother said, but she took the cup and sipped it gratefully standing at the great scrubbed wooden table. "The red bedroom smells of damp, and even with the window open, I don't know if the smell will be gone by tomorrow. Why, in the name of the Lord, did I say it was all right for everyone to come in late today, what with all the work to be done," Mary fretted.

"Sit with me," Lily begged, because she knew there was no point telling her mother to stop rushing for people who were not actually there and who wouldn't appreciate her rushing anyway.

"I'll sit for a moment," her mother said, and looked wistful. Her daughter was leaving home the next day, but Mary would be busy readying the staff for the big party. The family had been in Dublin for a week and were coming home the following day with a party of friends.

Normally, the place would be buzzing even at this early hour, with Eileen Shaw, the cook, huffing and puffing about how the cold, wet weather made her cough worse. Sean, who'd been the Major's batman in the last war and now worked as the family's butler, would be lighting his pipe and casting irritated glances at Nora, the latest maid, who was all fingers and thumbs, organizing Lady Irene's breakfast tray. Sean was generally easygoing, but there had been quite a turnover of housemaids recently and Nora, who was young and awed by the grandeur of Rathnaree, fell short of the butler's standards.

Last, there would be Vivi, Lily's best friend, standing outside and having a quick cup of tea and a cigarette before she started work. Lily loved Vivi: they were like chalk and cheese, Mam said, but they were best friends, had been since school, although Vivi had left at thirteen to come and work for the Lochravens.

Mam had insisted that Lily stay on until she was seventeen, which was almost unheard of.

"You're daft to keep at the books," Vivi used to say to her. "Think of the fun we'll have when you've a few bob in your pocket, Lily."

Vivi was short, curvy, and had recently gone to Silvia's Hairdressing Emporium to have a platinum rinse to her hair, doing her best to look like Jean Harlow, her heroine.

"But I'll have to work for bloody Lady Irene," Lily pointed out. That was the downside of having money. If it had to be earned in Rathnaree, she'd rather not earn it. Unfortunately, there weren't too many other options for her in Tamarin. There was no money in the Kennedy household for her to train as a nurse in one of the big hospitals, which was what she really wanted to do. So she'd ended up in Rathnaree after all, which had made Vivi happy.

Leaving her best friend behind was going to be one of the hard things about going to London, Lily thought sadly.

This morning was the last vestige of holiday for the staff. There weren't very many days when servants could lie in bed at their leisure. Tomorrow it would be business as usual with frantic dusting, cleaning and polishing, and Eileen in a lather of sweat preparing the pheasant for the party, cooking her special wild mushroom soup and making delicate pastry for the crème mille-feuilles Lady Irene insisted upon.

The fact that the family was away was the only reason Lily had come with her mother to Rathnaree in the first place.

She hadn't been there since the previous Christmas, when she'd left to work with old Dr. Rafferty in his surgery in the village. When Dr. Rafferty's daughter got married, Lily had leaped at the chance to take over her job tidying up after the doctor, helping him out sometimes, in the hope that she might somehow find a way to train as a nurse if only she had some experience behind her.

Lady Irene had been furious, although she had hidden it behind the usual veneer of disinterest.

"If you want to spend your life working with sick people, Lily, then I wish you luck with it," she'd said when Lily had formally handed in her notice.

Lady Irene's last lady's maid had been addressed by her surname: Ryan. But Lily, because she was the housekeeper's daughter and had been in and out of Rathnaree since she could toddle, had been spared the harshness of being called Kennedy. It was a great sign, Lily's mother said, pleased.

"She's very fond of you, love," Mam said with pride when Lily had been promoted, after just six months in the house, to the position of lady's maid. "And why shouldn't she be? You're so neat and clever, and I never saw anyone fix her hair the way you can."

Lily was quite aware that being able to dress the older woman's thinning dark hair was not necessarily a guarantee of her civility. Fifty years of having their every whim responded to did not endow a person with grace.

They all knew that Lady Irene was high in the instep and had been brought up with a fleet of servants, far more than she had now. There had been French chefs and an Italian lady's maid in her home in Kildare, not to mention two thousand acres of prime farmland, and an Italianate garden that lay spread in front of a vast Georgian mansion. All of which added up to the fact that she wasn't used to being thwarted by a mere member of her staff.

"I am surprised that you wish to leave," Lady Irene had added in her lethally soft voice, the pale patrician face showing an unaccustomed flush of red. Under the dusting of powder, the harsh smoker's lines around her tight mouth were like angry furrows.

"I thought you were happy here."

"I am, your ladyship," said Lily evenly. She'd learned to speak in calm measured tones when she'd been drafted to replace Ryan. Her mistress was mercurial and her mood could change in an instant. Her daughter, Isabelle, was exactly the same. Luckily, Isabelle was rarely home. She'd been schooled abroad, had gone to finishing school in Switzerland, and was now touring the Italian lakes with some cousins. The war was only four months old and neither the Major nor Lady Irene felt it was anything to worry about. Nobody thought it unsafe for Isabelle to be careering around Italy in a Hispano-Suiza with chums like Monty Fitzgerald and Claire Smythe-Ford. The unspoken message, one Lily heard loud and clear, was that money and class would see a girl like Isabelle Lochraven out of any difficulties.

"Why leave, then?"

So many answers ran through Lily's head: "Because I don't want to spend the rest of my life catering to your whims like my poor mother" was foremost. She suspected that Lady Irene knew this. It was a conversation Lily didn't want to have.

"It's been my dream to be a nurse since I was a child," Lily said, truthfully.

"Which doctor did you say you were going to work for?" Lady Irene pressed.

They were in the small sitting room beside her ladyship's bedroom. It was Lily's favorite room in the house. Her own home was a comfortable cottage with sturdy, much-loved furniture, and Rathnaree was very much a country house without frills and furbelows, but the small sitting room was the one room in the house that had been decorated to reflect Lady Irene's taste and it was a little oasis of femininity. The high windows were swathed in silk curtains decorated with pale pink and blue flowers; the heavy old fireplace had been replaced with a marble one where Roman nymphs frolicked with fauns, and the furniture was delicate and gilded.

"Dr. Rafferty," replied Lily.

"Oh, I don't know him."

The Lochraven family didn't bestow their custom on the local Tamarin GP. When the need arose, a doctor was driven from Waterford city.

"You must do as you wish, Lily," Lady Irene said, signaling that the interview was over.

Lily escaped gratefully. She disliked Lady Irene so much and lately she found it harder and harder to hide her dislike.

Lily wasn't sure when she'd lost respect for her employer: possibly round the time she was fourteen and her mother had fallen from her bike cycling home from Rathnaree late one night after having waited until two in the morning for the last of the dinner party guests to go home.

The next morning, she'd been back at work at seven as usual, black and blue with bruises and stiff from her fall. Lady Irene had mentioned finding some arnica for her—she'd never found it—and in the same breath had told Lily's mother about an impromptu shooting party the Major was having that day.

"Only seven guns, Mrs. Kennedy, nothing too much really."

Lady Irene called Lily's mother Mrs. Kennedy, as if respect was all about the correct titles and nothing to do with actually caring for the person.

She cared for no one. She didn't even care for her precious belongings—her clothes were left strewn on the floor as she stepped out of them. Lady Irene's clothes were exquisite—undergarments of crêpe de chine and finest silk, in peachy coral shades that flattered the skin, never the heavy woolen vests and vast interlocked gusset things the Kennedy women wore, grayed from washing, harsh against the skin, unflattering as could be.

If she ever had any money in her life, Lily swore, she too would have silken petticoats and negligees that swept the floor carelessly. And if she ever had money, she'd have someone to help her around the house, but she would treat that person with genuine respect. Irene Lochraven, Lily felt grimly, firmly believed that birth had made her better than Mary Kennedy.

Unfortunately, Lily's mam believed that too. Why couldn't she see that the only thing separating the Lochravens and the Kennedys was money, nothing more?

"You'll write, won't you?" her mother asked now, sipping her tea quickly, the way she did everything.

"Of course I'll write, Mam," Lily said. "Just 'cause Tommy's a hopeless letter writer doesn't mean I will be. I'll tell you everything."

"I'll miss you," her mother added. "I'll pray for you."

"I'll pray for you too, Mam," Lily said.

She felt guilty to be going, but excited too. When it became plain that the war was far from the little blip the Lochravens had insisted it was, she and Dr. Rafferty had talked about the opportunities for nursing in London. When Tommy had signed up, it had spurred Lily on. There was a whole world out there waiting to be discovered, and she was eager to be a part of it.

Two days later, Lily sat on the edge of the hard bed and patted the smooth coverlet washed to pansy softness. She was relieved that she only had to share a room in the nurses' home with two other students. The formal letter from the Royal Free Hospital in Hampstead had included few details of the residential arrangements, other than listing their new address: the scarily double-barreled Langton-Riddell Nurses' Home.

On the ferry to Holyhead, Lily had taken out the letter and smoothed it flat on her lap, wondering if she was doing the right thing. Yet when she'd reached London, she'd known she was.

It was her third city in as many days—Waterford, Dublin and now London—and instead of feeling scared in the crowded streets so unlike the rolling hills of Tamarin, she felt alive, excited, happy.

How could she have been scared? She loved this: all the people, the busy streets, cars and trams racing past, and vast elegant buildings that made Rathnaree look like a hovel.

Now that she was in the nurses' home, Lily was glad to see that her visions of dormitories with trainee nurses squashed together were wrong. It was a relief to find this lovely albeit tiny room under the eaves. So far, only one of her two roommates had arrived, a woman who was probably only the same age, twenty-one, yet looked a lot more sophisticated—and a lot less impressed with their quarters.

The room had all that Lily needed: heavy curtains for warmth, a washstand with floral bowl and matching jug, a rather elderly chest of drawers with a mottled mirror on top that looked quite serviceable as a dressing table, and beside each of the three iron-framed beds with their neat covers was a small stool, hastily conscripted into use as a night table. On either side of the door were nails for clothes to be hung on.

Lily had slept in much worse.

But the Honorable Diana Belton, who was now looking around her with something akin to shock, clearly hadn't.

Vivi, who was impulsive and always rushing in, would have

fussed over Diana, asking her if she was all right. And once Lily would have too. But today she held back.

She'd grown up beside a big house, had learned at her mother's knee that the people in big houses were different.

"Special," her mother would say when she sat wearing her eyes out mending a frippery of lace for Lady Irene. "Isn't this beautiful, Lily? Feel it—wouldn't it make you feel like a princess to wear it?"

Why did money and land and silken lace make them different? Lily wanted to know. Weren't they all the same, all God's people?

Here, in London, she wasn't Tom and Mary Kennedy's daughter who had made a very good lady's maid. Here she was the same as the Honorable Diana: a trainee nurse. She had no plans to strike up a conversation or to apologize for their quarters to this girl in her tweed suit, necklace of pearls and fur collar. The Honorable Diana might very well flick back her improbably blond hair and snub Lily: snubbing her inferiors was no doubt something she'd a lifetime's experience of.

Diana had remained coolly silent when the trainees had been welcomed by the stern Sister Jones.

"Up at six, breakfast at twenty past and on the wards at seven," Sister Jones had read out in her cool voice. "There will be lectures in the preliminary training school in the basement here and you will be issued your timetables for those tomorrow. For the first two months, you will work until eight at night with one day off every fortnight. Students are expected to be in the home by ten, when the doors will be locked. Late passes may be given at Matron's discretion, but only for special occasions: you will then be permitted to stay out until eleven. There are to be no visitors. Understood?"

"Yes, Sister," everyone had murmured.

Then the room assignments had been read out. Lily and Diana

had climbed the stairs with their bags in silence, and Diana hadn't spoken a word since.

She could suit herself, Lily thought irritably.

She got to her feet and took off the very plain worsted wool coat that had never clung to her figure the way Diana's suit did to hers even when it was new. And it was far from new now. Lily had bought it three years ago from Quilian's Drapers in Tamarin, which in itself had felt like an act of independence, because for years she'd bought her clothes under her mother's supervision in McGarry's Drapery. She'd felt pleased every time she saw the coat, pleased at that symbol of adulthood, and satisfied with her first purchase, chosen by herself and paid for with her own money. But now, faced with the glamorous Diana in marvelously cut tweed, she felt lumpen and ugly in it.

She hung her coat up and began to unpack her small cardboard suitcase.

When Diana spoke in a soft, hesitant voice, Lily was so surprised that she actually jumped.

"I'm Diana Belton. Awfully sorry we weren't properly introduced earlier. You must think me a complete boor, but I feel terribly out of my depth here."

Diana formally held out her hand, still in its suede glove.

"Lily Kennedy," said Lily, proffering her own hand stiffly.

"You're from Ireland! Oh, I love Ireland, wonderful hunting. Do you hunt?"

"No," said Lily evenly.

"No, sorry, no, of course," muttered Diana.

"Why 'of course'?" demanded Lily. "Why shouldn't I hunt?" She'd been on Lady Irene's hunter once, a huge roan named Abu Simbel. She'd only ridden him round the yard, and she'd been scared stiff the whole time. Lord knew how people raced over hedges and ditches on horses, galloping wildly after some poor fox. It was beyond her.

"I've offended you—I am so sorry." Diana clapped her hands to her perfectly red mouth. "I'm so frightfully sorry."

And she started to cry. "I have to make a success of this. My father says I'm behaving like a silly child and he's very angry with me. Can't understand why I didn't stay at home and go into the Auxiliary Territorial Service, says he's going to cut my allowance and, oh, all sorts of ghastly things, so I have to do this. I have to stick at it. This is what I want, to *do* something with my life."

Lily sat down beside Diana. They were almost the same size, she realized. Diana had narrow hips, long legs and a considerable bosom, as she did. She'd got Diana all wrong, she saw now. That cool poise had hidden terrible nerves.

"My father didn't want me to come, either," Lily offered. "Wants to know why I'm going off to nurse people in a war he says shouldn't have happened in the first place. He's not keen on war; we've had a fair bit of it at home. But this is the only way I'd be able to train as a nurse properly, and I wanted to do something too."

"Goodness, Daddy thinks war is the only answer," said Diana. "He's simply furious his gammy leg prevented him from rejoining his old regiment. He's stuck with the Home Guard. He doesn't believe I'll be any good at nursing. He won't disinherit me, though—nothing to leave."

Suddenly, they both began to laugh, and Diana was wiping tears away with a silk handkerchief.

"There's nothing for me to inherit, either," Lily said.

The door opened and a small, freckled face with a mop of fair curls peeped round.

"Am I in the right place?" she asked in a strong Cockney accent.

"This is room fifteen," Lily replied.

"That's me, then," said the girl, and came into the room properly, dragging a suitcase that looked bigger than she was. She was tiny, like an older version of Shirley Temple with those curls, but her laughing, cat-shaped eyes made her appear a little more grown-up.

"Maisie Higgins," she said. "Lawks, crying already!" She stared at Diana's tearstained cheeks. "I heard the matron was a bit of a tartar, but I didn't think she'd be cracking the whip already."

The first weeks in the grand old hospital on Gray's Inn Road were hard and exhausting. Lily and Maisie, at least, were used to getting up early—Maisie had been an apprentice in a hairdressers'—but Diana found it a nightmare. Food in the home was good, despite rationing. But the hardest part was getting used to dealing with actual patients. Anyone thinking there would be a lot of theory and lessons before they worked on the wards had been in for a shock.

Despite being students, they weren't shielded from the toughest parts of hospital life.

"This is wartime," said one of their nursing tutors that first day as she led them from ward to ward, letting them see the size of the great hospital. "Sad to say, but it's a great time to learn because you'll see things that you've never seen before. A quarter of last year's intake have dropped out, didn't have the stomach for it. So, ladies, it's up to you."

One of their number vomited at the sight of a burn victim having his dressings changed. Lily felt like joining her, but she forced herself to stand up straight and proud at the bedside. If she was to do this job properly, she'd have to learn to deal with worse sights. She would not be dropping out.

"You all right?" she whispered to Diana, who was looking very green under her starched nurse's cap.

"Not really," Diana murmured, wobbling on her feet.

"Think how hard it'll be for the poor man if we all run like headless chickens," Lily said, her eyes still on the patient's face, taking in the terrible charred edges of the burns and the raw pink skin underneath.

"Righto," said Diana, gulping. "I understand." She smiled at the man.

"Well done, Nurse Belton," said the tutor. "Thought we'd lost you for a moment there."

"Not a chance," said Diana, squeezing Lily's hand tightly.

Lily was surprised and pleased to discover that there were women medical students at the Royal Free.

"Wonder if they're like us and get the dirtiest jobs?" Maisie said thoughtfully.

"Not bloody likely," said another of the trainees.

The student nurses undoubtedly got all the worst jobs on the wards, mainly bedpan duty and sponge-bathing patients. One of the more sadistic ward sisters took an instant dislike to Diana and gave her all the most horrible jobs, including reapplying a dressing to a wounded man's groin area.

Diana nearly died of embarrassment, she told the other student nurses that evening in the home's tiny common room.

"I don't know which of us went pinker," Diana sighed, "him or me. Poor chap."

"*Poor chap!*" parroted Cheryl, a tough girl from Walthamstow who never missed the opportunity to tease Diana over her cut-glass accent. "Bloody toff," said Cheryl. "Who's she think she is—Lady Muck? She should have stayed at home with the butler. We don't want her sort here."

It had been another in a series of long days and Lily was dead on her feet. But even so, she could recognize that something needed to be done.

Easing her tired body out of her chair, Lily stood up and put her hands on her hips. "You've an awful mouth on you, Cheryl," she said coldly. "Diana doesn't look down on you, so you ought to stop looking down on her."

This stopped Cheryl in her tracks. "Me look down on her?"

"Do you look down on me too?" Lily went on. "Am I a big thick Irishwoman when I'm not here to hear it?"

"No," shot back Cheryl. "You're different. . . ."

"We're all different," Lily said sharply. "It's high time you got used to it."

"Or else?" Cheryl's pointed face hardened.

Lily drew herself up to her full imposing height. "I was raised right beside a farm. My father's a blacksmith and my mother's in service, and I can launder a lady's camis as handily as help shoe a horse. There were lots of knocks in my life before I came here and I'm not putting up with any more from the likes of you, madam. I don't believe in raising my fist to anyone, but if I did, I'd knock you from here to kingdom come and you wouldn't get up in a hurry, I can tell you. So leave Diana alone."

"The wild Irish girl!!" cheered someone.

"Fine," snapped Cheryl, and left the room in a huff.

"Thank you so much," Diana said, grabbing Lily's arm. "That's the kindest thing anyone's ever done for me."

She had tears in her eyes. Lily realized that at some point she'd have to explain to Diana that when she was feeling vulnerable, she adopted an icy demeanor that gave entirely the wrong impression.

"Think us three ought to stick together," added Maisie. "Lily can handle all the trouble, Diana can get us into the posh restaurants, and I can do our hair. What do you say, girls?"

The three of them looked at one another and grinned.

"Sounds good to me," Lily said. Who'd have thought that one of her friends would turn out to be someone every bit as aristocratic as Lady Irene? Wait till she told Vivi.

ten

Izzie, Anneliese and Brendan sat at the kitchen table around untouched cups of tea. The tea made Izzie realize she was home, for sure: only in her birthplace was everybody convinced that when all else failed, making tea helped.

Her father sat opposite her, looking much older than he had the last time. She hadn't been home in over a year—how was it that time between visits home seemed to expand the longer you lived abroad?

The plus of emigration was that you never spent long enough at home to be irritated by all your family's annoying little idiosyncrasies, stuff that niggled when you were in close contact. The minus was that your family aged so much in your absence.

Every time she came home, she had that feeling of watching another frame in a speeded-up piece of film.

Dad was sixty-seven, and when she said it fast, it didn't sound old at all, until they'd embraced in the hospital and she felt that he was no longer her solid father, just skinny, diminished and older. But then, she was older too.

Older, just not much wiser, she thought with bitterness. Joe had left two messages on her phone. One, a mere "Hello, talk soon." She'd listened to his voice and wished she had the strength to erase the messages without having to hear them. But she couldn't do that. Like an addict, she had to hear his voice, just in case he said what she longed to hear above all else: *I love you and need you. I'm coming to be with you, Izzie.*

But that wasn't what he'd said. Instead, he'd gone for a safe message that managed to say nothing: "I know you're upset, but please call me back. I hate to think of you away with us not talking. Call me."

Call me.

Izzie knew what she wanted to hear him say: *I was wrong, I love you, I totally understand what you want from me and I was stalling for time in New York.*

But even when she'd gone away from him, saying she didn't want to see him again, he hadn't said those words.

For the first time, she began to link up the two Joes—the one she loved, who was funny, warm and sexy, and the business version, who obviously hadn't become wealthy and powerful by being Mr. Pushover. Had she made the classic female mistake of thinking that underneath the tough businessman was a teddy bear only she could see? And all along the only thing underneath the tough businessman façade was a tough man.

"I do love you, but it's not that simple," he'd said.

She'd known it wasn't simple. And she'd done her best to block that out because the lightning strike of love was so strong that it had seemed it must be their destiny to be together. This wasn't a scheming, sex-fueled fling: it was the real thing. True love trumped a marriage that was a marriage in name only, surely? Or so she'd assumed.

Assume *makes an* ass *out of* u *and* me, as somebody once said.

Izzie Silver might be a dumb broad, but nobody was going to make an ass out of her twice.

"I've been thinking," said her father, clearly desperate to break the silence around the kitchen table. "Is it possible Jamie is a brother of Lily's, somebody who died when she was young and that's why we've never heard of him? Infant mortality was terrible eighty and ninety years ago. If Jamie was her little brother, it would all make sense . . ." Brendan's voice trailed off. "Maybe Edward knows, or maybe there's something in the family records."

Even in her exhausted, jet-lagged state, Izzie was astute enough to sense Anneliese sitting up uncomfortably when Brendan spoke. It was the mention of her uncle Edward's name that had done it, Izzie decided.

Dad had said something when he phoned her in New York about Edward seeming oddly reticent about speaking to his wife. Dad hadn't known what was going on, but Izzie knew now, without anybody telling her in words, that there was something wrong between her aunt and uncle.

"If Edward knew about another uncle who'd died, he'd have told us years ago," she said now, and again she could sense Anneliese relax a little. "You know how close Gran and I were. *She'd* have told *me* about a little brother who died, wouldn't she? There was just her and Tommy, I'm sure of it."

"Well," said Anneliese glumly, "we don't know who this Jamie person is, so maybe we don't know as much as we thought we did. Even when you know people terribly well, you can discover they have secrets from you."

"True," agreed Izzie, thinking of Joe and how she'd been deceived by him. Or maybe he hadn't deceived her. Maybe she'd wanted to be with him so much that she'd been blind to reality.

Still, it was harder to know people than you thought. And for whatever reason, dear Anneliese clearly felt the same way.

"Do you think Lily will ever come back to us?" Anneliese said listlessly.

"Nobody knows, love," her dad said. "It's up to God now."

The three of them had stayed in the hospital for an hour with her grandmother, and after that brief moment of lucidity when Lily had cried, "Jamie!" there had been nothing else, just her grandmother lying there, still absent. She hadn't opened her eyes or moved or said anything. All the hope that Izzie had felt on the flight over had melted away.

The young doctor who'd talked to them really hadn't known what to say.

"Sorry, there are no straightforward answers right now."

At least she was being frank, Izzie thought. The young woman's honesty was preferable to the "I am the doctor, I know everything" mode of communication.

"We've done a CT scan, she's on heparin to arrest progression or prevent recurrence of further strokes, but I'm afraid there has been a considerable bleed in your grandmother's brain. And when there's coma following a stroke, it does present an unfavorable prognosis. It's not all doom and gloom, there might well be spontaneous neurological recovery, but we really don't know if that will happen. It's a matter of waiting now, I'm afraid.

"The added problem is that because of your grandmother's age, there are other risks now, including heart problems and pneumonia. And I'm afraid her heart activity has been a little erratic in the past twenty-four hours. That's our primary concern."

"There's a problem with her heart too?" Izzie buried her face in her hands. It kept getting worse. "I thought, because she talked, that she might come out of this. It's got to be a good sign, hasn't it? It means she's coming back, right?"

"I'm sorry, it's not that simple," the doctor said. "Who knows what your grandmother is seeing or believing right now? People in her position can respond in some way to voices, so it is perfectly natural that your voice sparked something in her, but as to what she was thinking, I don't know. As to whether she will ever come out again, we don't know that, either. We're monitoring her and trying to keep her vitals stable."

"And if she doesn't come round properly?" Anneliese asked what Izzie couldn't bear to.

"Every case is different. If a person in her condition hasn't recovered in some neurological way within the first three weeks to a month, then it doesn't look good, I'll be honest with you. We'll have to wait and see. Right now, we want to keep her stable and see what happens next."

The first three weeks to a month? Izzie felt ill at the thought of watching her beloved gran fade away over a month. When they left the hospital, she was conscious of a sensation of emptiness in the world.

Twenty-seven years ago, when her mother died, she'd felt the same thing. It was, Izzie remembered, like part of the earth had crumbled away, leaving a huge, gaping hole.

The difference was that there had been some time before Mum had died, some warning. Not enough, but it had at least given Izzie a chance to say good-bye.

The thought of that good-bye gripped Izzie's heart tightly. Move on, think about something else, she told herself.

Anneliese moved her chair to sit beside Izzie. God, she was so intuitive, always had been. She and Gran had been brilliant when Mum died. It wasn't the same as having Mum to turn to, but they'd been there for her, forming a sort of parental triangle with her father. It was a new family of sorts: not conventional, clumsily made up, but still a family.

Now it was coming apart and there was another gaping hole there. But it had all happened so quickly. There had been no time to prepare, no time to say all the things that hadn't been said. Gran might die without ever smiling at Izzie again or telling her that it would be all right, that she was loved. . . .

Izzie couldn't bear it.

She squeezed her eyes shut. She wouldn't cry again because if she started, she genuinely didn't think she'd be able to stop the grief from pouring out, and it hurt too much. Anneliese reached out and wrapped her arms around Izzie, saying nothing, just holding tightly.

"Parish records," said Dad suddenly. "We could search the old parish records for births and deaths to see if there's a Jamie or a James anywhere."

"Yes, Dad." Izzie untangled a hand from her aunt's embrace to take his hand in hers, and they sat, making a clumsy, irregular trio around the old kitchen table. Sometimes Dad's habit of focusing on the not-so-important details irritated Izzie. But now she could see it for what it was: a survival tactic.

His mother-in-law had been with him for the darkest parts of his life and now she might be dying. Rather than face that cold, stark fact, Dad was training his sights on something else.

"Does it matter who he is?" Anneliese asked with a touch of irritation. "You heard the doctor: nobody knows what's going on in Lily's mind. Jamie might be someone important or he might be the postman."

"The postman's called Calum," said Brendan stubbornly.

"Not the postman, then," said Izzie quickly. It was unlike her aunt to be so irritable. She gave Anneliese a final hug to show that she was all right. Anneliese resettled her chair and pulled her cup toward her.

"Is Beth coming?" Izzie asked Anneliese to deflect the irritation, and felt guilty as soon as she'd done so because her aunt looked away as if she could hide the anxiety that had flared in her eyes.

"No, she can't come yet and I don't want to worry her," Anneliese said.

"Of course," Izzie replied, in the cheery voice that she used to clients on the phone who were telling her they didn't want to use one of the models on her books.

Not worrying Beth was a mantra she'd grown up with. In the family tree, Izzie was the one who had it all sorted out, who knew where she was going with her life. Beth was younger, the fragile, sometimes dizzy one, the one who wouldn't quite make it in the world. How wrong that had turned out to be. Beth was happily married to Marcus and Izzie had notched up another failed relationship. Not even a proper relationship, actually: a relationship with a married man. Who was the fragile, dumb one now?

Damn, she had to stop thinking like this. She was going

round and round in circles and her brain was numb. She should be thinking about her grandmother and not about bloody Joe Hansen.

Suddenly, Izzie felt so very tired. It was a sad, lonely homecoming with nothing but misery. She wanted it to be the way it had been before—before Gran was ill, before she'd realized Dad was getting old, before she'd known about something wrong between Anneliese and Edward. Before it had all gone wrong with Joe.

She got up from the table quickly. "I'm sorry," she said. "I think the jet lag is getting to me. I'm going to go to bed."

"Of course." Anneliese got up and gave her another hug.

Izzie sank into her aunt's arms and bit back the desire to burst into tears.

"I'll phone you later," Anneliese whispered, for her ears only.

"I'd like that," Izzie said.

Izzie woke up to light filtering in through floral curtains. She'd been having the most amazing dream and she wanted to tell Joe. They'd been on a holiday somewhere sunny, maybe Mexico, and she could feel the heat burnishing her skin. Then there was a ride in a teeny plane and now they were back in their lovely home, a light-filled loft apartment. She felt utter contentment fill her and she rolled over in the bed to touch Joe. Just then, she came fully awake. There was no Joe in the bed beside her. She'd never slept with him, she realized suddenly. It had all been a dream. Their sleeping together was relegated to small naps after those times they'd made love. Correction—after they'd had sex.

They would never live in an airy loft apartment in New York together; he'd probably hate it. She wasn't sure what he liked in apartments or houses. She'd never seen anywhere he'd ever lived. Instead, she was alone in her childhood bed in Tamarin, with the pale wallpaper she'd picked herself when she was eighteen and the apple tree banging in the wind against the window. Joe would never see this, he would never know about her childhood, he'd never come here, he'd probably never get to meet Gran.

"Izzie, you are a moron," she said out loud.

She rubbed the sleep out of her eyes, threw back the covers and got up. No looking back: it was time to look forward. It was after eleven. She'd slept for fifteen hours and she was hungry and thirsty.

Still in her T-shirt and pajama bottoms, she went downstairs. There was no sign of Dad, but there was coffee in the pot and a note left on the counter beside the coffee.

"Izzie, there's food in the fridge. Hope the coffee's drinkable when you get up. I'm on my mobile phone and I'm going to drop into the hospital later. Call me if you need a lift; otherwise, I'll be back at one."

Izzie drank her coffee, ate two rounds of Irish soda bread toasted and smothered with bitter marmalade, then showered and checked her messages on her BlackBerry. There was one from Carla, wishing her well, hoping that everything was OK, a couple more from people at work, another from Andy, who lived two apartments below her, saying he'd called and did she want to go to the movies with him and some friends?

She'd have to ring him later and tell him she was in Ireland. There was one from Stefan, about the SupaGirl! competition. More work, she'd pass that on to Carla. Nothing from Joe. Not that he'd ever emailed her before—he was far too clever to want electronic evidence of their fling, she thought acidly. But he had her email address, he could have emailed if he'd been that desperate to get in touch with her.

It seemed that when the going got tough, the tough found themselves other sex playmates. *Thanks a lot, Joe, delighted to find out that you could last the distance.*

Leaving a note for her dad on the counter—*Gone to the hospital, probably see you there. In case I don't, I'll be back this afternoon*—she stepped out the door and set off. She'd forgotten how small Tamarin was. One of the joys of Manhattan was that it was such a compact city compared to places like LA, but Tamarin was so wonderfully small, and she'd forgotten that. It was possible to walk from one side to the other in half an hour, and in the process one would probably have to stop ten times to talk to acquaintances.

As she walked, Izzie found herself wondering what it would be like to live in Tamarin again. Maybe that was the answer: get away from New York and all the toxic men she met, live somewhere simpler, where she belonged. But then, New York was the perfect place to live if you didn't feel you belonged anywhere else. Everyone belonged in New York.

Gran had never pushed her to come home. She wasn't the sort of person who laid guilt trips on people. Not once in all the years that Izzie had lived away had her grandmother complained about Izzie not phoning, writing, visiting or moving home.

Walking through the town where her grandmother had lived most of her life, Izzie wished they'd talked about it.

Why was it that when someone was ill you thought about all the things you hadn't said? Up until now, Izzie was pretty sure she'd said everything, and yet there were some gaps in the conversation, gaps she wished she could fill.

"Gran, I'm sorry I haven't got married and had kids. I know you'd love to have great-grandchildren, and you're so good with children. You were so good with me. But it just hasn't happened."

What else would she say?

"How do you find love, Gran? You loved Granddad so much. But how do you know when you've got that and how do you get it? Was it easier when you were young? Did you get married more quickly? Is it because we date people and have sex and go off them and don't have to marry them, is that the difference?"

Izzie thought she'd read somewhere that relationships where

people lived together for years before they got married were more likely to end in divorce than the reverse. It didn't make sense.

Knowing the person by living with them seemed preferable, but Gran could hardly have lived with Granddad Robby before they'd got married. The net curtains in Tamarin would have been twitched off the windows in outrage if that had happened fifty-odd years ago. Yet they'd stayed together, even though going from singledom into marriage must have been a big leap at a time when women were virgins before marriage and the marital bed was a place shrouded in mystery.

Did people stay together years ago because it was preferable to splitting up?

Izzie had reached Harbor Square and she sighed with pleasure at the beauty of it. This really was the heart of Tamarin, had been for centuries when the local market was held here, where the salty-fresh smell of fish mingled with the heat of farm animals penned up to be sold. Now there was no straw underfoot and the only creatures were the local dogs that congregated outside Dorota's café with their owners, but the sense of timeliness continued. The squat palm trees reminded Izzie that once ships had sailed into the harbor from exotic climes. The wide boulevard style of Harbor Square was a legacy of nineteenth-century mayor Emmanuel Kavanagh, who'd come from Argentina on a ship, stayed to marry a local girl and planned the elegant expanse of the square to rival the airy open spaces of his beloved Buenos Aires.

Seagulls wheeled around in the sky, calling to each other as they considered where to sit and watch the fishing boats unload their catches.

It was a busy scene but never frantic. Tamarin had a calming effect on people: as if the very bricks of the town murmured a message that there was enough time in the day for everything, and if there wasn't, whatever was left could wait till morning.

When she had a moment, Izzie decided, she'd come back and

sit in Dorota's and watch the town unfold around her, the way she used to when she was at school and would sit there with her friends, gossiping and pretending they didn't see the boys from school doing the same thing. For now, she only had time to buy a takeaway coffee of Dorota's strong Colombian blend. Gran loved that coffee and Izzie decided that if she sat at her grandmother's bed, the scent could drift over her. If Izzie's voice had woken her up yesterday, maybe Izzie's voice and that wonderful smell could wake her up today.

She never got to try her theory out because when she reached the hospital with her coffee cup in her hand, she saw her aunt sitting on a bench in the small hospital garden to the right of the ambulance bay. Anneliese didn't notice her: she looked as if she wouldn't notice a meteorite unless it landed directly on top of her. The hospital was built high up on the east side of the town and looked out at the harbor. Anneliese was staring out to sea blankly.

Watching her, Izzie fought the desire to go into the hospital and not confront whatever was troubling Anneliese. She didn't have the energy for someone else's pain. But that was the coward's way out.

"Hello," she said, sitting down beside her aunt.

"Hi, Izzie," said Anneliese dully, then turned back to the sea.

"It's beautiful here," Izzie continued. When in doubt, make small talk.

Anneliese nodded. "Beautiful," she repeated.

Izzie took a deep swallow of her coffee for moral courage. She figured that there was some problem in Edward and Anneliese's marriage. She hoped it wasn't serious. At home in New York, marriages flew into turbulence every day and such a thing was quite normal. But here it felt different. As if the "till death us do part" vow simply couldn't be broken.

"What's wrong, Anneliese?" she asked softly. "Do you want to talk about it?"

She'd expected Anneliese to pause and to tell her slowly. But no. Still looking out to sea and in a voice filled with emotion and anger, Anneliese said: "Edward left me for Nell. You remember Nell, my best friend?"

"What!" said Izzie. "I can't believe it. When?"

"Nearly a week ago," said Anneliese, matter-of-factly. "I would tell you exactly how many days and hours, but that sounds too much like a smoker working out how long it is since her last cigarette, so I won't do that."

"He left you for Nell?" repeated Izzie.

"I came home from Mass and they were together; not in bed together, although they might have been. It's funny," Anneliese added, almost thoughtfully, "that sleeping with someone else is seen as the ultimate betrayal. Fucking someone else is believed to be the worst thing, isn't it?"

Izzie winced at hearing her gentle, elegant aunt use such harsh, crude language. In all her life, she had never heard Anneliese speak in such a way.

"But you know, fucking isn't the worst thing," Anneliese went on. "The intimacy, the closeness, the sharing thoughts: they're the worst things, that's what I keep thinking every moment of every day. I keep thinking about what they were doing. Did Edward phone her or text her at night, saying, 'How are you, darling? I'm bored, wish I was with you'? And knowing it was all because he wasn't interested enough in me, I wasn't enough for him." She turned to face her niece. "Can you imagine what that feels like, Izzie?"

Izzie wondered if her face was red with the flush of guilt. She had no idea what to say to help ease Anneliese's pain. There wasn't a lot she could say. But she had no right to say anything. Somewhere in New York was a married woman just like Anneliese, and her husband was cheating on her with Izzie. He might have insisted he was no longer with his wife, but his actions proved otherwise.

"And what did Edward say?" Izzie asked, wanting to help, but knowing she wasn't the right person to do it.

"He didn't know what to say. I asked him to leave and then, when he left the room, bloody Nell insisted that I'd known about them all along. Because any fool would have known if their husband was in love with somebody else," she said bitterly. "And that's the thing, Izzie: I didn't know. I really didn't. After thirty-seven years of marriage, you think you know somebody. Of course, that's the other hard thing, one of many hard things." Anneliese almost laughed and she sounded a bit crazy, Izzie thought.

"There are so many horrible things, it's hard to pin down the worst, but certainly one of the startling bits of information out of this entire situation is the realization that you really don't know anybody. I thought he loved me. More fool, me."

Anneliese was quiet for a moment. "God, Izzie, I hope you're never betrayed like this. I wouldn't wish it on my worst enemy. I really thought Edward loved me. We'd been through quite a lot together and I thought we'd be together until the end. And now it's like everything wasn't true, everything we did together was a big lie. I was looking at our lives one way and he was looking at them another way. Perhaps that's where the expression 'rose-colored glasses' comes from," she said suddenly. "I had rose-colored glasses on. I was looking at the truth and I simply didn't see it. He must have been bored, fed up and hated me. Otherwise why would he want Nell?"

Izzie quickly scanned her mind for Nell. Nell was nowhere near as attractive as Anneliese. Her aunt had those huge blue eyes, a graceful face and the amazing silvery blond hair that made her look like a fey, otherworldly figure. As if she might dance down the street and disappear like a mermaid into the water. Compared to her aunt, Nell was shockingly ordinary. What had Nell got that Uncle Edward wanted? None of it made any sense.

"Did you tell Lily?" said Izzie. She knew how close her grandmother was to Anneliese. Maybe that had shocked her grandmother so much it had contributed to her stroke. But Anneliese had clearly followed her train of thought.

"No," she said, "I hadn't. I was too ashamed and embarrassed and all the things you are when your husband walks out on you for your best friend. Now I'm sorry I hadn't told her. That's what I do every time I see her: sit down, hold her hand and tell her, because she has that warmth, that wisdom. You understand, Izzie: you know you can tell her anything. There can't be too many nearly ninety-year-old women with her open-mindedness. I know Lily would have had no problem grasping the fact that Edward and I had split up, and she'd have been there to tell me how to move on with my life. I didn't tell her because I was so ashamed, and now I may not ever be able to tell her."

It was Izzie's turn to be silent. The shame overwhelmed the guilt now. Guilt was too insubstantial an emotion for what she felt: it was pure shame.

All her life, she'd been against the idea of dating a married man, and yet Joe had got under her radar before she'd had time to put up the barriers, so that by the time she'd realized just how complicated it all was, before her moral compass cranked into action in her head, her heart was trapped.

Loving him was the only option.

Hearing Anneliese's story was like having a magnifying mirror held up to the biggest blemishes on her face. She could see every giant pore and big spot. Anneliese's story had magnified Izzie's under the cruelest light.

Just as Anneliese had done, Joe's wife might still think her husband loved her. That he was there for her, didn't want anyone else to share his thoughts and dreams.

The only difference was that Edward had left Anneliese for Nell. He'd had the moral courage to walk away to be with the woman he apparently loved. But Joe hadn't. There was a nice simple message for her in all of this—Joe hadn't loved her enough. Whether he'd been lying or not when he said he and Elizabeth were no longer together was immaterial; he hadn't wanted to be with Izzie when she needed him.

Despite the guilt and shame, she felt as if she might cry.

Anneliese gazed at her niece and felt incredibly guilty for having told her what was happening. It seemed so bloody ridiculous that with darling Lily lying in the hospital, here she was having to reveal the sad details of her own life.

Poor Izzie, no wonder she was shocked, silent and tearful. And if Izzie was shocked, Anneliese didn't even want to think about what Beth would do when she heard. Oh, Lord, Beth.

Anneliese knew she'd taken the coward's way out by not telling Beth yet, but she simply couldn't face it.

She recalled her mother explaining the mother–child bond when she'd been pregnant with Beth: *It's the greatest love*, her mother had said. *The greatest. I can't explain it to you, nobody can. In a few months, you'll have this child who depends on you utterly, and nobody else matters, nobody, even Edward.*

Ma, don't be daft, Anneliese had laughed.

No, really, her mother had insisted. *Wait and see.*

And she had seen. Anneliese had never thought of herself as particularly maternal until she'd had her daughter. Up until then, she'd felt she was capable, almost masculine, in her ability to turn her hand to just about anything. She'd always loved the physical side of gardening—the digging, planting, hauling things around. She had such great strength and energy. So she thought she was one of those women who might not be terribly maternal. And then Beth had appeared, and it was like being hit hard over the head with one of her gardening spades: bash.

Suddenly, she was in love and enthralled with this tiny, squalling, mewling infant. The first six months of Beth's life, Anneliese had existed on practically no sleep.

She'd gone half crazy, thinking that she could manage through sheer force of will to push the depression out of her mind. If only such a thing were possible.

Her mother had been right: Beth had become her life. And now she had to tell that sweet, fragile person that her parents were splitting up.

She only hoped that Beth wouldn't stare at her and say, "You must have known!"

Anneliese thought of a politician she'd read about in the papers who'd told his wife he was gay an hour before he gave a press conference telling the whole world. His wife had stood beside him in front of the cameras and reporters, holding his hand, and somehow that became the most talked-about part of it all. *How could she? She* must *have known*.

The story was no longer about him. It came down to the question: How could she not have known?

Years later, the woman gave her side of the story and made sense of the strange events of that day. She hadn't known. They were married, they had a child, why should she doubt him?

When he told her, she was stunned, and was still stunned an hour later when they stood together.

"Anneliese," said Izzie, and Anneliese was sure poor Izzie was about to cry. She looked on the verge of it. "I thought I wanted this coffee but I don't, actually. I'm going to get myself some water from the coffee shop. Shall I get you something too?"

"No thanks," Anneliese said. She didn't feel hungry or thirsty these days. She couldn't feel anything other than the big black hole inside her.

With Izzie gone, she could go back to torturing herself, thinking about the past. It was a movie reel she couldn't turn off in her head. She kept going back over their lives together, analyzing everything, working out when Edward had been telling the truth and when he hadn't.

At Christmas, Beth and Marcus had come to stay and the house on Milsean Bay had been full of laughter and joy. Anneliese had loved it. She'd gone overboard with finding the perfect Christmas tree, decorating it, turning the whole house into a Christmassy bower with lots of holly, mistletoe, shiny gold balls and enough Santas to sink a ship. On Christmas Day, she'd had a lunch party for seven: her and Edward, Brendan, Lily, Nell, Marcus and Beth. Nell had brought her famous dark chocolate meringue, which they'd had with raspberries.

So often over the years, when they'd invited Nell to their house for something, Nell would say gratefully, "Thank you for having me."

And she hadn't said it that Christmas. Anneliese remembered it most clearly because at the time she'd thought, with pleasure, that Nell had finally accepted that they were friends, that she didn't need to thank them for their kindness every single time. How wrong she'd been.

"Can I do anything to help?" Beth had said, coming into the kitchen, looking like a Christmas fairy with her glossy dark hair curling around her face and wearing a beautiful moss green silky sweater over a gray velvet skirt that twirled around her legs.

"No, darling," said Anneliese, looking up from the cooker. She'd changed out of her Christmas outfit after church and had put on a pair of jeans and an old shirt for doing the cooking, which was terribly messy. She would change quickly as soon as dinner was ready. Meanwhile, Nell had covered up her finery in a big apron. Nell was looking great, Anneliese thought fondly. Edward and Anneliese had bought her these beautiful handmade earrings shaped like little fuchsia drops and a necklace with a fuchsia drop pendant. Nell wore them with pride.

"How's the turkey doing?" she asked Nell. Nell was the turkey expert.

"I'd say another twenty minutes, just to be on the safe side," Nell said, sounding professional.

"Right, I'll open the oven if you manhandle it in," Anneliese replied.

Edward had come in when they were finished. "How are my two favorite cooks?" he said cheerily.

"We're fine," said Anneliese, going over to poke around in the saucepan where the sprouts were steaming away.

"Everything is going wonderfully," said Nell. "Doesn't it smell amazing? I know you're ravenous, Edward—it's going to be fabulous though. Better to take that teeny bit longer and have it just perfect."

"You're the expert, Nell," he said.

And dinner had been perfect. Every moment of it. Anneliese had felt proud to think that so many people fought like cats and dogs over Christmas dinner while her family and friends enjoyed this warm, civilized meal where they laughed over appalling cracker jokes and reminisced about Christmases past.

That night, when everyone had gone home and Marcus and Beth were downstairs watching something on the TV, Anneliese and Edward had lain in bed and held each other.

"It was a lovely day, wasn't it?" Anneliese said.

She was exhausted. All that standing around in the kitchen was so tiring and she'd wanted to make the day just right. It seemed to have gone just right anyway, but she still felt the need to be watching, a bit like flying and never going to sleep, as though the psychic will of all the people with their eyes open could keep the plane in the sky, and if they concentrated hard, the plane would land safely. That's how she felt about days like Christmas.

"It was wonderful, darling," Edward said, giving her a chaste kiss on the forehead and turning over. "You're tired," he said magnanimously. "Let's go to sleep."

Once upon a time, they made love at night after big events like anniversaries and birthdays. It had become a part of their marriage, Anneliese remembered now. She should have realized there was something wrong then, when Edward didn't want to hold her and undress her gently, making love to her with the combination of passion and gentleness that came after thirty-seven years of marriage. She should have known something wasn't quite right. But she hadn't because she was so busy concentrating on the wrong thing.

Was that going to be her epitaph? *Anneliese kept her eyes open so the plane would stay in the air, but she'd watched the wrong plane?*

No matter how angry she was with Edward, Anneliese realized that she felt even angrier with herself. She hadn't seen what was happening and she couldn't forgive herself for that.

It was no good; she couldn't face seeing Izzie again and seeing the shock on her face, not when she felt this close to screaming. She'd come back to spend time with Lily later. Better to go home and have Izzie briefly wonder where she'd gone than to fall apart in front of her niece.

At home, she could give in and take one of the tranquilizers she had left over from years ago. There were a few left in a small bottle in her bedside table, enough to do her until she went to the doctor. There was no point putting *that* off, either. She'd fought it, determined not to have to go back on bloody antidepressants again, because taking them felt like such a sign of failure. But the time had come for the big guns: if Dr. Whelan had something to take away the grim darkness in her head, then she needed it. Lots of it. Otherwise, who knew what might happen?

It was seven that evening when she returned to the hospital, in a state of tranquilizer-induced calm. She hoped that Izzie's jet lag meant she'd have left and returned home to her father by then, but even if she hadn't, Anneliese could cope.

It was amazing how one little tablet could make her feel better. Well, not so much better, but calmer. As if she was on a tiny lifeboat in the middle of a huge, deep ocean, and with the little tablet inside her, she didn't need to look over the edge of the boat to see the vast inky blueness beneath her. It was still there, she knew that. But she didn't need to look at it. She could exist and not look, which was much nicer than forcing herself to stare at it and feel the anxiety flooding in.

The hospital was busy with visitors rushing to and fro, carrying flowers, bottles of mineral water and magazines in to their loved ones. Anneliese smiled at them all serenely. People were so kind, really.

When she got to Lily's ward, she was surprised to see a woman sitting by Lily's bed, holding her hand. It wasn't Izzie; it was a younger woman, perhaps late twenties, and she had long streaked blond hair piled on top of her head in an untidy knot, and wore the loose trousers and thonged shoes that Anneliese always associated with students on sabbatical in Thailand.

"Hello," she said curiously.

"Oh, hello." The girl leaped to her feet and her lightly tanned face looked anxious.

"I'm Anneliese, a relative of Lily's."

"Sorry, I didn't mean to intrude. I'm Jodi. I'm not a friend or anything."

Anneliese blinked at her in surprise. The girl's freckles looked Irish but her accent was pure Australian.

"I never actually met Mrs. Shanahan, but we talked on the phone. I came to visit her because I feel . . ." She bit her lip. "I feel responsible."

Anneliese stared at her, taking in the friendly, open face. She hoped the tranquilizer wasn't making her stupid, but this didn't make sense.

"How?"

"I phoned her, you see," Jodi went on, even more anxious now, "asking her about the history of Rathnaree, and she said she'd meet me, and Yvonne, who's my next-door neighbor, says Mrs.

Shanahan hasn't been to Rathnaree in years, but I still asked her, and then she had a stroke, and it's all my fault!"

"You poor thing," said Anneliese. "Don't be silly. It's not your fault."

"You don't understand—it is!" insisted Jodi. "She's an old lady and I knew I should have talked to somebody else about it. I upset her, I must have, because one day I'm talking to her on the phone arranging to come and see her, and the next Yvonne tells me she's in here in a coma."

"You didn't cause the stroke," Anneliese soothed. "You clearly didn't know my aunt. Lily could cope with just about any bit of news you cared to throw at her and the fact that she's an old lady doesn't matter a whit. She's young on the inside and she has the most open mind of anyone I ever met. If she didn't want to see you or if you upset her, she'd have said, I'm sure of it. Tell me, what particularly did you want to research?" Anneliese asked curiously.

"All about Rathnaree House. I found this photograph, you see, and I mentioned it to her . . ."

"Was there anybody called Jamie in it?" Anneliese asked.

"No, I've only got the name of one person, a Lady Irene. Why?"

"The thing is, Lily hasn't been conscious since her stroke, except for one moment when she called out 'Jamie.' None of us knows of any Jamie in her life and, well, her son-in-law thinks it might be important. Now that you tell me you were talking to her about the past, it makes sense that she was thinking about it. He might be someone connected to when her parents worked in Rathnaree."

"I could try and find out," said Jodi. "I mean, if you want me to, if it's not being intrusive. It's just that . . ." She stopped.

"That would be great," Anneliese said. "I think Izzie, my niece, and her dad would like to know who Jamie was."

"Oh, Izzie, she's the one from New York," said Jodi excitedly. "Yvonne told me all about her. It sounds so exciting."

"Yeah, it is," said Anneliese, who thought she would never find anything exciting ever again. But then, excitement was overrated. Calm was nicer. "The thing is," she added, "the doctors don't know if what Lily is saying is important or what it is. I suppose it's like dreams—nobody knows what they mean. So it might be useful to know who Jamie is, and then again, it might mean nothing."

"But it could put all the puzzle together and let her go happy," said Jodi.

Anneliese looked at this eager Australian girl with the kind eyes and open heart. To Jodi it was very simple. Lily was probably going to die and the best thing to do for her was to put all the pieces of the puzzle in place so that she could go happily, with her life sorted out. And of course, Anneliese thought bitterly, nobody's life was ever sorted out.

If she died right now, nobody would be able to put her pieces back together, or if they did, it would look like a pretty weird jigsaw puzzle.

In her pharmaceutically induced calm, she felt able to look distantly at her life and see how out of control it suddenly was.

"We could check the local records and the census," Jodi said enthusiastically. "I did some historical research and archaeology modules in college and I know how to research correctly. It's fascinating once you get into it. I feel there is so much history here, so much to be told. Would Mrs. Shanahan like that, do you think?"

Anneliese considered it. Normally, she felt as if she had the answer to most questions, but right now she had no clue what Lily would want her to do—if Lily would like the past gently opened up and examined, or if she would prefer it left alone, all neatly and mysteriously packaged up. None of them had ever heard of this Jamie person, so perhaps Lily had her secrets after all.

Perhaps Izzie would like this man tracked down. Izzie had a closer claim on Lily than she did. Yes, that made sense: Izzie could make the decision. Anneliese was fed up making decisions. All the ones she'd made hadn't turned out very well, had they?

"Jodi," she said now, "let's talk to Izzie. If she thinks it's a good idea, we'll go for it. But it might be a good plan to wait a few days before suggesting looking for clues. It's probably a little raw now. I know you think it might help her come out of the coma, but we'll give it a few more days."

"Of course," Jodi agreed. "I wouldn't want to do anything to upset her; she sounded so lovely on the phone. It's sad to think of her calling for somebody and we don't know who that person is. It's like in a film, isn't it? Like there's so much we don't know about other people."

Anneliese nodded. She couldn't quite trust herself to speak.

"You must be worn out," Jodi added kindly. "Would you like to go and get a cup of coffee or tea or juice? Hospitals can be tiring. My granddad died a couple of years ago and it was rough."

The idea of a simple cup of tea, with no intense conversation and no need to think of the person sitting opposite her mentally working out why Edward had left her and what she was going to do about it, suddenly seemed very appealing to Anneliese.

"That would be lovely," she said. "I'm just going to sit with Lily for maybe ten or fifteen minutes and maybe we could go then? We could go into town and have something there."

Tamarin shone like a little jewel nestled in the curve of the hills as they walked out of the hospital and down into the town twenty minutes later. Anneliese saw her home through Jodi's eyes and she thought how beautiful it must look.

Their path took them along the curve of Plunkett Street, where all the residents had painted their houses in pretty pastel colors like a row of houses in a child's coloring book. It had rained heavily the day before and the combination of the downpour and the beautiful sunlight of the previous few days had done wonders for the window boxes and small gardens. The fierce colors of hot pink and red geraniums blistered out at them, offset with snowy tufts of pale lilac lobelia.

It was all so calm and beautiful, and for the first time since Edward had left, Anneliese found herself able to take pleasure in its postcard prettiness.

"Dorota's?" suggested Jodi as they reached Harbor Square.

Anneliese was about to say yes, and then she remembered that she'd been avoiding it lately, in case she bumped into Edward and Nell. There were so many places she was avoiding, including the supermarket, except late at night, because she knew she couldn't cope with a chance meeting with either her husband or Nell.

Moral superiority was no match for the double whammy of betrayal and depression. Anneliese knew that no matter how much she'd want to glare at the two of them should they meet, she'd be far more likely to collapse in tears on the floor.

"How about we try The Nook?" she suggested. The Nook was a small bar-cum-restaurant with a cozy name but a modern décor. Anneliese wasn't much for minimalism, but they always had lots of pastries from Oma's Kitchen, the Austrian pastry shop next door. Although Anneliese hadn't felt hungry lately, the thought of a sugar hit from lots of almond, honeyed pastry made her mouth water. Plus, Edward hated the place. Perfect.

They ambled along toward The Nook, and once there, Anneliese pushed open the door. Standing directly inside, talking to a couple at a table set up for dinner, was Nell.

Anneliese stopped as if she'd been turned to stone.

Thanks to her late-night shopping and careful choosing of places to go in Tamarin, she hadn't seen Nell since that day a week ago when Edward had left. After so much time spent obsessing over her, it was odd to actually see Nell in the flesh and realize that she didn't have horns or a forked tail but was still a middle-aged woman with frizzy hair and pale eyelashes. At the table beside Nell sat Geraldine, a friend of both of theirs, and her husband, Benny.

The three of them looked shocked as well as guilty and Anneliese had a suspicion that she was the subject of the conversation.

The sharp pinprick of another betrayal struck Anneliese. Geraldine hadn't rung her to commiserate or talk, even though she clearly knew what was going on. Without Anneliese's realizing it, Geraldine had turned into an ex-friend. She'd already picked which side of the split she was on.

"I was going, I'm just going," said Nell hurriedly, her eyes dark with shock and embarrassment.

"Isn't this the cutest little place," said Jodi, who'd come into The Nook just behind Anneliese and was looking around the pub. "It's so pretty. Look at those suede purple seats. They're fantastic!"

Nobody answered her.

"Anneliese, I meant to call," said Geraldine, getting to her feet, clearly even more embarrassed than Nell. She attempted to hug Anneliese, but Anneliese shrugged her off. Every bit of staid conservatism seemed to have left her and the effects of the tablet must have suddenly worn off because she felt wild with rage. Who cared what people thought of her? She must have been mad to be avoiding her normal haunts—Nell deserved to face her rage.

"Don't touch me!" she snapped at Geraldine. "You've chosen your side and I bet you've been sitting here listening to Nell's story."

"It's not like that," Geraldine said soothingly. "We're worried about you."

Anneliese snorted. "Worried about me? You're not worried enough to pick up the phone to ask how I am when my husband walks off with this cow! And she"—she gestured fiercely toward Nell—"she's hardly worried about me, no matter how she tries to paint the situation in a flattering light. Isn't that right, Nell?"

Some core inside Anneliese told her she shouldn't be doing

this, that she would regret standing in a bar in Tamarin, screaming everything that came into her head. But she couldn't help it, she wanted to say it. She could as lief stop herself as the seawater could stop pouring into the harbor, ebbing and flowing in the tides.

"Actually, I'd give anything to know what Nasty Nell has been telling you, Geraldine. Has she been giving you the edited, 'poor me and poor Edward' version or the truthful version? Hmm, let me see: the edited one, I think."

Nell flushed even more. "I don't have to listen to this," she said. "This isn't the time or the place."

"You're the expert on everything these says—what is the time or the place?" Anneliese demanded. "I think the old conventions were smashed up when you took Edward off me. Yes, you took him, didn't you? Don't pretend otherwise. You sickened me the other morning when you tried to pretend that I must have known about you and Edward. You know damn well that I had no idea what was going on behind my back. I still thought you were my friend."

There wasn't a sound in the whole place: everyone in The Nook was listening. Even the waitstaff who didn't speak English were motionless with their mouths open, trying to follow the conversation.

"You knew almost every thought that went through my head, Nell, and if I thought Edward was having an affair, you'd have been the person I'd have confided in. I'm glad I didn't know because imagine telling you I suspected Edward was having an affair and you sitting there smiling and simpering and going 'Oh no!' only for it to turn out that you were the one he was having the affair with."

Outraged muttering noises could be heard coming from the other customers.

"I'm going," Nell said angrily, and tried to push past Anneliese.

"No you're not!" hissed Anneliese back. She was taller than

Nell and stronger. She was so angry that she wanted to hit out and wipe that simpering lipsticked smile off Nell's stupid face.

"Anneliese," said Benny, speaking for the first time. Geraldine's husband was a gentle giant of a man and he got slowly to his feet to intervene.

Jodi stepped in before he could.

"Anneliese," she said, "please, don't."

Anneliese felt Jodi's hands on her, gentling her the way someone would gentle a young horse. "You don't want to do this, not now." Jodi was stronger than she looked and somehow she managed to maneuver Anneliese away from the door. Immediately, Nell pushed it open and rushed off into the dusk.

Geraldine stood for a moment, staring at Anneliese.

"I'm sorry," she said, ineffectively. "Sorry."

"Sure," muttered Anneliese.

Jodi hauled her into the bar part of The Nook and found a corner as far away from the door and her ex-friends as was possible. There, Anneliese slumped onto one of the purple suede seats and put her head in her hands, not caring what she looked like or who saw. Let her life be lived in the open with her dirty linen fluttering around in the breeze for all to see. Nell would tell her side of the story anyway.

Jodi didn't wait for a server but went to where the mugs and coffeepot were kept for the waitstaff.

"Here," she said, putting a steaming mug down on the table. "Have this."

She sat as close to Anneliese as she possibly could and put her arm around her. "I know you're in shock, but have some coffee, it'll give you a jolt."

"I thought brandy was the answer for shock," Anneliese said, wrapping her hands around the steaming mug.

"Bad for the heart," Jodi said briskly. "I don't want to have to drag you right back up to the hospital on a stretcher."

Anneliese laughed weakly. "Thank you," she said. "Sorry you had to see that. Guess you aren't looped into the Tamarin rumor mill or you'd have heard that my husband left me for her, my ex-best friend."

"No, I didn't know," Jodi said. "Dan and I haven't lived here long enough to be in on the round-robin emails. Does Yvonne know?" she asked, referring to her next-door neighbor and Anneliese's friend from the Lifeboat Shop.

"I don't know." Anneliese shrugged. "I didn't tell her yet, couldn't face it. Although she's a good friend and she'd probably be on my side. God," she said, "why do there have to be sides in marriage breakups?"

"Most people don't want to take sides," Jodi replied.

But Anneliese wasn't listening.

"Actually, it's not a marriage breakup," she said. "It's a marriage grenade launch or landmine or something. *Breakup* is far too innocuous a word for it. *Breakup* implies you knew it was coming, and I didn't. I hadn't a clue. How stupid does that make me? Don't make that mistake, Jodi. Keep your eyes open in your marriage. Forgive me," she apologized. "You don't need my advice. You young people, you're better at relationships than my generation. We think we have to stay in them no matter what; it's a sign of weakness if you walk out. Maybe it's a sign of weakness to stay when it's all pretty crap. I didn't know it was crap, I thought it was OK. Forgive me," she said again. "You don't want to be burdened with this. The tawdry details of other people's marriages. I didn't mean to shock you."

"You didn't shock me at all," Jodi said, shrugging. "Breakups happen all the time. My parents are divorced."

"I'm sorry," Anneliese said.

"Don't be," Jodi replied. "It's better this way. When I was a kid, they did nothing but fight when my brothers and I were in bed, and then they'd pretend everything was perfect when we were up, like we were deaf and couldn't hear them shouting. It's better this way. They're both happy, just not together."

"And that didn't put you off marriage?" Anneliese inquired.

"No, it put me off arguments. Dan and I don't argue. I used to think there was something wrong with us. Everyone says you need passionate fights in a marriage, but we've never had that. We have disagreements and we both get really upset because we're fighting with the other person. I don't think we've ever had a stand-up screaming match. I wouldn't want to."

"Me either," said Anneliese, thinking that she wasn't likely to be having a significant other ever again, so her not liking marital arguments was very much in the past. "I didn't like screaming matches," she added. "We never had stand-up screaming matches in our marriage. Edward and I got on pretty well. Not saying it was always easy, but we had Beth and we had to try and just muddle through the hard times."

"Beth's your daughter? What does she think of all of this?"

"She doesn't know."

"You haven't told her?"

"No, I haven't told her. I'm going to have to because she's coming to Tamarin to see Lily and she's going to go crazy when she finds out that her dad and I aren't together."

"Why haven't you told her?" Jodi asked.

"I don't know how," Anneliese sighed. She thought of how she'd tried to keep things from Beth all her life. To make everything perfect. It was overprotectiveness, she knew, but she'd always felt it was the right thing to do. Beth was such a gentle, fragile soul that she couldn't cope with life's pain. It was Anneliese's job as a mother to shield Beth from the pain, and now there was no option but to land her right in the middle of it.

"I'm going to have to tell her. I just don't know how I'm going to do it."

"Say it out straight," Jodi advised. "That's what I'd like if I was your daughter. Your niece, Izzie, she knows, right?"

"Yes, I told Izzie. I told her today, actually, and she was pretty shocked." Anneliese winced at the thought of that conversation and how appalling it had been. "Izzie's very strong and sophisticated and the fact that she was so shocked really upset me. Made me wonder how I am going to tell my daughter the same news. I didn't think anything would shock Izzie, but this did."

"It might be hard for her to hear the news because she lives abroad," Jodi said thoughtfully. "When you're not living at home, bad news makes you feel guilty for being away. You've got guilt for that and then you're a teeny bit grateful you're away because it means you don't have to deal with it so much. That sounds awful, doesn't it?"

"No," Anneliese said. "Just honest. I wish I was far away right now, then I wouldn't have to deal with anything awful. But that's not an option. I have to be here for Lily and Beth and Izzie. You'd like them both. Beth won't be here long but Izzie has an open-ended ticket, so she'll be around for another week certainly."

An idea struck Anneliese. Inactivity wasn't normal for her niece and it was quite possible that Lily would remain in the same state for some time to come, so that Izzie would have nothing to do except sit at her grandmother's bedside.

It might be good for her to hang out with Jodi, doing a little investigating into Rathnaree and this Jamie person. It would take her mind off Lily. Anneliese was beginning to wonder if Lily would ever come back to them.

"She could help with the research. She's very clever and it's going to be hard for her to be here with Lily so ill. She left such a long time ago, and has lost touch with the place. It could help her feel a part of it all," Anneliese said.

"That would be great," Jodi replied. "I'd like that. She wouldn't mind, do you think, helping me?"

"No, Izzie's very hands-on, very clever. If you want someone to help you get to the bottom of a mystery, I'd say Izzie is your woman. She can charm information out of anyone and she's very driven and focused, which is why she's so successful in her job. I guess she's sort of married to it, really. It's a pity," Anneliese added. "She's a gorgeous-looking girl. But everyone makes their own choices and I guess Izzie's choice is to be on her own."

"Hard for her if Lily doesn't make it," Jodi said.

Anneliese nodded sadly. "Hard for all of us," she agreed, "but especially for Izzie. It would be like losing her mother all over again."

eleven

Breaking up with Joe had more or less cured two addictions, Izzie realized after a few days at home in Tamarin. She was going cold turkey on Joe and the ensuing misery meant she no longer checked her BlackBerry fifteen times a day in case she had email messages.

Before, she'd known exactly why it was nicknamed "Crack-Berry," because it was clearly almost as addictive as the deadly rock cocaine. But currently work, New York and Joe were all mingled together in her head and she looked at her BlackBerry warily, as if it might impart some more news with the power to hurt her.

Instead, there was a message from Carla, written in her usual crisp style.

> *Stefan from Jacobman keeps wanting to know when you're going to be back. Everyone here is wild about the competition for the girl to be the face of SupaGirl!—it's going to be worth millions. Best news is Stefan promises Laurel and Hardy won't be on the team.*

Izzie grinned. Stefan was a brat. They'd both have their knuckles rapped if anyone heard them talk that way. She was sure there was a piece of equality law that forbade naming irritating colleagues after a couple of lovable clowns.

> *He says they can fire his ass, he doesn't care, he wants you back. How cute. I'd say it must be love, if he wasn't such a hound.*

She and Carla had often talked about Stefan's roving eye.

Have you talked to your Uptown Man? Hope not, but whatever happens, I'm here for you. Take care. Tell me if you need anything. Carla

It was brusque, to the point, and very Carla, emanating warmth and friendship, with a bit of careful advice buried in there: *Stay away from Joe, he's no good for you.* Yeah, well, Izzie had worked that one out for herself by now.

Hi, Carla, great to hear from you. Glad you're coping with it all—if Stefan acts up, treat him like a dog. I think that's the only way to deal with him. Give him simple commands and he'll roll over!

No news from Uptown Guy. I haven't contacted him and that's the way it's going to stay.

If her willpower held out, that was. She felt so emotionally fragile that she longed to hear his voice, but she knew she couldn't allow that to happen. It wasn't just that Joe was bad for her, he was bad for every woman in his life. Since Anneliese had told her about Nell and Edward, the reality kept throbbing in her skull: her uncle Edward had left someone as wonderful as Anneliese because he was in love, but damn Joe Hansen hadn't been able to leave his wife—a wife he allegedly was no longer really with—for her.

Therefore he didn't love her, despite what he said. And she was no longer sure she believed what he said about his marriage being over—although she'd been so *certain* he was telling the truth about that. If it really was over, why couldn't he just walk away? The fact that he couldn't made her think what he'd said was just a handy excuse. Joe respected nobody except himself.

The alternative was that he did love her and still couldn't put her first. Which was worse?

I am over him. O.V.E.R.

Then she changed the subject.

Gran isn't great. There's been no change since the first day and Dad says he'd understand if I want to get back to the U.S. She could stay like that for a long time, nobody knows.

I hate to leave though. I want to talk to her again, and though Dad says I could hop on a plane quickly to come home if she improves, it feels like abandoning her if I go back to work. But he's got a point. I can't do anything here except sit with her and hold her hand and . . .

Izzie hadn't said this to her father or Anneliese

. . . it feels like she's not there. Like she's already gone.

Even writing it made her shiver. She couldn't quite imagine a world without her grandmother in it yet that world was already there. Despite sitting at Gran's bedside every day, she felt no sense of the woman she'd loved all her life. No, she couldn't think that.

Better go,
Love, Izzie

She quickly emailed Stefan. Of course they were thrilled. Being involved in a huge campaign to find the next SupaGirl! model would mean both prestige and publicity for the agency. The publicity would make them top of the list for aspiring models. As a bonus, they'd get first dibs on any good candidates from the competition.

The girl who won the competition would need a specific look for SupaGirl! but the search would draw out plenty of runners-up whom Perfect-NY could then sign. Well advertised competitions that made TV news drew out girls with model potential much faster than ordinary model searches that involved trailing around cities looking for prospective girls. Everyone in the industry talked about how the *America's Next Top Model* series had taken off. Izzie knew that a lot of those girls would not have come forward without the bonus of TV and the excitement the whole thing generated.

Carla said you would be picking a good team for us to be working with

she added, grinning. She dared not use the words Laurel and Hardy.

Really looking forward to working with you, let's talk when I get back, thanks, Izzie.

There was an email from Lola, who worked alongside her and Carla in Perfect-NY. A feisty Latina lady who had come into the industry working as a makeup artist, Lola had been with Perfect-NY so long that she was practically management. She was in her early forties but looked younger and was a tiny sprite of a thing, just five feet, and made Izzie feel like a giant beside her.

Hi, Izzie, just checking in to see how you are and how your grandmother is. We're all thinking about you here and hope you're OK.

Business is quiet right now. There is only one blot on the landscape and it's a pretty terrible blot. You know Shawnee, that gap-toothed girl from Florida with the short platinum crop? She's very sick, and

I feel like it's totally my fault. She's always been very thin, worked really well in editorial. She had that edgy, androgynous look going, but she didn't get picked for a couple of jobs recently and she's taken it badly. She collapsed yesterday because she hasn't been eating. She's in the hospital all wired up and they're checking her for heart problems, not enough potassium in her system, of course.

I just feel like it's my fault, I should have been watching her better. She's so young, for all that she does that cool "I can handle it" trip. Sorry, didn't mean to lay this on you, just needed someone to talk to, I guess. I tried to say it to Natalie . . .

Natalie was the company's boss.

. . . but she just doesn't see it the same way that I do. Shit, Izzie, it's a tough business out there.

Hope you're OK, give us a call.

Lola

Lola's email was a sobering wake-up call for Izzie. Her grandmother might be in a hospital bed looking like a fragile little collection of bones beneath papery fair skin, but at least she was an old lady who had lived her life. Izzie knew exactly which model Shawnee was. She had an almost photographic recall of all the models on the agency's books, which was what made her so good at her job—she never forgot a face, and therefore was always able to work out which model would work for which booking.

She'd never have figured Shawnee for someone who would end up in hospital. Shawnee seemed so together, so happy: all lightly sun-kissed skin and those amazing pale green eyes that gave her the edgy look Lola had talked about. And now she was ill, weighing who knows what, all because she'd felt that she hadn't got the last few jobs because she wasn't thin enough.

And it was all about being thin. Beautiful was important too, but thin was almost as vital, no doubt about it.

When she'd first started in the modeling industry, Izzie had been irritated by people who had spoken about how crazy it was to have these incredible slim women striding up and down catwalks, showing off clothes.

"Why are they so thin? Why don't you use real women?" was the complaint, and Izzie would roll her eyes and look for another industry person to back her up by explaining how it all worked.

"They need to be thin to show the clothes to best advantage," she'd say patiently. "That way, you see the clothes and not their bodies. It would be different if they all looked va-va-voom, J-Lo–style. You'd be looking at them, not the garments. That's partly how the supermodel thing went out of fashion—it became all about the models and not about the clothes they were wearing."

Sometimes people got it.

"I see what you mean," they'd say.

Sometimes they didn't.

"That's bullshit," a woman said to her at a party once in Washington. Izzie had been with her Irish friend, Sorcha, who lived in D.C., and they'd attended the launch of a book of political speeches. The crowd was very different from the sort of people Izzie usually mixed with and she'd been cornered by a woman with a bad haircut who wore a very masculine-cut suit and T-shirt and managed to make this fashion statement look drab.

"The fashion industry is bullying women to make them powerless," the woman said. "Wear this, eat this, don't eat this, be thinner. It's all bullshit to sell clothes. Thin is a feminist issue. Actual women don't have flat stomachs and no tits. The fashion industry is conspiring to turn real women into powerless little girls. You people should be working from the inside to change it all."

Izzie cringed to think how she'd responded.

"You don't know what you're talking about," she'd snapped, fed up with the politics-obsessed city where nobody ever talked about anything except Capitol Hill.

"Let's go, Sorcha," she'd said to her friend. "I've just been yelled at by this nutcase in a suit. I work in fashion—I'm not the industry spokesperson. Sometimes a dress is just a damn dress."

But that woman had been absolutely right, she thought sadly. At the time she'd dismissed her words, assuming that a woman without fashion sense couldn't possibly grasp what the industry was really about, but in fact the woman had put her finger on the problem with great accuracy.

There wasn't any real need for models to be that thin. People weren't stupid, they could work out what the clothes looked like on real women. Apart from the ones who'd bought into the whole thin-is-fabulous mental state, most of the people buying the clothes were real women, anyway. It would be handy to see how the garments moved and flared on similar figures instead of on six-foot beauties who wore size zero.

Even the beauties couldn't stay that thin forever, which was how girls like Shawnee ended up in hospital beds on heart monitors.

Izzie felt ashamed when she thought about the SilverWebb Agency she and Carla had been so excited about. She'd lost that excitement in the last few months because of being involved with Joe.

She bet he hadn't stopped improving his business. But she'd done that dumb woman thing of taking her eye off every single ball while she was with him. She'd also neglected her friends: she hadn't been to see Sorcha for months, even though Sorcha had been ringing her up, begging her to visit.

Naturally, Izzie hadn't been able to explain why she couldn't come.

"Just busy at work," she'd said.

"Come on," Sorcha had groaned, "you can't be busy all of the time. At this rate, you ought to own the company by now—or do they own you?"

And Izzie had promised to make the trip to Washington sometime in the future, but not just yet, because she couldn't very well tell her old friend that she didn't want to leave New York in case she missed spending time with her not-really-married lover.

Then there were Laura and Jacob, friends from Yogilates. The three of them had been friends for ages. Laura and Jacob had shared dating stories for years until one day they'd looked at each other in a different way and—kapow—cupid's arrow skewered them. They'd got married the previous Christmas and Izzie was ashamed to realize that she had only seen them once since.

Joe Hansen had taken over her life and she had nothing to show for it. Tish was another Joe casualty. How long had it been since Izzie had dropped in to see her and her new baby?

She was going to change, she decided. When she got back home, she'd phone all the people she'd neglected. The Joe days were over.

Dear Lola, I'm so sorry to hear about Shawnee. That's truly terrible. It's the one thing I really hate about this industry and I've hated it for a long time. It makes you wonder what's going on when someone like Shawnee looks in the mirror and hates what she sees. I know we all do our best to take care of the girls we work with, but it's a big world out there and we can't protect them from that, unless we try and change that world. I'd love to talk to you about it sometime when I get back to New York.

She dared not say any more; this email was being sent to the office, after all.

But it's wrong that someone as beautiful as Shawnee thinks she's not good enough. It makes you wonder what's going on in our world when girls like her look in the mirror and hate what they see. She shouldn't hate what she sees.

Things aren't good here. My grandmother had a stroke and still hasn't recovered. It's a waiting game now, and the longer she stays in a coma, the less chance there is of her coming out of it without neurological damage. I guess I'm saying good-bye to her.

Izzie wiped away the wetness that suddenly came to her eyes.

But I was thinking, before I wrote this, that at least Gran has lived her life. She's done so much, not like poor Shawnee. Talk soon, Izzie

Izzie wasn't entirely sure of everything her grandmother had done, but she knew it had been a packed life. A person didn't get the wisdom Gran had without having seen and understood a huge amount. Anneliese had mentioned that Jodi, the Australian girl, had offered to find out who Jamie was. Maybe Izzie should talk to her too.

"Everything happens for a reason," Gran used to say. She'd said it when Izzie missed out on a job in London and decided it was time to go to the States.

Perhaps Gran had called out the name Jamie so that Izzie would look into her past and learn something from it. The more she thought about it, the more sense it made. Looking into her grandmother's past would be as near as she could get to actually talking to darling Gran. Her brief moment of lucidity had to be a message to them all.

And this email from Lola was another.

Remember your dreams, was what it said. Before Joe, she'd had a dream about starting an agency where girls wouldn't have to starve themselves like poor Shawnee in order to be successful.

Perfect-NY was a good and reputable agency. They had never condoned the practice of checking how skinny girls were by measuring their fingers. It worked better than measuring wrists because some people were big boned, but fingers gave a pretty accurate indication of whether someone was thin or not.

Reputable agencies didn't do things like that. Nobody wanted sick models on their books and most of the companies had really good relationships with their models, but the industry itself had a dark, cruelly commercial heart that was oblivious to kindness.

If the darkness was to be driven out, the battle would have to be fought from inside the industry. SilverWebb could do it, Izzie hoped. But first she had to let go of Perfect-NY. And Joe Hansen.

twelve

Anneliese had changed the sheets in the spare bedroom for Beth and Marcus. She'd tidied and polished, and had even roused herself enough to buy fresh flowers for the house to lift the place somewhat. There was only one big housekeeping screwup and that was that Beth's father no longer lived there.

Anneliese hadn't the energy to practice telling her daughter the news. Goodness knows, she'd tried.

Darling Beth, your father and I have decided . . .

That wouldn't work because it wasn't true.

She hadn't decided anything; it had been decided for her. Try as she might, she couldn't put a Beth-friendly spin on this one.

Your father dumped me after having an affair with my so-called best friend sounded too like a television true-life confession. All she needed was a studio audience and an eager host with a microphone and a faux worried manner and her spiel would be perfect. So no, that wouldn't work, either.

Blunt was going to be the only answer. When Beth arrived, eager to see them, her father's absence would start the conversation rolling. Anneliese wished Edward was the sort of man who'd be able to tell their daughter the news, but she knew he wasn't. All the difficult talks in their house had been left to his wife.

Beth and Marcus were due in Tamarin at lunchtime, so Anneliese had cold chicken and salad ready for them and had tried to buoy herself up to deal with her daughter's tears.

But when she heard Beth's key in the door a little after one o'clock, Anneliese wished she could run away.

Why hadn't bloody Edward found the courage to phone his daughter and tell her . . . ?

"Mum!"

Beth stood in the kitchen doorway, her dark hair framing her face, and Anneliese instantly realized that her daughter knew.

"Dad told me this morning," Beth said.

"Ah," Anneliese replied flatly. "I'm sorry, darling, I wanted to tell you and I didn't know how."

"Mum, this happened ten days ago and you never said anything. Why didn't you tell me when you rang to say Lily was in hospital?"

Anneliese had no answer. Fear, she supposed: fear of falling apart when she told Beth the news and fear that if she began to fall apart, she wouldn't stop. For a woman who'd tried to face life head-on, this avoidance tactic felt strange but also, weirdly, like the only option.

Beth was still raging on. "If I hadn't rung on his mobile this morning asking if he wanted anything from Dublin before we came, I still wouldn't know. I found out by fluke! Dad assumed I knew and hadn't been phoning him on purpose. Did you ever plan on telling me? You're my parents, I love you. I could have come, you needed me, you both needed me, what with Lily being sick and everything."

Anneliese smiled. Beth had always been a fair person. Even now, in the midst of her anger, she was gently telling her mother that she loved her dad too, that she wouldn't be a pawn in any game between them.

"Don't worry," Anneliese said, "there are no sides, Beth—you know us better than that. There's no battle, no fight for your feelings. It's not the sort of news you can say over the phone, is it?"

"Of course it is. You could have told me when you phoned about Lily being sick, couldn't you?" Beth demanded. "I would have come right down."

Anneliese was about to say how she hadn't wanted to worry Beth, but Beth was too angry now and interrupted her.

"I can't believe you didn't tell me you'd split up. You're my parents, I have a right to know. You always think I'm weak and stupid, that I'm not able to cope with stuff and you can't rely on me."

She looked so furious that Anneliese reeled back in shock.

"I just didn't want to hurt you." *And I was hurting inside*, Anneliese thought.

"Life hurts people, Mum," Beth yelled. "Life hurts us all. You think you're in charge of it, you can control the hurt, but you can't. Lots of things hurt me and I have to deal with them, you're not in charge of them. Have you any idea how hurtful it is to find that you and Dad have split up and nobody told me? I bet you don't. But I know exactly why you were waiting till I got here to break the news to me. Because you were working out how to tell me, is that it?"

"Beth—" said Marcus. He was hovering in the kitchen doorway, as if waiting for the row to blow over before he came in properly.

"I'm sorry, Marcus, I have to say this," Beth said. "It's gone on too long. Stop controlling me, Mum. I'm not a child."

"I'm sorry," Anneliese said, and she felt as if the ground had been ripped away from under her feet. Beth didn't seem to understand that she was in pain and shock. No, Anneliese, who had always been in control, must still be in control in Beth's eyes. Somehow she'd also been cast as the villain of the piece. She hadn't broken up the family, Edward had, but she was the one getting shouted at. She'd hoped that she might get some sympathy from her daughter. "It hasn't been easy for me."

"I could have helped," shouted Beth.

You're not helping by screaming at me, Anneliese wanted to yell right back, but she didn't. She never yelled at her daughter.

"But you didn't give me the chance to be there for you. You are so controlling, Mum!"

"I wasn't trying to control things," Anneliese said with absolute honesty. Or at least, the only controlling she'd been doing was trying to keep her own life under some control so she wouldn't fall apart.

"Yes you were," Beth interrupted. "This is all about controlling how you told me, Mum. Please, give me some credit for understanding you. I'm not a child anymore, I have to face things, OK? And if you'd told me when it happened, that would be better, because then I wouldn't have to get all this information on the day when I want to tell you something very special. But you've ruined it now."

"What?" breathed Anneliese.

"I'm pregnant," Beth said. "Three months. Marcus and I are going to have a baby." She laughed, but there was no humor in her laugh. "I didn't tell you because I didn't want to worry you until I'd passed the three months' mark and knew everything was all right. You see, Mum, you've brought me up perfectly! You tell me nothing because you don't want to worry me and I tell you nothing because I don't want to worry you. We're a fabulous family. No wonder Dad left."

It was like being shot, Anneliese thought. She'd never experienced a bullet, but she imagined it must feel the same, that sudden arc of pain and weakness and the feeling of blood draining out of your body and everything going dark. How could Beth say that about Edward? Like it was all Anneliese's fault. He'd left her, didn't Beth realize? Or had he said she'd pushed him away? She felt sick at the very thought of what Edward might have said in an attempt at damage control, but she couldn't collapse, not here, not in front of Beth. Not after hearing this news.

She summoned up every ounce of strength from inside her.

"I am so thrilled for you both," she said. "It's the most wonderful news. I love you, darling, and you'll be the most incredible mother."

"Thank you." It was like a magic cloth had rubbed away the

anger from her daughter's face and now Beth looked serenely happy.

She'd been the same as a child: able to flick a switch between her passions. It was what made Beth so different from her mother. Beth's moods changed like quicksilver and Anneliese had always envied that ability. It was as if Beth's mind said, "OK, that's horrible stuff, let's not deal with that now, let's deal with something nice."

"Marcus, I'm thrilled for you both," Anneliese said, and she put her arms around Beth, willing herself not to faint. She would have a grandchild, how wonderful that would be. But the pain and the ache was still there, because there was a fault line in her relationship with Beth, and that was horrific. Beth blamed her for everything, and in her fury hadn't even acknowledged the pain Anneliese must be going through. The love of a beautiful new baby couldn't mend that, surely?

"Thank you, Anneliese," Marcus said proudly. "It's wonderful, but scary too!"

"It's taken me quite a while to get pregnant. We were trying for, well, nearly a year, and then just when we thought we better get some help, it happened! We had a scan—I've pictures here," Beth said.

The proud parents-to-be crowded round and they looked at the scan. Anneliese kept her arm around Beth and tentatively touched her daughter's gently budding belly. There was no kick from her future grandchild in there, and she thought of how often she'd longed for this news. How ironic that it had to come today of all days.

Yet she was happy to think that her daughter would experience that great mother–child love that she'd had. Except they never told you, when your baby was little, that it could bring such heartbreak too.

"I'm so sorry, darling," she said, a lifetime of suppressing her own needs allowing her to do so again. "I'm sorry that you had to find out about me and your dad today, but let's just forget about that, that's not important. *This* is important"—she touched Beth's belly again—"this new life. I am so happy. Let's focus on that. Maybe your dad and I are better off apart, who knows?" There, she was doing it again, making everything nice and safe and sanitized for Beth. And Beth seemed to like it.

"I hope you're right, Mum," she said. "I don't understand what's going on in Dad's head—" She stopped. "We don't have to talk about it if you don't want. I'm sorry I shouted at you. It's just that what with Lily and now this . . . I wanted everything to be perfect when I told you about the baby."

"Forget everything else," Anneliese insisted. "It will all work out in its own good time. Your news is what matters now."

Beth grinned. "It's so exciting. Will you come and stay with us when the baby's born? Because it's going to be difficult, and you know I don't know anything about babies. I was saying to some of my friends that they're lucky to have older sisters and brothers so they have nieces and nephews. But being an only child, well, I don't have that experience. I suppose I'll learn!" she laughed. "I was thinking that it's going to be hard to tell Izzie," Beth went on, "because, well, I never really knew if she wanted kids or not and there's nobody special in her life, so—"

She broke off and sighed. "I sort of thought there was someone. She referred to a guy in emails, but she sounded a bit vague about him so I didn't like to pry."

"She hasn't told me about anyone," Anneliese said, surprised. She and Izzie spoke a lot. But then, she hadn't been on the phone filling Izzie in with her own life-changing details, had she?

"She was probably afraid to tell you and Gran, because you'd be planning the wedding as soon as you heard and, well, it doesn't work like that nowadays," Beth said wryly.

Yes, Anneliese thought grimly, that's me—poster girl for marriage.

Once she'd started talking about the pregnancy, Beth kept going. Marcus took their bags upstairs to the spare room and got his wife some water, while she told her mother how she felt tired at night, how she hadn't really had morning sickness but the nausea had been quite intense, although it was improving now. And she'd developed a burst of energy the past week. Some people found that after the first trimester, she explained.

"You sound so knowledgeable." Anneliese smiled. "You must have been reading loads."

"Yes, tons. Actually, last night I was reading a baby magazine and it mentioned this new book about the first year with your baby. I'd love to get it," Beth said. "Maybe we could try the bookshop here?"

"Of course," Anneliese said. "I'll just run upstairs and brush my hair."

In her bedroom she found the tranquilizers and took another one. Right now she needed some help, and since divine inspiration seemed to be in short supply, medical inspiration would have to do.

After they'd bought a couple of books—Anneliese paid—the three of them went down to Dorota's and drank herbal tea, looking out over the bay. There was no fear of meeting Nell or Edward now, Anneliese decided. Nell wouldn't dream of turning up, and even if Edward did, she could cope with him, thanks to both her little tablet and the presence of Beth and Marcus.

After a while, Marcus went back up to the counter to order more tea.

"How are you feeling?" Beth asked, taking her mother's hand and patting it.

Anneliese smiled at her pregnant daughter.

"I'll be fine," she lied.

"Dad says there's a whale stuck out there in the harbor," said Beth idly when her husband came back. "Poor thing, how does that happen? Do they get lost or something?"

"Nobody knows for sure," her mother replied, looking out at the sea. It was such a beautiful, clear day, but there were volcanic-looking dark clouds over to the right on the horizon, a summer storm coming in. "There's a marine expert here and he says it's apparently something to do with the whale's sonar getting messed up. They get stuck and then they can't get out again. Quite often they die."

"How long has the whale been here?"

"Nearly two weeks. I don't think she's going to last much longer. They say she's weak."

"Oh, poor whale," said Beth. "Why can't they just put her to sleep, or does that not work?"

"I think they can do that if the whale is actually beached, but she isn't and it would cause her even more distress if they tried to get close."

"Oh," sighed Beth.

"They tried to coax her out into deeper water with a diving team, but it was a long shot and it didn't work."

Anneliese had watched the rescue operation from the high point between the two bays. Lots of people had been there in the harbor, silently watching and willing the plan to work.

Anneliese had brought her binoculars and she'd spotted the marine guy, Mac Petersen, in the middle of it all. Now that she knew who he was, she realized she had seen him before on the beach near Dolphin Cottage. He had a small boat, a curragh like the old island fishermen used to use, and he went out to sea in it occasionally. He had a dog too, a woolly scruffy thing that was just the sort of dog he ought to own, and she'd seen him on the beach with it.

When she saw him on the beach, she went the other way. She didn't have what it took to be polite to strangers anymore.

Thanks to her binoculars, she'd seen his head hang low on his chest when the rescue plan had failed, and she felt a pang of sorrow at having been so nasty to him the time they'd met. He did care about the whale, after all.

"You know, I think I might have another muffin," Beth decided. "I've been reading up on pregnancy food, and muffins are really good for giving you your energy back. Milk's good too. I'm drinking lots of milk. And then maybe we'll go and see Lily. I don't want to stay too long," Beth confided. "I don't know if I could cope with it. I don't think it would be good for the baby if I got upset, but I need to say good-bye to her."

"OK," said Anneliese, feeling her heartbreak. She didn't want Lily to go. But everything was changing in her life and it was as if she had no power to prevent it all.

She thought of the whale, lost in the bay, life ebbing out of her every day, and thought that it might be quite nice to dive in and sink to the bottom with the whale.

"Mrs. Kennedy," said Dr. Whelan, looking up from his writing as she entered the surgery. "What can I do for you?"

"A lobotomy," Anneliese said easily. "I just need a bit off. A trim, so to speak. It would be nice if you could do that with brains, take out the tricky, difficult bits, like removing split ends."

The doctor put down his pen. He was younger than she was, which Anneliese liked. Younger doctors were always up to speed on the latest treatment. Old Dr. Masterson had been a nightmare when it came to talking about depression. Despite the alphabet of letters after her name, she was one of the "pull yourself together" merchants who felt that depression was entirely controllable by thinking happy thoughts. Anneliese had ended up moving to another doctor in the center of town rather than visit her, but then Dr. Whelan had come along. He'd been in Tamarin for ten years, and in that time Anneliese had visited him twice over her depression. He'd been friendly, helpful and kind. But none of these things made it any easier to discuss her problems with him.

If Anneliese felt like a failure because her head was flattened by this black dog in her mind, then it was hard to convince herself that he would feel any different. He'd think she was a failure too.

"Lobotomies aren't much in demand nowadays," he replied, falling into the same light manner she'd used. "Certainly not on an outpatient basis," he added. "What's wrong, Mrs. Kennedy?"

Anneliese closed her eyes. She hated this, hated it. Being the supplicant in the surgery, having to ask for help.

"I'm depressed," she said. The desire to burst into tears was dampened down by the tranquilizer she'd taken before she'd driven there. It was her last one. "I need to go back on antidepressants."

Damn Edward and that bloody bitch for making her have to do this.

"Is there any particular reason?" Dr. Whelan asked, joking manner gone.

The little white tablet gave up the ghost and the tears came.

Half an hour later, Anneliese had a prescription for the antidepressant that had worked for her before, along with a short-term script for an antianxiety drug to tide her over until the big boys began to work.

"Come and talk to me anytime, please," Dr. Whelan said kindly as she left, trying to mop up her red eyes before she headed back into the reception area.

"Thank you," said Anneliese, knowing that she wouldn't. She felt as if nothing could help her, even the various tablets he'd prescribed. They were short-term things. She wanted a guarantee of happiness and she didn't know if that was possible anymore.

At home, she made herself some tea, took one of the antianxiety drugs and lay down on her bed. Her head ached from all the crying. Perhaps if she had a little rest, she'd have the energy to get up and cook dinner for herself, Beth and Marcus. They were going home the following morning and had been at the hospital with Lily that afternoon, giving Anneliese a chance to make her secret trip to Dr. Whelan. She hadn't told Beth how she felt and Beth hadn't asked.

It was understandable: Beth wanted to protect her unborn child from stress. Any mother would do the same. But still, Anneliese felt a part of her ache inside at this evidence of her daughter's ability to shut out other people's pain.

Beth didn't want to deal with her mother crying and alone, so she simply didn't deal with it.

Lying down with several pillows cushioning her and the duvet loosely over her, Anneliese looked around the room. Maybe she should sell up. It was a beautiful cottage but it held too many memories for her now. It wasn't as if she could redecorate it and make it different. As a beach cottage, it was perfect the way it was, all bleached wood, white walls and pale blue detailing. No, she couldn't decorate it and change it. Selling was the only option. She ought to talk to Edward about it—well, talk to Edward's lawyer. That would be next, she supposed: his lawyer talking to her lawyer. She didn't have a lawyer. There hadn't been much call in her life for legal help, but she'd have to get one now. Not from Tamarin, of course. Even if the lawyer was the very model of discretion, Anneliese winced at the thought of somebody local knowing everything about her and Edward's breakup.

She could imagine it. Nell, sitting in a lawyer's office, crouched like a witch on her chair, saying, "No, Edward, make sure you get half of everything—more than half."

Anneliese shuddered. She'd get a lawyer in Waterford and let them deal with it. She'd say she wanted it done as simply and cleanly as possible, like amputation. Cut the limb off, cauterize it and walk away. But where would she go then? Would she stay in Tamarin? If Lily wasn't there, she probably wouldn't, and Lily might not survive.

It had been over a week since her stroke and it was time to

face facts. Lily might never come back, and the more Anneliese visited her, the more she thought that Lily was getting older and frailer and more distant in the bed.

She could move to Dublin to be close to Beth and Marcus and her beautiful grandchild, but that might be crowding Beth; it wouldn't be fair.

Her family home had been on the other side of Waterford, but her parents were long dead and her brothers and sisters were scattered all around the country and the globe. There was no one place to call home anymore, except Tamarin. When she'd married Edward, Anneliese had made this place her home.

God, the tablets were great, she thought sleepily. They allowed her mind to roam into areas she'd previously locked off. Which had to be good—or was it bad?

She closed her eyes, allowed herself to stop thinking about what she'd do next, and somehow she fell asleep.

The sound of a car crunching up on the stones on the drive woke her up. Beth was back. She should have been cooking and she'd fallen asleep. Blast it.

She threw back the duvet and looked out of the window, but there were two cars parking, Beth and Marcus's car and Edward's.

Anneliese's chest tightened. She couldn't cope with Edward right now. Clearly, this was some idea of Beth's to bring him here and make him talk to Anneliese. But Edward and Anneliese didn't want to talk to each other. They'd had two weeks to do it and neither of them had so much as picked up a phone to speak to the other. There was simply nothing to be said and too much pain would emerge during the saying of that nothing.

Anxiously, Anneliese pulled on her sweatshirt and jeans.

"Mum," said Beth from the door of the bedroom. "Mum, I know you're not going to like this, but . . ."

"I saw your father's car," Anneliese said. "Beth, this isn't a good idea."

"Mum, please." Beth came into the room and sat on the bed. "Please."

"I'm not ready for this."

"But talking is good, Mum, and you haven't spoken to each other since he left, Dad told me."

"So?" snapped Anneliese, feeling suddenly angry. "What is there to talk about? That he's sorry and can we all be friends and do this amicably? I can guess what he wants to talk to me about, and I don't want to listen. Once upon a time, he told me he loved me, and all the time he was involved with Nell. So frankly, I'm not interested in anything your father has to tell me."

Beth looked taken aback. Anneliese knew she should apologize. It wasn't her daughter's fault, after all, and she never spoke to Beth like that, but she was fed up with considering everyone else's feelings before her own. That was the old Anneliese.

"Beth," said Anneliese firmly, "I do not want to talk to your father. Now get him out of my house."

"Please, Mum." Beth's eyes filled up with tears.

She looked so forlorn and Anneliese knew at that moment that she'd have to go down to talk to Edward.

"How did you get him here?" she asked.

"I told him to do it for me. He didn't want to come, but I know if the two of you would just talk to each other, it would help."

Anneliese raised her eyes to heaven. She knew that Edward, like herself, could never deny their daughter anything. Even now, when Anneliese couldn't bear the thought of being in the same room as Edward, she knew she would endure that because it would make Beth happy.

Nobody else would be able to make her do it. They were hardly at the family-mediation stage, unless mediation involved throwing kitchen implements and screaming blue murder. Oh well, she'd talk to him for five minutes, that was all. Anneliese glanced at herself in the mirror. Her hair was wild and her face tired. She looked like she looked when she came in from a wild, windy walk on the beach, except that then she might have some glow in her cheeks and now she just looked drained. There was no point primping or beautifying. Edward had gone. He'd hardly come back just because she was wearing lipstick.

"I'm ready," she said.

"But your hair . . ." began Beth.

"My hair's ready too," said Anneliese grimly.

Downstairs, Edward was standing just inside the front door, looking anxious. Sitting down on one of the armchairs was Marcus, looking more anxious. Anneliese was very fond of her son-in-law. He was kind and gentle as well as being a clever, thoughtful man. He probably thought it was an appalling idea to see his in-laws turning out-law and screaming at each other in the same room, but Marcus was another one who would do anything for Beth. She'd undoubtedly twisted his arm too to make him go along with this crackpot plan.

"Do you want to come in?" Anneliese said to her husband.

"I wanted to wait until you invited me in properly," Edward said formally.

"I think the time for formality is over," she snapped.

Edward sat on the edge of the armchair opposite Marcus.

"Come on, darling—let's go for a walk on the beach," said Beth, grabbing Marcus and hauling him to his feet.

"Yeah, sure. We'll be just outside if you need us," Marcus said, shooting anguished looks at both Edward and Anneliese.

Anneliese felt the faint stirrings of a grin.

"I'm not going to kill him," she said reassuringly. "I'll just rough him up a little bit, OK?"

Beth hustled Marcus out of the front door before he could respond to this.

"I'm really sorry about my turning up, Anneliese," said Edward, still formal. "It's just . . . Beth insisted."

"I know," said Anneliese. "I understand, not your fault."

"You're being very magnanimous," Edward said.

"I'm not magnanimous at all," Anneliese replied. "I'm just tired, and I don't have the energy for gilding the lily. We're here because we love Beth, she's pregnant and we don't want to upset her."

"Isn't it wonderful news?" Edward said eagerly, and then stopped, as if he suddenly remembered that they weren't normal would-be grandparents discussing their imminent grandchild. Anneliese thought the same thing.

She'd allowed herself to think about how she and Edward would react to the news that Beth was having a baby and this scenario had never figured in her imaginings.

"It is wonderful," Edward went on, "that something nice is coming out of all of this."

"You talk like there has just been a natural disaster and none of us are responsible for it," Anneliese snapped. "There's nothing natural about it at all. You cheated on me, left me for Nell. Nell! For God's sake, how could you do that, Edward? Nell was our friend. I used to feel guilty inviting her over all the time, in case you were fed up of there being a third wheel at dinner. How stupid of me: you loved having her here. I was probably the one you wanted to get rid of."

"No, it wasn't like that," Edward said.

"Well, what was it like? You know, now that you're here, you can answer some questions."

She sat on the edge of one of the chairs opposite him and glared at him.

"When did you start screwing my friend? Please tell me—not that I expect you're going to tell me the truth," she went on. "Because you won't, will you? That's one of the rules of infidelity, isn't it?"

"No," he said.

"Yes," she argued. "You make it sound like it was only going on five minutes and then, eventually, I'll learn you've been together months, years, so that everything I thought was real wasn't real at all. Talk about a recipe for making someone go mad. That's what I keep doing, Edward: thinking of the past and what bits were real and what bits involved you faking happiness so you could spend more time with Nell."

Anneliese slipped into the seat properly. She'd intended to sit on the edge in case she wanted to run out of the room because she couldn't stand to look at him any longer, but the weariness came over her again.

"Were you together at Beth's wedding, for example?"

"No," he shouted.

"Well, when then? Christmas?"

He didn't answer.

"OK," said Anneliese. "Christmas, then; you were together at Christmas. So when before Christmas did it start? Just tell me, so that I can draw a line under the time you were with her and remember the memories before that, because they were real. I hope they were real."

Another thought occurred to her. Had there been somebody else, other women? A man who could cheat once could have cheated before.

"Was there anyone else, before Nell?"

"No," he said. "There was never anyone else. I wish you didn't think that of me—"

"You mean you wish I didn't think badly of you," Anneliese interrupted. "How can I not think badly of you, Edward? You cheated on me. If our marriage was so terrible, you should have told me. You could have given me a choice. But you didn't. You played a game, where you stayed with me and waited for someone else to come along."

That was one of the biggest injuries, she realized with stunning clarity. Instead of walking away from their marriage, he'd waited, thoughtfully watching. "Is that what you did?" she demanded. "Waited, while looking around for someone, and Nell just happened to fit the bill?"

"It wasn't like that," he said. He leaned forward and put his head in his hands. "It wasn't like that at all. You were . . ."

"Oh, my fault again, right," said Anneliese bitterly. "I behaved in a particular way or I wasn't what you wanted, and that's why you had to look elsewhere."

"No." His voice was getting harsher. "I'm not saying it's your fault. I'm saying we, we as a couple, had drifted apart, that's all. I was vulnerable."

"Vulnerable to what?" she demanded. "Vulnerable to Nell boosting your ego, telling you how fabulous you were?"

He flushed and she sensed that she'd made a direct hit. "That's not a relationship, Edward. That sounds like something schoolgirls do. *You're so wonderful, Edward, why don't you leave your boring wife to live with me?* You know what, I wish you happiness."

She pushed herself off the seat. She didn't want to sit in the same room as him anymore; there was no point. He wasn't going to answer any of the questions she needed answers to, and this was too raw to talk about. She'd been doing it for Beth, and in truth, if Beth had understood either of them better, she wouldn't have pushed them into this.

"Edward, why don't you go. We have nothing to say to each other."

He got to his feet obediently. "I'm so sorry about Lily," he said. "I know it must be terrible for you. I know how much you loved her."

"Don't talk about her like she's already dead," snapped Anneliese, "because she's not."

The look Edward shot her was of pity. Anneliese turned around and went upstairs into her bedroom, slamming the door.

She heard a car door bang shut and then the sound of tires on the drive as Edward drove away.

Two weeks ago, Edward had been everything to her. They'd spent hours together, happy, content in each other's company, or so she'd thought. Except that they hadn't been happy, apparently. If it hadn't been for a simple migraine that made her come home unexpectedly, she mightn't have ever known that. The randomness and powerlessness of life hit her again. Why had she been so stupid as to think she had any control of her own life? Because she didn't.

thirteen

"Here we are," Jodi said as she drove over coral azalea petals lying like confetti on the driveway.

"Oh my," breathed Izzie as she caught sight of the house for the first time. It was early afternoon and bright sunlight painted the graceful façade of the house with a pale, shimmering gold. Set in the middle of a bower of trees and overgrown gardens, Rathnaree was like a graceful bride on her wedding day: no matter how lovely everyone else looked, your eyes were drawn only to her. "It's beautiful."

They parked beside the estate agent's car and Izzie began to wander around the garden, touching shrubs and small statues, admiring it all, astonished at this beauty, something she'd grown up so close to and yet had never seen. Here, buried under a Japanese maple and covered with lichen, was a marble goddess with a half smile on her lips.

Izzie ran her fingers over the smooth stone. Rathnaree was from another world and yet Izzie's own family had been a part of it. To think that her family had worked here in this amazing house, her grandmother and her great-grandmother. And all these years it had remained undisturbed, preserved as if waiting for her to walk in.

"Come on, Izzie," said Jodi, who'd seen the gardens and just wanted to get inside.

In the end it had been Izzie who had managed to persuade the estate agent to let them see Rathnaree. That she had managed to achieve this was a combination of her charm and the fact that she and the estate agent had gone to school together.

"Aggie, we just want to have a look around for this history that Jodi's writing. Look at it this way: anyone who is willing to put up the money to buy somewhere as massive as Rathnaree is bound to be egotistical enough to want a history of the place written. Rich people have egos the size of Mars, right, and having a history of their new house already written—well, it's got to be a selling point. You could put it on your marketing brochures. Can you see what I'm getting at? It's not just a massive old Anglo-Irish wreck in need of restoration—"

"I thought you were putting a positive spin on it," muttered Aggie, the estate agent.

"—it's a beautiful example of classic Irish architecture, with a fantastic history that links it to Tamarin and all the great events in Irish history."

"Such as what?" said Aggie.

"Well, I don't know yet. That's why we want to see inside, isn't it?" Izzie said. Honestly, Aggie was hard work.

"I'm not going to tell Peter about this," Aggie said, weakening.

Peter Winters was the man who owned Winters & Sons, the estate agency trying to sell Rathnaree. The company's motto was along the lines of *If you want to sell an exquisite family heirloom, with style and dignity and no nasty modern advertising, then come to Winters & Sons*.

That sort of ploy might have worked years ago, but it clearly wasn't working now, Izzie realized. Rathnaree had been empty for four years and there was no sign of anybody taking it off the owner's hands.

"Peter doesn't need to know anything," Izzie said. "We won't tell him, Girl Guide's honor."

"Were you in the Guides?" Aggie asked.

"I went to Brownie camp once," Izzie volunteered.

Aggie shrugged. "Fair enough," she said. "I'm warning the pair of you, Rathnaree needs a hell of a lot of work," Aggie went on as she found the keys for the house. "If a bit of plaster falls off and kills you, I'm not liable, right?"

The current owner was one Freddy Lochraven, a distant relative of the original family. According to Aggie, he divided his time between London and Dubai and had only visited the house once, shortly after he'd inherited it.

"Peter thinks it suits him that it hasn't sold on the grounds that with property prices rising all the time, it will make more money when it eventually sells."

"And he'd love, I'm sure, a detailed history of the place," Izzie interrupted.

"I suppose," said Aggie. "Fine. I'll let you in and I'll leave you, but don't take anything, please."

"Oh, Aggie, for God's sake," grumbled Izzie. "Don't be ridiculous. We just want to breathe in the atmosphere. Besides, you've known me all your life—and Jodi's the vice principal's wife; she's hardly going to start ripping the fireplaces off the walls, is she? No. We're doing you a favor."

"We have to go in through the kitchen," said Aggie now, jangling keys, "because the front door's a nightmare. The last time I was here, I could barely open it."

They walked around the side of the house to the big gate into the courtyard Jodi had peered into once before. She was so excited and was mentally urging Aggie to hurry up but the estate agent was taking forever, slowly inserting key after key into the lock, trying to find the right one and muttering as she did so.

"Hurry up!" Jodi wanted to scream, but she daren't. If Aggie changed her mind, they wouldn't be able to get in, and she just had to see inside.

Finally, the stiff lock yielded. Aggie unhooked it and pushed the creaking gate open. Jodi ran in first, looking around, trying to commit everything to memory. Photos! She'd better take photos.

The courtyard had stables at one end with arched doorways and horseshoes hung for luck all over the place. Jodi wanted to look everywhere, but she wanted to go inside too.

At the kitchen door there was another interminable wait while Aggie fiddled with the keys again. And then the door was open and they were inside.

"Holy smoke, it's an awful mess," said Aggie, sighing as they went in.

Jodi and Izzie exchanged a grin. Aggie had never been the most imaginative person in school, Izzie thought, and clearly, nothing had changed. All she saw was dust and cobwebs, while Jodi and Izzie saw history right in front of them.

"If you want to leave me the keys, Aggie, I'll lock up and bring them back to you in a couple of hours," Izzie said.

"Well, OK," said Aggie grudgingly. "I have a lot to do."

Izzie nodded as if this was indeed the case, although she didn't think so. The phone hadn't rung once when they were with Aggie in the office. Business didn't appear to be too brisk at Winters & Sons.

"Of course, you're busy," Izzie said briskly. God, the fibs she was telling. "I'll take care of this. And thank you so much. You have no idea what this means to us."

With Aggie gone, they could look to their hearts' content. Izzie almost didn't know where to start. She walked around the big kitchen with the huge old Aga and recalled Gran once telling someone about cooking on such a beast. Apparently, it was difficult to learn the vagaries of the giant Aga, and a total nightmare to relight it when it went out.

In one part of the kitchen were bells hung high on the wall with names for each room: library, drawing room, study, bedroom one, bedroom two, etc. There were three rows of bells and Izzie imagined staff rushing off at high speed when one rang.

To the right of the kitchen was a huge scullery with two vast sinks and lots of old wooden crates still lying on the floor. There were newspapers on the floor too, dropped carelessly there as if to mop up a spill. Behind the door they found the source of the newspapers, piles and piles of carefully tied-up newsprint. There must be years' worth there, Izzie thought.

It was a dark room with only a tiny light and in her mind's eye she could see a girl, her hands raw from scrubbing potatoes or peeling mounds of vegetables. Until now Izzie had never thought of herself as a particularly psychic person, but here, in this old house, the sense of the generations who'd worked their fingers to the bone seemed to permeate the very walls.

"Izzie, look—back stairs," came Jodi's voice. "Come on."

Izzie left the scullery and went out into a little hall. There were plain stone flags on the floor and it was cold, freezing even in the heat of a warm spring day. There were lots of little doors off it and she quickly opened some of them, finding a boot room with old footwear standing dusty and covered with the film of age, and another room with nothing in it but shelves of empty bottles and jars, along with a strange contraption shaped like a sideways barrel on a wooden frame with a big handle on one side. It was a butter churn, she realized, delighted with herself for recognizing it. Gran had talked about making butter when she was a child: the fun of separating fresh milk into cream and skimmed milk, and then the hours of winding away with the churn until the magical moment came and the golden butter began to appear like little knobs in the milk.

"Are you coming?" said Jodi.

They ran up the narrow stairs and came out via a small door into a large airy corridor. It was a different world, the difference between downstairs and upstairs. Izzie tried to take it all in.

The walls were covered with the palest green silken wallpaper that almost looked as if someone had painted exotic birds on by hand. With their wings spread as they flew, the little birds were rainbow bright: acid yellows, crimson reds and electric blues. Beneath their feet was a wooden floor covered with a long, threadbare carpet. Even though it was old, it had clearly once been very beautiful with an intricate architectural design along the edges and huge old roses tumbling over each other in the middle.

Jodi half ran down to big double doors at the other end of the hallway and pushed them open. Izzie followed her and they found themselves in a light, airy sitting room with huge sash windows and heavy silk curtains. The original furniture was still there, some draped in off-white Holland covers. A pair of gilded chairs sat in front of a beautiful fireplace, a vision of white marble with delicately chiseled Roman goddesses frolicking around the edges. Izzie guessed this must be the lady of the house's personal salon. Here her ladyship could sit and amuse herself, in sharp contrast to the women toiling downstairs in the scullery.

Next were bedrooms, two huge ones, for the master and mistress: his with a small dressing room and masculine bookshelves on the walls; hers with an enormous four-poster bed as centerpiece. Izzie recognized Indian carvings on the heavy bedposts, but the crimson and golden hangings had been badly attacked by moths and they hung in threads around it. It was such a shame. The wardrobes and the other furniture didn't match the Indian bed. The wardrobes were vast 1930s style, with simple lines and doors hanging open, smelling musty. There was candle grease on the small bamboo table beside the bed and Izzie had a sudden vision of the last of the Lochravens as a little old lady getting into bed on her own, with a candle to save money on electricity. Jodi had told her that Isabelle Lochraven had been ninety-five when she died. She'd never married and had lived here in the house all her life. Izzie knew her grandmother must remember Isabelle from a long time ago because Isabelle had been a young woman when Lily worked in Rathnaree, yet Izzie was quite sure the two hadn't met after that, even though they were of similar vintage. They must have shared many memories, but the servant/mistress divide was so great that even in old age they'd never thought to breach it.

Izzie thought back to her childhood in Tamarin. She couldn't recall hearing anything about the Lochraven family, apart from the odd reported sighting of Isabelle driving into town in one of her ancient cars. She was a danger on the roads, everyone said. Drove as though she owned the road, which a long time ago she had.

What a sad way to live, Izzie thought, touched with empathy for these people. They had so much, and yet because of their position, they cut themselves off from the people around them. They were part of the country and yet not part of it. How sad.

On the next floor up were children's rooms and a giant nursery, painted bright yellow with all sorts of old-fashioned children's toys lying in disrepair on the floor. There were cross-faced dolls with hard china heads and little wigs; a tricycle that must be at least a hundred years old, with its paint nearly all chipped off; and little books from another age, Kipling and Enid Blyton in tattered covers.

Farther along the corridor was another door that led up to the servants' quarters in the attics via a narrow and winding staircase. Here were the maids' bedrooms: tiny little box rooms separated by paper-thin walls. Some had iron bedsteads, but only one had a small fireplace. Perhaps with their tiny windows, the attic rooms weren't as cold as the rest of the house, but with so many chimneys it seemed heartless that these maids, after a day stoking the Lochravens' fires, would climb the stairs to shiver under the eaves.

Again, she began to get an understanding of why her grandmother resented the Lochravens. For a woman as proud and intelligent as Lily, it must have been hard to have to serve these people with their sense of right and privilege. Lily, who thought that respect should be earned, would have found it hard to admire people who thought themselves entitled by virtue of their aristocratic blood. They lived in the pretty gilded salon and dined on fine china while their servants were denied any comfort whatsoever.

Finally, she went back down to the first floor. The main stairs leading to the front doors were grand and at least six feet wide, carved out of the palest white marble with veins of gray running through them. On either side was a solid brass stair rail. There was a huge hall at the bottom, with a pattern in black and white Victorian floor tiles and ornamental columns topped by pots of dusty earth with no trace remaining of the ferns that once must have been planted there. An ornate grandfather clock stood against one wall and the mounted heads of several stags stared down at her through dusty eyes that hadn't gleamed with life for many decades.

"Here it is," cried Jodi. She'd found the room from her precious photograph: the room in which the glamorous men and women had posed for the picture marking Lady Irene's birthday. Without the sepia mystique of the photograph, the room looked sad and tired, for all its elegant proportions and huge windows and the giant fireplace with the club fender exactly as they'd seen it in the photo.

But there was no fire in the grate. The tables with the beautiful arrangements of flowers were gone, and there was no sense of music in the background or the feeling of laughing people enjoying themselves, holding up crystal tumblers to the camera.

"Isn't it wonderful?" breathed Jodi, enchanted.

And Izzie wondered exactly what was wrong with her, because all she felt was sadness in this place. Maybe she lacked the archaeology gene. Or maybe she was a lot more like her grandmother than she knew. She didn't long to be in this grand house playing at being a lady, with servants running up and down the back stairs every time she rang a bell.

There was too much imbalance here. As if something had kept Rathnaree going unnaturally, and now that the cycle was over, all that was left was this beautiful, sad shell which had witnessed so much. Many people had lived their lives out in the house, yet the only stories people heard about Rathnaree concerned the wealthy people who'd lived here. The poor people of Tamarin who'd served them had been forgotten. That felt wrong to Izzie.

"It's a pity we don't know more about the people who worked here," she said. "That's the interesting story, isn't it?"

"I agree, both stories are interesting," Jodie said, surprising her. "It's like there were two separate worlds here, independent and yet linking up: the aristocrats and the servants. Two different stories at the same time, how interesting is that! Oh, I'm so glad we got to come in here. Thank you, Izzie, for arranging it."

"You're going to work on it, then—the history from both sides?" Izzie asked.

Jodi nodded. "I love uncovering the past, don't you?" she said happily. "It teaches us about ourselves; that's what they told us in college, anyway."

Izzie stood in front of the big fireplace the way the people in Jodi's sepia-tinted photograph had stood and tried to imagine herself back in their world. She'd read a novel about time travel once, where a woman from the twentieth century had been whisked back to the seventeenth. The idea had fascinated Izzie. What would she bring to the past if she was transported back to 1936 right now? Would her wisdom be of any use then? Or would she find that instead of her bringing superior modern knowledge into the past, the past would turn out to be her teacher?

fourteen

When she was older, Lily found that the seasons reminded her of different parts of her life. Spring was always Tamarin, when the bare trees were dotted with pouting acid-green buds of new life, and the fields changed from heavy umber to palest green dotted with velvety new lambs on shaky legs. Autumn was Rathnaree, when the staff toiled to get the great house ready for winter and when Sir Henry invited cronies to shoot or fish with him. Outside, the woods came alight with the russets and pale golds of autumn, while inside, apple logs burned in the grates and the kitchen steamed up with cooking for the parties of gentlemen.

But summer—summer would always be London during the war when the sun shone more brightly than ever before, and life was lived with far greater passion and ferocity than she'd imagined possible.

May 1944 was one of the hottest Mays on record, and on the rare occasions when they weren't working, Lily, Diana and Maisie loved to sit on the tiny balcony on the third floor of the nurses' home on Cubitt Street, faded and frayed cushions behind them, letting the heat sink into their tired bones.

They didn't get too many opportunities to sit in the sun; time off was at a premium for third-year nursing students and Matron was an ardent believer in the mantra of the devil making work for idle hands.

She would have been scandalized if she had seen them sitting on the balcony with their stockings off and their feet deliciously bare to the sun. But it had been a hard week, Lily thought, leaning back, and what Matron didn't know couldn't harm her. In the delivery ward, Lily had been involved in the births of seventeen babies in that week alone.

She deserved a rest. That evening she and the girls were going out to tea in Lyons Corner House, and afterward to the Odeon to see *Gaslight*. She loved going to the cinema and immersing herself in the fantasy world on screen. Joan Crawford was still her favorite film star, but she could see the lure of Ingrid Bergman. Maisie, who was prone to flights of imagination, said Lily had the same eyes as Ingrid.

"Mysterious," Maisie insisted. "Like you're thinking of a special man somewhere."

"When she looks like that, she's thinking of what's for dinner," laughed Diana, who was much more prosaic and, like all of them, thought about food quite a lot. "I'll make us tea."

Lily remembered the huge surplus of food at home, fresh eggs every day and her mother's fragrant bread. She'd never realized how lucky she'd been. Now the shortages had even spread to Ireland, where flour was in short supply. "We're all eating black bread at the moment," her mother had written in her last letter. "Tastes like turf to my mind. Lady Irene's got very thin on account of it."

As the afternoon sun warmed her face, Lily wondered how she had ever lived anywhere other than here. It wasn't just food that made her think back to Tamarin and Rathnaree, her mother working hard, never seeing anything but the bloody Lochraven family, never thinking of more. Lily herself had seen so much now—she'd helped in theatre when the hospital was short-staffed and had stayed standing despite the stench of discarded splints and dressings from men wounded overseas. She'd spent many nights in the basement during air-raids, comforting patients while trying to remain calm herself, telling them it would be fine, that the hospital had never taken a direct hit and wouldn't now, when she knew no such thing.

She'd delivered two babies all by herself, and had felt a surge of pride when she'd heard that the queen said she was glad Buckingham Palace had been bombed so now she could look the East End in the eye. Lily liked the queen: she cared, keeping the little princesses in London despite the bombing. They were on rationing too, which was only right. Lily would have bet her last shilling that if the Lochravens had been running the country, they'd still be eating plover's eggs and lobster thermidor.

"Is it bad not to want to go home?" she asked Maisie.

"Depends on what there is to go home to," Maisie said pragmatically. "There's nothing for me to go home to, 'cept Terry's wife, and she won't be welcoming me with open arms." Maisie's mother had been killed during the Blitz as she'd opened the front door of her flat to rush for the Underground. Only her brother, Terry, was left of their small family, and he'd married a year ago when his girlfriend, a platinum blonde named Ruby, became pregnant. Ruby and Maisie didn't see eye to eye.

"Yes, sorry," said Lily, angry with herself for thinking out loud. "But when the war's over, what then?"

"You got listening privileges in the War Office, then?" Maisie asked. "How'd you know it's going to be over?"

"It can't go on forever."

"Says who?" Maisie found her cigarettes and lit one.

"Tea's ready, girls." Diana put three cups of tea down beside them, then swung her long legs down so the sun could warm them.

"Thanks."

"Thanks, Diana." Lily sipped her tea, still wrinkling her nose at the first taste. She missed sugar, but had decided it was far better to save her coupons for actual tea.

Diana had given up coffee altogether. "I can't bear the taste of Camp," she'd said, shuddering at even the notion of the coffee substitute. She'd told them once about drinking delicious prewar coffee in Juan-les-Pins in the south of France where she'd gone with her parents and sister, Sybil, and stayed in a fabulous villa with its own swimming pool and blue and white umbrellas to shelter one from the sun.

"Lily's going all maudlin on us, Di," said Maisie. "Wants to know what we're going to do after."

Diana's perfect nose wrinkled. "Darling, heaven knows. Daddy will want me to get married, I suppose, so I'll be off his hands, like Sybil. That's what he thinks war is about—defending the country so your daughters can still get married in the family chapel."

"You never said you had a chapel." Maisie sat up. "I thought Sybil was getting married in an ordinary church."

"It's only a small one," Diana said apologetically. "Lots of people have them. Not just us."

"Keep your knickers on, princess," Maisie sighed. "I've never seen a house with a chapel before. Christ Almighty, I s'pose I'll have to be on my best behavior for this bloody wedding."

You're not the only one, Lily thought. She still felt unsure about attending Diana's sister's wedding. It was easy to forget that Diana came from another world, the world of privilege. She shared their room and they saw her asleep with her mouth open, and had watched her cram a cheese sandwich into her face after a twelve-hour shift when they'd not had a second to stop for a bite. But her family would be another matter. They'd already met Sybil, who was everything Diana was not: proud, sulky and keen to maintain the class divide.

Unlike Maisie, who was dying to see "how the other half lived," Lily—who already knew exactly how they lived—was dreading the wedding. To Diana, she was a friend. To the Beltons, with their private chapel and grand house in London and prewar holidays on the Riviera, she would be a servant girl. The war might have changed many things, but it hadn't changed that much.

"It's going to be lovely," Maisie sighed happily.

At twenty-one, she was the youngest of the three and yet the one who tried everything first. She'd been first to go out with an American soldier.

"Very polite, kept telling me about his mother," she said mournfully when she got back to the nurses' home and the others pressed her for details. "Said English girls were ladies. We'd all be ladies if nobody ever put a hand on us."

"You'd be furious if he tried anything," pointed out Diana, who had finally got the measure of Maisie after almost three years of living in each other's shadows.

"Three hours hearing about his mother put me right off," snorted Maisie, not even bothering to respond to Diana's remark. They were all so comfortable with each other: like sisters, they squabbled but always made up. They'd been through the fire together. It had created an unbreakable bond. "It was like having my Nan in the room, squawking, 'If you let the dog see the rabbit, it'll end in tears, my girl! Get the ring first!' And talkin' of rings—I hope someone will take pictures of us at the wedding," Maisie added. "I want to see proof of me in my finery."

"Course they will," Diana said. "Pictures for posterity."

Lily didn't know what they'd have done for clothes if it hadn't been for Diana's generosity. She had trunkloads of stuff: evening gowns and day suits she'd donated to the Impoverished of Hampstead Fund, as they called it. Maisie's nimble fingers could take in or let out any garment. As Diana and Lily were almost the same size, not much alteration was required, but a few inches had to be taken off all the hems so they'd fit her.

Thanks to Diana's capacious trunks, Maisie would be wearing a gray linen and silk suit and a dashing little silver feathered hat for Sybil's wedding. Diana was to be a bridesmaid in one of her mother's old Mainbocher gowns in a sea blue that made her English cream-and-roses complexion look even more beautiful, and Lily was to wear a crêpe de chine navy spotted dress with a

Chinese collar, a nipped-in waist that made her look like a very slender hourglass and a swirling skirt. The only fly in the sartorial ointment was the lack of shoes. Diana's feet were much bigger than Lily's, too big for them to share shoes, so Lily would have to wear her hospital shoes, a pair of brown lace-ups sturdy enough to walk from London to the church.

"You'll still look smashing," Maisie had said loyally when they'd tried on their respective outfits.

With Diana's great-aunt's jade earrings bringing out the hints of viridian in her eyes, and her chestnut hair a mass of glossy curls, Lily knew she would look her best. But the shoes would not be the only thing to give it away.

Servants were far greater snobs than their masters and the person who'd said a good butler could ascertain a person's social class from just one glance had not been lying. Lily knew that her background would be immediately apparent to all belowstairs at Beltonward.

"Come on, girls," she said now, getting up from her seat in the sun. "Let's go out for cake: I'm starving."

Beltonward was Lily's worst nightmare. From the moment the old truck they'd got a lift on lurched over a hill and Diana cried, "Look, there it is," pride overcoming the politeness that made her play down her family's wealth, Lily felt her heart sink to the soles of her shoes. Beltonward was a vast mansion, built along the lines of the huge houses commandeered by the army, navy and air force as bases for their operations. The only factor that had left Beltonward in private hands was its location far from anywhere. It was perfect as a convalescent home for wounded soldiers, having acres of land for men to roam about and try to forget what they'd seen.

"Christ Almighty," Maisie said. "You must be a bleedin' princess, love, 'cause your dad would need to be a king to keep this place going."

"Oh, Maisie, shut up," snapped Diana, with an unheard-of irritability that showed Lily that she wasn't the only one anxious about the wedding.

Maisie shut up.

When the truck deposited them at the huge front door, two elderly gentlemen appeared.

"Daddy," said Diana, leaping forward to hug the shabbier of the two. At least seventy, with a few strands of silver hair on his brown, liver-spotted head, he wore a much-darned knitted waistcoat, a pale blue shirt and silk foulard, and an amiable expression on his lined, bespectacled face.

"Maisie and Lily, this is Daddy, Sir Archibald Belton, and Wilson."

Try as she might, Lily couldn't bring herself to call a man older than her father by his surname without some prefix. *Wilson*. No, couldn't do it.

"Hello, Sir Archibald, how do you do, Mr. Wilson," she said.

Sir Archibald's face didn't flicker but Wilson looked marginally shocked.

Oh well, thought Lily, in for a penny, in for a pound.

She picked up her small valise.

"Wilson can take your bags, m'dear," said the genial Sir Archibald.

"Not at all," Lily said cheerfully. "I'll carry it myself."

Beltonward might have been stripped of most of its artwork (the valuable stuff was in the enormous cellar, along with the dwindling collection of wine—Sir Archie was said to be desolate that all his precious hock was gone), but the building itself still held treasures. As Sir Archie led them inside, chatting happily to his daughter, linking arms with her, Maisie and Lily were able to look around a vestibule—far too grand to be a hall, Lily thought with a grin—with a huge staircase stretching elegantly in front of them. A few portraits still hung on the faded damask red walls.

Men with long Borzoi noses like Sir Archie, and powdered and beribboned women like poor horse-faced Sybil, stared down at them, as if to say, *Yes, we're rich and powerful and masters of all we survey*.

Plasterwork picked out in tattered gold leaf caught the light and the vast vaulted ceiling was painted with frolicking cherubs and goddesses scampering through sun-lit clouds.

Two giant cracked blue and white vases decorated with peeping Chinese girls stood at the turn of the stairs and Lily knew enough from Rathnaree to recognize that they were worth something.

"Christ Almighty," whispered Maisie as they climbed the marble steps, "I was never interested in marrying a toff, but I can see the attraction now."

"Not if you had to clean the steps yourself, you wouldn't," Lily whispered back, thinking of the yards of marble at Rathnaree and knowing that no matter how much money she had, she'd still hate to get another human being to clean her floors.

"Good point."

Maisie and Lily were to share a room and when they were alone, Lily sat down on one of the twin beds. The coverles were pure white quilted cotton. They were the newest things in the room. Everything else was very old and faded, including the heavy floral curtains and the threadbare carpet.

"Gawd, not quite the Ritz up here, is it?" Maisie said.

"Family rooms," Lily explained. "These are where family and friends of the children stay. The proper guest suites would be better, but nothing too showy. It's bad taste to have the place too grand."

"I would, if I lived here," Maisie sighed, opening drawers and poking around.

"That's why you and I would never make toffs' wives," Lily laughed. "We'd want round-the-clock heat, silk bedspreads like

Greta Garbo's and a Rolls-Royce, and the posh boy would want old curtains, no heating and us darning his socks rather than buying new ones. Rich people don't need to show off the fact that they're rich."

"They're odd, that's for sure," Maisie said.

They tidied themselves up to meet Diana's mother and the other guests.

"Mummy's in the little drawing room," Diana said as the three of them headed down the massive staircase once again. "She can't wait to meet you."

Diana had changed from her traveling clothes and looked younger somehow in a pair of old jodhpurs and a light jersey. Lily felt as if she were seeing a new side to her friend now that she was at home. Again she thought of her own home in Tamarin. She imagined taking Diana and Maisie there and showing them all the places she'd played as a child. The woods where she and Tommy played hide-and-seek, the stream where they'd lain on their bellies, dangling fingers in the cool water. She thought of introducing them to her mother, how they'd take to her instantly. Everyone loved Mam; she was so warm, so kind. Except her mother would be different with Diana because Di was one of *them*. Why did it matter?

The small drawing room was on the left side of the house, where the family lived, as opposed to the east wing, which was currently occupied by the sanatorium.

Diana's mother got to her feet and held out her arms as soon as she saw them.

"How wonderful!" she cried, with genuine delight. She was the image of Diana, only an older version, with the same sweet face, a dancing smile and hair dotted with gray.

"Hello, Lady Belton," said Lily formally.

"I do feel as though I know you, girls," she said. "I've heard so much about you, and how kind you've been to Diana. I can never thank you enough." She beamed at them with such warmth that Lily finally felt herself relax. Perhaps it was going to be all right after all.

Sir Archie, for all his amiability, was very much an old-style gentleman: charming, yes, but no doubt fully aware of his rank. But Lady Belton was much more in Diana's style: kind to all, irrespective of background. Lady Irene would not have liked her one little bit, Lily thought with amusement.

Dinner was "just the family," as Diana guilelessly put it. Lily, Maisie, Diana, Lady Evangeline and Sir Archie were joined by Sybil and her fiancé, the firm-jawed, largely silent Captain Philip Stanhope.

Sybil, two years younger than Diana and a million years away from her sister in terms of temperament, only wanted to talk about her wedding the next day, and fretted about her dress, the flowers and how awful it was that they couldn't have a proper society wedding because of the horrid old war.

Lily thought of the people who'd really experienced the horrid old war—people like Maisie, who'd lost her mother, and the young men in the other part of the house, battered inside and out by what they'd seen on the front line. Here in the idyllic world of Beltonward the war seemed a long way away. Sybil worked with the local Land Army, and Lily couldn't help wondering how Sybil went about supervising homesick nineteen-year-old land girls who'd signed up to help the war effort and found themselves miles from home, getting up at five to milk cows or drive a tractor.

"You come from a farm. You should join the land girls," Sybil said sharply to Lily, as if she'd been able to see into her head.

"Bit of a waste of my training, though," Lily said evenly.

"Yes, but you started in Ireland," Sybil said, as if that in itself rendered the training useless.

Lily felt the familiar flare of anger inside her. She dampened it down.

"I didn't, actually," she said. "I didn't nurse in Ireland at all. I worked for a local doctor."

"Sibs! Lily's a better nurse than I am," Diana said.

"If you say so," Sybil muttered, staring down her long nose at Lily.

"Where did you say you came from again, m'dear?" Sir Archie inquired.

Lily felt herself stiffen. She'd die, just die, if he knew the Lochravens. She couldn't bear a conversation about them, one that could only end with the realization that Lily had worked as a lady's maid at Rathnaree.

"Waterford," she said, which was correct, after a fact. Tamarin was in the county of Waterford.

"Oh, right," Sir Archie said.

After dinner they all retired to the small drawing room where Lady Evangeline sat beside the unlit fire to work on a tapestry of a unicorn in a verdant wood, and Diana, Sybil, Sir Archie and Philip played cards. Maisie and Lily, neither of whom liked cards—Lily had only said it because she was sure the games she'd played at home weren't the sort Sybil had in mind—sat on the window seat and talked as they looked out over the grounds.

Wilson, Philip and Sir Archie had assembled all the garden chairs on the small terrace beside the rose garden for the wedding party. The plan was to open the terrace doors so the guests could wander in and out at will. Sybil was still sulking because the convalescents hadn't been cleared out of the ballroom for her big day.

"Do you think she and the captain have done *it*?" Maisie whispered now.

"Sybil?" Lily shrugged. "Don't know. They don't look like they're at it like knives, do they?"

Philip and Sybil had known each other since childhood, and Lily couldn't discern any passion between the two of them. She'd seen some of the nurses come home from nights out flushed and with their lipstick kissed off, their hair disheveled. They always crept in—if Matron found them, there would be hell to pay. Lily always wondered what it would be like to feel such wild passion for a man. She didn't know if she'd ever experience it. She'd been out with men, of course, but she'd never felt the slightest passion for any of them.

"I'd sleep with my fiancé if I was engaged," Maisie said suddenly and surprisingly. Lily had always thought Maisie the most moral of them all. For all her Christ Almightys and jokes about frolicking with soldiers in backseats of the cinema, she had been brought up to follow a strict moral code. "He could go off to the front and you'd never have been together. At least if you were engaged and you fell pregnant, you'd have something of his if he didn't come back."

"I suppose," Lily said, shuddering. "There couldn't be anything worse, could there? Loving someone and having them shipped overseas to who knows what. How would you sleep at night?"

"Maybe that's why the three of us are pals," Maisie mused. " 'Cause we don't have sweethearts overseas. We're not mooning over men somewhere else, not like those girls who can't hold a conversation without turning it back to their beloved in Africa or wherever."

Lily laughed at that. "That's true," she said. "Besides, men complicate things. We'd have to leave the hospital if we got married, and we'd be out on our ear if we got pregnant." Neither was even a vague possibility for Lily. Romance was very low down her list of priorities; her job mattered most. And she worked such long hours that it was almost impossible to have a life outside the hospital, although other nurses managed it. Both Diana and Maisie went out to dinner and to the cinema with men, but she rarely did. "We see too many sick people and too much death. It puts you off love."

"Speak for yourself." Maisie laughed. "I'm still looking. Maybe there'll be some lovely bloke here tomorrow to whisk me off my feet."

"More likely some old duffer will get sunstroke and you'll have to sponge him down for the afternoon."

"Knowing my luck, you're right!"

The day of the wedding was every bride's dream: a sunny, cloudless blue sky without the fierce heat that would wilt the flowers begged and borrowed from every garden in the neighborhood. Lily was up early and she took a long walk through the gardens and into the pastures behind the house where a small herd of cows now grazed contentedly, swatting their tails lazily at flies. If she closed her eyes and breathed in, Lily could almost imagine she was in the fields at home with the familiar scents of the earth and cattle around her. She felt a pang of homesickness.

Back at the house, all was mayhem. Sybil's voice could be heard wailing about her hair and how someone had run off with her perfume.

"There was only a little bit left, and I was saving it for today!" she roared. "How could this happen to me?"

Lily and Maisie dressed quickly, and each fixed the other's hair.

"Yours is so glossy," Maisie said, standing back to admire Lily's rippling chestnut curls that she'd pinned up at the sides with two tortoiseshell combs. "Did you rinse it in beer or something?"

"Not beer," said Lily, grinning. "Perfume!"

"You're fibbing?" giggled Maisie.

"Yes."

"It would serve the horrible little monster right. I don't know how Diana stands her," Maisie said.

"Oh, she's not that bad," Lily pointed out. "She's just spoiled and hasn't seen very much. If she was living with us for a while, we'd rub the corners off her. A few days as an aide in the hospital would bring her down to earth."

"Thought you hated her."

Lily shook her head. "No, I was letting the chip on my shoulder bump into the chip on hers, that's all. I should know better. She's just a kid, really."

"You are a wise old bird," Maisie said. "Let's give Miss Uppity Knickers a chance, then."

"*Mrs.* Uppity Knickers after four o' clock," Lily added, laughing.

The chapel was indeed tiny and simple, with an almost puritanical stone altar and stone pews softened only by elderly velvet kneelers in old gold. Lily felt a gentle shiver of anxiety at just being there: Catholics weren't supposed to celebrate in other churches, she knew, but still, it was for a wedding, she reasoned. That must be all right, surely? She'd mention it at confession and be vague in her letter to her mother.

By four o' clock there were some forty guests assembled, including the vicar and a white-haired old lady seated at the organ to the right. Unlike prewar weddings, Diana had said, most of the family's friends would be unable to attend, and the few who could were simply rushing in for a few hours and then leaving again. With this in mind, Sybil was not allowed to be late, so it was only ten minutes after four when the bride appeared on her proud father's arm and the congregation let out a collective gasp. Not for her a wedding dress of parachute silk: Sybil's gown was Brussels lace, made over from a court dress of her mother's. She didn't have her elder sister's fair coloring or symmetrical features, or Diana's true loveliness, which came from within, even so, Sybil looked lovely on her wedding day.

The groom clearly thought so; his face softened as he turned to look at her. For the first time, Lily saw the face of his best man, a fellow naval officer. He was taller than Philip and for a moment his eyes met Lily's across the little chapel. Lucent gray eyes locked with Lily's startling blue ones, and she felt as if a little dart of fire had just lit inside her. Then his gaze was gone, and Lily was able to study him and catch her breath a little.

The ceremony was short and simple, totally unlike the Catholic marriage services that Lily was used to. When it was over, Sybil and her husband walked down the aisle, Sybil looking triumphant now that she'd got her man.

"I always cry at weddings," said Maisie, patting her eyes with a little lace-edged hanky as they made their way out of the chapel. "Don't know why. My mum always said I was daft for crying. Wish my old mum could see me now." For a moment, Maisie's eternal optimism appeared to desert her and her eyes shone suspiciously brightly.

"Mine too," said Lily, putting her arm around her little friend. She was lying. Her mother would be a bag of nerves to see her daughter hobnobbing with the aristocracy. "Your mum would be proud as punch to see you here," Lily whispered. "What's that thing she always said: Bless my . . . what was it?"

"Bless my sainted aunt." Maisie laughed. "Poor Mum never cursed, not like me. She'd have said, 'Bless my sainted aunt, Maisie, look at you drinking Gin and It with the nobs.' "

"May I refresh your glass, miss?" Wilson, still as stiff as a man with a poker firmly holding him upright, appeared beside them.

Lily felt the weight of his disapproval. Everyone else was lovely to Diana's fellow nurses; even Sir Archie was charming in that vague way of his. Only Wilson behaved as if they were two beggars who'd wheedled their way into the throne room to run off with the family silver.

"Why not?" Maisie drained the last of her drink. Straight gin and a full measure of Italian sweet vermouth: Gin and It, her favorite cocktail. "Thanks, love." She beamed at Wilson, her pretty face utterly unaffected by his stern demeanor. Lily envied her. How wonderful it would be not to care about the Wilsons of this world, to be blissfully free from that sense of not belonging. Maisie was comfortable wherever she was, the same as Diana. Both of them had an inbuilt sense of security that meant they never looked at anyone else and wondered what they were thinking. Lily never stopped.

Somehow Lady Belton had managed better than the two pounds of boiled ham that was allowed on ration cards for a wedding. Even though Sir Archie was very strict, even he had only muttered a little when Evangeline had got her hands on pork cutlets and some real bantam eggs for the wedding feast. She'd saved several weeks' worth of her own hens' eggs.

She kept four hens in the kitchen garden and looked after them herself. "I can't imagine Mummy looking after chickens before the war," Diana had said. "She's very resilient, you know. She can turn her hands to anything."

The eggs had made delicate egg and watercress sandwiches, while the bantams' eggs had been hard-boiled and were served with lettuces from the kitchen garden. There was no hope of having a traditional wedding cake so there were lots of little jellies with flowers for decoration and a tiny single-tier sponge cake. It all looked absolutely beautiful, and for once even Sybil couldn't complain.

Lily watched her losing her rigidity as she drank some of Sir Archie's precious champagne. It was a lovely day and people wandered out onto the terrace, sitting on the chairs to enjoy the mid-May sunshine.

Sybil and Philip had danced to a couple of waltzes first for the benefit of the older members of the party, then Philip's jazz records were played.

"I love this music," Sybil said dreamily as she whirled round in her new husband's arms.

Suddenly, their happiness got to Lily. Tamarin had been in her mind and her heart all day and she felt a huge pang of loneliness. What was she doing here? She took her glass and wandered out to the terrace.

When the war was over, she would go home. Whatever she'd been searching for wasn't here. At least at home she'd be among her own people, and if she felt out of step with them, well, she'd discovered that she felt out of step everywhere.

"Hello," said a voice.

She turned her head and found Philip's best man beside her, the naval officer. She wasn't sure of his rank: she'd never had Diana's ability to read insignia and battle-dress ribbons.

"Are you escaping too?" His accent was soft, a hint of a Scottish burr in there somewhere.

Lily gazed at him for a moment. She'd become an expert in saying the right thing—part of learning how to live in a different country was the chameleon ability to blend in. But at that exact moment in time she was fed up with blending in. Thinking of home made her sense of alienation spike.

"Yes," she said bluntly. "I feel as if I don't belong. I don't know anyone here except Diana and Maisie. I don't want to talk about old yachting trips in the Med," she added, her gaze on the bride as she whirled past the terrace door.

"War makes small talk difficult," he agreed, his eyes following hers and alighting on the new Mrs. Stanhope. "It's hard to care about trivialities when . . . "—he edited himself—"when so much is going on."

Lily looked at him with renewed interest. She'd half been expecting him to say, "Cheer up, old girl. Another drink?" As if blotting everything out with gin was the correct answer to all life's problems. But this man didn't have the gay, polished charm of Diana's officer friends, men who'd joke with that quintessential upper-class British charm even in front of the firing squad. He was rougher hewn, tougher. Even his wide square face with the flat prizefighter's nose and deep-set eyes gave him more the look of a peasant turned warlord than an aristocrat.

"My excuse is being an outsider, but surely you must know everyone here?" she probed.

"Quite a few of them," he agreed. "Philip and I were friends at school." He held out a big hand. "Lieutenant Jamie Hamilton," he said formally.

Lily stared at him. She took his hand and felt the same shot of adrenaline she'd felt in the chapel when he'd stared straight at her.

"Jamie, that and your accent tell me you're not from around these parts," she said to hide how jolted she felt.

"I'm Scottish, from Ayrshire," he said. "And you're Nurse Lily Kennedy from Ireland."

"Yes." She smiled. It would be plain to anyone listening to her that she was Irish, but she wondered how he knew her name.

"Difficult job," he said.

"Yes," she agreed, looking at him, "very difficult."

"Does it get to you?" he asked. "Seeing the injuries, the death."

Few people ever asked Lily questions like that. Perhaps it was because everyone in London saw the results of the war day in and day out. Plus the fact that most people would prefer to talk about anything else. Even when somebody died, the period of mourning seemed to be growing shorter and shorter, as if people were afraid to think about death. To acknowledge death, to linger over it, was too depressing; the only sensible survival option was to turn their faces bravely toward the next day and move on.

"Yes," she said to Jamie Hamilton now, "it does get to me. Especially the children. Last week two little boys were brought in—brothers, they couldn't have been more than ten or eleven. They were still in their blue-and-white-striped pajamas, looking like they'd just been plucked out of their beds, fast asleep. And they were dead, from a bomb. I keep thinking about them.

"It's four years since I started my training, and I think if I'd known then what I know now, I wouldn't have become a nurse. I had a misty idea that it was about helping people, giving comfort, being this kind being in the middle of someone's pain. And it's not like that: it's about desperately trying to keep people alive, all at a frantic speed, watching them die terrible deaths, being powerless a lot of the time. . . . I don't know how to describe it," she said. "But there's an adrenaline rush too, when you're working in theatre or on the wards on a very busy day and you've got to keep going because if you don't someone will suffer." She stopped, feeling out of breath from all she'd said.

"Do parties help you unwind, or just make it worse?" he asked.

Lily laughed. "A bit of both," she said. "It's lovely to forget about it all for a while and dance, and then I feel I shouldn't be forgetting about it."

She turned away from him to watch the dancers inside.

"I feel the same way," he said. "When you're in the middle of the war, you want to be away from it, and when you're away from it, you want to be there again."

"Where do you serve?" she asked him.

"I'm first lieutenant, second in command on a submarine. I was injured out a month ago."

She noticed he didn't tell her where in the world or how he'd been injured. Submariners, she'd heard, held their cards close to their chest.

"You work with Diana, don't you, in the Royal Free?"

She nodded. Two could play the game of keeping their cards close.

"Where do you come from?" he asked.

"A little place called Tamarin, in the south of Ireland. You won't have heard of it—it's on the coast, very pretty, very quiet, very unlike London."

"Why did you leave?"

"Because I wanted to be a nurse and I couldn't afford to pay for training at home. My father's a blacksmith and my mother is a housekeeper in a house not unlike this one, only not as big," she said. *I'm different,* she was saying. This is who I am. If you like me, you'll stay. But I won't pretend. I'm not from your world.

From inside they could hear the sounds of Maisie singing, "Doing the Lambeth Walk."

It was Maisie's party piece. She had a beautiful voice and would have them all dancing soon. It was a gift, the gift of charm and making people like her. Lily knew she didn't have that gift herself. She was too wary, too inclined to stand on the sidelines and watch.

Jamie was watching her now. She felt something inside her quiver at the way he looked at her, felt something shift.

"I think we're the only two people not laughing and joking," Lily said suddenly as great peals of laughter came from inside. "I'm surprised Sybil hasn't had us thrown out. She's very keen on the whole wedding being done perfectly."

Jamie moved closer so that he was standing right beside her. "I don't know about you," he said, "but I'm enjoying myself."

"Are you now?" she asked, moving past him. "I do hope you keep enjoying yourself, Lieutenant. If you'll excuse me."

She went to the lavatory, where she splashed water on her flushed face, then tried to repair the damage with a dusting of the English Rose powder that didn't really suit her but was all she had left. Her precious Chinese Red lipstick was down to the very stub and she used a hairpin to eke a last bit out to smear onto her full lips.

Bright eyes shone back at her in the mirror and she felt an unaccustomed surge of pride in her appearance. Her skin was flawless cream without a single freckle and it contrasted with the rich chestnut hair swept back from a fine-boned oval face. The spark of intelligence in almond-shaped eyes shifted her looks from mere prettiness to an arresting, wild beauty.

After she'd told Cheryl off, the other nurses had taken to calling her the Wild Irish Girl. It had been a compliment, she supposed, showing that they saw her as self-composed, strong and confident. She had something to be grateful to the Lochravens for. Watching Lady Irene had taught her the virtue of calm self-possession and Lily's determination to be different from every other member of the servant class on the Rathnaree estate had given her a queenly bearing.

"You're not looking bad, Nurse Kennedy," she told herself.

The gramophone was playing Glenn Miller when she returned to the drawing room, and everyone was dancing, determined to squeeze the last bit of enjoyment out of the day. It was nearly eight and she knew that many of the guests would be leaving soon, hurrying back to barracks or their postings before nightfall. The party was winding down.

Diana had whispered to Lily that the groom's leave had been canceled: nobody knew why, but there was some talk about a big offensive. Sybil didn't know yet.

"He's going to have to leave this evening. The honeymoon's on hold. Wouldn't like to be him, poor boy."

Lily stood and watched the dancing, breathing in the melody and swaying on her feet. She tried to shut out the speculation about the big push that would be taking the menfolk away. Whatever it was, they'd soon find out the hard way, when the casualties were wheeled in and a twelve-hour shift turned into an entire night with both shifts working in tandem.

"Do you care to dance?"

He was beside her, taller than she was, and suddenly Lily could think of nothing she'd like more.

"I'd love to," she said. "I'm not very good—"

She was too tall and most partners seemed to prefer smaller women.

"Me either," Jamie said with a smile that lit up the hardness of his face.

He was lying. From the moment he took her hand, Lily felt his rhythm and energy join with hers. It was like being sprinkled with magic dancing dust. The music was loud, all-encompassing, and they fitted into a space on the floor seamlessly. Lily wondered whether everyone else could see the electricity between them. Surely they must. Jamie's hand pressing into the intimacy of her back felt as if he was touching her flesh, stroking her skin erotically, and not the silken crêpe fabric. She could sense the great strength of his wrist as his other hand held hers tightly, and under his uniform her fingers felt powerful shoulder muscles move. It wasn't like dancing, it was like making love.

The music rippled to an end and they stopped dancing and stood staring at each other.

"Let's hear it again!" cried Sybil like a child, and someone scratched the needle over the gramophone record.

Lily hadn't realized she'd been holding her breath until the music started again.

"I don't want it to stop," he said, his voice close to her ear. Lily closed her eyes and allowed herself to be pulled closer. While around them couples danced with exuberance, she and Jamie moved as if to different, slower music.

She stared up at him as his dark eyes bored into hers, telling her that he wanted her just as much as she wanted him.

A whoop from behind made them turn to see Maisie being whirled by one of Philip's American friends, a blond army captain who was matching Maisie's fabulous jitterbugging, swinging her as if she was a doll, her skirts flying.

Seeing Maisie broke the spell. Lily gave herself a mental shake. What had come over her? She'd been around too long to dally with a handsome man in uniform. That wasn't her plan. And Jamie, no matter how attractive she found him, was from that other world, Diana's world.

"If you don't mind, I think I'll sit down," she told him quickly, determinedly not noticing the disappointment briefly etched on his face.

"Can I get you something to drink?" he asked, a mask of politeness up.

Lily would have preferred it if he'd said, "What's wrong with you?" But his type never would. That was the one joy of the upper classes: they took it all on the chin. A lad back home from Tamarin would have demanded to know why she'd stopped dancing.

"No, thank you," Lily said, just as politely. "I got a bit carried away there with the dancing." *And with you*, she wanted to say. "I think I'll sit the next one out." She spied Diana standing on the fringes of the group, watching and smiling. "Diana's a marvelous dancer."

"I know," he said, jaw solid.

"Good, then you know what a wonderful girl she is too," Lily added. She wasn't sure why she was doing this: urging Jamie to go over to Diana. But he was everything Diana wanted in a man and Lily loved Diana like a sister. Diana longed to be in love and Jamie was, Lily sighed to herself, special.

"You're sending me to dance with Diana?" he asked, mildly amused.

Lily felt a spark of anger at his amusement. What was he laughing at?

"She's probably more your type," she said. Damn, that sounded wrong. "I mean, you come from the same—"

"—background?" he provided.

"Yes," she snapped.

They'd moved away from the dancers now and were at the other end of the room where people were sitting in sofas and chairs, chatting and drinking.

"Is that important to you?" he asked. "Background?"

"I bet it is to you."

"Not really. Not with the right person."

"Good luck finding the right person," she said sweetly, then went to sit beside Diana's maiden aunt Daphne, who was stone deaf.

That would show him, she thought, shouting greetings at Aunt Daphne and all the while watching Jamie, who was still standing close by, smiling at her in a way she could only describe as wicked.

He caught her eye and one dark eyebrow lifted marginally, as if to say, *I see your game, my dear*.

"Lovely music," she shouted at Aunt Daphne, then cursed herself because poor Daphne couldn't hear very much of anything, much less the music.

"What?" screeched the old lady, cupping an ear with one hand while the other held a glass brimming with one of Wilson's Gin and Italians.

After half an hour of Daphne, and watching Jamie out of the corner of her eye, Lily felt some of the tension leave her when she saw Sybil storm by in tears. If Philip had to leave that night, she assumed that Jamie would go with him. When Jamie was gone, she could relax.

Fifteen minutes later, a red-eyed Sybil and the rest of the wedding party assembled in the vast hall for the leave-takings.

"I can't throw my bouquet," Sybil wailed to her mother, who was fussing over her, trying to dab at Sybil's face with a handkerchief.

"Chin up, darling," said Lady Evangeline.

"I can't!"

"Oh, darling, we'll have another party for your wedding, soon, I promise," Philip could be heard saying.

"Promise?" sniffled his bride.

"Promise."

"Poor bloke, I feel sorry for him," Maisie whispered to Lily. Maisie was definitely tipsy now, rosy-cheeked and sleepy from the cocktails. "Doesn't know what he's got himself into, I reckon. He'll soon find out."

"Here goes!" shouted Sybil.

"Girls, watch out!" shrieked Diana.

The bouquet was high in the air and then Lily looked up to see it falling, falling, right toward her. At the last second, she grabbed Maisie and shoved her in its path.

"Lawks!" squealed Maisie as the flowers fell quite literally on top of her.

Everyone laughed, especially Lily.

Then she felt a strong hand on her waist, gripping her body in the navy spotted crêpe de chine, the heat of the embrace burning through to her skin.

"I wanted to say good-bye, Nurse Kennedy," said Jamie, his face bent so it was inches away from hers.

In the throng of the crowd, they were pushed against each other.

Their lips met, fiercely and hot.

And then, in an instant, he drew back.

"Till we meet again?"

Lily could do nothing but look at him as the two men went out the door, comrades and relatives crowding them.

"Here comes the bride," sang Maisie tunelessly, waving her bouquet and putting her arm around Lily.

"Wasn't it lovely?" she sighed.

Lily's eyes were on the door where Jamie had been moments before.

"Lovely," she breathed, and touched her lips where he'd kissed them. She'd been kissed before but never like that. Why had she played stupid games with him? Why had she walked away when they were dancing?

She felt furious with herself. That inherent spikiness in her character had let her down again. Now he was gone and who knew when she'd see him again?

September 1944

Sybil had pulled out all the stops for her wedding party, part two, but even so, it fell short of the grand celebration she'd hoped for.

Instead of a formal dance, she had to put up with having nothing more than a small dinner party in Philip's grandmother's house in South Audley Street, a rather grand mansion that had been closed up since 1942, with every stick of furniture shrouded in Holland covers. After dinner, the party was moving on to The 400, a glamorous nightclub which Diana often frequented and where Lily had never been.

Lily was quite sure Sybil had only agreed to invite her to the party because they'd need an extra pair of hands to help with the cooking and the tidying up. She could imagine Sybil balking at the idea of Lily being a guest, and almost hear Diana, shocked, insisting that she wouldn't dream of asking her friend to help if she wasn't invited.

"It's going to be super," Sybil said blithely the day of the party, as she, Diana and Lily surveyed Philip's grandmother's house and tried to work out what to do first. Sybil had been there since the day before and appeared to have done not one iota of tidying up, Lily decided, looking at the layers of dust everywhere.

"We're going to be exhausted by the time we've made this house presentable," snapped Diana, who, along with her mother, was furious with Sybil for going ahead with the party in the first place.

"It's not safe in London anymore, Sibs," she said. "Even Philip says it's not safe because of the V-2s. I don't know why you wouldn't listen to Mummy and settle for a small party at home at Christmas."

Since D-day, even Londoners hardened to the sound of air raids had learned to fear the scream of approaching doodlebugs. And now there was a new, even deadlier threat in the shape of V-2 flying bombs, which came with no warning and left entire streets devastated.

For the first time during the war, Lily was in a state of constant fear.

"It's bad enough I had to miss out on a honeymoon. I'm not going to let this silly Baby Blitz ruin my party," Sybil sniffed.

Lily stopped what she was doing. "Listen, Sybil," she said, between gritted teeth, "I'm here on my day off because of Diana, not you. So please keep quiet about the 'Baby Blitz' because you wouldn't call it that if you'd seen its aftereffects in the hospital every day."

For once, Sybil shut up.

"Sorry," Diana muttered to Lily when Sybil had gone off to another room, ostensibly to find a vase for the late roses from the garden. "She doesn't understand."

"I don't know why," Lily said angrily. "I know she's insulated at Beltonward, but honestly, Diana, she must see what people are living through. You tell her what you see every day; how can that not touch her?"

Diana shrugged elegantly. "Sibs is like Daddy: she only understands something if it affects her directly. Don't let this ruin tonight; we all need some fun. Please, Lily? You're going to love The 400."

Lily allowed herself to smile. She longed to ask if Lieutenant Jamie Hamilton was among the guests, but didn't dare. She hadn't so much as mentioned his name since that night. She didn't want anyone, even Diana, to find out how she'd felt about him.

Anyway, if he was there, she thought, she'd ignore him. If he was that keen to see her again, why hadn't he made an attempt to get in touch? The D-day push that had put paid to Sybil's honeymoon was long over; he'd had three months to get in touch and he hadn't.

No, if he was there, she wouldn't even speak to him, that was for sure.

"Hello, Lily," he said that evening at eight, his voice just as she remembered. He was more tanned, and he looked wonderful standing in front of her in his uniform.

He was one of the last of the party of twelve to arrive: everyone else was standing around the dining-room table finishing their drinks. Thanks to Sybil's flowers and Lily's skill in laying a table, it all looked perfect. Diana had toiled away stewing the chicken—"Think it's rabbit, actually," she'd told Lily—that Sybil had brought with her from the country.

"Hello, Jamie," she said.

"I hoped you'd be here tonight," he said.

"And I am," Lily replied. She wasn't going to make it too easy for him. Once she'd realized he was coming, from reading Sybil's careful table plan, she'd felt her excitement grow.

"I wanted to get in touch with you," he began.

"Did you?" asked Lily lightly.

He nodded.

Lily watched him scan the place names and then reach down the table to swap names so that he would be sitting beside her.

"We can take our seats now," he murmured.

"Sybil will be very cross with you," she murmured back.

"I can take it," he said. "I'm only here for one reason and it's nothing to do with Sybil."

The quiver she remembered from before rippled through her body again and Lily had to sit before she fell.

She knew the protocol for elegant dinner parties well enough to know that for one course she was expected to talk to Jamie and for the next she was to turn politely and talk with the man on her other side. But Jamie was having none of it.

"Let's not bother with that," he pleaded with her when they'd finished the lukewarm minestrone soup served up by one of Philip's grandmother's old retainers, Mr. Timms, a frail white-haired man with shaky hands. Lily hated watching him serve them. *He's too old to be working,* she wanted to shout.

During the first course, they'd talked about the past three months of war and the chances of it being over soon. Now, her tongue and her heart loosened thanks to a glass of wine and a predinner cocktail, Lily wanted to ask Jamie why he hadn't written to her. But something held her back.

Instead, they talked about their childhoods, and for once Lily wasn't economical with the truth. The other guests faded away as they talked and talked. She told him quietly about Tamarin and Rathnaree.

"You're an admirable woman, Lily Kennedy," he said gravely at the end.

"Why does admirable not sound like a compliment?" Lily demanded.

In response, Jamie took her hand under the table and stared into her eyes.

"All right, you're a beautiful woman and I haven't been able to think of anything else since I met you," he said so softly that nobody else could hear.

Lily's heart skipped a beat.

There was an almighty clatter of dishes from outside the dining room. Lily leaped to her feet. It had to be poor Mr. Timms. Nobody else moved a muscle. The wine had been flowing freely, the gramophone was playing loudly in the background, and the rest of the party were enjoying this respite from war far too much to care what calamity had befallen the hired help.

Outside the dining room, she found Mr. Timms nursing a sore knee and the whole of the lemon syllabub lying in creamy globules on the parquet.

"Mr. Timms, let me see that knee," she said in her professional voice.

"Sit here," said Jamie. He'd followed her out and now led the elderly man to a chair in the hallway.

While she checked Mr. Timms's knee, Jamie managed to scoop most of the syllabub from the floor.

"I should strap it up, and then you'll need to rest that leg," Lily explained.

"I could lie down in the butler's pantry. There's an old pullout bed from when the butler before last was here. He had a bad back and needed to be able to lie down," Mr. Timms said, and then collected himself. "But what about the next course?"

"They can do quite well without another course," Lily said briskly.

Jamie took coffee to the laughing, chattering horde in the dining room and told them they'd have to sing for their syllabub.

"The plan is to go to The 400 in a few minutes," he said, coming back downstairs to the kitchen where Lily was washing her hands in the old Belfast sink.

"Did our hostess even ask after that poor man?" Lily demanded. Mr. Timms was now installed down the corridor in the butler's pantry.

Jamie took her hand lightly as if to lead her back upstairs: "I'm afraid dear Sybil isn't too worried about the welfare of others."

"Don't I know it," Lily replied grimly.

Suddenly, they were inches away from each other, holding hands. Jamie shut the kitchen door, leaned against it and reached out for her. Lily pressed herself against him and reached up with both hands to touch his face, while he wrapped his long arms around her body, tightening her to him.

Without a word, their bodies melded against each other. Lily felt her breasts hard against his uniform buttons and she wanted nothing more than to strip her clothes off and lie naked against him. His hair was silky and spikily short. Her fingers gloried in it, twisting, touching, then sliding down the strong column of his neck to find his uniform buttons.

He found the tender skin behind her ear and nuzzled there, making her moan with pure pleasure, and then his strong fingers were cupping the curve of her breasts, finding the buttons on the collar of her dress, sliding in urgently to find naked skin. They moved slightly and Jamie's hand reached beneath the satin of her brassiere to touch the hard peak of her nipple, on fire from his caresses. She gasped and leaned into his touch.

No man had ever touched her so intimately.

He opened her dress fully at the front, unbuttoning it so that he could see one heavy breast and take the rose peak into his mouth.

"Oh, Jamie," she groaned, and let herself fall against him.

Suddenly, he'd pulled her over to the kitchen table, a huge wooden thing with a scrubbed surface. He sat her on it and moved between her legs, so that he was imprisoned between her thighs. She could feel the scratchy wool of his trousers against the soft flesh above her stockings. His body was urging hers closer, so that her legs were almost wrapped around him.

Jamie was strong, vibrant and fiercely male: she could feel him hard against her, his body responding to hers in a primeval way. And she wanted him.

"You are so beautiful," he moaned, finding her mouth again and kissing her. "Do you want me to stop?" He was serious.

"No, no," she said. "I don't. I never want this to stop."

For a brief second, they stared at each other, the spell momentarily broken.

"I don't want it to be like this," he said gently, "on the kitchen table in someone else's house. But oh, I want you, Lily."

"Where, then?" she asked, her fingers instinctively caressing him, letting her hair brush against his face as her mouth traced the hard edge of his jaw. He moaned softly.

"I don't know. I won't be able to stop," he said, "if you don't stop what you're doing right now."

"We don't need to stop," she said, unable to believe herself. She, the girl who'd never been with any man, never let any man do more than kiss her, was writhing against this man, panting for him.

"We do." He pulled her closer and held her, enfolding her, as if by stopping her moving he'd stop his body's animal response to her. "Not here. Trust me."

"I do," she said, and she did. "I've never done this before." It was important he know that because the war had loosened many people's morals, not to mention their knickers elastic.

"I know."

"How do you know?"

He grinned. "I just do. Philip told me about Sybil's sister's friends long before I ever met you. The wild Irish girl with ice and fire running in her veins. And I can tell. There isn't a false bone in your body. I can feel it."

She laughed loudly, exploding with the humor of the situation. "You can certainly feel every bit of me," she said affectionately, wriggling her hips and feeling his body react instantly.

"Jamie, Lily—I hope you're not eating all the chocolates. Leave some for the rest of us, you greedy pigs!" It was Sybil.

"Jesus!" Lily struggled away from him at the sound of Sybil's high heels marching toward the kitchen.

"Nobody else wants liqueurs: they want to dance," Sybil went on, "but I've got to have something sweet after dinner."

She was getting nearer. How awful if she found them semi-dressed.

Quickly, Lily did up her buttons and smoothed down her hair. Reaching up, she rubbed a smudge of red lipstick from Jamie's mouth.

"Coming, Sybil," Lily said loudly. "Can't find the chocolates." She put her hand on the doorknob to open it. They were both respectable again, if a little flushed.

"Lily—" Jamie sounded urgent.

Lily turned the knob and opened the door. Four years of fear of Matron made her anxious about even being seen to do anything wrong. Whatever Jamie had to say to her, he could do it later.

"There's something I must tell you," he said.

Sybil was outside the door. "There you are," she said, smiling.

"Sorry, Sybil," Lily said, doing her best to sound breezily unconcerned. "I had to bandage poor Mr. Timms's knee."

"Really," said Sybil, and Lily could instantly tell from her voice that the other woman knew exactly what had been going on. It was so subtle, but it was there, and Lily felt the stain of embarrassment on her face.

Now Sybil linked one arm with Lily and held the other out for Jamie to take.

"I'm longing to dance," she said in a confiding voice. "You'll love The 400, Lily, it's such fun. She's never been before, Jamie. Imagine that? Jamie and Philip almost lived there once upon a time, didn't you, darling?"

They were at the back stairs now, and Sybil briskly let go of Lily's arm in order to walk up with Jamie because there wasn't room for three of them together.

Lily felt a sense of unease at Sybil's bright, acid tone.

"Some people prefer The Florida or the dear old Café de Paris, but I just adore The 400," Sybil went on, in a falsely wistful voice. "What about Miranda?" Sybil inquired. "Which club is her favorite?"

Lily's unease grew. Jamie wasn't saying anything; he was walking beside Sybil as stiffly as if he was at a funeral.

"Miranda is Jamie's wife, Lily. She's such a darling, we all love her. Such a pity she's stuck in Scotland, isn't it?"

Lily felt herself falter on the steps and Jamie looked back at her, reaching out an arm, but she drew back from him sharply.

Jamie was married. He wasn't free to make love to her, he was betraying his wife, and he'd just betrayed her.

Bile rose in Lily's throat. Irrespective of how it looked or how Sybil would gloat, she had to get away from him.

"Excuse me," she said, "back in a moment—"

She turned and fled downstairs to the lavatory, slammed the

door behind her and sank onto dusty parquet flooring beside an old, cracked toilet. There was no relief when she'd been sick: the nausea was still there. She felt so confused and empty. A lightning bolt had hit her. It was like nothing she'd ever felt before, and now it had been whipped away just as quickly. Except now she knew what it was like to feel that volcano of emotion, and once she'd felt that way, she couldn't un-feel it.

Her body still tingled with the rasp of his mouth on it, and yet here she was, crouched on the lavatory floor, alone and feeling used. She wanted to die. No; she wanted him to die. She wanted him to suffer the way she was suffering.

He was there when she came out a few minutes later. She'd been sure he'd be too much of a coward to wait for her, yet there he was: tall and concerned, not looking like the cheater he was.

"Lily, please let me explain—"

"Don't touch me!" she hissed at him, spitting fire.

"I wanted to tell you—"

"Keep away. I never want to see you again as long as I live."

She ran up the back stairs and into the dining room, where Diana, darling Diana, was waiting for her. There was no sign of Sybil. The rest of the party must have gone down the main stairs to the front door.

"I'm so sorry, Diana, I don't feel well. I'm going back to the nurses' home."

"What?" Diana was stunned. They had arranged with the home sister to stay in South Audley Street for the night: a special dispensation that had required a week of wheedling. And now Lily wanted to go back to their tiny little room in Cubitt Street.

"Please," begged Lily, looking anguished. "I'm sorry." She grabbed her small handbag and fled through another door, thanking her lucky stars that this house was so enormous, like a palatial warren. She made it upstairs to the bedroom she'd planned to share with Diana, then shut and locked the door. She didn't turn on the light but sat on the bed in the darkness, waiting in case Jamie came looking for her. Hopefully, if he asked Diana, she'd make him think Lily had gone back to the nurses' home. So she'd be safe here. Safe to lie on the bed, feeling the twin fires of shame and pain, and let the tears flood down her cheeks. She heard the huge front door slam shut. That was it, then: he was gone from her life forever and she could try to forget the white-hot heat of passion and how it had felt. She never had to think of Lieutenant Jamie Hamilton ever again.

fifteen

There was nothing more beautiful than the sight of New York's skyscrapers soaring into the sky on a sunny morning, Izzie decided as she sat in the back of the cab. She loved New York, even loved this patchouli-scented cab with its dangling beads that rattled off every surface like mini-castanets for the entire trip.

The city spoke of fresh starts—it was impossible to come here without starting again, without thinking of reinvention. In New York you could be anyone you wanted to be.

And from now on, Izzie vowed, she was going to be a totally different person from the Izzie Silver of three weeks ago.

She'd thought about it on the long flight across the Atlantic, hemmed in between two chatty German girls on their first trip to America.

They were going to see so much, do so much, and Izzie naturally thought of herself ten years ago and her plans. What exactly had she done in those ten years but get caught up in the sort of bullshit that was the same the world over—trying to fit in, trying to make money, trying to catch some impossible dream. Doing it, she'd lost sight of all the things that mattered, and she'd become a victim, tossed along on the storm.

She'd let everyone down: darling Mum, who'd wanted her to be happy; Dad, who thought only the best of her; and Gran, who'd taught her to be strong, honest and courageous. Dear Gran. It was hard to think of her lying in that hospital bed without any light or expression in her eyes. After three weeks in Tamarin, waiting for her to wake up again, Izzie had realized that her beloved grandmother might never wake up again.

But despite the pain of all the things left unsaid, Izzie knew she couldn't fail Gran now. She'd start again in her life and do it all right this time. She had a second chance and she didn't want to screw it up. The first change was going to be Joe. She'd been hoping for what could never happen and crying into her pillow when it didn't. No more. It was over between them, but not with her as the wronged heroine, screeching pain at him. It would be over in a dignified manner.

Her apartment felt like an icebox when she opened the door. The air-conditioning was playing up again. Switching it off, she phoned the super to get him to look at the unit, then opened the windows to let a little summer morning heat in.

By the time the super arrived, she'd unpacked, piled her dirty laundry into a bag for the launderette and stripped off her traveling clothes for a pair of sweatpants and a T-shirt.

"Hey, Tony, thanks for coming so quickly."

"No problemo," Tony replied, and set to work.

"You want coffee?"

"Yeah, cream no sugar, please."

While the coffee brewed, Izzie clicked on her answering machine to pick up her messages.

There were a couple from friends she hadn't got round to telling she was out of town, a cold call from a telemarketer and one from Joe. He'd stopped phoning her cell phone when she was in Ireland after his first five calls went unanswered. This message was from last night.

"Hi, Izzie. I hear you're home tomorrow . . ."

How had he heard that?

"I wanted to say hi and I'm thinking about you, honey. Please call me when you get back."

"I've got to get another tool," said Tony, shuffling into the hall. "Back in a moment."

"Yeah, sure," she said absently.

She'd removed Joe's cell phone number from her speed dial, but she knew it by heart anyhow. She keyed the number in and thought about pressing the Dial button.

What would she say: *Bye, and it was fun knowing you?*

No. She pressed Cancel, put the phone down and poured the coffee.

Carla arrived at half nine on her way to work with pastries from the deli on 29th and some gossip magazines.

"Sustenance," she said, dumping it all on the coffee table. "I figured you wouldn't have gone to the market yet to stock up." She hugged her friend tightly. "How are you?"

"I'm fine," Izzie said, and immediately began to cry.

"Oh, baby girl, cry," sighed Carla. "I knew you sounded too perky last time on the phone. How's your granny?"

"Still in no-no land," Izzie sobbed. "She's just lying there in the bed. Within the next week they'll move her into a nursing home. The longer she's in a coma, the less chance she has of coming out of it. That's all that's left for her now: she'll be left in a bed in a home, and I can't bear to think about it. It's such a horrible end to her life. She deserves so much more. . . ."

The apartment phone rang and Carla automatically got up to answer it.

"Yes? OK, who's calling?" Carla's sharp intake of breath made Izzie look up. "No, you can't talk to Izzie, you asshole. She can do without you right now. She needed you three weeks ago, and you couldn't be there, so don't think you can skip the queue this time. . . ."

Joe. Nobody else could make Carla sound so furious.

"Let me talk to him," Izzie said, holding out her hand for the phone. "I'm OK, honest," she added.

Grudgingly, Carla handed over the phone.

"Hello?" Izzie said.

"Hello, you," he replied, soft as honey.

His voice was so comforting and she felt that pang of knowing that she'd have to turn her back on its comfort. Or it would kill her. What was the point of living a half life with a man who'd never be hers? Endless sacrifices, being on her own for every Christmas, squirreling time away on birthdays, taking trips where they'd know nobody, going to off-the-grid restaurants in case someone walked up to either one of them and said "Hello!" in a knowing tone. She knew what their future held if Joe stayed in his tangled-up life, and she didn't want that.

She knew it would ultimately destroy her. And them.

"What do you want, Joe?" she asked tiredly, as if she'd lived out her thoughts in real time and was suffering from exhaustion.

"To see you and hold you," he replied.

"You know what's wrong with you?" she asked. "You say all the right things at the right time and it's killing me, Joe. Why can't you be a straightforward bastard and let me hate you? It would be easier for me that way."

"Do you think I'm a bastard?" he said.

"Yes," she said candidly. "I do. You came into this game with a loaded deck and I have only myself to blame for playing along. I wish I hadn't."

"Can I come round?"

Straight to the point—the captain of industry who realized he was on to a loser and knew that taking the meeting in person would work.

Izzie didn't have the energy to fight. "Yes." She sighed, and hung up.

"You got rid of him?" Carla asked.

"Not exactly—"

"He's not coming here, I hope. Because if he is, I'll give the son of a bitch something to remember me by—"

"Carla, don't. I'm going to tell him it's over."

"Hope so. He doesn't deserve to have two women fighting

over him, and that's what'll happen, Izzie. Men like him want to have their cake and eat it. He wants you *and* Mrs. Charity Lunch Bitch."

Izzie laughed. "Thank you," she said.

"For what?"

"For hating his wife even though she's done nothing to either of us."

"I'm just following the script," Carla said, grinning. "The girlfriend's girlfriends have to diss the wife and say she's a heartless hustler who's in it for the money, and the wife's girlfriends have to say exactly the same thing."

"Oh. I thought we were mold breakers and did things a new way," Izzie remarked.

"Sorry, girlfriend, there ain't nothing mold breaking about this story. You think prostitution's the oldest game around? No, baybee, it's the love triangle."

"I'm a cliché, huh?"

"'Fraid so. Tell me, does Uptown Man have a key, or can we hit the grocery store and come back safely?"

"No key."

"Cool. Let's take our time and make him wait."

Joe was sitting in her apartment chatting with Tony, the super, when they got back.

Izzie still felt her heart jump when she saw him, and even the disapproving presence of Carla and her own vow that she wouldn't touch him couldn't stop her moving toward him to kiss him.

"Honey, I've missed you," he murmured, holding her tightly.

Briefly, Izzie let herself relax into him, sucking comfort from his presence. Then she pulled back. She shouldn't have let him come round. She could never resist him in person.

"You must be Joe," said Carla.

"And you're Carla—pleased to meet you," Joe said, all charm.

She'd seen him charm people before but had forgotten how good he was at it.

Tony had finished up working on the air conditioner and he left. Joe settled on the couch, leaning back into it, long legs spread, utterly relaxed.

He chatted to Carla about Perfect-NY, and when she began to talk about their idea for setting up their own agency, Izzie silenced her with a look. She'd spoken to Joe about it before, but now, now that she was giving him his marching orders, she didn't want to talk about it in front of him. He'd only try to invest in the firm and then she'd never be free of him.

Finally, Carla got up to go.

"Work: curse of the shopping classes, huh?" she said. "Talk to me later?" she added to Izzie.

Izzie nodded. The two women exchanged a look. Carla shrugged; she knew it was no good trying to persuade her friend to send Joe home. Izzie had to do it in her own time.

"Just don't hurt her anymore," Carla said to Joe, "or you'll have to answer to me."

"I won't hurt her," he said.

Carla stared at him and then at Izzie. The look on her face said she didn't believe him.

They were alone again, and when Joe moved over to where she was sitting and began to caress the line of her collarbone under the cotton of her T-shirt, Izzie let him. This is the last time, she thought.

He brushed his lips softly across the silk of her skin and she felt her body curve under his caress.

The last time.

His fingers closed around her breast, making her liquid with desire.

The last time.

He kept her close to him, naked skin to skin, afterward. He didn't move to light a cigarette, just held her as if he knew what was in her mind.

"I don't want this anymore," she said, breaking the silence. "I want you, sure, but not everything that comes with you."

"We can work it out," Joe said, still holding her.

"No, we can't. I thought a lot while I was away—all I did was think," she admitted, "and I want what I wanted from the start, Joe: a proper relationship. You can't give me that and I was stupid to get involved with you in the first place. I knew something wasn't right."

There, she'd said it: what she'd barely admitted to herself until now. She'd had the strangest feeling that something wasn't right and she'd still hoped it might all work out.

"People being ill or dying always makes us think about our lives, but we can work it out—" he said.

"I don't want to," Izzie interrupted. "I love you, Joe, but I'm asking you to walk away from me, please. Leave me alone, stop contacting me."

"You don't mean that," he said.

Gently, she disentangled herself from him and the bedclothes.

"I do," she said sadly. She leaned down and put a hand on either side of his face, a face she loved so much. If she cried now she wouldn't be able to do it, and she had to. There would be pain and heartache for a while, but eventually she'd come out of it.

If she didn't end it, the pain would drift along for years and it would destroy her. She loved him and she knew she'd put up with anything because of that. Anything.

So now, while she still had the strength, she wanted him to leave her alone.

"Please go, my love. Just go."

He stared at her, his face expressionless.

"You mean it?"

"I mean it. There's no future for us."

"You're wrong, Izzie. This is special, what we have. It doesn't come every day, please don't throw it away. I just need more time—"

"It's not special enough anymore," she said sadly. "If it's that special, why do I feel so sad?"

He didn't speak as he showered and dressed, although several times she caught him staring at her as she sat on the bed and watched. Watching the man she loved preparing to walk out of her life was one of the hardest things she'd ever done, but Izzie knew she had to do it. It was her gift to herself, but, God, it hurt.

When he was ready, he turned and came to the bed.

"Good-bye, Izzie," he said, and bent his head for one last kiss.

At that brush of his lips, Izzie felt her resolve collapse and she bit out the words: "Please go, Joe. Leave me alone."

"If it's what you want," he said, "it's what I want."

He went. When the door shut, the apartment seemed to shrink to half its size. With him it was the center of the universe. Without him, it was a cage.

He'd left the thin navy silk scarf he'd been wearing, she realized. She picked it up, holding it to her face and smelling the scent of him, then sat cradling it on her lap like a talisman of their life together. Only then did she allow herself to cry.

Tomorrow she'd start her new life, but today was for mourning.

A month later, Izzie walked around the enormous loft, taking in the airiness of the space and admiring the high ceilings, pale oak floor and outer brick walls. It was the biggest loft she'd ever been in, and it looked like it should have either a ballet barre and a mirror at one wall, and a mirror at the other, or else it should be hung with vast canvases in progress and a barefoot guy in paint-splattered jeans with a cigarette in his mouth staring at the walls.

"Wow, imagine this as an apartment," sighed Carla, peering down at 34th Street below.

"Nobody could afford this as an apartment," laughed Lola, who'd found the place for the casting, and was busy setting up camp at the large desk beside a small, very old stereo system. "It's been everything from a gallery—"

"I knew it," Izzie said, thrilled to be right. She'd felt art breathing in the space.

"And some guy used it as a yoga studio. Asthanga? Whatever, I don't know—I get those yoga types mixed up. It's too big to ever make it as a home. The realtor says an ad agency is desperate to get it."

"Figures," Carla said, returning from the window to put her things down beside the table. "I can just see a group of anal-retentive ad types arguing over who gets the biggest desk space and where to put the basketball hoop, because they have to have a hoop so they'll look like homeys, even though the nearest they get to a basketball court is wearing Air Jordans."

"Do I detect a note of bitterness about advertising men?" Lola asked naughtily.

"Bitterness? Me? Not at all." Carla laughed. "But if the ad agency guys who are interested in this place are called Worklt Ads, then tell me so I can buy a couple of tuna steaks and hide them under the floorboards where a guy called Billy sits. Oh yes, and I want a standing order with the local porno video shop to send round dominatrix movies every afternoon. Come to think of it"—she paused—"Billy's probably weird enough to like that. Strike the porno movies."

Everyone laughed.

"Pity we can't afford this for more than a day," Izzie sighed, mentally shaking her head to get Joe Hansen out of it. It was a futile gesture. He inhabited her every moment and it hurt more than she'd thought possible. If she hadn't had the new agency to think about and all the organization it involved, she'd have gone crazy.

So much had happened in the past month. She and Carla had given in their notice, Lola had said she wanted to join them, and suddenly they were raising money, looking for premises and ready to cast their new models.

They had just signed the contract for the SilverWebb Agency's first office suite. It was lovely but the location was so perfect that something had to suffer, and that something was floor space.

There was enough room for reception, a small conference room and a four-desk office, along with a tiny kitchen area. But there was no space for a start-up casting, hence their presence in the former yoga studio.

"If there's anyone else you can wangle money out of, Izzie, then we can rent it," Lola said. "Where are all the *Fortune* 500 moguls now, huh?"

Carla shot Izzie a sympathetic look. They both had a certain *Fortune* 500 mogul in mind, but neither of them cared to phone him up and ask for a check.

"When a man's the answer to your question, you're asking the wrong question," Carla joked, checking to make sure the Polaroid camera was working.

Normally, on a casting, the models had their own portfolios and model cards. Today's was the result of a lot of ads looking for "plus-sized" models—Izzie hated the term with a vengeance as it summoned up visions of women too big to walk—so lots of the prospective models wouldn't have model cards. Both Izzie and Carla liked Polaroids for instant memory refreshing.

Izzie laid out sheets of paper and pens so everybody could write down their contact details.

"I hope we get a good turnout," she said to Lola anxiously. "There's nobody here yet."

"There's half an hour to go before the start time on the ads," Lola said. "It's only nine thirty. We said ten."

"Yeah," Izzie fretted, "but I've been to find-a-model castings where girls have been queuing all night to be first in line."

"That's ordinary models." Lola shrugged. "They're a whole different story. Too much caffeine and nicotine makes them jittery. Being normal makes you less desperate."

Izzie laughed. "Hope that's true," she said. It was so simple, it probably made perfect sense.

She thought back to her first casting years before when she'd been utterly in love with the world of fashion and modeling, and watched endless leggy gazellelike creatures sway in and out of the room, each one more beautiful than the last.

When one girl had erupted into tears as they looked at her and the panel had raised collective eyebrows, the girl had rushed from the room and Izzie had hurried out after her.

"It's the zit, isn't it?" the girl had said, shaking with nerves and misery. She'd pointed to an almost invisible bump on her cheek, which she'd expertly hidden with concealer. "I knew they'd notice it, I knew it. And I'm so fat. Look!" She'd reached down and tried to grab nonexistent flesh around her concave belly.

She wore tight, low-rise jeans that revealed her bones jutting out like knobs on a Braque sculpture.

In a shoot for designer clothes, with her hair carefully windswept and a dusting of St. Bart's tan over her body, she'd look amazing. In the flesh and with tears on her hauntingly thin face, she looked like a fragile child-woman. Izzie had been horrified at the girl's obvious self-hatred and by the easy way the other people on the panel were able to dismiss her.

"But she's so upset, Marla," Izzie wailed afterward to her colleague from Perfect-NY when they all took a coffee break.

"That's why we're not seeing her again," Marla whispered. "If she cries in front of us, what'll she do in front of the client? It's about more than looks, Izzie. She's got to toughen up if she wants to make it."

That was the first time Izzie had seen the reality of fashion. For her, it might be an exciting female-friendly industry where women's beauty and brilliance were prized. But it could also be cruel.

By eleven that morning of the first SilverWebb casting, Izzie knew she'd made the right move. This was genuinely unlike any other casting she'd ever been at. It was like being in the backyard of Goddesses R Us, where Zeus was trying to find the perfect example of womanhood.

Women of every shape and color crowded down one end of the loft, and whereas at normal castings wariness was a tangible currency, these women squealed and laughed and chattered at full blast.

"I can't believe I'm here!" shrieked one woman.

"This is what I've been waiting for all my life!" yelled another.

"I'm never going to be 00 but my daddy says I'm OhOh!" laughed a third.

"I'm going to get coffee."

"And cake?"

"Better get some for everyone."

Izzie and Carla grinned. At normal castings, diet soda, black coffee and cigarettes were the only staples. Here, muffins and lattes might work better.

Seven hours later, they had signed up eight models, and the last one was a triumph. Six feet, statuesque and blond, Steffi had been a school gymnast and cheerleader, but she'd always been too big for "normal" modeling.

She moved with the grace of a lioness and her face was poetry with a sexy smile that lit up the room. When they'd finished, Steffi had said she wanted to treat everyone to a drink to celebrate. Her boyfriend wanted to come over and celebrate too.

"Sounds good to me," said Lola, rubbing a stiff neck.

"Sure," said Izzie, who had nowhere else to be. It had been

a very successful day and they had another casting tomorrow: SilverWebb was due a little downtime.

"There's a nice bar around the block," Carla said.

Steffi, Lola, Izzie and Carla piled in the door of the bar.

"Hey, I like this place," said Steffi delightedly. She really was gorgeous, Izzie thought, and everyone in the bar clearly agreed with her, because they all stopped what they were doing to look at the tall blonde with the long legs and wide, all-encompassing smile.

"Now where will we sit? Over here by the window so we can see what's going on?" She walked over to a banquette by the window and sat down, beaming out at everyone, happy with the world. Her happiness was infectious. Grinning, Izzie went and sat down beside her.

"You do realize that every man in the bar is staring at you?" she asked.

Steffi laughed, a rich, sexy, throaty laugh.

"I know," she said mischievously. "And I like it! Hey, girls, let's celebrate my new career. I can't believe I'm going to be a model!"

"You should believe it," said Lola, sitting down beside her. "You've got a great look."

"You say the nicest things." Steffi squeezed Lola's arm happily. "It's gonna be such fun working together, and I can't wait for you all to meet Jerry. You're going to love him!"

Carla came back from the bar carrying a tray with four glasses and a bottle of white wine.

"This moment deserves champagne but this was all they had," she said. "I got peanuts too. Wine and peanuts are major food groups, right?"

"Right." Izzie nodded.

"Fantastic," said Steffi, grabbing a pack of peanuts. "I'm starved."

The three SilverWebb women looked at each other and laughed.

"You are so different from most models we know," Lola remarked.

"You mean that I eat?" said Steffi between mouthfuls. She even ate sexily, Izzie thought with admiration. "I hate girls who don't eat. Like, why?"

By the time Steffi's boyfriend, Jerry, arrived with a couple of his friends to celebrate, the girls had finished their bottle of wine and were dickering over the idea of ordering a second.

"Jerry!" squealed Steffi when she saw him.

He was tall, good-looking, maybe six or seven years older than Steffi and clearly besotted with her. With a brief hello to everyone else, he caught her and grabbed her in a bear hug, whirling her around the bar floor, not caring who saw him.

"I'm so proud of you," he said.

"Baby, right back at you." Steffi beamed and they kissed, slowly, with the burn of real passion.

"Way to go, man," said one of his friends, clapping.

"Isn't she something?" Jerry said, still holding on to Steffi.

That was when the emotion of the day finally got to Izzie. Gorgeous Steffi seemed to symbolize everything the SilverWebb Agency stood for: beautiful, real women who were at peace with who they were.

And yet finding Steffi for their agency highlighted just how much of an outsider Izzie felt and how badly she'd got it wrong. Steffi was hugging the man in her life on this special day and Izzie was sitting there smiling, drinking celebratory wine—knowing that when her glass was empty she'd be going home to an empty apartment.

Izzie guessed there was probably the same age difference between Steffi and Jerry as there was between herself and Joe Hansen, but Joe had never whirled her around in pride at her achievements or showed her off to his friends saying, "Isn't she something?"

Instead, he took her to quiet, out-of-the-way restaurants lest they meet anyone. She'd been essentially hidden, whereas Steffi was feted and adored in public.

How ironic that as one of the bosses of the new SilverWebb Agency, she was supposed to be the wise, clever one, running models' careers, yet right now she felt like the novice who knew nothing. Pre-Joe, she'd been so shrewd and sensible, but not anymore. It had taken Joe, and Gran's stroke, to show her that she didn't know diddly-squat.

"I have to go," she said, reaching around for her handbag.

"No," shrieked Carla, Lola and Steffi in unison.

"You can't," said Lola. "We haven't celebrated enough."

Then she corrected herself: "But if you have somewhere to go . . ."

Izzie thought of where she had to go: home, then maybe to the launderette. She needed to buy a few groceries. She was out of coffee filters and granola.

"You don't need to rush off, do you?" asked Carla gently, gazing at her friend with worry on her face.

Carla knew that Izzie had no vital appointments except with her television remote control.

"OK," Izzie said. "I'll stay for one more."

An hour later, Carla was getting on like a house on fire with one of Jerry's pals, and even Lola, who had never quite decided whether she preferred men or women, was talking animatedly to his other friend.

Somehow Izzie had got stuck in the corner seat and she felt like a spiky, uninhabitable island in a sea of loved-up couples. She couldn't do small talk anymore: she'd lost the knack, along with her sense of humor and her sense of knowing what life was about.

Two glasses of wine had given her a headache and she thought maybe some orange juice would help. She wriggled out of the corner, hauling her handbag after her, and went up to the bar, where the bartender proceeded to ignore her.

"Hey," she said loudly, "seeing as how I'm invisible, should I use my superpowers for good or for world domination? What do you think?"

The bartender turned around and she noticed, in a dispassionate, model-agency-scout kind of way, that he was pretty good-looking. Younger than her, of course: everyone was younger than her now. He was midthirties and athletic. Once upon a time, she might have expected him to flirt mildly with her but not anymore. Nobody was ever going to flirt with her again because she couldn't bear it and they seemed to sense that.

"Superpowers, huh? What sort of hero are you precisely?" he asked, leaning against the bar.

"I don't know, possibly Really Bad Flu Woman," Izzie said. "Or else Shield Woman, in that I have an invisible shield that keeps people away from me. It's a *Star Wars* vibe, very modern, very technological."

"Ri-i-i-ight," said the bartender, stretching the word out into several syllables.

"Yeah," Izzie went on. "It's an invisible shield and people bounce off it if they get too close, so they just stop coming. Invisible Shield Woman, that's me. Could I have an orange juice, by the way?"

"Do you want that with a side of Xanax?" he asked.

"Oh, what the hell, give me a side of Xanax too." She sat on a barstool. This was clearly the way her life was going to be: no relationships, but possibly lots of interesting, if strange, conversations with bartenders and waitresses. That was what happened to women on their own, she decided. They talked a lot to strangers.

"You're not feeling the party spirit?" the bartender said, slapping down the orange juice.

"No," Izzie sighed. "I have an antiparty shield thing going on too. Do you ever sit and watch people having fun and just not be able to join in?"

The guy raised his eyebrows. "I'm a bartender," he said. "That's what I do for a living—watch people party and not join in."

"Yeah, sorry," she said. She drank her juice quickly. "Could you send over another bottle of wine to the party crew in the corner?" she said. "I'll pay. I better get out of here before I destroy the atmosphere altogether."

"Is this a work party?" the guy asked.

"Sort of," said Izzie, and then the confessional nature of the barstool got to her and she blurted out, "We run a model agency and we've just had our first casting. Steffi"—she gestured over to where the beautiful blonde woman was sitting—"is our newest signing."

"Yeah, she's a fox," said the bartender.

The way he said it made Izzie feel about a hundred and ten years old. He was looking at Steffi with pure admiration. He hadn't looked at Izzie that way. Once, men in bars had looked at Izzie, taking in her curves and her beautiful hair, admiring the feistiness in her. Not anymore. Her feistiness and her attractiveness had all been sucked out by Joe.

She put some money on the bar. "Keep the change," she said, her voice dull, and she walked out quickly before anyone could see her go.

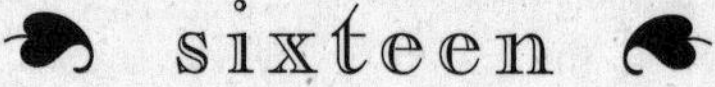

sixteen

Tamarin in late September was breathtakingly beautiful. Summer had been patchy with rain squalls, as if the goddess who ruled summer had been fractious, had thrown her toys out of the pram and cast a pall over weddings and barbecues and parties. Then in September, her mood changed, bringing glorious sultry days. The drive from Waterford meant a road that cut through a sweep of hills and suddenly Tamarin lay in front of you.

Jodi wanted her mother to sit in the front seat beside Dan so she'd get the full effect of the beauty of Tamarin when they arrived, but because Aunt Lesley was on the trip too, Jodi's mum had suggested that Lesley take the front seat.

"You're going to love this, Karen and Lesley," Dan said, purposefully cheerful as he looked back and winked at his mother-in-law.

Karen smiled at him but Aunt Lesley just gave her usual sour glare.

When her mother had suggested bringing Lesley on the much-talked-about trip, Jodi had groaned over the phone.

"Mum, please, no. I've wanted you to visit for so long and Lesley will hate it."

Three weeks of her mother was a pleasure for Jodi, but three weeks of her aunt would be the reverse.

"You know your aunt's been a bit down ever since Uncle Philly left," Karen said.

Jodi was only surprised it had taken her uncle so long to actually leave. The man deserved some sort of a medal for staying with her all those years.

"I've got to cheer her up, Jodi. She's my big sister, after all. We'll have fun, don't worry."

Fun and her aunt Lesley were not concepts that went together, Jodi decided.

"I'm sorry about this," she said to Dan later.

"Nonsense," said Dan, who took everything in his stride. "It will be great. If my parents come too for a week, we'll all have a blast. We haven't all been together since the wedding."

"Right," said Jodi. She'd planned to show her mother around Rathnaree and talk to her about everything from the miscarriage to the research she'd been doing, but she couldn't imagine doing that with Lesley.

Lesley had a way of trampling dreams and ideas underfoot. Jodi couldn't see herself sobbing in her mum's arms over the miscarriage with Lesley tapping her toe impatiently in the background. And she wanted to talk about it; talking helped.

She and Dan had gone to a miscarriage support group a couple of times and it had been the most enormous help. Just not feeling alone and hopeless: that was what made it so useful, Jodi thought.

But there would be no chance of talking with bloody Lesley here.

And then a thought had come to her: poor Anneliese was still very down, for all everyone else said she was getting over it and wasn't she a marvel. If she asked Anneliese to come round with her, Mum and Lesley, then things might be bearable.

Anneliese would be the perfect person to accompany them—a catalyst, so to speak, for Lesley's misery, and if she was with the three of them, then Anneliese wouldn't have so much time to spend sitting on the beach looking sadly out to sea, which was where she appeared to spend most of her time.

Jodi was worried about her, but unsure what to do about it.

"I can't very well phone Izzie up and say, 'Your aunt is crazy and has lost the will to live,' now can I?" she said to Dan.

"Tell Yvonne," he replied. "They work together in the Lifeboat Shop and Yvonne would know what to do."

Jodi thought of their chatty, scatty next-door neighbor and then of Anneliese, who didn't take too many people into her confidence. Jodi felt honored that Anneliese talked to her so much. Since that awful night they'd encountered the woman Anneliese's husband had left her for, they'd become friends.

"You've seen me at my worst," was how Anneliese put it.

Despite their closeness, she just knew that Anneliese would die of embarrassment if Jodi approached Yvonne about her behavior.

But she had to do something. The past couple of weeks, she'd dropped in on Anneliese to update her on the admittedly slow progress she was making on the Rathnaree history and each time Anneliese had seemed even more disconnected and distant.

The only positive in Anneliese's life was that she'd gone back to work in the garden center outside town: at least that way she met people. But Jodi had an uncomfortable feeling that this wasn't enough.

Everyone's life had gone back to normal except for Lily's and Anneliese's. Izzie was in New York, Beth was happy in Dublin waiting for her baby to come along, and even Nell and Edward had been seen walking through Tamarin one night hand in hand, a fact which had scandalized a good part of the population.

Lily was now in Laurel Gardens, a large nursing home on the Waterford Road and apparently wonderful. As for Anneliese—well, she was stuck, it seemed to Jodi. Her life was frozen, not going forward, not going backward, just stuck in a sad limbo.

"I know it's a cliché, but isn't it all so green?" said Jodi's mum happily.

"It's very small though, Karen, isn't it?" said Lesley. "The way you talk about Tamarin, I thought it was a big place, Jodi, but it's not. Sort of a two-horse town."

Jodi didn't look at her mother, but she knew that if she had, Mum would be shooting her an anguished "Sorry, but she is miserable over Phil" glance.

As Dan drove down through the streets of Tamarin, Jodi resigned herself to the fact that her aunt wasn't going to be impressed. It was so different from home, from the sense of space in Brisbane. Tamarin was small, its houses clustered together in a way that was so very European, so Irish, lots of dwellings perched close beside each other as if huddling for warmth against the wind and the rain. And now, with the sun beating down, much of the town looked quaint and otherworldly. There were whole rows of houses dating from the early nineteenth century, and the odd big house from a moneyed merchant. And farther in, near the harbor, were the fishermen's houses, tiny, cramped and yet so pretty with their sea blue doors.

Jodi loved it here now. Finding the photograph of Rathnaree had been the catalyst. Until then she'd stood on the edges of the town and hadn't become involved. And then she'd gone to Rathnaree, poor Mrs. Shanahan had had a stroke, Jodi had met Anneliese and Izzie, and somehow she'd become tangled up in their lives and in the lives of the local people. She had friends here, a life, and she loved the strange charm of the town. If Lesley didn't, that was her loss.

"Here we are," Jodi said brightly as Dan pulled up outside the Harbor Hotel. Tamarin boasted two hotels, a cluster of guest houses and several B and Bs. The Harbor Hotel was definitely the grandest of the bunch, although it was certainly in a different league to the Intercontinental in Sydney, which Lesley insisted was her favorite hotel.

Originally named The Tamarin Railway Hotel, back in the days when the trains had come this far out, it was a cheerful building, with long, wide windows, an entrance hall with two giant pillars and lots of flowers in pots going down the steps at the front.

Lesley glanced at it with a hard eye.

Cow, Jodi thought crossly.

She loved the Harbor Hotel. It was gorgeous inside, with a

"Laura Ashley meets the Ancient Mariner" style that meant lots of sprigged, floral soft furnishings and plenty of seafaring bits and bobs hanging around, including a giant fish hung over the fireplace in the lounge bar. Dan and Jodi were never quite sure if it was a real fish, despite the writing underneath it, or a plaster-of-Paris copy. It always looked far too vivid and cheerful to be an actual marine creature caught midbreath.

When the pair were checked in, Lesley said she wanted to go to her room and lie down. Jodi and Karen looked at each other again. Jodi wanted to sit and talk to her mother, but she knew that probably wouldn't be possible because Karen would be trying to take care of Lesley, who wanted no doubt to go upstairs and glare around her room, complaining that it wasn't what she'd expected and she was jet-lagged and, really, what on earth was Jodi doing stuck here in the middle of nowhere in some God-forsaken town that didn't even have its own airport.

It had been a source of great irritation that Tamarin didn't have an airport because Lesley set great store by flying. That didn't mean she enjoyed it; Jodi knew the flight from Australia would have been a nightmare, what with her aunt growling at the poor stewardesses because no matter what they did, it wouldn't be right. She glowered at her aunt. The excitement she'd felt over the past few weeks waiting for her mother was diminishing every second she spent in Lesley's presence.

"Lesley, you must look at this. I know you're so interested in boats," Dan said suddenly, and pulled her over to the wall, where there were several big framed pictures of old-fashioned ships coming into the Tamarin harbor. Darling Dan, Jodi thought, he knew her so well. He knew her aunt was annoying the hell out of her.

"Sorry, sweet pea," said her mum, giving her a hug. "She's just tired. She'll be fine tomorrow. We need a good sleep. It's been a killer trip. We should have stopped over in Hong Kong, but I didn't want to waste a minute more away from you."

"I don't want to waste a minute, either, Mum. I know Lesley will be OK when she gets some rest," Jodi said, which was a kind fib between the two of them. "I'm just so glad you're here. We're going to have a lovely time and I want you to meet all my new friends. You're really going to like Anneliese too. She's your age, actually."

"She's the one you told me about, the woman whose husband left her?" Karen asked. "How's she doing?"

"Well"—Jodi paused—"not bad on the surface, but you might be able to get more out of her, Mum. She might talk to you. I don't think she's coping underneath the brave face, and I feel sort of responsible for her."

"You crazy girl," Karen said fondly. "You're always getting yourself mixed up with other people and taking care of them, aren't you?"

When they got home to Delaney Street, Dan sat down at the kitchen table to go over some work for school the next day, while Jodi went into the small second bedroom she was using as an office. If it had just been her mother visiting, Karen could have stayed here, but Jodi drew the line at facing her aunt morning, noon and night.

She sat down at the desk and looked at her notes on Rathnaree and Tamarin. Jodi had just finished editing a book on Roman legends for her old employers and it had taken up a huge amount of her time, so the Rathnaree stuff had been shelved for a while. But she couldn't resist flicking through her notes again. Her work schedule was now clear. The Roman book was finished and she had nothing else on except spending time with her mother. She could quite easily fit in some more research.

Not that it had been easy so far. The only easy bit had been researching the Second World War to find out what life would have been like in Tamarin then. Everything else was hard: in fact, the only analogy she could come up with was that it was like looking for a needle in a haystack.

Originally, she'd thought that finding out all about Rathnaree would be a simple task: finding clues laid out simply on a path, a bit like Nancy Drew unearthing information at high speed with minimum effort. But it hadn't turned out like that. Instead of finding a great hoard of stuff, she'd found nothing but the odd mention of Rathnaree in newspapers and periodicals online in the library. It didn't appear to be mentioned in any books about the War of Independence or farther back.

She'd had no luck tracing the mysterious Jamie, either. There were plenty of men named James in the parish records, but without a surname or some clue of the link to Lily or Rathnaree, the paper trail was stone cold.

The fact that the first person she'd tried to interview had suffered a stroke had shocked Jodi into retreating back into the simplicity of the internet, but eventually she realized she'd have to dig up information the hard way. She needed to talk to actual people again.

With Dan's help, she'd drawn up a plan of action.

"Dr. McGarry is on the school board and so was his father before him," Dan said. "His father's got to be in his eighties, but I don't think much passes him by. He'd be good to talk to."

She'd never got around to phoning him. But today, with nothing else to do, she decided to make the call.

Dr. McGarry Sr. was thrilled at the notion of talking to Jodi about the past.

"Nobody wants to know about the past," he said. "It's all future this and future that, but we can learn from the past too."

"That's what I think," Jodi agreed. "Can we set up a time to meet?" she asked, her diary in front of her.

"I'm free now," said Dr. McGarry eagerly.

Dr. McGarry lived on the seafront in a tall narrow house with an attic converted so he could sit and watch the sea from up high. Jodi followed him up there carrying a tray of tea and biscuits. A very old spaniel waddled up the stairs between the two of them, and sank panting onto the floor.

Once the tea had been dispensed, the doctor sat back in his chair.

"Medicine was different during the Second World War," he intoned, and Jodi could imagine him forty years before, leaning back in a similar chair in a lecture hall with students listening to his every word. He liked telling stories, she realized. No wonder he'd been so keen to talk to her. "The war changed everything. Before, we didn't have penicillin. It's hard to imagine now, isn't it? There was sulfa powder—bless me, the old sulfa powder." He sighed and gazed into the distance. We put it on wounds to fight bacterial infection. It didn't always work, mind you. When penicillin came, I used to think of the people it could have saved. It was a wonder drug, really. We'd all heard about it and we were waiting for it, like a cure for AIDS today, I suppose. It was miraculous to us. Cut the rate of infection right down during the war, although it wasn't freely available outside the military until a few years later. It came into its own in Ireland in the fifties, you could say."

"What was the war like here?" Jodi asked.

"We didn't have a war here, such as it was," he amended. "Ireland never got involved. We were neutral, or neutered, as some people called it. What we had was described as 'the emergency.' Terrible bloody name. Apologies for swearing, dear. Afterward, when we knew it all and heard the stories, it was so limp calling it a bloody emergency. Millions of people died and we had an *emergency*. Very Irish. There was some rationing too, but here, in rural areas, we didn't go short for much. Forgive me." He collected himself. "I've gone off on a tangent as usual. Where were we?"

"Did you ever talk to Lily about her work as a nurse during the war?"

"A little," he said. "Mrs. Shanahan wasn't a patient of mine, but it's a small town and we met up. Medicine hadn't changed that much from the First World War, and I was interested in what she'd seen in London. Although she wasn't that keen to talk about it, to be frank. I've found that before: people involved in brutal times don't want to talk about it, and those on the periphery never stop.

"She worked as a theatre nurse and that was a tough job back in the day. A person would need to be in the whole of their health to handle that. Dealing with patients was only half of it. The surgeons weren't easy to get on with. Like kings, they were. Theatre nurses had backs of steel, we used to say." He thought some more, spinning his mind back to before Jodi was born.

"I do remember we talked about how surgeons used human hair for suturing sometimes. They did marvelous things then. The hospitals were run so well, of course. There was none of the cross-contamination or infections we get now. No MRSA, I can tell you. Hygiene was very strict. Those old-time matrons who ran hospitals when I was a medical student—well, we were all scared out of our lives by them. Not that you'd let on, oh no. We used to tease the matrons. Lots of joking got us through. My favorite joke was that the treatment was successful but the patient died. Gallows humor, I'm afraid, m'dear. Doctors are very bad for it. Tell me," he said suddenly. "What are the youngsters up in the hospital saying about her? Any use?"

"They're not that hopeful," Jodi said sadly. "It's very sad. Izzie Silver, her granddaughter, is devastated. It doesn't look like Lily's going to wake up."

"It's a pity," Dr. McGarry said. "She was a nice lady. Beautiful in her day too, let me tell you. When she came home after the war, she could have cut quite a swath through the town. There was no end of young men who'd have liked to put a ring on her finger, but she had no interest in going out. Then she married Robby Shanahan. Nice fellow; quiet, though. Could never see why she'd settled for him. She could have had anyone, the pick of the town and Rathnaree too. Still, people will always surprise you, and that surprised us all."

He talked for a while longer but he didn't have any more information. He couldn't think of anyone called Jamie at all, never mind one connected with Lily.

"Hope I didn't say anything I shouldn't," Dr. McGarry said finally. "My wife says the dog shouldn't wear the muzzle, I should." He roared with laughter at his own joke.

"No, you didn't say anything you shouldn't," Jodi assured him. "Just one more question: Why were people surprised at Lily marrying Robby Shanahan?"

"No reason, just a feeling," he said. "It seemed like an odd match, to my mind. I've had a flash of inspiration: you could talk to Vivi Whelan. She's got to be pushing ninety-five and if she's compos mentis, she'd be a good person to talk to. Back in the day, nobody knew what was going on in Tamarin like Vivi.

"Married to the butcher, you see, and the butcher knows everything because, one way or another, the whole town comes into your shop to buy their dinner." He tapped the side of his nose. "The butcher, the post office and the chemist: they're the places where they know everything that goes on in a small town. I think Vivi might be your best bet for solving this mystery."

As she walked home from talking to Dr. McGarry, Jodi thought about what she'd learned. All the stories certainly painted very different portraits of Lily Shanahan. From Izzie Jodi had the picture of a vibrant, strong and, above all, motherly person, who took care of her family with kindness and courage. Dr. McGarry had drawn a picture of a career woman who'd been at the top of her game during a world war, when the human casualties were unimaginable to modern eyes. What were the other sides to Lily?

In the second bedroom, Jodi closed the file. Tomorrow she'd bring her mum and Lesley to visit Anneliese and perhaps they could talk about Lily. Kill two birds with one stone, as Dan might say.

seventeen

Anneliese found a saddle of scrub grass on the dune and sank upon it, letting her legs stretch out in front of her. She was tired, bone tired. Walking normally invigorated her but now it exhausted her. Her muscles ached all the time and even climbing the staircase left her shattered. She wondered, could shock make you ill? Surely some of those autoimmune diseases hit people who'd been emotionally battered? Perhaps she should look them up on the internet.

Then again, why bother?

When she'd been thirty-five or -six, she remembered, she hit a very deep depression that coincided with Beth at her teenage worst. In time-honored tradition, Anneliese had managed to hide her own bleakness in order to deal with her daughter's problems.

Somehow the family had clambered out of the depths and Beth's outlook had been transformed when she fell in love with her first boyfriend, Jean Paul, and Anneliese had been able to relax long enough to think about herself. Standing still had done it: the depression hit her like a slow punch out of nowhere. It was more intense than it had ever been and the intensity panicked her.

Fear, bleakness and the abyss of her life gaped in front of her. Intellectualizing didn't help. There was no point telling herself that she had so many things to be grateful for, that she had a lovely husband and daughter, that this too would pass. Her mind took all the platitudes and considered them, and the big dark hole inside her stamped on them. Nothing worked, even the tablets.

Every morning, she dropped Beth at school, went to work and sat in terror all day. She decided that listening to music might help and put a Vivaldi tape on her Walkman. It didn't work.

Reading happy books might do the trick: she consumed every self-help volume she could find. That didn't work.

Seeking solace with God could be the answer: she sat in St. Canice's and begged for help, but none came. There were no heavenly beams of light falling through the stained-glass windows as a personal message for her. She was still lost and alone.

Finally, she took to walking. She walked miles and miles, burning up roads as she tried to walk the pain out of her heart because she wanted to feel better *now*.

And finally, slowly, something began to repair inside her.

The problem was that all those cures took a long time to work and Anneliese didn't have a long time. She wanted to feel better now. It was months since Edward had left and she still felt worn and battered by the black wave that engulfed her every day.

It was fear of life itself. Nameless, almost inexplicable fear of what would happen.

The fear meant it was better to stay insular, keep away from people and places so you wouldn't get hurt.

So many people had tried to help.

Dear Brendan invited her to dinner several times a week.

"I've told Edward he's a stupid fool," Brendan said to her, "and I won't have Nell here, no matter how long they're a couple."

"That's very kind of you, Brendan," Anneliese had said, "but there's no need to do that." She supposed that as someone who'd always championed women, she should point out that both Edward and Nell had betrayed her and therefore why should the punishment be meted out only on Nell? But try as she might, Anneliese couldn't be that forgiving. Sisterhood hadn't worked very well in the reverse, had it?

Yvonne phoned every day to say hello and on the days when Anneliese worked in the Lifeboat Shop, she insisted that the two of them have lunch.

"You could do with feeding up," Yvonne said, regular as clockwork. "You're far too thin, Anneliese. At our age, you have to choose between your face and your figure, you know, and if the figure's that thin, the face gets cadaverous. Not that I'm saying yours is or anything, but—"

Lovely Yvonne, she tried so hard.

Even Stephen in the garden center talked to her, and for Stephen, who made shyness into an art form, that was something.

He'd been delighted when she asked for her old job back, saying, "I'd love it, we missed you," which was practically a speech from him.

Anneliese couldn't help but realize that she'd only retired because Edward had been telling her to do so for such a long time.

"You don't need to work anymore, love, you've worked enough," Edward had been saying to her for a couple of years. Funny, then, that when she finally handed in her notice he hadn't seemed so keen. Probably because of Nell.

Beth had had her to stay in Dublin and it had been a disaster from start to finish. Beth was in baby mania and everything revolved around her pregnancy and what would come after. Lightning could strike down the houses on either side of her pretty little town house and she wouldn't have cared in the slightest—apart from worrying over whether lightning-blackened bricks were dangerous to her baby.

The moment she arrived at Beth's, Anneliese knew she'd made a mistake. She felt too raw, too sad to deal with her daughter.

"You see, the developers thought it would be easier if there weren't individual gardens." Beth sighed as she and her mother looked at the patch of scrub grass outside their home. It had seemed like a good idea when they had bought it, a couple of years before.

"It's not suitable now, of course," Beth added. "We need a back garden for the baby, even if it's only a sliver of grass, just so we can be outside. It will be such a pain to have to sell the place, you know, keeping it tidy every evening for viewings and everything."

"I know, it's annoying, isn't it," said Anneliese automatically.

She had been responding to a lot of her daughter's statements like that. Since Beth had picked her up from the train station there had been a constant monologue about all the difficulties involved in the new baby. The house was wrong, for a start. There were only two bedrooms and they really needed three, for people like Anneliese who would be coming to stay with them when the baby was born. Every time her daughter mentioned this in such a blasé way, Anneliese prayed that by the time her grandchild was born she'd have recovered some of her energy and enthusiasm for life. As it stood, she couldn't imagine taking care of a baby. Babies needed kindness and love, and Anneliese felt like a big slab of ice.

Beth's car would have to go: two doors were no good for getting a baby in and out of the back. Work was a problem too. Beth was a chartered accountant and it wasn't the sort of job you could do on a part-time basis—not in her company, anyway.

Try as she might, Anneliese couldn't summon up any enthusiasm for Beth's worries. It was odd. All Beth's life, Anneliese had been consumed with interest in her; no detail was too small. From her anxiety as a small child over having a book to read for book day to various worries over how she had done in her accountancy exams. But now, all of a sudden, Anneliese felt so distant from her daughter.

It wasn't Beth's fault: it was her. Edward leaving had suddenly sheared their family into three different compartments. It was as if in making Anneliese redundant as a wife, he had somehow made her redundant as a mother as well.

The depression added to it all too. Anneliese hated this feeling of distance from her beloved Beth and, damn it, she hated Edward for having done this to her.

"Are you OK, Mum?" said Beth as they got inside the house.

She hadn't asked this question yet, although Anneliese knew

it was coming. She knew it as soon as she set eyes on Beth and realized her daughter had noticed how tired and drawn she looked, and how she hadn't dressed up the way she might normally, if she was going to visit her daughter in Dublin.

For a moment she was about to launch into her standard "No, I'm fine, really," speech—the way the old Anneliese would have done. And then she changed her mind.

"No, Beth," she said. "I'm not fine, I'm not OK. I'm heartbroken."

"I wish I could do something," Beth said sadly. "I don't think I'm much help to you, Mum, I'm sorry."

"You're a great help," Anneliese said passionately. "But there is nothing you can do. There's nothing anyone can do. I just have to get through it."

"But if Dad came to his senses and came home, it would all be OK again, wouldn't it?"

She was like a child, Anneliese thought wistfully. A child hoping that Mummy and Daddy could get back together and everything would be the same as it ever had been.

"It's not that easy," she said. "Even if he turned around and came home now, I couldn't have him back. It wouldn't be the same. He's broken my trust and it's a very fragile thing, you know."

"He's sorry, though. I know he is," Beth insisted.

"Did he say that to you?" Anneliese asked.

"Well, not in so many words."

"Not in *any* words, you mean," said Anneliese. "This isn't something that can be easily fixed, Beth. It's over. We'll just have to put up with it. I'm finding it hard to deal with it, but that's my battle, not yours. Now, can we talk about something else?"

"Sure." Beth looked mildly shocked, but said nothing more on the subject as she showed Anneliese to the spare bedroom and began to outline the plans she'd made for the two days that Anneliese was going to stay in Dublin.

Sitting at Lily's bedside, watching her disappear, the idea of going to Beth's had seemed like a good one.

When she was there, with lots of outings arranged to cheer her up, she felt even more miserable. At least in her own home she could be miserable if she felt like it. There she'd be forced to smile and put a brave face on things.

She'd endured the trip, and on her return home she'd slipped back into her quiet life, working at the Lifeboat Shop twice a week and working with Stephen in the garden center on Saturdays and Sundays.

September was always an interesting time in the garden center. The crazy summer rush of people realizing that their back gardens were neglected was over. Everyone had bought the sand boxes and wading pools and potted shrubs to brighten up the gardens. September was a new beginning, school time.

It was time for battening down the hatches and tidying up after the summer. It was also the time to plant bulbs for Christmas. For years Anneliese had planted vast quantities for the Christmas market, and then last year she hadn't done it at all. She'd spent all yesterday sitting out behind the big greenhouse with bags of compost and peat beside her, along with giant bags of hyacinths arranged by color. There was something comfortingly familiar and monotonous about lining the pretty pots with crocks and then filling them up with peat and soil and compost and planting the bulbs carefully. White hyacinths were her favorite. There was something about the combination of the pale subtle green and those strongly scented tiny white flowers that she loved. At home she used to pot up two blue china bowls with bulbs and they'd always bloomed in time for Christmas. They were part of her Christmas decorations. She hadn't bothered doing any this year.

Her bones ached and she moved off the scrub grass, getting to her feet to walk the stiffness out.

Walking on sand was supposed to be springy, but she'd never felt that. Perhaps she'd seen too many bad films when she was young where quicksand lured people in so that they sank into it, drowning in sand instead of water. To her, sand was not as benign as everyone thought.

Gazing out at the harbor from the dune, she thought of the poor whale. The marine expert guy who'd tried to save her was still in Dolphin Cottage. Anneliese avoided him whenever she saw him walking that bedraggled big black dog of his. He'd done his best for the whale, though.

It was sad to see such a beautiful sea creature die simply because her sonar had become messed up and she couldn't find her way out to sea again. Like me, Anneliese reflected. My sonar was Edward and Beth and now they've gone and I have nothing. No safety, no security, no reason to be.

Did the whale drown? she wondered. Drowning was supposed to be quite comforting once you let yourself go—but how did anyone know that? Surely if you'd actually drowned you couldn't tell anyone.

Anneliese felt the texture of the sand beneath her feet change. She looked down and realized she'd moved farther down the beach and was now walking in sand drenched in seawater. The waves were out but suddenly a large wave swept in. She didn't move, just let the seawater surge over her shoes. It felt interesting not to step back, the way she would normally. The salt water slowly drenched her feet in their light running shoes.

It was a cold, gray day after a week of glorious September sun, yet weirdly the cold wasn't shocking. Instead, it was almost soothing, the soothing of nature's logic. You stood in seawater and it was cold, like a mathematical equation: $x + y = z$ and always would. Nothing else in life worked out so logically or mathematically.

Just to see how it felt, Anneliese walked a little farther out. The seawater lapped around her ankles now, on the bare skin under her jeans. She could feel goose pimples on her legs, and it still felt strangely all right.

The sea was the same as it always had been: vast and somehow not frightening any more. It was the rest of the world that was frightening. With the natural world, you got what you expected. It was so-called civilization that threw curveballs at you.

Anneliese stopped and let her mind flow around her the way the water was flowing around her ankles.

Would the sea embrace her? Would the cold numb her so that she no longer felt anything, just began to float? Yes, that's what it would do, what she'd do. People were animals, just organic matter, after all, so what could be more normal than going slowly into something else organic, being consumed by the planet? It would be like the whale dying slowly in the harbor. It made perfect sense.

People would be sad when they heard. Death was sad. But they'd get over it. They had other things in their lives, other people.

Beth had the baby. Anneliese tried to stop herself thinking about the baby, her grandchild. The baby was part of a future life and she didn't want to think about it. There was no place for her in that future, no place at all. She'd given everything she had to everyone else and now she was done, finished.

This was her choice.

She walked farther into the sea until the seawater came up around her torso, waves creeping up, wetting her clothes so that the water moved up over her breasts, reaching up toward her shoulders. It was cold. Walking in this way was different from running in when you wanted to swim or creeping in gently, screaming with the cold and laughing with people teasing you and urging you on. That's what she used to do at the seaside as a child.

This was different, and yet she wasn't afraid. The sensation of doing this was stopping her from thinking, and stopping thinking was what she wanted to do so much. Her mind was so full all the time; it never stopped.

At night it woke her up, tormenting her with the same questions and the same sense of hopelessness, and she wanted it to stop. No tablets could do that. Nothing could, not unless she was so drugged that she couldn't keep her eyes open, and what was the point of living like that? This was safer.

This would support her: the sea would take care of her. Suddenly, she couldn't feel the sand anymore. She was treading water and she'd have to stop that, wouldn't she? Because you couldn't drown if you were treading water. Or maybe you could and you just waited until you got tired, like the whale. She wasn't sure. It was so cold that she tried to stop and closed her eyes. The weight of her clothes and her shoes pulled her down and her head went under the surface.

Cold shocked her face. She could feel her hair rippling around her, like fronds of seaweed. What did she have to do next? She had a mission, a plan, didn't she? Every thought was slow, as if she was in an alternate universe, where real time took much longer.

She would close her eyes and keep them tightly shut and just *be*. That's all she wanted to do: just be. Not have to think, not have to move, not have to tread water. Just be and let the sea decide what was going to happen to her, because she was fed up of deciding.

"It's OK, I've got you," said a deep, frantic voice.

She was grabbed and the shock made Anneliese gasp, taking in a huge gulp of seawater. She coughed and began to choke, and suddenly fear grabbed her. She was in the sea, up to her neck in the sea. Jesus! Then she was being grabbed forcibly by somebody very strong. She was coughing so much and felt weak, but they were hauling her out of the water onto the beach where cold, icy cold, claimed her.

eighteen

She knew she shouldn't be making such an effort for a lunch with her ex-lover, but Izzie couldn't help herself.

When Joe had phoned and asked her to lunch, for one final goodbye, she'd agreed and had shocked herself by instantly wondering what she could wear so he would think how well she looked.

"I hope you're not going," Carla had said. She'd overheard the conversation because Izzie had taken the call at her desk. In SilverWebb lack of space made privacy nothing more than an amusing concept.

"Think of it as closure," Izzie replied.

Beautifully dressed closure, she decided, as she picked out a clinging wrap dress very like the one she'd been wearing the first day they'd met. It was over, she knew it was over, but that didn't mean she didn't want to look good, did it?

Besides, he'd chosen to meet her in The Amber Room restaurant, a sign if ever there was one that their relationship was over. The Amber Room was in the financial district and would be full of people he knew. Only an idiot would bring someone he was having an affair with there for lunch, and Joe Hansen was no idiot. This was final proof that Izzie and Joe were no more.

In the cab on the way there, she put on a coat of the richest red lipstick and layered gloss over it: war paint as modern armor. "I'm ready for you," it said.

And then she applied an extra-thick coat of mascara, because no woman could possibly cry when she was wearing mascara or she'd be left with spidery trails down her cheeks. Izzie Silver was not going to cry today. She mentally cloaked herself in self-possession as she walked into the restaurant, walking tall in her high shoes. The maître d' brought her to Joe's table. He was already waiting for her, and at first glance she realized he must have caught some sun recently, because his skin was tanned and it stood out against the crisp icy white of his shirt. As usual, he was impeccably dressed, but there was that hint of a street fighter under the cashmere elegance.

"Izzie," he said formally, and got to his feet, placing a sedate New York kiss on each cheek, the way he'd greet a friend.

"Joe, sorry I'm late," she said, even though she wasn't sorry at all. She'd been late on purpose.

They exchanged idle chitchat while a waiter hovered, took their drinks order and carefully laid Izzie's napkin on her lap.

"You look well," she said to Joe. "Have you been up to the Cape?"

"Yes, I went for a few days' sailing," he said easily. "The weather was fantastic."

Izzie thought how that would have hurt so much before, the reference to the family's place in Cape Cod. It still twinged, except now it was different; now she wasn't allowing herself to be hurt. He had a wife and children, and no matter what the state of his marriage, she was no longer a part of his life. He could go wherever he wanted: sail, get a tan, go to Acapulco and dance on the beach. It was nothing to do with her.

There, she could do it, she was over him.

"It was a lovely weekend," she agreed. "I flew to Washington to see a friend of mine—lovely girl, works on the Hill as a journalist. We came over from Ireland at the same time."

When Sorcha had phoned, Izzie had felt so guilty because it had been months since they'd met. The plans she'd made in Tamarin, to see Sorcha, had come to nothing because of the buzz of setting up SilverWebb. Luckily, Sorcha wasn't the sort to sulk or hold grudges.

"Good to hear from you finally, you mad thing, and that's great news about the business. I had this idea there was a guy involved somewhere and that's why I hadn't seen hide nor hair of you for ages," Sorcha had said on the phone when Izzie rang to apologize and explain how busy she'd been with SilverWebb.

"Well," Izzie deliberated, "before I started the business, there was a guy . . ."

"If you want to come down here and cry your eyes out with me, you're welcome. You do realize that for every eighty-nine men in Washington, there are a hundred women. Those are terrible odds. I'll be crying too."

"I won't be crying," Izzie had said confidently. "I'm over him."

Sorcha had said nothing, a very loud nothing.

"Good for you, Izzie," she said finally. "I don't believe you, but you sound like you mean it. Fake it till you make it, right?"

"Washington, what a great city," said Joe appreciatively. "I do business there sometimes."

She imagined him having meetings in elegant Washington hotels, power brokering with other moguls, which was the rich man's equivalent of paintballing.

The maître d' finally left after much table tweaking.

"You look beautiful," Joe said. His voice was different now.

Izzie glared at him.

"So, again, tell me about this new business of yours," he said, as if forcing himself to lay off the compliments.

Izzie grinned. She knew not many people slapped Joe Hansen down.

"Well," she said, "we've got a beautiful office space; there are three of us: Carla, whom you've met." She was sure he would never forget Carla and the day she'd snapped at him for breaking Izzie's heart. "There's Lola Monterey, whom you probably don't know. She was a coworker at Perfect-NY. And then there's me. We had our first castings, which were brilliant, and we're pitching for lots of work. New York Fashion Week gets under way on Friday and we're involved in two shows, which is quite amazing for a plus-size agency. But the tide's turning in terms of model sizes. They're exciting times for us. Also, I was working on this big contract with the SupaGirl! cosmetics people before I left for Ireland, and we've got some meetings lined up later in the fall to talk about the possibility of casting SilverWebb models for some of their products. It would be a big step for them, but if it works, fabulous."

"Could it work?" he asked.

"Absolutely," she said. "A couple of companies are using normal women to advertise their cosmetics. Mainly skin-care lines rather than the more lucrative makeup, it's true, but all it needs is somebody to take the plunge. A lot of people don't agree with using ultrathin models anymore, but skinny, beautiful girls have been selling products for years and most companies don't want to upset the status quo. We're offering something different, and while people might agree with us intellectually, the bottom line comes first."

"I think that's changing to an extent," Joe said thoughtfully, steepling his fingers. "There's a lot more ethical business going on, companies that have made enough money to be able to think ethically."

"Isn't it sad, though, that the idea of using normal-sized models should be seen as some affirmative action or an ethical move?" she said.

"Just don't forget about your bottom line," he warned. "If your business fails, you're not doing anything for anybody." He switched subjects. "Have you found any fabulous new signings, the supermodels of the future?" he asked.

Izzie smiled at him coolly. "How did I know you'd be interested in that?" she said. "*Cherchez la femme*, right? There's got to be a chick in this for you to be interested."

"I didn't mean it that way," Joe said. "I'm not in the market for another woman."

The waiter came with their drinks and there was a moment of fussing with glasses and rearranging cutlery.

"I just meant it from a business point of view," Joe said when the waiter was gone again. I didn't know this was going to be such a tough lunch." His words were cool but his eyes were anything but.

Izzie could feel him almost breathing her in across the table.

"It's not supposed to be tough," she said. "It's supposed to be about closure. I'm trying to say a civilized good-bye to you, to end it all," Izzie said. All the calmness seemed to have deserted her and the deep breathing she sometimes did when she was stressed suddenly appeared like a very stupid way to make yourself calm. He unnerved her in every way. She must have been mad to think she could sit with him for a civilized lunch when just being with him made her both mad and lonely at the same time. She wanted him like crazy and she must have been delusional to think she was over him. But even though she wasn't, she knew she had to end it or else she'd be sucked back in. It was time to put a lid on this box.

"You know what, Joe, I'm not blaming you for everything, don't get me wrong. I walked in, theoretically, with my eyes open. Except they weren't open, I wasn't thinking. I was so dumb, I didn't really register about your still being married and what that meant," she said, more to herself than to him. "Perhaps that's because I've never been married myself or had children; I didn't understand what was going on with you. I thought"—she sighed heavily at this proof of her stupidity—"that you'd sort everything out, the kids would be happy, you could start again. Am I dumb or what?"

He made as if to interrupt, but she kept going.

"When I went home to Ireland, my aunt Anneliese told me that she and my uncle have split up because he cheated on her. He walked out on her for the other woman. When she told me that, I felt . . . I felt . . . oh"—she held her fingers up to demonstrate, about two inches high. No, make that one inch high—"She was devastated and she had no idea what was going on until she found him and this other woman in their house. He walked, and that was thirty-seven years down the drain. It made me think of two things, Joe. One, that my uncle had the courage to deal with the mess he'd gotten into. And two, it made me think of the other person in this triangle—your wife. I never thought about her before. I assumed it was over between you, so she didn't count. But it wasn't over, was it? So she did count."

"It wasn't that straightforward," Joe said slowly. "It was complicated, Izzie, you know that. It was over with me and Elizabeth, still is, but it was all about timing—when I could tell Elizabeth and the boys—"

"Yeah, timing is everything, that's for sure," said Izzie.

"Seriously, it *is* about timing. I want to be with you, Izzie, I just need more time."

Izzie wasn't listening. "When I began to think about Elizabeth," she said, "I began to wonder why it is that the wife always picks on the girlfriend and never on the guy who committed adultery. The person who betrayed them was their husband, but they don't blame him most. It's as if men are wild animals who can't be tamed or trusted, and if they stray, you have to blame the woman who made them stray."

She stopped to take a breath.

"You betrayed both of us, Joe. You told me we had a chance, and you hadn't gotten round to telling her that it was over. I never thought I'd date a guy who was a cheater. When a guy cheats on his wife to be with you, he can cheat on you to be with someone else."

"I wasn't cheating on my wife," he said in a low voice. "I told you, it's over between us. Aren't you listening?"

"Aren't *you*?" she snapped. "My problem is that you lied to me. You wanted both of us, and I don't care whether your relationship with Elizabeth was over or not, that doesn't work. You can't love two people. I don't buy all that stuff about men being able to compartmentalize their love lives or that evolution has made them unsuited to monogamy. I don't think you can share a man—and I had to share you every day. I don't want to share the person I've fallen in love with."

The speech felt like a clumsy elaboration of everything she'd been thinking about, but even if it hadn't made total sense, she'd said it.

"You don't want to share me with my kids, then?"

"This isn't about your kids," she replied angrily. How dare he imply that because she didn't have children she didn't understand the love a parent had for them. She'd never said she didn't want children, damnit. She did. His, actually. She'd wanted his kids, but he'd never known that. "If you're half the person I thought you were, you'd want to be there for them," she said quietly. "If I didn't understand they're a huge part of your life, then I'd be Ms. Moron of the Year. That's not the issue. You had a choice: you could have stayed home quietly, lived your separate lives and been there for your kids. You didn't want that—you wanted home, kids, *and* me, the whole enchilada. Not fair to any of us, I think."

"You think I'm a shit, then?" he said. He drank some of his cocktail. It was clear and had an olive in it. Izzie knew he wasn't much of a drinker, but she could smell the alcoholic reek of a gin martini from where she was sitting.

"Yes, I think you are a bit of a shit, actually. You weren't thinking about anybody except yourself."

"I wasn't lying when I told you we didn't have a marriage," he said. "I never gave you any of that 'my wife doesn't understand me' crap, because I thought you were better than that. *I* was better than that. We were worth more than those stupid lines. But I don't have a marriage," he said fiercely. "When I got married I thought it was for life and it turned out not to be like that. I'm not a saint, I've had a few affairs along the way, but they didn't really mean anything. They were"—he looked her straight between the eyes as he said this—"just sex."

She recoiled in her seat.

"I figure it's no fun for you to hear me say that, but that's what they were: just sex, for the comfort and the gratification men get from sex. But you, Izzie, you were different. When I met you, it was like a light had come back into my life, a light that had gone a long time ago. I thought that part of me was finished. I thought that loving and kindness, wanting to curl up beside someone in bed and not move and let the day dwindle past—I thought that was over. I figured it happened when you were twenty-five and then it was gone forever. But with you, Izzie Silver, I got that back again. So that's what you brought me. And I guess you're right, I wasn't strong enough to do anything about it. I didn't have the courage to tell Elizabeth what we both know, that it's been over for years. I couldn't bear what that would do to our family because I knew it would be tough, dirty. Elizabeth wouldn't want a divorce—not an easy one, that's for sure. So I took what I could from you and I didn't give you what you wanted back. But now . . ." He paused. "Now I want to give you everything."

He'd been staring at her so intently that it was almost hard to look at him. It was like he was in court, making his impassioned statement to the jury, who were about to send him to the chair.

"What did you say? You want to give me what?" Izzie asked, confused.

"I want to be with you."

She blinked. "No, you cannot be doing this, Joe. Don't play me. I'm not some idiot you can fob off with words and then, ten years down the line, I'm sitting here in the girlfriend seat and nothing has changed."

"I'm not doing that," he said. "I'm saying I want to leave Elizabeth. Tell her we can't mess around with this separation thing anymore, that it can't be on and off all the time. I'm ready to make the break."

He reached out and held her hands. And in that startling instant, Izzie believed him because of the gesture. Her mind couldn't compute what he was saying because it was so unbelievable, but his taking her hand *in this restaurant*, a restaurant frequented by people he knew, where a person couldn't step in the direction of the restrooms without fifteen people noticing them—his taking her hand here meant something. It was a declaration.

I'm with this woman, he was saying, loud and clear.

"Joe, I don't know what to say."

"Say yes," he said calmly. "That's all you have to do. Say you want to be with me."

A month ago, she'd have burst into tears on hearing him say those words, because they were everything she wanted to hear. But now, after everything that had happened . . .

She hesitated. He'd let her down so badly when she'd needed him. Inside her still was the memory of flying home to Ireland, heartsick and lonely without his support. She could remember the misery she'd felt going to her grandmother's bedside after having heard the man she loved telling her he couldn't be with her.

Her grandmother's bedside had felt like church: Izzie had gone there to be absolved of her sins, to feel Gran's love, but there had been no blessed relief. Gran hadn't woken up, and Joe had abandoned her.

His betrayal had left a wound so deep that even with fresh scar tissue on top, it was raw underneath.

"Joe, I don't know if I can do this," she said. "I think it's too late."

To his credit he didn't gasp in surprise.

"I didn't think it would be easy for you," he said, "after I let you down before."

She nodded and then smiled slowly.

"Is that why you brought me here—to back me into a corner so that we'd be all over the gossip columns tomorrow and there'd be no way for either of us to back out?"

Joe grinned and his eyes lit with that sexy sparkle she still adored. She felt the magnetic pull of him and how easy it would be to say yes.

Joe Hansen wanted her. He wanted to leave home to be with her. And yet to do that, he'd have to tell Elizabeth, tell their children, pack a bag and walk out the door and leave his key on the hall table, or whatever passed for a hall table in his mansion on the Upper East Side. Perhaps he'd told Elizabeth already? No, she thought, he wouldn't do that, he'd wait to see. Joe was pragmatic. Wait to see if Izzie said yes; and if she said no, no harm done.

"Tell me," she asked, holding the stem of her water glass, "have you told Elizabeth you're leaving?"

"This is the million-dollar question, isn't it?" Joe answered. "No, I haven't. I was waiting to see what happened today. That doesn't mean that she and I are going to stay together if you say no, because it's over between us and there's no point in dragging it out any longer. This separation thing has gone on for years, on and off."

"You say all the right things," she said. She could recall having said that to him before. He really did say all the right things. It was like he could see into her mind and work out precisely what she needed to hear. Except once upon a time he hadn't said the right thing, and that's what she couldn't forget. She wasn't going to be a fool the second time around. She had to know everything.

"So tell me, this really being together: Are there rules?"

"Rules?"

"Second-family rules," she said.

He still looked blank.

"Rules like you want to be with me but no wedding rings, no kids . . ." Her voice trailed off; it was almost too painful to talk about. Children. Babies. Her baby. Damn, but the biological clock was powerful. Not so much a clock as a time bomb. Babies kept popping into her head, and now they'd popped into this conversation too.

She and Joe had never discussed children. Well, how could they? It hadn't been a relationship where they'd had the chance to talk about such things. Like a sports car, they'd gone from zero to sixty too fast for that type of discussion. She glanced up at his face and saw the surprise still written there.

"What—you had me down as a tough-cookie career girl who'd prefer a Fendi bag to a baby?" she asked, somehow managing to hold back the hurt.

He laughed. "No, not exactly. But I didn't think you were the maternal type."

"Not the maternal type," she repeated dully.

"I didn't mean—"

"No, that's fine," she said quickly. Too quickly.

He saw his mistake. "You never said anything about kids," he pointed out. "How could I know?"

"Did Elizabeth talk to you about kids before you got married?" she asked.

He thought about it. "Well, no—"

"But it was a given, right? She was going to be the mother of your children?"

"Yes."

"That's my point, Joe. We never had that talk, but you didn't even rate it as a possibility. What does that say about us and our future?"

"I don't really want more children," he said helplessly. "I have to be honest. Children complicate things. If you had them, you'd understand. And it would make the breakup even harder for my boys if you and I had more children. Added pressure. I'd hate them to think they weren't the most important people in my life."

She nodded. She was getting very good at this nodding at important moments when she felt as if her heart was breaking.

"But we can talk about it," he said. "I mean, I never thought—I don't mean we can't have any, it's just . . ."

"I think we've got a deal breaker," Izzie said tightly. "I don't want to walk into a relationship where the boundaries are mapped out because you've already been there, done that. I'm sorry." She began to get up.

"Don't go, Izzie," he begged. "We can talk about this," he said.

"Later," she said. She leaned over and kissed him on the cheek quickly, not lingering in case he grabbed her and then she'd really be lost, because Joe Hansen wanted her and when he wanted something, he went after it. She wouldn't put it past him to grab her and to kiss her passionately in the restaurant, with everyone watching. So she moved away quickly.

"As they say in all the best business circles, 'leave it with me,' " she said, and got to her feet gracefully. "I'll call you." And with that, she turned and walked out of the restaurant, conscious that a lot more eyes were on her as she left than had been on her when she entered. She looked straight ahead as if she was already thinking of her next appointment but instead only one thought was going through her mind: What was she going to do now?

There was only one option: phone Carla. She sat in the back of a cab, hoped the driver didn't speak English because she didn't particularly want to share her pain and dialed.

Her friend was between calls, between coffees and sounded irritable.

"When are you back in the office, Izzie?" she said. "It's crazy here today and the espresso machine's broken down."

"He's going to leave her."

"What?" said Carla.

"I said," repeated Izzie, "he's going to leave her. Joe is going to leave his wife."

"Well, paint me pink and mail me to Guam," Carla retorted. "I didn't see that one coming. Thought you were meeting him today to finish it in style."

"I was," Izzie said. "I was. I had it all planned and then I was halfway through my spiel and he said he wanted to be with me."

"Honestly, straight-up wants to be with you or just semi wants to be with you?" demanded Carla cynically. "Like, he plans to stay married to his wife and give you a better class of present to keep you happy?"

"No," Izzie sighed. "He never gave me presents in the first place. It wasn't that sort of relationship, you know that."

"Hmm, yeah," said Carla. "I'd have understood that better. Mercenary relationships have rules and I like rules. Well, if he's going to leave her, wonderful. That's what you wanted, isn't it? But you don't sound very happy. Why not?"

"He doesn't want kids, my kids," Izzie said flatly.

"Ah."

"Exactly. Ah."

"He said that?"

"More or less. More kids would hurt his sons, and he pointed out that kids change everything and if I had them I'd know that."

"Cute," Carla commented. "Cute to say that to a woman who doesn't have any. Tactful."

"That's what I thought."

"What are you going to do?"

Izzie rubbed her eyes. She had no idea what she was going to do. "Think about it, I suppose."

Think about what it would mean to go back to him, think about her aunt Anneliese too. Her thoughts ran to Anneliese often: How was she doing now without Edward?

"Do you love him enough to have him without the kid thing?" Carla asked.

"That's the million-dollar question, isn't it?" Izzie wished she had a crystal ball so she could find the answer. Did she love Joe enough to be with him knowing that she was giving up the chance to have children? He'd said they could talk about it, but she knew he'd been speaking from the heart when he said he didn't want more children. Did she want to have a baby with someone who didn't want a child with her?

"Well?"

"Well, I don't know," Izzie said. "You know, Carla, every time I think I have all the answers, they change the freaking questions."

"I don't know what to say, Izzie," Carla said. "Except come on in. I don't have the answers either, but hey, you'll be among friends. What do you say?"

"See you in five," Izzie answered dully.

When she got home that evening, the message light was lit on her answering machine. For a moment, she thought it might be Joe telling her he'd changed his mind, he loved her and would love to father her babies.

Eagerly, she pushed Play.

"Hello, Izzie, love." It was her father and he sounded very tired and old. "Sorry to be giving you more bad news over the phone—"

Izzie's hand flew to her mouth. Gran?

"—but your aunt Anneliese tried to kill herself today. Drown herself, I should say. Somebody pulled her out of the sea in time. She's in hospital. Edward and I were just with her." She could hear the shock in his voice. "Phone me when you get this. Love you, bye."

Izzie shuddered. Her poor darling Anneliese. Only today Izzie had been thinking about her and wondering how she was surviving without her husband. Izzie had tried not to think about that because she didn't want to compare Anneliese's story with her own. She didn't want to cast Anneliese and Elizabeth in the same role. She couldn't bear to do that. There was nothing about her and Joe that mirrored Nell and Edward, was there?

nineteen

The day after Anneliese Kennedy tried to drown herself, Jodi bought herself a pregnancy testing kit and when Dan had gone to school, she went into the bathroom and used it. She would never have thought of such a thing had it not been for her mother saying that she'd had a shock, and instead of doing any sightseeing the next day, wouldn't it be a good idea if the three of them did something relaxing, like taking spa treatments in the hotel.

"Sounds great, Mum," Jodi had said. "I'll go along to reception and book."

They'd been having coffee in the lounge and trying to plan their day when an acquaintance of Dan and Jodi's had walked by and told her the news.

"Trying to kill yourself is not the answer to anything," had been her aunt Lesley's sniffy comment about it. "Just as well we never met her. I don't like being around negative people."

At which point Jodi's mum had finally told Aunt Lesley she was being rude and why didn't she leave them alone if she wasn't going to be supportive.

Lesley, unused to her sister standing up to her, had stomped off furiously, leaving Jodi and her mother to talk.

Finally, Karen had suggested the spa treatments. "You need something lovely to help you chill out," she said. "I love those aromatherapy massages, they really take the strain out of your whole body. Lesley would hate that, though. She's more of a manicure person."

At the reception desk, Jodi had been put on the phone to the spa where she'd talked to a friendly therapist who'd listed their treatments.

"We've got a lovely mum-to-be special on this week," she added, "if that applies to anyone in your party."

Jodi had been about to say no, it didn't apply, when a thought occurred to her. She had a very clear memory of sitting in Dorota's with Anneliese and having to rush to the loo because her period had come. The cramps which always followed at high speed had made her feel so awful, she'd had to go home, and Anneliese had gone to the drugstore to get some painkillers for her.

That had been six weeks ago—one and a half menstrual cycles. Two plus two equalled baby. She felt the same wild burst of excitement she'd had the last time, but she felt fear too. The last time, she'd miscarried. She couldn't bear to go through that again.

"On second thought, could I book treatments for two instead of three?" she said to the therapist. "A facial, mani and pedi for my aunt, Lesley Barker, who's staying in the hotel, and an aromatherapy massage and facial for my mum. Eleven o'clock for both? Great."

"Mum, I've booked you both in, but you know, I forgot that I'm going to see this lady in the nursing home tomorrow—it's part of my research for the Rathnaree story." This wasn't precisely true. Jodi had been meaning to see Vivi Whelan for days but hadn't got round to it. Still, the trip would give her an excuse to get away from Aunt Lesley. Right now, between the possibility of her being pregnant and the sadness over poor Anneliese, she needed to be as far away from her aunt as was humanly possible. If she was pregnant, she didn't want her baby raised by someone else because she was in jail for manslaughter.

In her bathroom, she sat on the side of the tub with her eyes closed and then opened them to look at the little window. Two fat blue lines sat side by side. Two lines meant pregnant. Pregnant. Jodi sat with her hands clasped to her mouth and rolled the idea around in her mind. If only she could be given a guarantee that this time everything would be all right, then she might allow herself to feel happy. But nobody could give her that.

The meetings with the miscarriage support group had shown her that some people endured many miscarriages before carrying a baby to term. She didn't think she'd be strong enough to cope with the pain a second time round.

"Don't panic," she told herself, and put the kit carefully away in her knicker drawer. "Don't panic. Keep yourself busy and don't panic."

She gathered up her notebook and tape recorder. Seeing Vivi Whelan would be a good way of letting everything percolate in her brain.

Laurel Gardens was a long, two-story building surrounded by beautifully kept gardens. Anneliese went there every few days to visit Lily, Jodi knew.

"I came to visit Mrs. Vivi Whelan?" Jodi said at the front desk, wondering if there was a security system in place to protect the people in the home, and ready with an explanation about why she was there.

"Great. She loves visitors," said the woman behind the desk cheerily. "Go on in, take the first left down the stairs to the garden room and buzz there. They'll let you in."

"Er, OK," said Jodi, surprised at the lack of vetting. Anneliese had said it was a lovely place, but she hadn't mentioned this laid-back approach to visitors.

On the inside, Laurel Gardens was the sort of place a person might rest in very happily. It was decorated in soothing shades of apple green, soft classical music drifted out of a radio somewhere, the smell of baking permeated the air, and there was no roaring or screaming from discontented people. Instead, the doors were open to a large garden and residents sat inside on armchairs or outside under the shade of parasols. The staff wore white but they weren't bustling round like they might in a hospital: here, they sat beside their patients, talking, smiling, patting an arm here and holding a cup up for someone there.

"I'm looking for Mrs. Whelan?" she asked one of the nurses.

"She's over there, sitting at the last table in the sun."

Vivi Whelan was a rounded lady with little wisps of white hair curling round her face and a beaming smile which she presented to the world. A nurse was feeding her a bowl of cut fruit and as soon as Jodi sat down beside her, Mrs. Whelan said, "Sarah! Lovely!" and smiled at her with the distant benevolence of one who had long since lost touch with reality.

The lack of vetting at the desk suddenly made sense to Jodi: she'd had to be buzzed inside the garden room area and the garden itself was surrounded by a high fence. There was no way the residents could get out, and it soon became apparent that not that many people came in. The garden room was carefully locked because most of the people there were living in their own world.

Jodi felt sorry she'd never been to visit Lily now; she hadn't wanted to be intrusive, but now she realized that visitors were important in a place like this, proof that the people weren't forgotten.

"No, it's not Sarah," said the nurse gently. "Sarah was her sister," she explained to Jodi.

"Hello, Mrs. Whelan. I'm Jodi Beckett," Jodi said gently. "I came to talk to you because Dr. McGarry said you might be able to help me."

Mrs. Whelan nodded happily.

"I don't want to be here under false pretenses," Jodi said, directing her conversation to the nurse. "I'm trying to write a history of Rathnaree House. Dr. McGarry—old Dr. McGarry, that is—said I should come to see Mrs. Whelan because she knows all the history of Tamarin, but if it's not appropriate, then I'll go."

"Vivi loves talking about the past," the nurse said. "She doesn't have that many visitors, just her immediate family, so it's nice for her to have a new face and a chance to talk. You're not doing her any harm. The past is another place for her, somewhere she's comfortable. The present and the recent past are her problems. But if you want information, her daughter, Gloria, might be able to help. I'll give you her phone number."

Gloria sounded so bad-humored on the phone that at first Jodi assumed the other woman was irritated by Jodi going near Laurel Gardens and her elderly mother in the first place.

But it soon became apparent that irritation was her normal state.

"We've lots of papers of my mother's, all her bits and bobs. I'm fed up with dragging them around with us. You see, we've moved three times in the past five years," Gloria informed her testily. "My husband's job. When we got back to Waterford last autumn, I told him if he needed to up sticks again, then he was on his own."

"Perhaps I could drop in and talk to you sometime," Jodi said hesitantly.

"I don't know much," Gloria went on, "but I could give you a look at Mother's things. I'm at home now."

"Now?" Waterford was a forty-minute drive away.

"I'm a busy woman."

"Give me your address and I'll be there as soon as I can," Jodi said. In for a penny and all that. And she needed to keep her mind off the two blue lines on the pregnancy kit. Driving miles to Waterford would certainly fit the bill.

By the time she got to Gloria's house, Jodi was sorry she'd started. Despite her best efforts, all she could think about in the car was her baby and the miscarriage. She'd been mad to think of doing this right now. The trail to Rathnaree was bare and the flicker of excitement she'd felt at the start was waning. There had to be stories behind that wonderful old house, stories surrounding the people in the faded sepia photograph. But they were going to remain hidden.

Gloria's home was a semidetached house on a busy road near

the bishop's palace, and Jodi's sense of irritation with the whole project heightened when she had to circle the area three times to find parking, and then walk ages to find a ticket machine to pay the parking fee.

I must be mad, she thought as she finally pushed open the gate to the house. When Gloria opened the door and seemed pleased to see her, Jodi was a little surprised.

"You won't believe what I'm after finding," Gloria announced, ushering Jodi in.

"What?" asked Jodi, not convinced that it would be anything to do with her search. Already Gloria struck her as a bit of a fruitcake.

"I knew we had papers and stuff, but it's mainly old doctor's bills and X-rays and things. Mother's health was never good. But look at this: a box of old letters and all sorts of things. There's nothing valuable in there, mind. I looked. I was hoping for a diamond necklace!" She squawked with delight at her own joke. "Take care of it all."

"Oh, I will," Jodi said, her heart leaping as she looked at the box of papers and documents. Suddenly, the surge of excitement about uncovering the past came back to her.

"But I want it all back, mind. And if you do a book, will you say that you got all the stuff from me?"

"Of course," said Jodi, who'd have offered her own left leg at that precise moment just so that she could get her hands on the precious bits of paper.

"This is fabulous," she said, picking up an old newspaper clipping gently. Gloria had pulled it all out on the floor and Jodi quickly came to the conclusion that the best thing to do was to put it all away, take it home, and sit down and sift through it all carefully. She felt like Howard Carter, closing up King Tut's tomb and saying he'd come back later when he had more time.

"I promise I'll write you a detailed list of everything I found in the box," she said, "and I can photocopy stuff and take photographs of it and then you can have all the originals back." She knew the right way to document archaeological finds.

"It might be a load of old rubbish," Gloria said, "but it's the sort of thing you were looking for, isn't it?"

"Exactly what I was looking for," Jodi agreed.

Jodi had turned the second bedroom into her office and once there she carefully took out every piece of paper, listed all items and tried to organize them into chronological order. There were letters in a tiny, neat hand on filmy notepaper—letters from Lily Kennedy to her best friend, Vivi McGuire.

Jodi made herself comfortable on the office chair and began to read.

twenty

October 1944

Lily knelt on the bare floorboards in her thin cotton nightie, and through a chink she'd made between the blackout curtain and the window, stared out at the ghostly city in front of her. It was freezing; even on the surgical ward, always guaranteed to be warm, she'd felt the cold that day.

The ward had been short-staffed, and in between holding the hand of a man who'd come back from theatre after the trauma of having surgery for colon cancer, Lily had ended up on bedpan duty.

The patient, a corporal who'd seen action in Africa, had begun to cry the last time she'd left him.

"Don't go," he said, grabbing her hand weakly. He was pale under his desert tan, and although he'd insisted on shaving that morning before surgery, he already had stubble on his face, making him look somehow more vulnerable.

Lily knew she was no good as a nurse if she couldn't detach a little, but this man, drowsy and sick after the anesthetic, seemed so desperate for her attention.

With his coal black hair and sad face, he reminded her of her father: a kind man stuck in a difficult situation. When he'd been half delirious after the operation, he'd muttered constantly about the noise of the tank guns.

"Will I write to your family and tell them how you are, Arthur?" she asked.

His daughter worked in an aircraft factory near Slough and his wife was at home in Liverpool, taking care of their two smaller children.

"It would be lovely for them to hear you got through this and that you're getting better."

"Thank you, Nurse Kennedy," he said, choking back tears.

At the door to the ward, Lily could see Matron standing, her searing gaze taking in every patient and every nurse. It was nearly teatime and Lily had other duties to attend to, but when the two women's eyes met, Lily read Matron's agreement for her to stay with Arthur.

Matron was a woman nobody dared to cross, but Lily liked her for all that. Lily had been trained to work quickly and efficiently, and she applied those skills whatever the task. What was more, she never quailed under Matron's fierce glare.

Matron's favorite catchphrase was "Your best isn't good enough, nurse. I want it to be my best."

She never said this to Lily.

Whether it was taking care of patients or general drudge duties that came with nursing training, Lily did it all.

Diana definitely suffered more under Matron, who did her utmost to ensure that her few debutante nurses didn't receive any special treatment.

It was the first time Lily had realized that being born into privilege could work against you: nobody expected anything of her because of where she came from, but with Diana they anticipated a lady-of-the-manor haughtiness. It was unfair because there was nobody with fewer airs and graces than her friend. From sharing clothes to sharing her godmother's house, Diana gave everything she had, including her love and friendship.

The plus of being in their final year of training was that Lily, Diana and Maisie had been allowed, grudgingly, to live outside the nurses' crowded accommodation. Two weeks ago, they'd moved into rooms in a small house at one end of a mews just off the Bayswater Road that belonged to Diana's godmother, Mrs. Vernon. Quite bare, because Mrs. Vernon had moved a lot of her furniture down to her house in Gloucestershire, the house was, nevertheless, a blessing for the three nurses. Diana's parents owned a great town house in Kensington that had been damaged by a bomb during the Blitz and left uninhabitable: the three of them had gone there to rescue a few bits and pieces to make their new home more comfortable. Diana had thought of asking Philip's grandmother if they could take a couple of pieces of furniture from the big house in South Audley Street, but Lily had winced and said no.

"We've got everything we need here," she said, worried in case Diana suspected the real reason why she didn't want a single item from that house near her. South Audley Street meant Jamie, and Lily didn't want any reminders of him. He was in her head often enough as it was, without having to look at a chair or a table from that damn house to ram it home.

Lily's room in their new home was at the back of the house and looked out onto a small square of garden that she'd considered growing vegetables in. If nearby Hyde Park could host pigs and vegetables, she could supplement their rations with produce from Mrs. Vernon's little garden. But since they'd moved in, she'd changed her mind. They were all working such long shifts, and their time off was much too precious. It was far nicer to spend it lying on the couches in the drawing room, listening to the gramophone and occasionally, when they could lay their hands on some coal, lighting a fire.

Mrs. Vernon had quite a collection of orchestral music and Lily loved lying back on the couch, closing her eyes and losing herself in the music.

Diana had long since realized that Lily felt her lack of education badly, and she'd been more than happy to talk about art and literature, with Lily eagerly listening, keen to learn. The National Gallery's treasures had been hidden in caves for safekeeping, but once or twice they'd been to the lunch-hour concerts in the gallery where, for a shilling, they listened to great musicians.

Sometimes Diana talked about her life growing up, something she hadn't done much before because she sensed the vast differences in their lives made Lily uncomfortable. Yet now, in this house where they could relax, and having come through so much together, it seemed more apt to be honest about their lives.

"My best friend, when Sibs was small, was the cook's daughter, Tilly," Diana said. "We used to play hide-and-seek in the orchard, and sit in the nursery and play with my doll's house. I'd had governesses but I can't say I ever learned anything. Mademoiselle Chamoix was the best, and but she only stayed a year. Then, when I was nine, Mummy and the rector's wife cooked up a scheme where her sister, who was getting over a love affair, would come and teach me.

"Her name was Miss Standing and she was a bit of a bluestocking, but nice with it. She encouraged me to play with Tilly—she was a great believer in social reform. Of course, when Daddy found out Miss Standing was a Fabian he nearly died. Sent her packing, I'm afraid. After that, poor Tilly was teased over being friends with me, and she began to not want to come to play and I was left with Sybil. I didn't have many friends until I came out."

"What was it like?" Lily asked. "Coming out and all that?"

The question wasn't quite as unconcerned as it sounded: ever since Sybil's wedding, Lily had listened avidly for mention of Miranda Hamilton, or whatever she was before Jamie married her. Miranda Hamilton. It was strange that the name of a woman she'd never met had such power over her. But Lily found she could think of almost nothing else.

Jamie was foremost in her mind, but he was followed closely by the mystery of his wife, a woman from Diana's world of wealth and privilege.

"Who were your friends?" she'd asked Diana idly one day, hoping for some snippet about Miranda. Maybe if she knew about her and Jamie, the spell would be broken. But she couldn't say a word of what had happened between her and Jamie to her friend. For all her work in the hospital, Diana remained at heart very innocent.

"I keep hearing how it was all so different before the war, but coming from Ireland, I can't tell what's changed and what hasn't."

"Golly, everything's changed," sighed Diana. "Before the war was practically another world, Lily. I can't begin to tell you . . ."

But once prompted, Diana had gone on to describe a world that was indeed alien to Lily. She talked about being presented at court in a stiff satin dress with flowers in her hair, and dancing the night away with debs' delights in Claridges and nightclubs like The 400. The name made Lily feel sick: they'd been going there that night.

"We weren't supposed to go to nightclubs," Diana revealed. "But we all did. I liked The Florida best. It was so much fun."

Chaste kissing was as far as Diana had ever gone with a man, even now. Lily remembered in their early days of training thinking it was strange that a nurse could know so little about sex. Having grown up with farm animals all around, Lily had a working knowledge of what must happen between a man and a woman. Diana, in contrast, had seemed clueless.

"Nobody talked about you know what," Diana said. "All we were told about were men who were NSIT—not safe in taxis."

She was on first-name terms with dukes and foreign princes, had spent a year at a finishing school in Paris where she and ten other young ladies had been watched like hawks in case they escaped from their patroness's establishment, and had perfected their French and spent many hours in Parisian museums. As a young girl, she'd learned to dance at Madame Vacani's, where she'd met and giggled with other young, female British aristocrats of the same age.

There was no doubt in Lily's mind that her friend would marry one of the wealthy titled men from her world, but she was that rare creature: a person without snobbery. The difference in their upbringing genuinely didn't bother Diana.

Yet it seemed clear to Lily that the old world was changing—birth and privilege meant nothing to a person lying in blood after a bomb had hit. Bombs made no distinctions between the rich and the poor, although a wealthy woman might have a fur coat flecked with blood around her when she arrived as opposed to a poorer one who'd be in an old, darned wool coat over a nightie.

Lily shivered again in the cold. She was so tired but sleep was out of the question.

Nighttime was the worst, when Lily, exhausted until she lay her head on the pillow, replayed every aching moment over and over again, from the spike of knowledge that told her Jamie was hers to the agony of finding out that he couldn't be.

She replayed the scene in the kitchen again and again.

Had he been about to tell her . . . ?

"Lily, there's something I've got to tell you—"

And she could see the viciousness in Sybil's eyes. Amazingly, Sybil hadn't told Diana. Was it guilt at being such a cow, or did she prefer that Lily should suffer in silence? Lily had no idea.

Still, it was better this way, better that nobody else knew.

When Jamie's face haunted her, sleep was out of the question. Since that night, over a month ago, there had been many nights when Lily sat at the window both here or in their old room in the nurses' home, pulled the blackout blinds up and stared out at the dark streets of London.

Tonight she felt so lonely that she knew she'd almost welcome the roar of the air-raid sirens and the darkened stumble down the stairs into the Anderson shelter in the garden. There at least she'd feel a sense of camaraderie instead of this awful being alone.

The air-raid siren began to wail and Lily got stiffly to her feet, feeling cold from kneeling so long by the bedroom window.

On nights like tonight she didn't mind the siren: it interrupted the raging fire in her brain and the pain in her heart. But she wondered, as she peered out of the window to where the searchlights now lit up the sky, if Jamie was safe. She hoped so.

In early November, Philip was back in London and Sybil quickly arranged to come up to meet him on Thursday evening. Before they knew it, a party had been organized, starting with cocktails somewhere, then on to dinner and hopefully a club.

Diana had said she was meeting Sybil in Haymarket first as it was so central.

"Sibs says she wants to go to the Savoy for cocktails. Silly girl. I told her you can't get into the Savoy—it's full of visiting American colonels waving dollars around. 'Jolly good,' she says, 'I love Americans!' 'Really, Sibs,' I told her. 'You're married, and besides, the war isn't a giant cocktail party. The Goring is the most darling place and it's much cozier . . .' but she won't be swayed. Do say you'll come, Lily. It'll be such fun. Philip has asked lots of pals too."

But Lily couldn't risk it. She knew that Jamie might easily be part of the group, if he was still in England. He might not be, he might have rejoined his submarine, gone off to whatever theater of war was important. Stupid phrase, theater of war. As if it were a show. If women had their way, there would be no show. Women didn't want to lose people.

Even if there was a crowd of Philip's friends there, and Jamie was just one of many talking and drinking, she'd have to leave. She wouldn't be able to sit there in his presence, feeling so betrayed, and with Sybil gloating maliciously in the background.

"No, Diana," she said. "I'm too exhausted. Count me out."

Maisie was dating an American soldier she'd met in the Café de Paris and had gone out to dinner with him. The house felt very empty with them both gone, so Lily tried to amuse herself by having a bath with the regulation four inches of water. Even with a kettleful of hot water added, it was still too cool. Finally, she got dressed and went out for a walk. She decided to head over to Hyde Park and breathe in the nearest thing to country air she was likely to get in the city.

It was dusk as she began walking home and her heavy shoes were killing her. She'd had a pair of plimsolls that were a lovely relief from her work shoes but they were too worn down now and buying shoes was always such a hard task. Her feet were very narrow with high arches. She often thought she had such trouble with shoes because she'd gone barefoot so much as a child, running over the stones on the back avenue to Rathnaree, her little feet with beetle-hard skin. If Lily closed her eyes, she could feel the cool ticklish flicker of grass on her feet as she ran through the fields, trailing hands through the stalks of rushes.

A bus roared past her on the Bayswater Road, inches away. Lily's eyes shot open and she rocked back from the edge of the footpath, realizing that she'd nearly walked shut-eyed into the road.

"Watch out, love. He nearly had your head off." The speaker was a tiny, shrunken man with a stick.

"Thank you," said Lily, shaken.

This was ridiculous; she could have been killed or at the very least ended up in her own hospital on a gurney.

But the streets kept shimmering in and out of her mind, being replaced by a vision of the Savoy, with Diana rushing in, hair flying and a cloud of Arpège trailing in her wake, saying, "Sorry I'm late." Diana was always late, Lily thought fondly.

She'd be there by now, garnering admiring glances as she sat with her sister and her brother-in-law's friends. Lily had been to the Savoy with Diana once before, had drunk in the heady atmosphere of the exquisite Art Deco palace and the frisson that this, *here*, was where it was all happening.

For once, she wished she were back in the nurses' home: at least in the common room there would always be someone to talk to and a radio to listen to. Right now she felt so isolated, so not a part of anything anymore.

And then she heard it: the low drone of the siren. Instinctively, she looked up, trying to see the deadly V-2 rockets in the sky, as if seeing them would keep her safe from being hit.

Once you could see them, you were safe, surely? Not true: the wards of the Royal Free were full of people who'd seen and yet still ended up destroyed with bomb fragments.

The siren grew steadily louder. As familiar as the sound was, it had taken on a new, terrifying aspect since the advent of the V-2s. Her heart was racing as she tried to remember where the nearest shelter was. Of course: Lancaster Gate Underground.

She joined the river of people streaming toward the station steps and in moments she was caught up in the crowd, being jostled down into the entrance, past an old MAKE DO AND MEND poster with the ends curling up as it came off the wall.

Normally, Lily hated the Underground and steered well clear of it. Some people loved the camaraderie of bedding down on the station platforms at night, joining in with the sing-songs and taking advantage of the tea provided at dawn. But not her. For Lily, the thought of being buried alive in a narrow, airless tunnel beneath the ground made this a far-from-safe haven.

New panic clawed up inside her as she reached the ticket hall. The only way down was the lifts. She hated lifts, and especially now, when they'd be full to bursting. Crushed in the human river, she had to fight to breathe. If the entrance was bombed, she'd be buried alive in a small metal box at the bottom of a lift shaft. She knew she had to get out.

Even the V-2s couldn't be as bad as a slow death in an airless coffin.

"Let me out!" she shrieked, and turned, pushing against the human river trying to force its way in. It was all she could do to keep breathing, let alone move against the flow, but she knew she couldn't turn back now.

"Lily."

She thought she heard somebody call her name but she couldn't be sure. It was like being in a nightmare—she didn't know what was real or not.

"Lily!"

It was the voice she'd heard in her dreams, and the last person she'd expected to see here today. *Jamie*.

He was behind her in the crowd with his hand held out, fingers reaching toward her.

"I have to get out," she shouted wildly. "I can't go down in the lifts."

"Hold on," he yelled back. "I'll get you."

She knew it was madness to climb back up to the street, but she didn't care. Only one crazy thought gripped her: Once she was with Jamie, she'd be safe.

With a final surge of energy, she reached his fingers first, then his strong hand gripped hers and hauled her against him. Her face was crushed against the scratchy wool of his navy uniform, and she breathed in, inhaling his scent and the sensation of being safe.

The crowd was thinner now, and with Jamie holding her, they made it up to the street.

It was only a few minutes since she'd heard the siren, yet it seemed like hours. The streets were nearly deserted, like a ghost city banked up with sandbags: only the foolhardy weren't seeking shelter.

"Here." He pulled her into the doorway of a big, imposing house with a huge portico above them. "It's as safe as anywhere aboveground."

His arms were around her and Lily held on to him tightly. From the east came the low rumbling of the bombs. Like counting thunderclaps when she'd been a child, Lily felt a guilty relief that the bombers were targeting somewhere else.

"What are you doing here?" she said.

"I came to see you," he replied.

Lily looked up into his face. His eyes were the most extraordinary color: a lucent gray that appeared lit from some powerful inner force. They weren't the sort of eyes that could lie. Searching them, she found nothing but truth.

"Why?"

"You know why," he said in a low voice.

She kept looking at him, wondering how she knew his face so intimately when she barely knew him. The dark eyebrows, the scar that bisected one and made her long to run her fingers wonderingly over it.

"I've been keeping away from you," he said. "I made myself stay away. I told Philip I couldn't meet him later. But I couldn't help myself. I had to see you again. When I went to the Savoy and Diana told me you weren't coming, I knew I had to see you."

"It's wrong," she said. She couldn't look at him. He'd come to find her and she wanted him so much, but it was wrong. He had a wife. Under the eyes of God, he couldn't betray that wife. She couldn't betray his wife. If they gave in, they would be committing adultery, a mortal sin.

Would God forgive that?

True, her faith had been rattled during the war from what she had witnessed. How could God allow this much pain and death?

Jamie took one of her hands and brought it to his lips. She could hear his breathing deepen. They'd have to think about God afterward, there wasn't the time now.

She brought him home, led him up the stairs into her bedroom. It was a large and dark room, with heavy alizarin crimson wallpaper, a vast bed and wardrobe in a rich wood and no carpet on the wooden floor.

Jamie shut the door, locked it, then grabbed her. It was hard to say which of them was fiercest: Lily wanted to meld herself to him, and it seemed as if he wanted to devour her with his mouth, tasting her with his lips, his tongue plunging into her forcefully.

Her fingers ripped at the buttons on his uniform. Briefly, they separated as he opened his jacket, then tore at her cardigan.

There was no moment to think about what she was wearing; suddenly, she was naked, pressed against him. They fell onto the coverlet, bodies on fire against each other.

Lily had never felt a man's hands on her naked skin and she arched herself against him, loving the feeling of his mouth on her nipples, biting, licking, sucking. She could feel his erection long and hard against the smoothness of the skin of her thigh and she wondered how she'd ever thought sex must be a strange business, from years of looking at men's flaccid bodies in the hospital. They were ill, lethargic; Jamie was strong, powerful, and a ferocious energy burned within him.

Furious intense ardent aggressive ferocious.

She stroked the long angry red scar on his hip, the scar from the wound that had brought him home the first time they met. He barely limped now, she realized; when they'd met at Sybil's wedding, the limp was noticeable, but not anymore.

"Is it painful?" she asked.

"Not now," he breathed, fixing his mouth over her breast again.

Lily closed her eyes and gave in to the sensation.

"I don't want to hurt you," he breathed.

"I don't care."

"I do," he said. "I want you to want me again."

"I do."

"And not be hurt." One long finger reached inside her and Lily felt her body spasm with pure pleasure.

"We don't have to—"

"We do."

She thought she'd die if she didn't consummate this now. She swung herself underneath him and straddled him, reaching down to touch him and marveling at the sensitivity of his body as he gasped in pleasure.

"Tell me how—"

He positioned her over him and their eyes locked—lucent gray on pure blue—while their bodies slowly moved. Then she felt him nudging inside her and she couldn't breathe. Still, he stared at her and she could sense him falter, and knew it was for her sake.

Then she moved her body, sliding so that she was impaled upon him and the huge surge of him inside her made her cry out.

"Oh, Lily," he groaned, and then they were moving together, clinging tightly, his hands gripping the soft curve of her buttocks until Lily felt the slow burn of ecstasy ripple out from somewhere inside her and she gasped, arching herself on top of him, reaching, stretching, and then he was with her.

They lay curled together afterward, with the curtains still open. The moon was a sleek crescent curve in a dark sky.

"You've no idea how many nights I've looked out of the window and wondered about you," Lily said, snug in the curve of his arm. "I wondered, could you see the same moon, where were you, what were you doing, and if—if you ever thought about me."

"I haven't thought of anything else," he said with humor in his voice. "They're not best pleased with me in the War Office. Think I'm going back to the sub soon."

There was silence. Not talking about where they were going was a part of a submariner's life, and intellectually Lily understood it totally. Emotionally, it hurt. If he had to go, she wanted to know where, so she could follow every moment in the newspapers, on the radio and in the newsreels. That way, at least, she could be close to him.

She knew so little about submarines, only that, unlike battleships, once they were hit, there was little hope for survivors. The sea was cruel and unrelenting. He could die so easily, locked underwater in that claustrophobic tube. The terror of his dying like that pierced her.

"We shouldn't have done this," she said. "I'm afraid that we're going to be punished. You're married, and in my faith that's for life. How can we have a future?"

"I'm fed up with concentrating on the future," he said in a low voice. "Life is all about the future. If we win this campaign, if the Allies advance here, if the Axis fails there . . . What about now? What about how we feel now? What about me making a mistake seven years ago when I got married and now having to deal with that every day of my life since I met you."

"You made a mistake?" It was what she wanted to hear. Jamie had married the wrong woman. But she was Catholic. Mistakes didn't matter when it came to marriage. Marriage was for life. God was watching, He was tallying it all up. If she disobeyed the rules, she would pay with her immortal soul. That was absolute; there were no gray areas when God talked to you.

"Tell me," she said.

Lying in each other's arms, he told her about Miranda, the girl he'd grown up knowing as almost a best friend. Their mothers had been bridesmaids at each other's weddings. In 1937, they'd got married.

"I knew it was a mistake even then," Jamie said. "On our wedding night—"

Lily flinched in the bed beside him.

"—Miranda locked herself in the bathroom and cried. She wouldn't come out. I told her we didn't have to do anything, that I wouldn't touch her, but she refused to come out."

"Why?"

"She was frightened of me, frightened of making love. She'd led a very sheltered life and she had no idea what was going to happen. Whatever her mother had told her had terrified her. She'd kept up the façade until we were alone and then it all spilled out."

Lily hugged him more tightly.

"What did you do?"

"I slept on the floor," he said. "It was hardly the ideal wedding night, but that wasn't what worried me; it was the thought of the future. A woman who's that scared of you isn't going to get over it easily. She loved me well enough during the day, but at night she was terrified of me."

Lily could hear the remembered pain in his voice.

"She'd been led to believe that men were like beasts, that once the doors closed, we couldn't control our appetites. She told me that, later."

"Couldn't you talk to her about it?" Lily asked. "Or speak to her mother . . . ?"

"Her mother was the problem," Jamie said. "She was the one who'd told Miranda about men being beasts. There was no one I could ask for help. We had to get through it."

"And did you?" Lily asked quietly.

"No," he replied. "We didn't. My mother and, ironically enough, Miranda's are always inquiring about the patter of tiny feet and when we're going to start filling the nursery. Before the war, I thought about divorce, but then I joined up and it was easier to do nothing. Divorce felt like failure and I'd never failed at anything in my life before Miranda. Then I met you. . . ."

He turned to face her. "I fought it, Lily, because it wasn't fair to flirt with you when I was still married. That's why I didn't write to you after the wedding. You deserve someone who's free, you deserve the best. But . . ." He kissed her face, moving from her forehead to her eyelids, down the bridge of her nose, to the softness of her lips. "I couldn't help myself. That's why I made up my mind to talk to you tonight, to tell you I could get a divorce. Miranda wasn't a failure, after all—our sham of a marriage meant I was waiting for you. You're my future."

Lily felt her heart ache.

"I'm sorry, Jamie. There can't be any future for us. Even if you divorced your wife, I couldn't marry you. A Catholic cannot marry a divorced person. I'd be excommunicated. I can't do that, I can't live without my faith."

Jamie didn't say anything for a while and Lily felt angry, angry that he didn't want to understand.

"You must see how it is for me," she said. "I was raised like that, my faith is part of me, part of my family. It's different for you. God's important to me."

As she said it, she could see her parents at Mass on a Sunday, praying, believing utterly. She could see herself in the virginal white of her First Holy Communion dress, her heart bursting with pride on this special occasion. Didn't he see that she couldn't marry him because she'd never be part of her church again? God might forgive her this, but not more, not marrying a divorced man.

"Do you honestly believe that?" he demanded. "That God gives a damn who you marry? How does He work it out, then? Remember when we first met and you told me about those little boys you saw in the hospital, looking like they were asleep in their pajamas. Who decided they would die? God? Did He make a good choice? I don't think so, and I bet their parents don't think so, either. Who decided that war was a good idea? Are you telling me that ordinary people want it?" He was almost shouting now. "Ordinary people in Germany, do they want their sons killed and their daughters bombed? No."

Lily was shocked. She'd often questioned the concept of war. Mopping up blood and comforting patients who'd woken to find themselves facing life as an amputee had that effect. But she'd kept her doubts to herself. To question would be disloyal, as if she was undermining the war effort.

"If God is running the whole world, then I don't like the way He's doing it," he said grimly. "This war isn't solving anything. If the Allies had done the right thing about Hitler a long time ago, we wouldn't be here now. We behave like sheep, Lily. Somebody else will work it out, somebody like God or the government. If you cede power to somebody else all the time, then you get what you deserve."

"I still believe in God," she said.

"But why does there only have to be your precise God? Why can't somebody else's God be enough? It's fear, you see; I don't like religions that rule by fear. Believe us or else you'll burn in hell. That's not a loving religion. We're all living in fear right now and I can't believe that it's the right way to live. I should add that I'm not saying that to get my hand on your leg, Lily," he said gently.

Lily smiled, grateful that his anger had dissipated. "You got rather farther than my leg," she said.

"Did I? Hmm, I might have to try that again."

He began caressing her again and Lily felt her blood stir. They didn't have much time.

Diana and Maisie would be home soon.

"I'll be gone before they come, I promise," he said, and then quieted her with a kiss.

Lily lay under him, reveling in the feel of his body on hers, and wished she could quiet her racing mind as easily as he'd quieted her talking. This was wrong, so wrong, screamed her head, but still she couldn't stop. There was no going back now.

He left at twelve, heading off in black streets with only a torch to find his way. Lily didn't ask if she would see him again; she knew she would.

She climbed the stairs and got into a bed still warm from the imprint of his body, hugging the sheets where he'd lain close to her. She felt exhausted and sated, but sleep wouldn't come. All she could think about was what she'd done.

She'd betrayed her upbringing, her religion by being with Jamie. She didn't have to tell anyone to be cast out from the Church; the Almighty already knew.

She thought of the picture of the Sacred Heart of Jesus that decorated every Catholic home in Ireland. A red lamp was always lit under the Sacred Heart, and beside it would be a beautiful box-frame with Pope Pius XII's picture, and the papal seal underneath.

She could see her mother blessing herself each time she passed it, and the guilt overcame her.

But one question remained in her mind: If their love was such a powerful lightning strike and made her feel whole like nothing ever had before, then how could it be so wrong?

She'd never really questioned her religion before, even after all she'd seen at the hospital. Questioning was the enemy of faith. But were the old instincts so wrong, the powerful instincts that drove her as a woman?

A strong voice from a little old lady came into her mind.

"Trust that," said the voice, laying a small hand, clawed from the ravages of arthritis, on her breast bone just over the heart. "The heart never lies, *mo chroi*." *Mo chroi*, Gaelic for my heart. Like saying "My love."

Granny Sive, Dad's mother. Lily hadn't thought of her in years. She was dead, God rest her, had died when Lily was only nine or ten. And even though Lily had been a child, she'd known that her grandmother's death was like the end of an era of some sort. The passing of history, her dad had said.

Indeed, Granny Sive—Lily had lisped the name when she was a small child, could barely say it: *Sii* and then *Va*, all rolled together into one syllable—had been the last of what her father called "the old people," and he wasn't talking about age.

Granny Sive had gone to church and was on nodding acquaintance with the priest, but her Christianity sat side by side with the old Mother Earth religion of the Celtic peoples.

She could tell the time without heed to the kitchen clock, she knew what way the weather was going to turn from looking at the way the birds were flying back to their nests, and she studied the phases of the moon carefully.

Granny Sive told Lily tales of the warrior goddess Brigid, who had powers to heal the sick. For the old people, Granny Sive explained, lighting candles to honor Brigid on the first of February was as important as Easter to the priest. Imbolg, the Celtic festival around Brigid's day, heralded the birth of spring, the lambing season and the prospect of warmth. Mountain ash and whitethorn grew outside her house: magic trees, she told Lily.

And she told stories of the mother of all the Irish goddesses, Danu or Dana. Lily's middle name was Dana. Mam had favored Lily, the name of one of Lady Irene's sisters, but Granny Sive had pushed for Dana. In the end, they'd compromised. She became Lily Dana Kennedy.

What would Granny Sive have made of Jamie? Would she have invoked the crucifix and eternal damnation? Or would she have pressed her old hand to Lily's heart and said, "Trust that"?

Lily wished she was more like Granny Sive.

twenty-one

The hospital psych ward in Tamarin was tiny and consisted of a small four-bed section in the middle, with another four rooms leading off from the communal area. Overlooking the sea was a television room, a quiet room, the nurses' station and a consulting room.

Anneliese had been there for five days and she was fed up with asking the chief psychiatrist, Dr. Eli, if she could go home. Once again he was dragging his heels.

"I'm fine," she said. "It was an error of judgment brought on by numbing myself with tranquilizers," she added as they sat in the small consulting room and Dr. Eli gave her his grave but friendly look.

"Trying to drown yourself is quite a statement," he said, in a voice so calm and measured that Anneliese would have hit him over the head with something if only there had been a single blunt object in the room that wasn't nailed down. Clearly, people had tried this before. In the psych ward, the knives and the chairs were plastic. There was nowhere to vent any anger.

"Lapse of judgment," she insisted. "I can't believe I did it. I'm not mad, right. Plus, if I wasn't mad before I came here, I'm going mad now. I hate, *hate* being in rooms where I can't get out, and there's nothing to do and nobody to talk to. It's like being stuck on a reality TV show without the cameras or the choice about food. Let me go home."

"You know you're only in the locked ward because we've no beds anywhere else in the hospital," Dr. Eli said. "I'd like to keep you in for a few more days to make sure you're doing as well as you say you are."

"I am well." Anneliese groaned. "You can't fake it—I tried and, believe me, I now know the difference between not being well and being well. I want to go home, breathe fresh air and feel healthy again."

She wanted to leave because the atmosphere of sadness that permeated the ward was hard to live with. Compared to the teenage boy locked in his own head from drug addiction, and the young woman with empty eyes and bandaged wrists from trying to cut them, Anneliese knew she was basically well. Her being here was a stupid mistake. With those kids, it was much, much more, and she knew she couldn't heal until she was away from the ward.

"Plus," she added, "I never want to see a tranquilizer again in my life. I don't want to be out of my mind. I've decided I like being in it. Numbing my brain was the problem. I numbed too bloody much and stopped thinking straight."

"How does it feel, talking about this, about why you did it?" he asked.

Anneliese had regretted her walk into the sea many, many times. Trying to explain her actions to Beth was the worst, but telling Dr. Eli came a close second. The man was a bloody monolith of calm—nothing upset him—and he asked the same questions again and again, as if the repetition would make her give in and supply the real answer.

Except Anneliese had given the real answer already: I don't really know why I kept walking into the sea, it's sort of hazy in my mind. I wasn't thinking properly, but I know I don't want to do it again. I made a mistake, really, a mistake.

"Oh, Dr. Eli," she said wearily, "what is the correct answer to that question? What's the answer you want to hear? That I've got Dalí-esque shapes in my head bleeding their life out onto the floor? That giant cockroaches are under my T-shirt? You know what was wrong with me? Life.

"My life sucked. I haven't lost my marbles, I didn't have a hallucinogenic dream where Noddy French-kissed me or where I turned into a horse and wanted to trample my mother and marry my father. I don't want to be a paper on Freudian analysis for the middle-aged woman. My problem is simple: I reached rock bottom, tried to numb my head and ended up in a numb blur that saw me walk down the beach and keep walking."

There was a pause before the doctor slid seamlessly into the space with a question. "How does it feel to say that?"

A roar of laughter bubbled up inside Anneliese and escaped. The noise shocked her for a second because it was so long since she'd laughed. *How does it feel to say that?* You couldn't make it up, she decided. She felt as if she was trapped in an episode of *Frasier* crossed with *One Flew Over the Cuckoo's Nest*.

"Do you ever watch *Frasier*, Dr. Eli?" she asked. "You know, the sitcom with the psychiatrist who has a radio talk show in Seattle."

"Not really," muttered the doctor. "I don't watch much television."

"It's very funny," Anneliese said. "You should watch it. You'd love it, although you've got to be able to laugh at yourself to enjoy it, and that's not always easy—"

"Back to you—"

"No, not back to me," Anneliese interrupted. "Not trying to be rude here, Dr. Eli, but I'd like to go home and stop this. Can you discharge me?"

"One more day?" he said.

Anneliese thought it would be easier for Beth if she was discharged properly instead of her just charging out by herself, saying she was fine. Legally, Anneliese knew she didn't have to stay, but she felt guilty for stressing out her pregnant daughter, and playing by the rules seemed a good solution.

"One more day," she agreed. "Now, *I Love Lucy* is on—you need satellite television in here, Dr. Eli. Paramount Comedy would help a lot of us get better much faster."

"You think so?" he asked.

She nodded. "Sitcom therapy should be a recognized form of analysis, part cognitive-behavioral, part laughing at yourself. And I'm smiling just thinking about it, so isn't that progress?"

After Dr. Eli had gone, Anneliese wandered into the television room and sat in one of the windows, looking out at the sea. The windows had bars on the outside. To keep the crazy people in or keep the rest of the world out—Anneliese didn't know which. Strangely, she was used to the bars now. Those first twenty-four hours, when she'd lain numbly in her bed, she'd hated them and all they represented. Her downfall.

It had been instantaneous: one moment she'd been standing on the beach, still being Anneliese, mother of Beth, sort of wife to Edward, stalwart of the Lifeboat Shop. And a fraction of a moment later she was the woman who'd tried to drown herself in the deceptive currents of the bay. Just a flicker of doubt and her whole life had changed.

Edward had come to the hospital after she'd been brought in and she hadn't cared about him seeing her.

"Go away!" she'd cried hoarsely at him, clad in a hospital gown because her sea-sodden clothes had been removed. "Go away."

He'd gone and even though Anneliese knew he was devastated by what had happened, she didn't care about his hurt. Let him hurt. Let him feel what it was like.

Beth was different.

"Your daughter's coming to see you, Anneliese, isn't that nice?" said one of the nurses, the tall one with the dark hair, the next morning. That was when the shame coursed through her. Her darling pregnant daughter was driving to see her and had presumably been phoned the night before with the sort of news nobody ever wanted to hear. Anneliese pictured the confusion and hurt on Beth's face; she could imagine her leaning against the wall to rest her back, hand on the mound of her baby, saying, "No, it can't be true."

She'd done that. Her. The woman who'd spent her life taking care of Beth had spectacularly abandoned taking care of her. Beth could have gone into early labor with the shock, anything, and it would have been her fault.

For the first time since she'd been admitted to Tamarin Hospital the day before, Anneliese emerged from her locked-in state and began to cry. She'd thought she could simply disappear off the planet and nobody would care. But she'd been wrong.

Beth hadn't arrived until nearly lunchtime. From her bed, where she was propped up against the pillows because she felt so bone-numbingly weary, Anneliese could see Marcus and Beth enter the ward. Even the strain on her face couldn't diminish the glow of imminent motherhood. Beth's skin really was blooming and her hair fell lustrously around her shoulders. She looked like an ad in a pregnancy magazine. Except that pregnancy magazines never featured pictures taken inside psychiatric wards.

Anneliese gulped and the gulp turned into a sob.

"Mum!" Stopping only to gesture to Marcus to stay back, Beth rushed to her mother and hugged her. "I was so worried, Mum. I couldn't believe—"

"I know: that I'd done something so stupid. I'm sorry, so sorry," Anneliese sobbed.

"Mum, how could you think of doing that? How could you?"

Anneliese hugged her daughter and the promise of her first grandchild and felt the raw heat of the shame again. Look what she'd *done*.

Anneliese knew there was only one way to fix it and she took a huge step back into her old life: "It was a mistake, my love, I wasn't thinking straight. I'm so sorry. I can't tell you how sorry I am. I'd taken too many antianxiety tablets and I did something I'll always regret. It was a stupid mistake, please believe me."

"Oh, Mum."

Anneliese could feel some of the tension leave Beth's body and she knew she'd done the right thing.

"I was so worried, you've no idea. Dad phoned and I couldn't take it in at first. I mean, you would never—"

"I'm sorry," said Anneliese softly, "so sorry." She wanted more than anything to tell Beth the truth about how she felt, but she couldn't. Not now, with Beth pregnant. Probably not ever. A long time ago, she'd made the decision not to raise her daughter to stand in the front lines.

She'd tell Beth what she needed to hear and pray that telling Beth it had all been a mistake would take away the raw red shame inside her for having hurt her daughter. So, she wasn't being honest. But she might die of pain if she told the truth. And now, with Beth holding her, Anneliese realized that she didn't want to die after all.

"It's going to be all right," Anneliese soothed, and was astonished to realize that it *was* going to be all right. At that precise moment, when she should be feeling worse than she ever had, she felt a strange surge of relief because she'd been through the absolute worst and had come out the far side, still breathing, still *there*. Despite the fear, she'd got through it. She could get through anything. That thought brought her a ray of sheer peace.

It was like jumping into the abyss and instead of falling endlessly, she'd hit a trampoline—or "bouncelina," as Beth had called them when she was little—and she'd been bounced back.

We don't want you—so you'd better bloody well get on with it, the other world had said irritably.

"It's going to be all right," she repeated, and this time she meant it.

"Why didn't you phone me and tell me how you were feeling?" Beth went on. "Mum, I'm here for you, you know that."

"I'm sorry," Anneliese repeated, hugging her.

Eventually, Marcus had come over to sit on the bed, and they'd skirted round why his mother-in-law was in the psychiatric ward. Dear Marcus, he was a good man.

She'd told him as much when he and Beth left.

"Take care of her," she'd whispered to him. "I'm sorry for all of this, Marcus. It's going to be OK, though. I'm not planning on trying it again."

Marcus nodded and she could see a telltale gleam of wet in his eyes.

Beth had come back the following day, and Anneliese had summoned up the energy to look sprightly and tell her daughter to go home, that she'd be fine.

"Are you sure?" Beth asked.

Anneliese, inhabiting the in-control-mother zone, nodded. " 'Course I am," she said firmly. "You go home and work on this baby. I'm going to be fine. I'll be out in a few days and I'm looking forward to going home and putting all this behind me."

She managed to say it with brio, as if what had happened was a little glitch instead of a suicide attempt.

"Well . . ." Beth faltered.

"Darling"—Anneliese used the voice she'd used when Beth was at primary school and didn't want to get out of bed on cold winter mornings—"I'll be fine."

"OK, Mum," said Beth, accepting it.

Anneliese felt relief that she'd convinced Beth she was fine, even though she wasn't. But mingled with the relief was a certain sadness that her daughter had believed her so readily.

Anneliese had never known her mother's secrets, any more than she'd known dear Lily's secrets. But she'd somehow thought that she and Beth would share each other's lives. But they didn't. The fierce bond between mother and child didn't include that. Perhaps the bond would be weakened if it did.

Mothers were meant to mother, not spill their souls.

Beth didn't need to know that Anneliese now bore two scars that would never heal. The first was how much she'd hurt Beth by trying to kill herself. The second was that she'd reached that place where death seemed the best option. It was like a spot on a mythical road trip, somewhere that altered a person so much that once they'd visited, they were never quite the same again.

When Beth had gone, Anneliese let the in-control feeling flood away. She could summon up the mother persona if required, but to get out of this place, she needed to let go of the old Anneliese.

"Anneliese."

She looked up from the window seat in the television room. It was her favorite nurse, the tall dark-haired one.

"Hello, Michelle," she said.

"You've a visitor, Anneliese," said Michelle.

"Who?"

"Me, the man who pulled you out."

She'd thought the big figure behind Michelle was another patient, but it wasn't. It was the marine ecology guy. Mac, the man she'd tried to avoid on the beach, the man who had pulled her out of the sea.

"I'll leave you to it," said Michelle, walking off.

Anneliese stared at Mac and embarrassment flooded through her. He'd been there that day; it was like him seeing her naked.

"How did you get in?" she demanded. She was all out of politeness.

"I was visiting someone and I thought I'd come over and say hi. I wanted to see how you were. I was the one who pulled you out, after all."

"I didn't ask to be pulled out," said Anneliese irritably. It wasn't entirely true, because she had wanted to be pulled out. He'd saved her life.

"I'm sorry," she said abruptly. "You did pull me out, thank you. It's just that I don't have much social grace in me at the moment," she added. "This isn't the sort of place for pretending and smiling politely. I seem to have lost the ability for hiding the truth."

Also not entirely true. She'd pretended everything was fine for Beth. But she wasn't going to do it for anyone else. No more pretending she didn't mind that Edward had left her. No more pretending politeness and happiness. How liberating.

"You want to go and get a coffee?" he asked.

Anneliese looked at him in surprise. "It's a locked ward," she said.

"Time off for good behavior," he said. "I've been here before and I know the rules, I can bring you out, if you'd like to go and have a coffee with me, in the hospital coffee shop? Of course, if I don't bring you back at the prescribed time, they'll set the dogs on me. But we'll get a head start on them."

Anneliese laughed. It felt great to really laugh again.

They sat at a table in the small coffee shop. It felt good to be out of the ward where she'd spent the last five days, and Anneliese enjoyed watching the world move around them.

"Thanks for the coffee," she said, "although I should be buying. I owe you, after all."

"You don't owe me anything," he said. "I just happened to be there at the right time."

"You're very laid-back about this whole saving-woman-from-killing-herself thing," she said curiously. She couldn't imagine many other people sitting there so calmly with someone they'd pulled from the sea, yet Mac wasn't watching her warily, as if expecting her to wail and throw herself onto the table with grief.

"I've been on the edge myself a few times. I sort of understand it," he said. That's what life is about: teetering on the edge."

"How do you know all this?"

"Just do," he said.

"Been there, done that, got the T-shirt, huh?"

He smiled slowly. "I bought the factory that makes the T-shirts."

"Tell me about it," she said.

"You don't want my life story."

She grinned. "Actually, I do. Before the Sea—should I have an abbreviation for it, BS (Before the Sea)?—I'd never have been so blunt, but now, After Sea, I am. The new and improved Anneliese tells it like it is. Confess all."

It took another coffee for him to tell his story of alcoholism, a failed marriage and two little girls who he hoped more or less forgave him for it all after ten years of recovery. He couldn't give them back their childhood, though, any more than his alcoholic parents could give him back his.

"Do you ever wonder why it happened to you?" Anneliese asked. It was the one thing she had trouble sorting out in her head: Why had it all gone wrong? A man who'd been born into addiction must surely understand that?

"This wise guy once told me that when someone falls in a hole, they think, How do I get out of the hole? But when an alcoholic falls in a hole, they think, Why did I fall in the hole?"

Anneliese laughed.

"Makes sense, doesn't it?" Mac said.

She nodded. "Works for me. Actually, it *does* work for me. Every time I fell in a hole my entire life, I wondered why instead of just getting out of it."

"The *why* is the killer for some people." He shrugged. "How about you just accept it? Stop asking why, move on and try to find peace."

"I have peace," she said with a certain pride. "Before, I tried everything for a sign that it would all work out. I read books, tried to meditate, listened to CDs, and finally I sat in St. Canice's and prayed for a sign, and there was none. But I was looking in the wrong place. The sign is me. I'm still here, so I guess I must be meant to be here. That's my sign.

"Mind you, this feeling-at-peace thing is very strange," she added now to Mac. "I daresay it's a gift. I asked for help and it came. Sort of last minute," she added wryly. "You can't get more last minute than that, but the help came. You came. Angels, God, I don't know who did it. But whoever it was, I'm grateful."

"Glad I was there."

A woman Anneliese knew saw her and waved, then stopped still and her hand dropped and her face fell.

Anneliese kept smiling and waved back.

"Poor old thing," she said kindly, "probably forgot for a millisecond that I'm here for trying to kill myself and now doesn't know what to do. I might not have managed to kill myself, but I've probably committed social suicide." Then she laughed. "We should go out together, Mac. Wouldn't that be apt—you're an alcoholic and I'm a failed suicide." She beamed at him. "We'd make a lovely couple. People would be terrified to invite us to their houses: they'd be worried in case you saw a bottle of wine and freaked out, and they'd be worried in case I tried to impale myself on the kitchen knives."

"And every time they'd mention the beach or the sea, they'd all go silent and gasp in case you started to cry."

It was so ridiculous, they both started to laugh. Anneliese knew people were probably looking at them but she didn't care. She'd come out the other side of the abyss. Wasn't that something?

"How did you get involved with marine rescue?" she asked.

"It was the only liquid I hadn't tried to drink," he deadpanned.

Anneliese shrieked with laughter.

"OK, why didn't you consider stand-up comedy?"

"I'm not depressed enough."

"Have you ever been depressed?" she inquired slowly.

"No. I was never anything. Whatever I felt I flattened with alcohol. I didn't have any feelings left to be depressed about. You?"

"Yeah, for most of my life. It's not quite the mountain on top of you that some people talk of. For me, depression is so subtle, it creeps up like a colony of termites eating away at your house, nibbling through all the—what are those important bits called?"

"Joists?"

"That's it. Joists. The termites ate away at the joists. They messed me up, turned me into a bit of a control freak—or at least that's what my daughter says." She winced, remembering Beth accusing her of trying to control everything. "And . . ." She stopped.

"And?"

Anneliese sighed. "Can I say anything to you? I feel as if I can, but can I?"

"Say anything," he replied. "I'm unshockable."

"I think I probably ruined my marriage." There, she'd said it out loud, the horrible thought that had been haunting her for the past few days. That she was more responsible for making Edward leave than silly Nell had been. That her retreat into her sadness had pushed him away.

"I don't know if you know, but my husband left me earlier this year for my best friend. That's partly what pushed me over the edge. But I'm realizing that I wasn't easy to live with. Not in the slamming-doors-and-dropping-crockery sort of way, but in my own quiet way. I wanted to cope with it all on my own, so I shut Edward out and didn't talk to him about how I felt. In the last five days I've told the doctors here more about what's been going on in my head than I've told Edward in our whole marriage."

Mac said nothing. He just listened. He was a good listener, she decided: he didn't let his attention flicker even for a second.

"I hate admitting that it was my fault. It's like I've failed, and I can't bear failure, but I have to take the blame, or most of it, anyway. I shut him out, and if it was the other way round—if I was married to someone who shut me out of that part of their life—I'd want to leave too. When our daughter was grown up, I shut down even more."

Anneliese felt her throat tighten thinking about Beth. It wasn't her darling daughter's fault, but when Beth was young there had been someone there for her to fight for. Beth needed protecting and Anneliese would do that; if it meant laughing, smiling and singing at the top of her voice in the morning, she would do whatever it took to make their world happy and normal.

With Beth gone, there was nobody left to protect. The fire in the husband-love corner had long since gone out while Anneliese had tended the daughter-love one.

"Nell said I wasn't interested in him anymore," she said slowly, "and she was right. I loved him, cared about him, yes. But not in the way I used to."

There was something immensely freeing in saying what she'd thought out loud. In her head, the words had such dark power, but when she spoke them to another human being, and he didn't cringe away in horror, she felt enormous relief.

Anneliese wasn't sure that talking about problems endlessly helped—it had never helped her. But speaking the absolute, unabashed truth and not flinching—*that* helped.

"Would you have him back?"

Anneliese didn't know why, but the question lacked the breezy informality of all the others.

"No," she said. "I doubt either of us could go back. I've changed. It's different now. I don't want to be the old Anneliese again. I can't go back. When he left me, I wanted it all the same as before, I longed for that, actually. What was hard to grasp was that I'd believed in one reality all along and I was wrong. Edward was deceiving me and so was Nell. I'd thought the world was flat and it was round."

"And now?" he prompted.

"Now I know *I* was deceiving me too because I was living as if we had a wonderful marriage, and we didn't. In the end, neither of us was sharing our innermost thoughts with the other. I kept mine to myself and he shared his with Nell. Not a textbook happy marriage, I think."

"My wife and I split up in my second year of recovery," volunteered Mac. "She'd lived with me through the drinking, through the nightmare of the first year of recovery, and then I left. She'll never forgive me for that, but I'd changed too much. It was time to let go of the old stuff and move on."

Anneliese understood. Going back would be lovely, but it wasn't an option.

"Not that Edward is asking me to have him back, but even if he did, I wouldn't be able to. I like the freedom of now."

Mac grinned at her.

"Freedom to be me," she went on. "It's so liberating. I can say what I like."

"Such as?"

"I want to tell dear Corinne who works in the Lifeboat Shop with me that if she waves another smelly little potion under my nose and tells me it will change my life, I will strangle her with her moonstone necklace."

"Moonstone?"

"Good for life energy."

"Is she energetic?"

"No, poor dear, she's the least energetic person I know," laughed Anneliese. "Her idea of exercise is sitting back in her chair and telling the rest of the world where they're going wrong."

"So the moonstone's not working, is it?"

"No, but I couldn't tell her that," Anneliese groaned. "Don't want to hurt her."

"I thought you were saying what you wanted to. You are nice, after all."

"Yes," she sighed, "I am nice. I don't want to hurt people."

"Who else, then?" he asked. "Who else can you tell what you think without hurting?"

"I'd quite like to tell Nell that fixing her hair, wearing lipstick and moving in on your supposed best friend's husband isn't the recipe for long life and happiness. She's not right for Edward, actually."

"Is this advice coming from your intellect or your heart?" he asked. "Bitter part of you speaking or rational part?"

"What I like about you is that you don't sugarcoat it," she said.

"Sugarcoating is for wimps. You don't get in the door of AA if you sugarcoat."

"Not even saccharine-coating?"

"Especially not. In fact, coats are out, full stop. We meet in the nude. It's hard to hide things when you're naked."

"What a horrible picture that conjures up," she laughed. "The advice is from the head and not from the heart," she added after a few moments' consideration. "Edward is complex, for all that he appears like a straightforward individual, and he needs someone who understands that. Nell is pretty straight down the middle: what you see is what you get. Apart from the running-off-with-my-husband bit," she amended. "But generally, Nell is Nell. No sidebars, no hidden extras. Edward likes the hidden extras, although I think he got fed up with mine."

"You don't have hidden extras so much as hidden labyrinths," Mac said.

"That's very forward, coming from someone who's only just met me," she said lightly. But she wasn't offended: far from it.

"When are you getting out of here?" he asked as they walked back upstairs to her ward. "Or are you planning to stage a hospital breakout?"

"Tomorrow, as long as I don't lose the run of myself tonight and go mad."

"Tomorrow, then," he said. "Do you have someone to collect you?"

She was touched. It was clear he was offering himself for the duty.

"I'm going to ask my friend Yvonne. We've known each other for a million years and she's one of the few people who probably won't be fazed by coming here."

"See you around," he said, and touched her hand briefly in good-bye.

Back in her bed, Anneliese lay on her pillows and closed her eyes.

Letting go. Mac had talked about letting go of the past. It was a nice idea: like cutting all the old bonds and letting them trail away, leaving her free to start again. Letting go; yes, she liked that idea, she liked it a lot.

twenty-two

Izzie had always adored New York Fashion Week. Twice a year, beautiful Bryant Park on Sixth Avenue was transformed into fashion central, and the world's top designers, models, fashionistas and celebrity dogs—plus owners—descended upon it to watch. By Friday morning, after an enormous amount of work, several huge white tents sat in the middle of the pretty little square, with all the iron tables and chairs having been moved out of the way under the trees.

It was lunchtime on a sweltering September day and people were taking advantage of the square's khaki table umbrellas, shading themselves from the sun and sipping coffees and diet sodas as they waited for the next show to begin. After getting out of her taxi in a traffic jam on 42nd Street to walk the final few hundred yards, Izzie felt that Bryant Park was like an oasis of calm snoozing under the watchful eye of the surrounding tall buildings.

The calm was strictly surface, though. Izzie had the spring/summer schedule in her hand and there were shows running from ten in the morning until five in the evening, every hour on the hour. Not all the designers used the tents, either—some showed in hotels and restaurants nearby, and for people working in the modeling industry there was a lot of rushing around from venue to venue, hoping everyone had turned up, frantically phoning for replacements if they hadn't and generally trying not to panic.

Bookers only got to go if they were lucky enough to get precious tickets from the designers, and when she'd worked with Perfect-NY Izzie had managed to see quite a few shows every year.

This was her first time at Fashion Week as boss of her own company, and though there really wasn't any absolute need for her to be there, SilverWebb had models in one of the shows, so Izzie had made sure she'd got her hands on tickets and backstage accreditation for today. High-fashion designers almost never used plus-sized models but Seldi Drew, a vibrant new design company run by a couple from Florida, based its whole range on ordinary women. They were showing in the main tent at two, but there was another show ahead of them, which meant that backstage the makeup, hairstylists, dressers and production people for that show would be taking up all the space.

Izzie had eight girls in the show and they'd already had a run-through with the Seldi Drew producer, making sure they moved at the right pace to a throbbing, rhythmic beat. Sometimes after shows she'd watched in the past, Izzie found she had a headache from the music, but models always said that walking down the runway was easier with a heavy beat, so they loved the bass thump of runway music.

By half one, all the SilverWebb girls were in makeup and hair, all the models for the show had turned up, and there had been only one minor catastrophe, when Feliz Guadaluppe, one of the Seldi Drew stylists, had discovered a model wearing a black thong instead of a nude one.

"Why would you do that?" he shrieked to the startled girl. "It might be seen through the clothes!"

Izzie felt a moment's relief that the guilty party wasn't a SilverWebb girl.

"Feliz, settle!" she commanded. "It's not the end of the world. Here you are," she said to the girl, pulling a new three-pack of Gap G-strings out of her bag. She mightn't have spent much time backstage at shows, but she knew enough to be prepared.

"You're a regular Girl Scout," laughed the model.

"That's me," agreed Izzie, and hugged Feliz briskly to break the cycle of horror. He leaned against her, a quivering mass of gym-toned, Hedi Slimane–clad fashionista.

"I'm fine, I'm fine," he said, fanning his face with his hand. "The shock, you know?"

"I know," Izzie said.

Crisis over, Feliz whipped round to continue styling the models. Izzie's cell phone, which she had stuck into her trouser pocket so she'd feel it, began to ring.

"Hey, you, how's it going?" said Carla.

"Great," said Izzie.

"Someone phoned looking for you," Carla went on, "a Caroline Montgomery-Knight."

"Doesn't ring any bells with me," Izzie said. "She leave a number?"

"Yeah." Carla read out the number and Izzie jotted it down. She really had to clean out her handbag, she thought—it was full of bits of papers and numbers, and with the agency's model cards tucked carefully into a hard folder in the outside pocket, not to mention necessities like G-strings, it was like hauling around a sack of potatoes.

She dialed the number, got a WASPy-sounding woman's voicemail with no clues as to whether it was a private or a business line, and left her name and cell number. If this Caroline wanted to talk to her, she'd ring.

Izzie didn't care much either way. It was hard to get worked up over anything these last few days. She was still reeling from her lunch with Joe. He hadn't phoned her since and she was glad. Glad because she still didn't know what she was going to do.

She and Carla had talked it over endlessly.

"How badly do you want your own kids?" Carla would ask, devil's-advocate-style. "Could you settle for not having them?"

Each time, Izzie came back to the same answer: she didn't know. She loved Joe, but she had a vision of them in the future, with this question coming back to haunt them. Would she wake up someday when she was too old for children and resent the hell out of Joe for stopping her conceiving? If she pushed him into having a baby, would he resent the hell out of her for affecting his relationship with his older children?

And could they ever accept her? Could Josh, Matt and Tom ever learn to love her either way?

There were no answers to these questions, and therefore no peace for Izzie.

When her cell phone rang again, the situation backstage in the big tent was at fever pitch. Someone was screaming in one corner of the tent, a model was yelling that she didn't see why she shouldn't smoke just because there were bloody signs up everywhere saying she shouldn't, and the buzz of hair dryers and loud conversation made hearing what the caller was saying nearly impossible.

"Izzie Silver?"

"Yes?" roared Izzie.

"Caroline Montgomery-Knight," said the woman. It still didn't mean anything to Izzie.

The woman said something else but the screaming had reached a crescendo and she couldn't hear.

"Sorry, I didn't catch that. It's a bit noisy here," Izzie yelled. "I'm at Fashion Week, down at Bryant Park."

There was silence and Izzie thought the connection must have been broken, but then the woman spoke again.

"If I come down, can I meet you there?"

"Izzie! My hair, look!" Belinda, a tall girl from Idaho, stood in front of her, on the verge of tears. Look!" shrieked Belinda again. She held up a blond ringlet that seemed perfectly all right to Izzie but which bore the faint smell of singed hair.

"The show's just starting and it should be over by two twenty. I could see you at three thirty?" That would give them twenty minutes for the show, and over an hour for the postmortem. "I'll meet you at the Bryant Park Grill, you know it? The restaurant with the green awning and the trailing plants hanging down from upstairs."

"At four then."

Izzie scribbled a note on a corner of her notebook. Caroline Montgomery-Knight. The name was vaguely familiar, that was all. Still, it would be appalling to lose business just because she'd had a momentary blip and couldn't remember who the woman was. She'd know her when she saw her, presumably—otherwise, Caroline would have asked what Izzie looked like.

The show was a fabulous success: the clothes looked wonderful, so did the models, and there was an admiring buzz from the fashion press that said, louder than any front-page headline could, that Seldi Drew had produced a breakout collection.

There was prestige in being associated with such success and Izzie was glowing with contentment when she made it to the restaurant at half three and ordered a bottle of icy Pellegrino. Her water had just been delivered and she was about to take a sip when someone addressed her.

"Izzie Silver?"

She looked up to see a tall blond woman staring coldly down at her. Caroline Montgomery-Knight, she surmised.

Izzie didn't know why, but there was something about the way the woman was looking at her that sent chills down her spine.

"Yes," she said with a confidence she didn't feel. She didn't know this woman, that was for sure. Ms. Montgomery-Knight was tall, Park Avenue slim and had a Nordic blond bob. In the midst of the fashion crowd, she stood out like a very elegant sore thumb in a mocha-colored twin set, real—and not ironic—pearls, and Capri pants finished off with soft ballet flats. Izzie had never seen her before but . . . wait, she looked a little like—

"You're the bitch sleeping with my brother-in-law," the woman said flatly.

Too late, Izzie realized the woman looked *exactly* like Joe's wife, Elizabeth Hansen.

For what felt like the first time ever, she was utterly lost for words.

"You want to do this here?" Caroline Montgomery-Knight gestured around the room. "Or outside?"

"Outside," said Izzie, gulping.

Izzie followed Caroline out of the restaurant, clutching her big handbag with one hand and trying to feel her way through the crowd, as if she was blind, with the other. She might as well be blind, she thought: blind drunk, blind stupid, blind something. This was an absolute nightmare, coming face-to-face with her lover's sister-in-law. How had it all come to this? She knew she could always run away, but that wasn't Izzie's style. There was no running away from this; she had to face the music. A few yards from the restaurant, Caroline whirled around and stopped, folded her arms, and faced Izzie, her expression diamond hard.

"I suppose this isn't the first time you've done this," Caroline said harshly. "It must be tough, finding the right rich guy. Though perhaps finding them isn't the hard part, I guess. Getting them to leave their wives, *that* must be harder. I guess because you're still working for your little agency"—she spoke as if Izzie's job was a mere step up from streetwalking—"you mustn't have got the right guy yet. And Joe's not your guy."

Izzie stared at her and felt sick at being the focus of such hatred.

"My sister wouldn't lower herself to come here to meet you. She doesn't know I'm doing it. Let me tell you, she's worth ten of you."

Still Izzie said nothing.

"Joe's not a bad person," Caroline went on. "Dumb, though. Dumb enough to think he can have it all if he leaves Elizabeth. They can't, you know: the fathers can't have it if they leave. They might think the money will fix it, but you can't fix Daddy not being home every night. Money doesn't make that work. Elizabeth and I grew up with that. Our parents divorced, and let me tell you, she won't let it destroy her boys. They have a good marriage and they've three great kids. Did he mention that to you? Bet he didn't. Men never do when they want to get you into bed."

Izzie felt herself recoil at the venom in Caroline's voice. But painful as it was, she felt that in some way she deserved this venom. She had hurt this woman's sister—not out of malice or greed for his money, but in the belief that Joe couldn't be interested in her if he still had a marriage left.

Now Caroline was saying something different.

"You know, Elizabeth thinks that if he wants to go, he should." Caroline glared at Izzie. "I'm not handing him to you on a platter, no way. You need to hear it all. He's done it before—screwed around, that is."

Izzie took the punch and remained standing. But she'd had enough. She hadn't gone into the Hansens' marriage with a crowbar—she'd met one half of the marriage who'd wanted out. The damage they'd done themselves to bring Joe to that point was not her fault.

"I'm going to stop you there," Izzie said. "Yes, I was seeing Joe for a while," she added, knowing she had probably broken the number one rule of difficult discussions by admitting blame in the first five minutes, but she had to, there was nowhere else to go. She had slept with Caroline's sister's husband and she could understand what had driven Caroline to storm down here to confront her.

"Bragging about it, are you?" replied Caroline, and for the first time her carapace cracked. Her eyes looked suspiciously watery.

"No, that's not it at all," Izzie said. "There is no point pretending it didn't happen. To get the facts straight, Joe told me his marriage was over and I believe him—he wasn't making that up.

Whatever's gone on between the two of them is their business, but don't try and blame me for it."

"How can you say—" began Caroline.

Izzie interrupted her. "Your sister's relationship with her husband is none of my business."

But Caroline came right back at her. "Oh, so that makes it OK to take him away from her, does it? Don't think about anything else, just take the guy. I hate women like you. You're after one thing: money. You've probably run around with every guy in New York and then, when the Botox stops working so well, you decide you're going to snatch somebody else's guy. If he wasn't rich, don't tell me you'd have looked at him twice."

As she finished, she began to cry: sad, slow sobs that had been building up.

Izzie reached into her bag and found a tissue. First G-strings, now tissues.

"Here," she said, handing it over.

"Thanks," mumbled Caroline.

"Do you want to sit down?" asked Izzie. She must be mad. She should be running away from this woman, not giving her tissues.

They found two seats near the tents and Caroline sank onto hers with the weariness of someone who'd just about fired themselves up with enough energy to complete a horrible task, and then collapsed when the task was over.

She was the task, Izzie realized grimly. She was the monster Caroline had come to slay. With her anger dissolving in tears, the other woman looked normal, like a slim, tired woman with lines around her eyes, a woman who'd come to fight for her beloved sister.

"Sorry if it sounds like cliché central, but Joe is the first man I've ever been involved with who wasn't single or had his divorce papers in a drawer," Izzie explained. "And what I feel—sorry, felt—about Joe has nothing to do with money."

Caroline appeared all out of talk, so Izzie went on.

"I ended it with him because I didn't want a relationship where he was still living with your sister, even though he told me it was over, finished."

"Joe would never say those things," Caroline protested weakly. "He loves Elizabeth."

It was like revenge tennis, Izzie thought: *he* said, *she* said. What else could Caroline do but defend her sister?

"Listen, it's not up to me—or you, for that matter—whether they have the perfect marriage or not. Who knows who's telling the truth? Have you tried to talk like this to Joe?"

Caroline shook her head.

"Why me first?" Izzie asked. "He's the one you know; he's the one who is married to your sister and was betraying her, as you put it. Shouldn't he be the person you'd see first and beg to stop, not me?"

Again, the other woman said nothing.

"And what about Elizabeth? Maybe their marriage is awful"—Izzie stopped and held out a hand as Caroline opened her mouth—"but either way, you and I aren't responsible for that. It's theirs to fix or break."

"You're not what I thought," Caroline said. "You're older."

"Thank you," Izzie said pleasantly.

"That's not what I mean," Caroline said quickly. "I had you figured out for one of those women who trap married men, but you're not."

"Who are those people, those man trappers?" Izzie asked. "I'm not saying there aren't women out there messed up enough to break up marriages for fun, but I've never met one. The way people talk about them, you'd think New York was awash with them, and it isn't. Who in their right mind would do that?" she said. "There's no fun falling for someone who happens to be married. You don't fall in love with them because they are married, you just fall in love with them, and then you discover they *don't* have the divorce papers in the drawer after all, and it's all thrown on its head."

"You could have walked away then, when it turned out not to be so simple," Caroline remarked quietly, and Izzie had absolutely no defense, because she could have walked away and she hadn't.

It was the crux of the matter. Something in her had said that what she felt with Joe was so amazing, so special, so different to anything she'd ever felt before, that it was real. It could only be real if he loved her back and he would only love her back if his own marriage was already in its death throes. She wasn't killing what was already dead. But there was no point in explaining that now. She didn't want to fight.

"I shouldn't have come here," Caroline said, getting to her feet. "But I'm glad I did. You're not a bitch, I see that. But for their family's sake, leave him alone."

"I have," said Izzie angrily. She thought she'd explained all that.

"Seriously, they love those boys. They love each other, they really do."

Izzie nodded. She wanted Caroline to go. She felt so tired. Being with Joe was like some huge quest, full of pain and heartache, and she wasn't able to deal with it anymore.

"No, they really do," Caroline insisted. "Why, just last month Elizabeth had a pregnancy scare. She thought she might be pregnant with their fourth child. 'At my age!' she said to me. She's forty-two, by the way. Lots of women have babies at her age, but it happens she's not pregnant after all. Still, it made them think, you know, about another child. Could that happen if they didn't love each other?"

Izzie didn't answer the question; she felt too much pain inside her. She'd never asked Joe whether he still slept with his wife or not. Such a thing was beneath both of them. In the beginning, she'd assumed not, since he and Elizabeth lived separate lives. Then, as time went on, she'd hoped that it wasn't the case. She'd thought about it, how two people living in the same house could come together over wine and shared experiences.

But that wasn't what hurt most. The baby did that.

Still, it made them think, you know, about another child, Caroline had said.

And another child would be an option. They had three beloved sons. They shared so much. Another child wouldn't be the disaster it would be if Izzie was its mother.

In this situation another child could be the glue that put the Hansens' marriage back together.

"Caroline, I have to go now," Izzie said formally.

"Of course." Caroline nodded.

They stood awkwardly for a moment. It wasn't the time or the place for handshakes.

"You're a good sister," Izzie blurted out suddenly. "Good-bye."

Whirling around, she walked in the direction of the big fashion tent, her head flooded with images of Joe and Elizabeth having a baby. She kept seeing a baby in her mind, except it wasn't Elizabeth's, it was hers, Izzie's.

"Hiya," yelled a voice.

She looked around. It was someone from another agency who'd clearly also sneaked down to watch the shows.

"Yeah, hi," she said, trying to look as if she was madly busy, not wanting to talk to anybody. There was no need for her to go back into the tent for the next show, but she just needed to be alone with her thoughts, and this was the only safe place right now.

In the tent chaos still reigned, but somehow Izzie tuned out all the noise.

A baby. She'd never have a baby, not with him, not with anyone.

Izzie slipped out through an emergency exit and found a quiet corner behind the tent, where she sat down and began to write an email on her BlackBerry. It took her an hour to compose the email, a ridiculous amount of time given how short it was.

She'd put "private" on the subject line because even though Joe had told her the address he'd given her was his private email address, she'd never sent anything to it before and she wasn't sure if his secretary went through all his emails, private or not.

Hello, Joe,

I got a phone call from a Caroline Montgomery-Knight. I didn't know who she was until she met me down in the middle of Fashion Week. I was here for my agency and then along came your sister-in-law to tell me that you and Elizabeth have a strong marriage, and that just a month ago, Elizabeth thought she was expecting another baby.

I'm taking the coward's way out because I can't talk to you again. I'm sorry.

Go back to them all. Leave me alone. It would never have worked. It's better this way.

I

She didn't want to sign herself "Izzie." That was too personal. She reread it all, adding a comma here, tweaking there—"Oh fuck it," she said out loud. Why was she bothering with grammar? All she needed to convey was a simple message, and when he read this, he'd get it. She pressed Send. It was gone, like Joe, out of her life.

She left Bryant Park and walked aimlessly along the sidewalk, stopping in a coffee shop for a latte that she barely tasted. It was nearly six when she made it back to the office. Their assistant,

Sasha, was out on the last coffee run of the day—the espresso machine was still broken. Lola was on the phone and so was Carla.

Carla held up a hand in greeting, then registered the look on Izzie's face. As much as she'd tried to disguise it, Izzie could tell that her pain was evident.

"What's up?" mouthed Carla across the room at her.

Izzie shook her head, afraid to speak in case she cried. She would not cry; she had wasted enough tears on Joe. She would never cry over him again. If she had to go down to the voodoo end of town and get some Haitian queen to come up with a spell involving chicken innards and rabbit's feet to get him out of her mind, she would. She was never going to talk to or see him again.

"Hey, what's happening?" said Carla, hanging up.

"I . . ." Izzie knew she was going to sob now. She turned and rushed toward the women's room with Carla hot on her heels.

"What's wrong?"

"What do you think?" said Izzie brokenly. "Joe Hansen, that's what's wrong."

"What now?" said Carla.

"His sister-in-law was the woman trying to phone me—Caroline-Bloody-Montgomery. She turned up at the Bryant Park Grill."

She had to stop and find a tissue to blow her nose.

"And . . . ?" asked Carla ominously.

"She told me Joe and her sister had a brilliant marriage and that"—Izzie could barely bring herself to say it—"that Elizabeth thought she was pregnant a month ago."

"Oh." Carla hitched herself up so she could sit on the vanity unit and lean her back against the mirror. "Honey, I knew that guy was up to no good the first moment I heard about him."

"You're wrong," Izzie said, startling her friend. "He's a good guy—too good. I wasn't up against his wife, I can see that now. I was up against his family, his kids. And that's not what I want or wanted: to compete with them for his love. He wouldn't be the man I loved if he didn't adore them. And he does."

She blew her nose again.

"There's no future for us and it's not because he slept with his wife. He's not ready to leave his family, no matter what he thinks. If he did, it would hang over us for the rest of our lives."

"The specter of the first family?" Carla said.

"Yeah, the three people he loves most in the whole world thinking he'd left them. He couldn't take that, and neither could I."

"So it's over? You told him?"

"Email."

Carla winced. "Probably the best way. You'd bleed to death if you had to see him."

Izzie managed a smile.

"Age does matter, doesn't it?" Izzie said to Carla that evening as they shared a cab home. Somehow Izzie had sleepwalked through the rest of the day, barely functioning and refusing to answer her phone in case Joe rang.

"No, of course it doesn't," Carla said, the way she always did. But Izzie interrupted her.

"You're wrong, it does. It matters for women—it matters because you can't have children."

"What about Madonna?" said Carla. "What age was she when she had her last baby? There's loads of other movie stars who've had kids late."

"Oh yeah," said Izzie, "and for every movie star who manages to have a baby, there's four hundred other women who didn't. You only hear about the successes, Carla, not the failures. Most of those people have guys in their lives: husbands, lovers, whatever. What do I have? Nothing. At least if you go down that whole trying-to-have-a-baby-chemically route, you should have somebody with you, somebody to moan about it and cry about it with. I wouldn't have that. I'd have nothing."

"Don't call your friends nothing," said Carla, pretending to be insulted to jerk Izzie out of her misery.

"I don't mean it like that," Izzie said quickly. "But if you're going to go on the baby quest, you do need to have somebody doing it with you. At least somebody to provide the sperm—otherwise what do you do, get donor sperm?"

"Plenty of people do that too," Carla said.

"Yeah, and that's a valid way of doing things. I'm not disrespecting it. But it's not an easy option, either. What do you tell the child? By the way, your daddy is Test Tube 453? I'm sorry, but it does make it more difficult. If that's the only option, fine, that's the only option, but wouldn't it be easier to have a guy you made love with and get pregnant? Wouldn't that be nicer than all these moral dilemmas of what you tell the children in the future? 'The test tube and I really loved each other, kids.' "

"You sound so defeatist," Carla said. "I never thought you were going to turn into one of those crazy baby ladies who had nothing in her life except misery and wishing she'd had a child. You can still do it, if you want to."

"You don't feel that way about kids, do you?" Izzie asked.

Carla shook her head. "No, and I'm really grateful, because I've seen it eat people up. I never thought you had that hunger, Izzie."

"I never did," Izzie said sorrowfully. "I always thought there was time for everything. Time for me to fall in love, time maybe for the baby to happen. I thought I was young and, look, now I'm not."

"Thirty-nine isn't old."

"Forty in two months," Izzie corrected her. "It's the whole Joe thing. I'm in mourning, I guess. Him and me, and me reaching forty and still not having had a child—all that is the end of something, and when you reach the end of something, you have to mourn. It's the end of my romance and baby chances, I know it is. That's hard to take."

The cab pulled up outside Carla's building.

"Forget about him," she urged. "You're better than him, you've so much going on. Look, we've got the company, we've so many plans, it's an exciting time in our lives."

Izzie nodded. Carla was right; everything she said was the truth. SilverWebb was going from strength to strength. On a professional level, everything was right in Izzie Silver's world. But on a personal level, the ground had just fallen from under her feet.

All the certainties in life—her grandmother being there and the notion that one day she'd find love and perhaps a family—had vanished.

"Yeah, you're right," she said, trying to sound cheerful for Carla's benefit. "Everything is going to be fine," she said. "Fake it till you make it."

"Way to go," said Carla. " 'Fake it till you make it': words to live by."

Izzie didn't notice Joe sitting on the steps outside her building until the cab had driven away.

Oh God, he was here. She couldn't cope with this, not with seeing him. She'd cry and then she'd never stop. . . .

"Izzie?"

He sounded so forlorn, not Mogul Man anymore.

"I can't talk to you, Joe," she said. "Please leave me alone."

"I don't want to leave you alone," he insisted. "I'm sorry, sorry about Caroline and the baby and what I said to you—"

Izzie stopped him. She knew what she had to do and nothing he could say would change her mind. It was over. All she had to do now was let him go, make him go.

"Joe," she said, fighting back the tears, "I'm telling you to go, right? We could never make each other happy. You'd be swallowed up with guilt about your kids, and I'd be swallowed up with resentment about my lack of kids. Don't you see? It could never work. We'd hurt each other and them too. You'd never forgive me for that. So leave me alone. Go back to them. It's what you want, really."

"It's not," he said frantically.

"It is," she said, feeling pity for him because he was still fighting it. Not like her: she'd stopped fighting. He wanted his family more than he wanted her. His mistake had been thinking he could have both. "I'm letting you go, Joe, for both our sakes. Won't you just go?" she pleaded.

He faltered, and at that moment Izzie knew she'd both lost and won.

"But—"

"No buts," she said.

He stood aside as she walked up the steps to her building. With shaking fingers, she found her keys and stuck them in the lock.

"Good-bye, Joe," she said, and pushed the door open without turning back.

Inside, she waited for the tears to come but they didn't. Maybe later. She had all the time in the world, after all. All the time in the world to cry on her own.

twenty-three

Yvonne chatted nineteen to the dozen on the trip home, as if, Anneliese thought, constant conversation would block out their having to discuss the elephant in the room, that Anneliese had tried to commit suicide. Anneliese felt that it must be the same as when somebody had cancer. Everyone tried so desperately hard not to talk about it, when the person with the disease didn't mind talking about it. They accepted that it was a huge part of their life and there was no getting away from it. They didn't have the choice of ignoring it.

There had been huge excitement in the Lifeboat Shop, Yvonne said, when someone had handed in a genuine Hermès Kelly handbag.

"I wouldn't recognize an Hermès handbag if it bit me on the bottom," Yvonne went on, "but this was it, the real deal. We put it in the window."

Anneliese had a hazy memory of hearing that such handbags cost thousands of euros.

"What are you selling it for?" she asked.

"Four hundred euros," Yvonne revealed. "I don't think we've ever sold anything for four hundred before—well, apart from that lawn mower."

Another topic that Yvonne considered suitable for discussion was the forthcoming autumn market in Harbor Square. It was going to be running for the next two Saturdays. Yvonne's daughter had been making crystal earrings for weeks now and was all set with her stall. Yvonne was being supportive, although really she felt that Catriona would have been better studying something practical in college instead of spending hours with teeny-weeny beads and jeweler's wire.

"What can you do?" she said. "I'm limited to saying, 'That's great, Catriona. Fair play to you, love.' My mother would've hit me over the head and told me to go out and get a proper job if she saw me wasting my education like that—Catriona got five As in her Leaving Certificate!—but being a parent is so different these days."

The final subject was that dear, sweet Jodi was pregnant.

"How wonderful," said Anneliese with pleasure. Jodi had come to see her once, bearing magazines and chocolate, and was one of the few people who hadn't seemed embarrassed by the locked ward.

Other, older friends had sent cards and notes but seemed to be scared to come in, as if mental illness was both contagious and so incomprehensible they were afraid to dip their toe in the water.

"She's absolutely delighted," Yvonne said. "Her mum, Karen, is going to stay in Ireland until after the baby's born. She teaches yoga—imagine that! I know Jodi wanted to tell you the good news when she went to visit you, but I told her she would want to be careful . . ." Yvonne's voice trailed off. "We didn't want to upset you or anything."

Anneliese was far too fond of dear Yvonne to let her go on torturing herself.

"Listen, Yvonne," she said, "life goes on, and I'm happy that it does. All I can say is, I was having a very bad time and I did something I'm sorry for. Telling me about the real world isn't going to stop me doing it again, if I wanted to—which I don't," she added hurriedly. "If someone wants to kill themselves, they will, they'll find a way. I think maybe what I did was a cry for help and it's shown me that I *do* want to be around. So tell me everything, Yvonne, *everything* that's gone on in the town. Don't be keeping little bits of news from me in case you upset me, because they won't, really."

"Oh, Anneliese," wailed Yvonne, who then swerved wildly on the road. "Sorry, sorry," she said, hauling the car back on track.

"Jesus, when I talked about killing myself, I didn't mean now, in your car," Anneliese joked, and suddenly they were both laughing.

"I never thought we'd be breaking our hearts laughing over this," Yvonne said. "I was dreading this, you know—I thought I'd be tiptoeing around you, not knowing what to say. I said to Frank, 'It's going to be different, because ideally the person who'd be picking her up would be Edward,' but . . ." She paused again, as if she'd realized she'd made another big boo-boo.

"Edward did offer to pick me up, actually," Anneliese said, "which was very sweet of him, under the circumstances."

"I'm sure that cow, Nell, would be foaming at the mouth if he came to pick you up. Not that she has a leg to stand on, I mean, considering what's happened . . ." Yvonne went on.

"Really, it's OK," Anneliese said. "There's nothing like a near-death experience for getting you to make your peace with the world, Yvonne, and I have. I told Edward it was really sweet of him but that we had to move on and I didn't want to fall into the trap of relying on him, as if everything was the same as it was before, because it isn't. It's so kind of you to come and get me. I really appreciate it."

Yvonne's kindness was evident in the house too. She'd been in with Jodi, given the place a thorough cleaning, and there were other signs of kindness around the cottage: fresh flowers on two of the tables, a bottle of wine on the counter in the kitchen.

"I didn't know," said Yvonne carefully, "whether any drink would be suitable or not. I thought, God, you might be on medicine and wine would send you completely over the edge. But then Frank said I was overthinking and that a little drop wouldn't kill you."

Anneliese smiled. "I bet it won't," she said, "and I'm not on any medication, except for some new antidepressants, and I can have half a glass of wine with them, I think."

Yvonne was fascinated. "So you're not taking things to calm you down and flatten you out or whatever?" she said. "My mother was mad for them you know, addicted, really. That was in the days when they handed them out like sweets, 'Mother's little helpers'—or was that gin?"

"They did try to give me medication when I was in the hospital," Anneliese admitted. "When they realized I didn't want everything blotted out or to be numb, that was fine, they stopped. Their aim is to get you better, and you're not going to get better if you're in a daze of Happyland. Nothing wrong with Happyland," she added, "but it just wasn't for me. So no chemical numbing, but a bottle of wine will do very nicely, thank you."

The doorbell rang at that moment and Yvonne went to answer it. The caller was Corinne from the Lifeboat Shop, smelling heavily of scented oils and waving a big bag that contained, no doubt, all sorts of organic, smelly goodies that would make Anneliese feel perfect—*Naturally, darling*.

With her was Stephen from the garden center, hidden behind a huge selection of plants in an old cardboard box. "I thought a bit of planting would do you good, Anneliese," he said, shoving the box at her.

She grinned. The gesture was so kind, bless him.

Yvonne opened the wine she'd bought.

"That shop-bought plonk is desperate," Corinne was saying. "My homemade elderflower wine . . ."

"Yes, I know," said Yvonne, "it's totally natural. But, Corinne, it still tastes like cat's piss. We're not drinking it, even if you have three pints of it in the back of your car, right?"

Corinne giggled. "It was only a suggestion," she said. "There're fewer antioxidants in the homemade stuff."

"And more alcohol," said Stephen.

"Exactly. *That's* why you like it, Corinne," added Yvonne. "One glass and everyone is lying on the floor, plastered."

Corinne had brought an enormous poppy-seed cake, which she cut up and they began to eat. Her wine aside, Corinne's cakes were legendary.

"Real food," said Anneliese sighing. "I'll tell you, I don't know why people go to health farms to lose weight. They just need to go into the psychiatric unit of Tamarin's local hospital. The food is appalling. Anyone would lose a few pounds in there."

"Do you think that could be a new diet?" laughed Yvonne, uproarious after one glass of wine in the afternoon.

"Ah no, it's a bit radical," Anneliese said.

"There's always liposuction," suggested Stephen, and the other three looked at him in complete astonishment. Stephen was so otherworldly that the thought of him knowing anything about liposuction was very strange.

"Well, there was this woman in the garden center the other day. She's just moved into Tamarin and she's renovating one of those houses down near the harbor and, well, you know, we got to talking." He went puce and Anneliese kindly changed the subject.

It would be gorgeous if Stephen found somebody to love. He'd been single forever. If the others teased him, he'd never mention it again.

She was saved by the bell ringing for the second time.

"Lord, it's like Grand Central Station here," said Corinne happily, getting herself another hunk of her own poppy-seed cake.

Anneliese opened the door to find Mac standing at it and suddenly something pale and woolly bashed into her, rushed between her legs and ran into the house. She whirled around, aware of a definite scent of wet dog. "I thought your dog was a big black thing?" she said to Mac.

"It is," he said, and looked marginally sheepish. "This isn't my dog. She's your dog."

"What do you mean, my dog?"

"She's a rescue dog, I thought you might take her on, being . . . seeing as how . . ."

Anneliese looked at him. "You rescued me, so I'm having a rescue dog—or is it that I need more rescuing and rescuing her will rescue me or—"

He shrugged. "Yes, all of the above."

"Mac, I don't want a dog," Anneliese started. "I'm . . ." And she stopped because there was no reason why she couldn't have a dog; it was just that if she got one, she'd want to get one in her own time and not when somebody else turned up with one. She looked into the living room, where the dog was standing, shivering and sniffing the air. She was so not Anneliese's type of dog. Anneliese liked medium-sized, smooth-haired dogs and this thing was, well, big with pale woolly fur and in severe need of a bath. It definitely hadn't seen hot soapy water for a very long time, and God knows how you'd put it in a bath. The dog looked Anneliese right in the eye and blinked innocently, huge coppery canine eyes boring into hers.

"Oh well," Anneliese said, "I suppose maybe we can rescue each other. What's her name?"

Mac shrugged. "She didn't say."

Anneliese bestowed one of her killer glares on him but he just grinned.

Eventually, the poppy-seed cake was gone, so was the wine, and everyone waved happily at both Anneliese and the dog as they left.

The dog was still content to look blankly and slightly nervously at Anneliese, and cowered close to the bottom of the couch when she tried to pet her.

"Please don't cringe every time I come near," Anneliese begged.

The dog still looked at her suspiciously.

"Right: house rules. If you're moving in, you have to let me pat you occasionally and allow me to give you a bath. Ah, you can understand human." The dog had definitely shivered a bit at the mention of the word *bath*.

"So we understand each other after all."

By the time she'd finished, the bathroom was a sodden mass of towels, with shampoo foam everywhere. She'd found an old bottle of dandruff shampoo, and decided that that was suitably doggy for the task. It was also very lathery, and it had taken all of her strength to hold the dog in the bath in her attempts to wash all the suds out of the dog's coat. Finally, she was out, clean but wet, running around the house at high speed in absolute delight and shaking herself all over everything. "You're like a puppy, really," Anneliese said, laughing.

It was so lovely to be able to laugh, she thought suddenly, and she thanked the dog for giving her those few moments of humor.

"Thank you, puppy. But you're not a puppy, are you?"

Mac said he'd got her from the local vet, who reckoned the dog had to be five or six years old. As to a precise age, it was anybody's guess. She looked quite well cared for, if a little thin.

The cowering must mean that somebody had hurt her. Nobody would do that here, Anneliese told her firmly.

"I suppose I could call you Nell, because being a female dog, you are theoretically a bitch," Anneliese said, looking at the dog. The dog stopped running around and threw herself down on Anneliese's feet, wriggling and rubbing her back into her new mistress's ankles, as if trying to get a back massage.

"No, naming you Nell would be cruel, and beneath me," Anneliese decided. "What do you want to be called, darling?"

Finished wriggling around, the dog sat up, leaned her back against Anneliese's legs and tilted her head backward, so that her silky ears hung down and her eyes looked up beseechingly at Anneliese.

Wet, the dog resembled nothing so much as a seal or a silkie, Anneliese thought. Silkies were the mythical creatures who were reputed to live off the western coastal islands, half human, half seal. "You're a silkie," she said. "Silkie, that's a nice name."

Silkie wagged her wet tail.

"I guess we're stuck with each other," Anneliese said. "I suppose you'll want to sleep in my bedroom?"

Silkie wriggled some more against her.

"Fine. I just hope you don't snore."

twenty-four

Six months later

Izzie stretched her legs out and said a mental thank-you that SilverWebb was doing so marvelously well, or else she'd still be counting her dollars and be stuck back in steerage as usual. She'd never flown home to Ireland in the business class section of the plane before and it was lovely not to be squashed in the middle of a row of four.

She didn't allow herself to think about the flights on the Gulfstream with Joe. They were part of the crazy dream sequence of the previous year and symbolized a time in her life that she didn't want to return to. This—sitting in an airplane seat she'd paid for—was what her life was about now. Not flying in luxury with Joe.

Joe. She closed her eyes and let him flood into her mind. She didn't do that much lately: give him head space. Because when he got in, he took over. Even the imaginary Joe had so much charisma he overwhelmed everyone and everything, she thought ruefully.

The real-life version had phoned five times in the past six months, but somehow she'd forced herself not to take his calls, just let him leave a message and then listened to it.

I wanted to say hi, I'm thinking about you. Think about you a lot, Izzie, as it happens. Call me.

She'd erased the last message after listening to it three times, but she could still recall every word. *Call me.*

She longed to do just that. Just to see what he wanted to talk about, if he was still with his wife, if he'd realized how much he'd hurt her, and how much of a sacrifice it had been for her to walk away. . . .

"Would you like some champagne, madam, or orange juice?" the steward asked her, proffering a small tray.

Izzie smiled at him, grateful on two counts. She took orange juice and a glass of champagne for later.

Joe was the past—the present was about this trip to Ireland to see Mitzi, her cousin's baby, for the first time, and to see Gran.

Not, she hoped silently, for the last time. Gran was still in a coma, alive but not alive, her life slipping away in the nursing home.

Anneliese had warned Izzie to be ready, that it would be hard to see her: "She looks very frail now, Izzie, love," Anneliese had explained on the phone. "She's still Lily but she's not there, if you know what I mean."

Izzie had mumbled in response and pretended that she wasn't crying. She'd done nothing but cry for the past months, it seemed. Over Joe and over Gran. Two huge voids in her life.

"Mitzi is a little darling," Anneliese had gone on. "You'll love her, Izzie. She's the image of Beth when she was that age, although, as I keep saying to Beth, Mitzi sleeps."

Mitzi was nearly five months old and the grand family reunion was for the occasion of her christening. If she was totally honest with herself, Izzie hadn't really wanted to fly home for the event. Mitzi's birth was still a very raw place for her—not that she begrudged her cousin her darling baby, but it hurt so very much to think that even Beth had managed what she hadn't. She'd told nobody how she felt because she was so ashamed of her feelings. Surely only a horrible person could allow themselves to feel sad that they didn't have a child when their cousin gave birth.

And then, six weeks after the baby was born, when Izzie had tried to assuage her guilt by sending an elaborate baby layette and a vast toy giraffe from FAO Schwarz over in the post, Beth phoned.

It was late New York time and Izzie was slumped on her couch, slobbing in sweatpants and a sweater, flicking through the TV channels.

"Beth!" she said in surprise. They hadn't spoken since Mitzi's birth. "How are you?"

"Shattered," sighed Beth. "Mitzi's sleeping pattern is all over the place, and no matter how much I try to get her into a routine, I can't. Marcus is so busy at work and I'm doing it all myself—night feeds, day feeds, you name it."

Izzie felt a brief flicker of annoyance at her cousin for not realizing what riches she had, but she kept it to herself.

Finally, after a certain amount of talking about how marvelous New York must be compared to boring old Dublin, and how Beth had seen a magazine interview with Steffi, SilverWebb's most successful signing, and how fabulous it must be to work in modeling, Beth got to the point.

"The thing is, Marcus and I would like you to be Mitzi's godmother," she said.

"Me?" Izzie couldn't have been more stunned.

"Who better?" said Beth.

"But I don't know anything about kids," Izzie said, and knew as she said it that it was a stupid thing to say. If all godparents had to be child experts, then the worldwide numbers would surely be halved.

"You don't have to know one end of a baby from the other," said Beth cheerily. "It's supposed to be about moral guidance."

Izzie winced. Not, she felt, her area of expertise either.

"But really, it's more about whether you'd be there to take care of Mitzi if Marcus and I were run over by a truck. Not that we're planning on that happening. Do say you'll do it. The christening's in March in St. Canice's in Tamarin. We decided to have it there because it's such a pretty church and Mum would love it. She doesn't go to church as much as she used to, mind, but still, we all love it. Please?"

"Of course, I'd be honored," said Izzie, because there was simply nothing else she could say.

When she'd hung up, Izzie hugged her knees to her chest and cried. She felt so unworthy of being this new baby's godmother. The only thing Mitzi meant to her was the dull ache of craving a child of her own. What good could she do for the little mite under the circumstances?

In the end, she'd all but decided to call Beth and decline, risking family fury rather than do this special thing for all the wrong reasons. She'd come to the christening because she wanted to visit Gran, but she wouldn't be godmother.

And then she'd changed her mind because of Lola. After many years of dating both men and women, Lola had finally made her choice and moved in with a Danish photographer named Paula. Paula was tall and fair to Lola's petite darkness, and together they made a striking couple. They had also decided to adopt a baby.

Neither woman appeared to have any worries about embarking on such a plan after only a few months together. Nor did they seem anxious about encountering any difficulties as a same-sex couple.

"Why should we?" Lola said with a shrug. "We would give our baby a wonderful home."

Self-doubt was what Lola lacked, Izzie realized with a jolt. Lola knew she'd be a wonderful parent and she was chasing her dream, even if the combination of biology and sexuality made it difficult. She was going for it. Self-doubt wasn't holding her back.

Izzie thought about what she'd done to fulfill her own dreams—she'd fallen at the first fence. She'd accepted the fact that it was unlikely she'd give birth to her own child because of her age and the lack of a suitable man. So she'd closed that book and begun to grieve.

"How hard is it for single people to adopt?" she asked Lola, who laughed uproariously.

"A hell of a lot easier than for two gay women, let me tell you!"

It was like a chink in the darkness, a chink that allowed the possibility of being a mother to enter. Izzie Silver could be a mum after all. It would take courage and effort, but it was possible. The door didn't have to close just because there would be no Joe to share it with.

She filed the idea in the back of her mind until later.

Life was good after all. She was doing something she believed in, working with women who loved themselves. That felt good, although it would never balance out the ache in her heart where Gran and Joe used to be. Not that Gran was gone, really, but at night, when she was in bed and she thought of morning dawning across the Atlantic in Tamarin, it felt like it.

The horrendous pain she'd felt after saying good-bye to Joe was lessening and the times when she wanted to phone him and beg to get back together were few and far between. She'd made her choice and she was living with it. Perhaps she hadn't got everything she ever wanted, but then who did?

Anneliese could feel the muscles in her arms cording with the exertion. "I don't know how much longer I'm going to be able to keep up here," she whispered, feeling her legs wavering. This was only her third headstand and Karen was hovering close by, ready to leap into action if Anneliese faltered.

"Stay a bit longer, you're doing great. Keep your arms strong, Anneliese," she commanded in her soft Australian accent.

For someone so sweetly gentle in ordinary life, Karen became quite fierce when she was teaching yoga. But it worked: in the four months Anneliese had been going to yoga classes, she'd progressed quickly, and it was absolutely due to Karen's pushing her to the limit. When she'd first come, she'd groaned every time she did the simplest move, and now she was upside down parallel to a wall in the yoga studio, balancing on her forearms and elbows, with her legs straight up in the air.

"They make you do it on marble floors in Pune," Karen went on. Pune, in India, was yoga central for Iyengar yoga devotees and was where she'd finished her training.

"They're sadists, then," Anneliese gasped. "I thought yoga was about mind, body and spirit—not bashing your skull on marble floors."

Karen laughed. She loved Anneliese's wacky sense of humor.

"OK, you can come down now. You went up with your right leg so lead down with your left."

With a grace that astonished Anneliese, she brought her left leg down toward the floor, fluidly followed by the right.

"Wow." She knelt on her yoga mat and breathed heavily. "I never thought I'd be able to do it without leaning my legs against the wall," she said.

"You're a natural at this," Karen said cheerfully. "Shona, do you want to try now?"

As Karen helped another member of the small Friday-morning class to perform a headstand, Anneliese let the feelings of achievement flood through her. It was strange how utterly exhilarating yoga was, both physically and mentally. Unlike the keep-fit classes of Anneliese's youth, where it was all about fighting with your body and bouncing madly to keep in shape, this type of exercise worked with you. No matter how wound up she felt, an hour in the yoga studio above the art-supply shop on Stone Street calmed her down.

The ten-minute meditation session at the end of the class was better than any antidepressant, she'd decided. It had been a good day for her in particular, and for lots of Tamarin women in general, when Jodi's mother had decided to stay on in the town for the birth of her grandchild. Now that Jodi's baby had been born, a fluffy-headed little tyke named Kyle, who looked the image of his dad, Karen had started murmuring about staying here permanently.

After yoga, the ten women from the class always headed down to the town for tea and buns in Dorota's. Today Anneliese and Karen walked together, Anneliese feeling that glorious sense of well-being that came from warmed, stretched muscles and a mind that had managed to still for at least ten minutes.

"Are you all set for tomorrow?" Karen asked.

"Pretty much," Anneliese replied. "I'm glad we're having lunch afterward in the Harbor Hotel. It would be too uncomfortable to have it in my house, for all that things are good between Edward and me. A christening should be about creating new memories, not being flattened by the weight of old, bad ones, so a neutral venue is best."

"You seem happy about it all," Karen commented.

Anneliese grinned. Karen had become one of her closest friends over the past few months. What made it different was the fact that they were friends by choice, and not by the fact that they lived near each other or had kids in the same class at school. They'd simply bonded, although as Karen once remarked, "It helps that you've split up with your husband too." Anneliese knew what she meant. There were definite cabals within the groups of women in the town. Widows fitted into one category because they'd had their men taken from them. Divorced or separated women made up another group. And happily—or even unhappily—married women were in a different group altogether.

It was more challenging being friends with the latter, Anneliese had found. Intuitive married friends worried that talking about their state of blissful coupledom might upset Anneliese, while the less perceptive blithely discussed their husband, his shortcomings and how they'd love to kill him without for a moment thinking of how this sounded to a woman on her own.

With Karen, none of this mattered.

"I'm happy about it. As happy as I can be," Anneliese replied now. "It makes me sound like a bitch to say so, but it is easier since Edward moved out of Nell's house. For all that I don't want him back, I feel a certain smidgen of relief that Nell wasn't any better for him than I was, that she failed too. Does that make me sound like a total cow?"

"Yes," deadpanned Karen. "The mayor is putting a statue of you up in Harbor Square as we speak, immortalized in marble as a big cow. No," she insisted. "It makes you sound normal. However happy you are now, it would still hurt to see Edward and Nell acting like love's young bloody dream all around town. I think you've been brilliant about it all. If it had been me, I think I'd have walloped Nell every time I saw her. Or," Karen added thoughtfully, "put her phone number and the words 'Madame Whiplash' on all the call boxes in County Waterford."

Anneliese burst out laughing. "The thought did cross my mind," she joked. "Seriously, though, what would be the point? If someone wants to leave you, they will. It's taken me a while, but I've realized that there's no point taking it out on the person they happen to leave you for. That's sort of missing the point."

"But she was your friend," said Karen.

"True. That did hurt. If he'd left me for someone I didn't know, it wouldn't have been so bad. But leaving me for Nell was hard. You wouldn't believe how I tortured myself thinking about every occasion the three of us had been together, trying to work out when they were together, and if they'd been secretly discussing me behind my back. 'Anneliese is down today, isn't she.' That type of thing." She shuddered. "Still, it's over now. I feel sorry for Edward."

"I take it back," Karen said. "The mayor's not putting up a cow statue—it's going to be you as a saint. Saint Anneliese."

"No, honestly," Anneliese said. "I'm being serious. Women are better at being on their own. Nell's been on her own for years and I actually enjoy it. But Edward—he's going to be lost."

It was Yvonne who'd told her. Yvonne had heard it from Catriona who'd heard it from Calum, the postman.

"Edward's living in Freddie Pollock's spare room. He's been there for a week. Nell told Calum that she wasn't taking Edward's post anymore," Yvonne had said.

Anneliese had been silent for a beat. "Well," she said finally, "I guess I'm not surprised. I never saw them as a natural couple." But then, perhaps lots of people hadn't seen her and Edward as a natural couple, either.

"He might want to come back," Yvonne said hopefully.

In spite of the emotions whirling round inside her, Anneliese smiled. Yvonne was so innocent. In her mind it was simple: Nell had stood in the way of Anneliese and Edward being together, and now that Nell was out of the picture everything could go—almost—back to the way it had been before.

"I doubt it, Yvonne," she said. "I don't actually want him back."

"Oh." Yvonne sounded shocked.

"I like my life the way it is now," Anneliese explained truthfully. "There isn't any room for Edward in it. I've let him and the past go."

"It's Mac, isn't it?" Yvonne said.

Mac was indeed a part of Anneliese's new life, but only as a friend. She cared for him deeply but their relationship would never be anything more. She was a long way from being ready for another love in her life. But to people looking in, it might easily appear as if Mac was next in line for a romantic entanglement.

"It's not Mac," she told Yvonne firmly, wanting to nip this idea in the bud. "He's a friend, nothing more. If I fall in love, Yvonne, I promise I'll tell you, but I don't see it happening any time soon."

"You must be lonely, Anneliese," Yvonne said. "I worry about you, being there all alone with only that daft dog for company."

"That daft dog is all I need," Anneliese said warmly. "I'm happy, truly I am."

"At least you don't have to worry about inviting Nell to the christening," Karen said. They'd reached Dorota's, and although it wasn't a cold March morning, the group elected to sit inside.

"Beth was the one who was worried about that," Anneliese whispered as they stood in line to order. "When I mentioned it to her, she shrieked down the phone at me. In the end I told her I didn't have a problem with it. Besides, the world doesn't revolve around me, I told her. So she relented, but now it's not an issue. Poor Nell. She's cut off from everyone. Yvonne and Corinne barely talk to her, and she doesn't have Edward, either."

"I'm a bit rusty on the whole religion thing, so help me out here. What's next up from sainthood?" Karen asked. " 'Cause you're definitely in line for it."

"Oh, stop it," chided Anneliese. "You've got to be positive." She gazed at the edible goodies under the glass cabinet in Dorota's. A succulent cream cake topped with almonds drew her eye. "I'll have that evil-looking million-calorie thing, and hope all the positivity burns the fat off!"

Beth and Jodi walked in companionable silence along the harbor wall, pushing their babies in front of them and luxuriating in the silence of both little people. Mitzi, at nearly five months, was growing into a curious little girl who stared up at people with huge greeny-blue eyes and smiled the most adorable smile that showed off dimples in both cheeks. She wasn't all fair weather, though, and Beth was used to the bouts of inconsolable crying that she'd finally worked out were colic. She was getting the hang of this motherhood thing, she decided, which was why it was nice to walk with Jodi and baby Kyle.

Kyle was only ten days old and looked so small in comparison.

Jodi was slowly getting over her fear of dropping him. She was still slightly shocked that she'd been allowed to bring him home from the hospital.

"How do they know I'll know what to do?" she'd asked Dan tearfully two days after the birth, when they brought Kyle home.

" 'Cause they can tell you're a great mum," said Dan confidently. He'd been well primed by his mother-in-law, who'd explained that postpartum blues were way worse than anything the premenstrual hormones could throw at a man.

Today Jodi had felt a little tearful too, but when Beth had rolled up for their walk, she'd felt her spirits lift.

"It does you good to get out of the house when they're little," her mum had said, before suggesting she go for a walk with Beth, who was in town for Mitzi's christening. The previous day, the two mothers had walked a circuit from one side of Tamarin to the other and had enjoyed it so much that they'd arranged to do it again, and were now at the harbor, planning to stop off for coffee if both babies remained asleep.

They'd talked about sleep, feeding and colic.

"It sounds awful," Jodi had groaned when Beth told her about colic.

"Don't get me started," Beth sighed. "I thought I must be doing something wrong. For the past three weeks, every evening at five she starts to cry."

In her stroller, Mitzi started to grizzle.

The two women looked at each other.

"Let's get coffee now before she wakes up?"

"Deal."

"Has Izzie recovered from her jet lag?" Jodi asked as they walked quickly to the coffee shop.

"Izzie's a trouper, she never gets jet lag," Beth said. "I'm going to ask her to babysit Mitzi tonight."

"I might drop by later, then," Jodi said. "I've never shown her the stuff I've written up on Rathnaree. I meant to email it, but it was so untidy, and I wanted it to be perfect before I sent it."

"I'd forgotten you were doing that," Beth said. "Mum told me. Did you uncover any family skeletons?"

Jodi smiled ruefully. The letters and documents Vivi Whelan's daughter had given her had proved to be only mildly useful. There had only been a few letters from Lily to her friend, and the ink had been so faded it was hard to read them.

The diary was different. Jodi was sure it told the whole story.

She'd found it the month before she'd given birth to Kyle, when she and Anneliese had gone to Lily's house to find some treasures from Lily's to decorate her bedroom at Laurel Gardens.

Anneliese had tidied up a little, doing her best to hide her tears as she plumped cushions on Lily's couch, clearly thinking that Lily might never be home again to sit on them.

Jodi had tried to distract her by chatting about how much weight she'd put on.

"Eleven kilos," she moaned to Anneliese. "I've put on eleven kilos. Can you believe it?"

"You'll soon lose it," Anneliese had said kindly, and then sighed heavily. "I think of Izzie coming home and seeing Lily's newspaper still open at the crossword page beside her chair, and the cups on the draining board . . ." she said. "It would be so sad, like Lily had only stepped out of her life for a moment."

Anneliese headed toward the stairs to get some nightclothes for Lily.

Jodi sat down on a big comfortable armchair and wriggled to get comfortable. If she moved the chair, she could put her feet up on a little stool. The chair bumped into a cardboard box that had been carefully placed on a pile of old newspapers, and the box tipped over. The untaped top opened and the contents spilled out: yellowing bits of paper, sepia-tinted photographs and a small hardback notebook with marbled edges.

Embarrassed at her clumsiness, Jodi hurriedly got to her feet to shove the contents back in the box.

"What's this?" asked Anneliese, appearing from upstairs.

"I knocked it over trying to get comfortable," Jodi said. "Sorry."

They both looked at the notebook. Anneliese bent and picked it up and opened it to reveal filmy pages covered with Lily's handwriting.

"Her diary," breathed Jodi.

"Jesus," said Anneliese. "I never knew Lily had kept a diary." She ran her fingers over a line of the writing, as if she could touch Lily through the pages, then snapped it shut again.

"I don't want to read it," she said. "It's still Lily's and she's not gone yet. If anyone should have it, it should be Izzie."

Jodi's fingers traced the cover longingly. She wanted to read it, wanted to know Lily's story.

"Izzie should have it," Anneliese said again.

"Of course," said Jodi, the historian in her bowing down to her sense of friendship. "Izzie's the right person to have it."

Anneliese patted her hand.

Jodi and Beth had reached Dorota's. The babies were still blissfully asleep.

"No," she said firmly, although she didn't really know one way or the other, "no family skeletons." If there were, it was up to Izzie to lay them to rest.

Izzie had unpacked her suitcase and hung up her dress for the christening. Tomorrow would be packed with activity, Izzie knew, although she was looking forward to it now. Holding Mitzi had been incredible: she'd half thought she'd only get a little cuddle with the baby and had been surprised the evening before when she'd gone to visit Anneliese and Beth had simply handed Mitzi to her, then vanished out of the room for twenty minutes.

"What do I . . . ?" began Izzie, left with a just-waking-up baby and a soft bit of rag that Beth had hurriedly draped over her shoulder. But she was alone.

"Just you and me, babe," she said to Mitzi, who crinkled sleepy and unfocused eyes at her. "Don't cry."

Mitzi's gaze began to focus. She realized that she was no longer in the comforting arms of her mother. Who was this woman?

"Oh, Jesus," said Izzie as Mitzi let out a roar that belied her tiny size. How could something that small make so much noise? The roar was followed by a squelching noise and a feeling of heavy warmth in Izzie's arms, and then a very bad smell took over the room. How could something so small make such a bad smell, either?

It took ten minutes for Mitzi to calm down, by which time Izzie had gone through her entire repertoire of nursery rhymes twice. She was reduced to murmuring "Bootylicious" in a singsong voice when Mitzi finally stopped crying and smiled.

"Oh, you're lovely," sighed Izzie with relief. "Will we change that nasty old nappy?" Mitzi gurgled up at her.

"We will, won't we?"

One messy nappy and at least a quarter of a pack of baby wipes later, Izzie felt as if her baby learner plates could be taken off.

"How was she?" asked Beth, breezing back in.

Izzie grinned. "Great. Tiring, though."

"You don't know the half of it," Beth sighed, grabbing her baby and hugging her.

Six weeks before, Izzie would have wanted to kill Beth for being so blithe about her baby, but now she was able to nod in agreement. "Worth it, though," she said with feeling.

"For sure," said Beth.

She went off to give the baby her bath and Anneliese breezed into the cottage, red-faced after a brisk walk on the beach with Silkie.

"Hello, darling." Izzie cuddled the dog happily. "She's adorable, Anneliese. Any chance I could steal her?"

Her aunt laughed. "She keeps me sane, so the answer is no. I'm only kidding," she added, seeing the anxious look in Izzie's eyes. "I don't need anyone keeping me sane, Izzie. I'm doing fine."

"I can see that. Dad told me you were."

"The family grapevine still working, I see."

Izzie smiled. "In the nicest possible way," she said. "You really seem happy, Anneliese."

"So do you," Anneliese replied. "You weren't when you were here last year."

Izzie shuddered. "That was a bad time in my life," she said, "apart from what was happening to Gran."

They were both silent for a moment and the only noise in the room was the sound of Silkie panting happily on the rug. Anneliese rubbed her dog's ears absently.

"Lily's slipping away, you know."

Izzie bit her lip. "I know," she said. "Dad told me that, too. I'm going in tomorrow morning."

"Just . . ." Anneliese halted. "I want you to be prepared, Izzie."

"I am."

"No, *really* prepared. It's time to let her go, Izzie. I have this feeling that she's been hanging on, waiting for you to come back."

Izzie could only nod because she was crying.

"Jodi never did find out who Jamie was . . ." Anneliese went on talking so Izzie could cry in peace. "She found some letters from Lily to her friend Vivi—she's kept them for you—but they stop before the end of the war. She must have come back to Tamarin."

"I'd like to read them," Izzie managed to say.

"But Jodi and I did find something else," Anneliese went on. "A box with some bits in, including a notebook. We think maybe it's a diary. Lily's diary. I haven't read it. I just felt Lily didn't want me to read it. Or perhaps she didn't want anyone to read it, but . . ." Anneliese's voice trailed off. She'd thought long and hard about this. The box had been carefully taken out from some hiding place and she had a sense that Lily had done it for a reason, to show to someone. That someone could only be Izzie.

"The box is upstairs," she added. "I'll give it to you when you're leaving, OK?"

"OK," said Izzie. She was kneeling on the floor, cuddling Silkie to hide the tears in her eyes.

Anneliese gently held out her hand to help Izzie up. "It's cold but it's still a nice evening. Come sit on the porch with me and Silkie and look out at the bay. It's calming. Reminds you that we're only specks on this planet and that we all have to leave one day."

By the time Anneliese and Izzie came inside, night had fallen.

"Thank you," Izzie said, hugging her aunt again. "I knew it was going to be hard, but being here," she sobbed, "it's so difficult."

"I know." Anneliese held her tightly. "Do you want the diary and the box, Izzie? I don't want to upset you more."

"Oh no, I want it."

Anneliese nodded. "Just stop reading if it's too much for you. I have no idea what's in it, but if Lily wrote it, it'll be wise, that's for sure."

When Izzie drove off in her father's car, the precious box with the diary inside it sat on the passenger seat beside her.

She wasn't sure if she was going to be able to read it. Reading Lily's diary now would be like saying both hello and good-bye to her at the same time.

The small room on the ground floor of the Laurel Gardens nursing home was very pretty even though it was mostly occupied by patients who couldn't open their eyes and admire the wallpaper with the blush roses on it. Heavy cream curtains kept the chill out at night, and although the bed itself was a standard hospital one, the covers were not standard, being a soft dusky pink that went with the walls. Bits and pieces from her grandmother's house decorated the room: a china vase with a rabbit on it stood on the dresser, filled with daffodils. Several silver-framed photographs, including one of Izzie standing hugging her grandmother, were placed on the locker beside the bed. A tapestry cushion of an elephant that had once rested on the armchair beside the fire in the Forge was placed on the chair by the bed, as if waiting for Lily to get up and sit against it.

But Izzie knew that her grandmother would never sit in the chair or admire how thoughtfully Anneliese and the nurses had arranged the room. As soon as she entered the room, Izzie felt the sense of death in it.

There was nothing left of her beloved grandmother now. Lily might have been frail in Tamarin Hospital the previous year, but now she was a wraith under the covers, as if her corporeal form was dwindling day by day. Her once-beautiful face was hollow, a mask of death like the old pharaohs' faces Izzie had once seen in the Cairo Museum of Antiquities.

Izzie put her hand over her mouth to stop herself crying out loud. She'd cried so much all night as she sat up with Lily's diary, deciphering the handwriting to read a story she'd never heard before.

"I'm sorry," the nurse said, gently patting her shoulder. "I did tell you she was a lot worse."

Izzie nodded. She couldn't speak. The nurse, a reassuring middle-aged woman named Rhona, had said the pneumonia Gran had developed had taken a lot out of her, but Izzie hadn't expected this.

Izzie turned back to the door. "I can't," she sobbed to Rhona.

Lily was so vibrant in Izzie's mind after she read the diary—the strong, passionate, young Lily, not this frail woman slipping out of life.

"Of course you can," Rhona said briskly. "I've heard all about how she practically raised you. Think of her, that woman, and you can do it."

Somehow Izzie stopped crying and managed to sit holding Gran's hand. It was too much to bear, watching her like this.

How selfish had she been to want Gran to remain like this, a living death, just so she wouldn't have to face the actual death. She'd been living her life and her darling Gran had been hanging on by a thread.

"I'm sorry, Gran," she said. "Please forgive me for not being here with you."

She touched the curve of Gran's eyebrows, thinking of the pictures of her as a young woman with lustrous hair shimmering about her face, and those clever eyes sparkling out at the world.

Izzie felt angry with herself for daring to think that age was cruel at forty—it was crueler now.

"I promise I won't waste my life anymore," she said. "That's what you learned, wasn't it? Sometimes you have to let go."

That was what the diary had told her—that and so much more. There were so many lessons in there: lessons she'd need to reread to digest. Her grandmother's life had been so full of stories Izzie had never heard before, stories about life, death and survival.

But the strongest feeling she had after reading it was that she'd made the right choice in letting go of Joe. It was as if Gran had been reaching out of the diary, patting her hand and saying, "You did the right thing, my love."

For the past six months Izzie had tortured herself over Joe, wondering if she should have stuck it out in the hope that one day he'd be free.

Her grandmother's words made her see that there were no simple answers, no black and white. Just as Gran knew that Jamie Hamilton could never be hers without hurting others, Izzie could see that it was the same with Joe.

There was too high a price to pay for their love, and the only thing she could have done was walk away.

Izzie thought of the world she'd been brought up to believe in—a modern world with rights. The right to have a baby, the right to love whoever she wanted . . . Yet it wasn't so simple after all. Gran's world had been ruled by conventions Izzie could barely understand: the fierce power of the Church hanging over people and the barrier that was class. The modern world might have abandoned some of those strictures, but it had created new ones. Like the awareness of how divorce affected children, for a start.

Leaving Joe was the hardest thing she'd ever done, but last night, reading her grandmother's diary, Izzie felt the comfort of knowing that her beloved Gran understood.

"Gran," she whispered now, "I wanted so much to tell you about Joe, but I thought you'd never understand. Now I know I was wrong, you'd have understood totally."

If only her grandmother could answer her, Izzie thought.

"I know about Jamie now," she went on softly, "I know it all. Thank you. Thank you for leaving your diary for me. I wanted to tell you how much it's helped me."

Izzie wiped away a tear. She was not going to cry, not yet.

"You've seen so much, Gran, and I'm sorry I never sat you down and asked you about it all—about the war, about Rathnaree. I was young and selfish, but I love you so much. I hope you know that."

For a moment she sat silently, watching Gran's beloved face, hoping for some response. But there wouldn't be any; somehow she knew that. She had to face it. No point running from the truth.

"I love you, Gran," she whispered again.

Lily's fine white hair was mussed up and Izzie went to ask Rhona for something to brush it with. Gran had always looked beautiful; she should look beautiful today too.

Rhona produced a soft pink baby's brush that she used on patients like Lily.

"Thanks," said Izzie, and went back into the room.

Gently, she brushed the fine white hair.

"You like your hair nice, Gran," she said as she worked, smoothing the flyaway hairs down. Next, she took her moisturizer out of her huge handbag and warmed a few small droplets in her hands. Slowly, she smoothed the cream into the papery skin of her grandmother's face, petting and stroking as delicately as she could. Her hands were next. Izzie had a wonderful Aveda hand cream that smelled of flowers.

"This stuff is the best there is, Gran. The hand models use it, you know, but your hands are more precious."

She took a frail hand between her two, stroking softly until the cream was absorbed before turning to the other hand. She thought of the times those hands had held hers, and the comfort she'd drawn from that touch. It must have been so hard to be mother and grandmother to a motherless girl, but Gran had done it.

"Perfume next. I don't have any of that Arpège you love, but I have this."

This was L'Occitane's honey perfume. She spritzed it onto her own hands and dabbed a little on to her grandmother's wrists and temples.

"Now, isn't that better?" she asked, then sniffed the air.

It was strange: she'd used the honey perfume and yet the dominant smell in the room was of lavender. It brought back a faint memory of her grandmother's closets and the scent of lavender that some of her clothes gave off. It seemed as if the lavender was stronger than any other scent in the room, a heady, soft smell that reminded Izzie of the lavender bushes outside the Old Forge.

Gran loved the purple herb and was assiduous in caring for her lavender bushes, cutting them back carefully, removing the woody stems and replacing the plants when necessary, so she could smell the cool scent wherever she stood in her home.

Izzie sniffed, taken back to her childhood. Where was the scent coming from?

April 1945

In the mews house off the Bayswater Road, Diana danced around the room, prouder in her mended gown than she'd ever been in any of her coming-out finery. The violet silk dress was the result of three women's sewing skills and meant more to her than any other dress because it was the dress she was wearing to her engagement party.

Tonight was the first step toward her becoming Mrs. Anthony Smythe, and Diana had never been happier. The party was being held in Claridges and everyone was coming, even her parents from Beltonward, which was a miracle in itself.

"You look beautiful," Lily said, smiling at her friend. She was sitting on the floor with a pincushion on her wrist for any last-minute alterations.

"So do you, darling," said Diana, beaming. In her pure happiness, she wanted everyone to be just as happy. "We ought to go, you know. I've made such a fuss to everyone about being on time, it would be ghastly if I was late."

Lily hid a smile. Anthony had said he knew his beloved would be late.

"Just one more thing I love about her," he'd said mistily to Lily the day before.

He was a sweetheart, Lily thought. Almost as gorgeous as Jamie. She allowed herself to close her eyes and think of Jamie for one bittersweet moment. The war was nearly over, everyone knew it.

Soon Jamie would be back in England and he'd want to talk about their future, and then Lily would just die. There could be no future for them for so many reasons.

Her faith came first. She wondered how she'd ever be able to explain to Jamie about Catholicism, about what it was like to grow up in a world where faith mattered.

No matter how she railed against God for what He was doing, letting innocent people die every day from this stupid war, she believed in Him. And God didn't believe in half measures when it came to marriage: it was for life. In her mind Lily tried to imagine her darling mother and father hearing about Jamie, that he'd been married before and that he loved their daughter.

First and foremost in their minds would be the fact that Jamie was not a Catholic and, worse, he was divorced.

She could almost hear her mother's words: *If you marry him, you'll be excommunicated, Lily. For the love of* God*, don't do it!*

Jamie might be able to talk her round on an intellectual level, but on a soul level, it was different. Loving Jamie went against every tenet of her religion, and when he wasn't with her, when she wasn't in the white heat of passion, she felt the weight of that betrayal.

Then Diana had inadvertently stuck a rapier into her side when she was talking about her forthcoming wedding.

Dear Diana, who Lily was sure still knew nothing about Jamie, was discussing the wedding guest list. Most of the people who'd been there when Sybil got married would be coming. Diana was trying not to obsess over the details of her wedding but still, she carried her list around with her and added to it when she remembered someone.

"Gosh, must ask dear Jamie and Miranda," she said one day, and Lily, who was used to Diana's name checking, stood very still, afraid to speak in case she betrayed herself in some way.

"Bit of an odd fish, Miranda," Diana went on blithely. "Not the sort of girl one would see Jamie marrying. *Entre nous*, Mummy's always said she's very highly strung. Jolly pretty, though. Mummy was up in Oxford and says she bumped into Miranda there—she'd been staying with Jamie's grandmother and he'd wangled some leave so he could see them both. Mummy says Miranda looks marvelous."

Lily now wouldn't have been able to speak even if required to. Jamie had been with Miranda at his grandmother's house in Oxford. He hadn't mentioned it to her. And he wouldn't, either. No matter what he said, he was still tied to Miranda.

Jamie's visit hadn't been for the purpose of telling his wife about Lily: no woman would look marvelous if her husband had just told her he was in love with someone else.

And then Sybil, nasty, cruel Sybil, had plunged the last poisoned dagger in and made Lily see that it was over for her and Jamie. It was simply up to her to let him go.

She and Sybil could barely cope with being in each other's presence, and Lily did everything she could to avoid it.

But Sybil was in London for the engagement party and although Lily had pleaded exhaustion when Sybil had rolled up to take her sister out for dinner, she'd still had to endure half an hour of her company. Sybil waited until they were alone, when Diana had gone to fetch her coat before going out.

Lighting a cigarette, she stared hard at her sister's friend.

"Daddy's been to your home, you know," she said.

"What?"

"Rathnaree, isn't it?" Sybil went on. "You were always very coy about it all, told us you came from Waterford, but I asked Diana and she told me exactly where your mother worked, where you worked. For the Lochravens." Her face was hard now. "Daddy knows them, went to a big birthday party there once for Lady Irene. Total darling, he says. The thing is, I wonder how Jamie's family will feel when they find out he's sleeping with a lady's maid? Not too impressed, I shouldn't wonder."

"Why do you do this?" asked Lily tiredly, knowing that Sybil was only putting words to her own darkest fears. "Why do you want to hurt me so much?"

"Because you look down your nose at me as if I'm some spoiled child!" shrieked Sybil. "Well, I'm not the one sleeping with someone else's husband, am I?"

There was no answering this. Sybil's condemnation was nothing compared to the recriminations she'd leveled against herself. There were so many obstacles to her and Jamie ever being happy. On their own, each would be enough to finish them off. But together, they made it impossible.

This, combined with what Diana had inadvertently let slip about Jamie seeing Miranda, made the end inevitable.

"Sybil, you're not worth fighting with," Lily said tiredly, and left the room to sit on her bed and cry.

It was over between her and Jamie, over almost before it had time to begin. It was up to her to end if before it destroyed them both.

Sitting on the bed where they'd made love so many times, she remembered the last time she'd seen him in the hotel in Torquay. It had been the only night in their whole relationship where they had managed to stay together until dawn.

Torquay was a perfect place for them to be together; there was so much military movement on the coast that nobody would look twice if they happened to see Lieutenant Jamie Hamilton walking with a woman they didn't recognize.

In her head, she knew what she was doing was wrong. She lay, open-eyed in the dawn, feeling the length of his naked body next to hers, warm despite the chill of the room. She'd never slept naked before, and now wondered how there was any other way.

Of course, you needed another body beside yours—a body like his, hard with physical exercise, taut and lean, not an ounce of flab on him and fiercely strong.

Yet he was so gentle with her. His hands with their tender pianist's fingers had drawn whorls on her pale skin the night before, his eyes shining in the soft light of the dim bulb.

With his hands on her skin, her body became like nothing she'd ever known before: a treasured thing made for being wrapped up with his and adored.

"You're so beautiful. I wish this moment could go on forever," he'd said in the low voice she loved. There wasn't anything about him she didn't love, really.

He was perfect.

And not hers.

Their time was stolen: a few hours here and there, holding hands under the table at dinner, clinging together in the vast hotel bed like shipwreck survivors on a raft. For those hours, he was hers, but she was only borrowing him.

The awfulness of separating rose up again inside her. It was a physical ache in the pit of her stomach.

He'd wake soon. He had to be gone by seven to get his train.

If she had been the one who had to leave the hotel room first, she knew she simply couldn't have done it. But he would. Duty drove him.

It was dark in the room and only the gleam of the alarm clock hands showed that it was morning. She nudged her way out of the bed and opened a sliver of heavy curtain to let in some gray dawn light. It was raining outside; the sort of sleety cold rain that sank cruelly into the bones.

There were early morning noises coming from the street below. Doors banging, horns sounding, traffic rumbling. Ordinary life going on all around them, like worker ants slaving away in the colony, nobody aware of anybody else's life. Nobody aware of hers.

He moved in the bed and she hurried back into it, desperate to glean the last precious hour of their time together. If she closed her eyes, she could almost pretend it was night again and they still had some time.

But he was waking up, rubbing sleep from his eyes, rubbing his hands over his jaw with its darkening stubble.

Soon he'd be leaving.

She was crying when he moved hard against her, his body heavy and warm.

"Don't be sad," he said, lowering his head and kissing the saltiness of her tears.

"I'm not," she said, crying more. "I mean, I don't mean to. I'll miss you, I can't bear it."

"You have to, we both have to."

She'd never known that love could be so joyous and so agonizing at the same time. Every caress took them closer to his leaving. Each time he touched her, she couldn't block out the thought: Is this the last time he'll ever do that? Will I ever see him again?

She could barely stop the tears. But she did, because she had to.

In the end, she lay silently in the bed watching him get ready. Just before he left, he sat beside her, pulled her close and kissed her as if she was oxygen he was breathing in.

Her hands clung to him, one curved tightly around his neck, the other cradling his skull. They kissed with their eyes closed so they'd never forget.

"I have to go. I love you."

She couldn't speak in case she cried again.

"Good-bye."

He didn't look back as he left and she wondered if that was the difference between men and women. Men looked forward, warriors focusing on the future. Women's eyes darted everywhere. Searching, wondering, praying to some god to keep the people they loved safe.

She lay back in the bed still warm with the imprint of his body, and wondered if she would ever see him again.

Lily had slept little of the night; instead, she'd lain there and thought about how it would never work out for them. Jamie loved her, she knew that. But there were too many obstacles to their love.

Her God wouldn't forgive her for being with him. Neither would her family. Could she give up everything and everyone for him? Could they really make each other happy, or were they fooling themselves, were they just two more star-crossed lovers caught up in a wartime passion with no hope of making a life in the real world?

Their worlds were too different, anyway. He could cross into hers easily enough, but she would never cross into his. The barriers were too high. Breaching them would destroy him. He was a man of duty and he had a duty to his family, his parents, his world.

No, it had to end. And she was the one who had to be strong enough to let him go.

"Darling, *you're* going to make us late this time," said Diana cheerfully, snapping Lily out of her reverie. "That'd be a first! Can you see everyone's faces if I'm late for my engagement party and it's your fault!"

"Sorry," said Lily. She wished she weren't going. She didn't have the heart for a party tonight, not even for her beloved Diana. She wanted to be at home with her thoughts; she wanted to mourn her relationship with Jamie.

He wouldn't be there tonight, she knew that. But she longed to see him, longed to tell him it was over between them. Perhaps then she would be able to carry on with her life.

She wished she could write, but you couldn't say any of this in a letter. Yet she needed to say it, to tell him it was over, now, before she lost her courage and changed her mind. There could be no future for them. One of them had to be brave enough to end it and it would have to be her.

She and Diana were late getting to Claridges.

"Sorry, my fault," yelled Diana apologetically as they arrived.

Everyone crowded round her, drinks were proffered, and Diana laughed and said she'd have a cocktail, just one, to celebrate.

"Lily," said a voice.

It was Philip, Sybil's husband.

Lily never felt as if she knew him very well, despite having been at many family events with him. She was normally so busy trying to avoid Sybil that she ended up avoiding Philip too, but he was Jamie's best friend and for that she loved him.

"Hello, Philip," she said, lifting her cheek for a kiss, one eye warily looking for his wife. She was not going to lower herself to even speak to Sybil, not tonight. Sybil had brought her nothing but pain when it came to Jamie.

"Lily, I've got to tell you something," said Philip, his voice low.

Lily knew what it was. She felt her legs weaken.

Philip was shielding her from everyone else at the party with his body. Lily looked down at her shoes, she couldn't bear to meet his eyes: she knew what he was going to tell her.

She remembered sobbing to Jamie that if something happened to him, she'd be the last to know.

"They'd all know you were dead, *she'd* know, but I wouldn't. I couldn't grieve because I'd be waiting for you! Waiting for you to never come back!" she'd wept, hitting him on the chest with her fists, so full of pain and hurt that she could only hurt him for all that she loved him so much.

"My love," he'd said, and pulled her close so her beating fists were crushed against their bodies. They were sitting on her bed in the mews; the bed was in disarray after their lovemaking and now it was time for them both to go back to their everyday lives.

Wearing only the little satin slip that Jamie had peeled off her just hours before, Lily sank against him and buried her face in his chest.

"I can't do this anymore, Jamie," she cried. "I can't lie to everyone and pretend I'm happy, that I haven't got a sweetheart, that I don't ache every time the radio reports the casualties. There's no hope for us. I'm going slowly mad worrying about you and trying to hide it."

"Somebody does know, I promise you, and if anything happens to me, he'll come and tell you."

"Who?" she said.

"You don't know him, but he knows who you are and if . . . something happens to me, he'll come. I promise." He'd kissed her then, through all her tears, but he'd had to leave. And when he was gone, she lay curled on the bed and cried hot, hopeless tears.

Now that day was here. Jamie was dead and it was Philip who'd come to tell her: solid, dependable Philip, whom she'd never have suspected of knowing.

"Lily, please look at me," Philip said softly.

Lily wouldn't look up at him. She kept her head low and bit her lip. If he didn't tell her, it wasn't true, was it? But then she began to shake. She couldn't control it, it was as if her limbs no longer belonged to her. Her legs gave out and she half fell forward.

Philip grabbed her and she smelled that familiar scent of a sailor's uniform, the same scent that surrounded Jamie. She thought of how many times she'd lain close to Jamie's chest, fingers starfished as she touched him, felt the warmth of him, loving the sense of his strong heart beating beneath the heavy woolen uniform. But his heart wasn't beating any longer.

Somewhere he was lying dead, maybe on a deserted beach, maybe in the cold coffin of his submarine, with nobody to cradle his beautiful head in their arms and kiss him, close his eyes, stroke him one last time. Why hadn't she been there with him, to tell him it would be all right, like she'd done for so many other men? Why couldn't she have been allowed to do the same for her man?

All around them were people laughing and cheering. Lily could only think of Jamie, cold in the sea, unloved at the end when she'd had so much love for him and it was all spent. Where was God now? What was God doing when Jamie had died? She'd been willing to give him up for God, so why hadn't God paid her back by taking care of him?

The train from Euston to Holyhead was jammed. There weren't enough seats and people were left standing outside in the corridors.

Lily had been lucky because she got there early and she had a seat at the window, where she was squashed by a man in a corporal's uniform next to her, dozing on her shoulder. It felt slightly surreal to be going home. She'd only been back to Ireland once during the war and it had been a totally crammed ten days of leave.

Mam had done her best both to feed Lily up and find clothes for her. There was no clothes rationing in Ireland and Mam had saved some of Lady Irene's beautiful castoffs, although the combination of rationing and hard work meant that Lily was too thin for them.

"Lord bless us, look at you! You're skin and bone, there's not a pick on you," her mother had said worriedly.

It had been a lovely visit, a little refuge in the middle of the war. Lily remembered it as if it was a dream, almost as if it had happened to another person altogether.

Now there was no sense of refuge in going home. The whole world seemed so happy and the atmosphere of sheer joy after VE Day permeated everything. But as much as Lily had longed for the conflict to end, now that it had, she couldn't share in the joy. None of it mattered. Jamie was dead. Her world was in darkness. How could she ever be happy again?

The hospital hadn't wanted her to go.

"Just because the war is over doesn't mean that the hospital has no need of nurses," Matron had said sternly. "I'm not sure why you want to go home, Nurse Kennedy, but we'd like you to stay."

Lily thought of the past three months when she had struggled to get out of bed every morning, working until tiredness finally engulfed her at night. Every time she looked out the hospital windows at the streets of London, all she'd seen in her mind's eye were places she had been with Jamie.

There was no relief from the pain. Even in bed, she lay there and thought of him, crying herself into fitful sleep most nights.

In the end, she decided that she had to get out of London—

there were too many memories for her there. She thought back to the time she'd blithely told Maisie that she didn't know if she wanted to go back to Tamarin after the war. She'd been wrong; she did want to go back to Tamarin. She'd feel safe there, and maybe one day she could feel a little bit happier. Or at least if she was miserable, she'd be miserable somewhere she hadn't been with Jamie.

The mail boat from Holyhead was no longer blacked out as it had been in her previous wartime crossings, but it was still packed and she felt sick, sitting on the top deck in a too-big life jacket. When the boat sailed into Dún Laoghaire, it felt strange to see the beautiful town all lit up, elegant and untouched by bombs. She was so used to London, where so many beautiful buildings had been destroyed. She could sympathize with shattered walls and crumbling roofs: she felt the same herself, shattered and crumbling.

Here, many of the people looked healthy, well fed. They weren't wearing patched, tattered clothes, they looked happy and prosperous. Somehow Lily felt irritated and resentful that some of her countrymen and -women had remained untouched by the war. But then, she felt angry with the whole human race, because she had lost the man she loved.

It wasn't their fault they hadn't been ripped apart by the war, she decided. They weren't guilty. No, that honor went to God. Her rage against Him was fierce and powerful, and because of that, there had been no refuge in prayers for her.

She'd found it so hard to pray when she was with Jamie because each prayer reminded her she was breaking God's laws. Now, when the reason for breaking those laws was gone, she still couldn't pray. Losing Jamie had made her lose herself.

The train to Waterford was half empty. She had the whole seat to herself and watched the countryside changing as she got closer to home. It was a beautiful August day and she had to stop herself thinking, *Wouldn't Jamie love this?*

He'd talked of their visiting her home, when the war was over, when he'd told Miranda, when he was free.

In Waterford she learned that the next bus to Tamarin wouldn't leave until seven that evening, so she left her suitcase with the station porter and walked down to the quay to sit on a bench and look out to sea.

The sun glinting off the water made her think of Torquay and how she'd decided that she had to let Jamie go. That was one mercy: that she hadn't told him and he'd died not knowing.

But now she had to live out the rest of her life without having let him go. For her, there was no sense of closing that chapter of her life.

The bus rattled out of Waterford, rolling past beautiful countryside that Lily barely saw. In her head she was still in London, hurrying through tired gray streets, looking up at the shimmering sun bursting through the clouds, thinking of Jamie . . .

"Will I let you off here?" the bus driver said loudly, jerking Lily back to the present. The bus had stopped as close to the Old Forge as it could and she stared out at familiar countryside.

"Yes, thank you," she said.

When the bus had driven off again, Lily looked at the suitcase she'd hauled from London and thought that she really didn't give a damn if she left it on the side of the road; she didn't have the energy to drag it half a mile up the lane to the house. She shoved it into a hedge and stood facing in the direction of her home.

Rathnaree was hidden behind the trees to the left and Lily felt a surge of hatred for it and all it represented. Those class barriers had driven a wedge between her and Jamie, even without Sybil and her venom.

The Lochravens, the Beltons and the Hamiltons were from another world, and it made no sense that people couldn't cross between the two. Well, Lily wasn't setting foot near Rathnaree or its like ever again. That world had hurt her too much: she would stay in her own from here on.

She wiped away a tear and, for the first time, allowed herself to breathe in the clear country scent of fields and trees and wild garlic. There was another scent: lavender. She stood close to the drystone wall and peered over it. There, in one corner of the field, were around twenty lavender bushes. She half remembered there having been a single bush there, but now the lavender had spread until there was an entire copse of it, richly scenting the air with that evocative smell. Lily climbed the wall, hopped down the other side and walked toward the lavender. On impulse, she took off her shoes and stockings and felt the softness of the grass under her feet. Then she sat down, drew her knees up to her chest and closed her eyes. She could remember Granny Sive talking about lavender being a very old herb, and there was some connection to the fairies, or "the little people," as Granny Sive referred to them.

Here, in the protective copse of the little people, Lily sent a silent prayer: "Help me," she said, and began to cry.

She didn't hear him until he'd scaled the wall and was striding toward her: a giant of a man with a tanned face, hair the color of copper and the kindest blue eyes she'd ever seen.

"I saw you from the road," he said, concern in his voice. "I had to see if you were all right. Are you?"

Lily just stared silently at him.

"Don't be frightened, miss," he said. "I'm not going to hurt you, I was only worried. My name's Robby Shanahan. Can I see you home or anything?"

Surrounded by her fairy lavender, with this kind giant looking at her with a gentleness Lily hadn't experienced in so long, she felt a warmth flood her body. It was a lightness, a feeling that, if she closed her eyes now, she'd sleep soundly and the pain and sorrow would go away for a little while. *Thank you.* She wasn't sure who she was thanking, but some deity had brought a little peace into her heart for the first time since Jamie died.

She smiled at the gentle giant. "I'm Lily Kennedy," she said. "You could carry my suitcase home."

At midday Rhona came in with a cup of tea for Izzie. Izzie could smell dinners being served in the rooms along the hall, but she didn't feel hungry. She felt strangely as if she was waiting for something that was just about to happen.

"Sometimes people need to be told they can go," Rhona said.

Izzie stared at her. Rhona had the look of a woman who wasn't prone to flights of fancy. It seemed such a strange thing to say; but then, hadn't Anneliese said much the same thing?

"You have to tell her she can go," Rhona went on. "She's been waiting for someone, for you, so she could go."

"How can you tell?" Izzie asked.

"You learn things during twenty years of working with dying people," Rhona said.

Izzie winced at the word *dying*.

"It's all right to say it," Rhona went on. "She knows she's going. She's at peace. Some people fight so hard. It makes me think of that Dylan Thomas poem I learned in school: "Do Not Go Gentle into That Good Night." Some people don't go gently, they really do fight. Your grandmother is happy to go, she's not fighting it now, but she has been holding on for dear life until you came."

Izzie didn't realize she was crying until she felt the tears drip onto her shirt. She reached up to find her cheeks were wet. Rhona fished in her pocket, found a tissue and handed it to her.

"I'll leave you."

Izzie nodded.

She sat on the edge of the bed and smelled the lavender again.

"Gran, I love you," she said, "but you can go now." Suddenly, she thought of the words in the diary, written over sixty years ago: *I know I have to let him go. I don't want to but it's the right thing to do. We'd end up hating each other and I love him too much for that.*

"You can let go, Gran. Thank you for sharing it with me—your life. I love you, Gran. I will miss you so much."

She felt tears sliding down her face and she mopped at them

with the tissue. "It's OK, we're all OK. Me, Dad, Anneliese, Beth—all of us. Even Mitzi. You'd love her—she's such a little pet. So you can go. We all love you, you know. And thank you for everything, Be happy wherever you're going, be happy, you deserve that—I love you."

Unable to go on, she lay down beside her grandmother's frail body, hugging her one last time.

Lily found she was wearing an old dress she'd had in London when she, Diana and Maisie lived in Diana's godmother's house. It was green chiffon, with flaring panels in the skirt, and it brought out the chestnut of her hair. "Where have you been, dress?" she said to it.

She was young again too; how strange. Her bones didn't ache and her skin wasn't wrinkled around her elbows.

Now where was she? In a field, that's where. Close to the Old Forge, the field with the lavender in it, where she'd met Robby for the first time. There were deck chairs arranged among the lavender bushes with people relaxing happily in them. Diana and dear Maisie were there.

Lily smiled at them, pleased to see them. It seemed like only yesterday they'd been writing to each other, bridging the miles and the years with their letters.

There was Lady Evangeline, Philip, Matron, Isabelle Lochraven too—so many people from her past lined up.

There was Mam, sitting smiling, and Dad beside her; there was her darling brother, Tommy, with Moira, his wife. How wonderful to see them.

Lily ran past them all, waving, motioning that she'd be back, but first she had something to do.

Then she saw him: Jamie, in his uniform and looking as handsome as ever. Behind him, in the distance, coming running to her, were two people: one a tall man with copper hair and the other a slim woman with dark hair and her father's kind expression. Robby and Alice.

Lily beamed at them. "Just a moment," she whispered. "I'm coming."

She turned to Jamie and touched his hand.

"Thank you," she said to him. "Thank you for teaching me how to love. I don't think I knew how until you taught me. And I'm sorry I had to let you go, you know that."

Robby and Alice were closer now.

Jamie's hands slipped through hers. He was smiling, disappearing somehow.

Lily looked past him at her husband and daughter.

They'd waited for her; she'd always been afraid they wouldn't and yet here they were, smiling, holding out their arms. And she ran to them, to the two people she loved most.